NIKI SANDEMAN

Stranded on hostile ground, she vows to take back what's hers . . . to love and not to be abandoned.

PEPPER HYLAND

Once she seduced Niki with promises of the family she had never known. Now the sleek sophisticate in L.A. may surprise her half-sister with bitter betrayal, or something even worse.

DUKE HYLAND

It's a rare wom [illegible] his money—and h [illegible] ip to Niki can destro [illegible] eep.

W [illegible]

The handsome land manager and rising country singer, he will teach Niki what it takes to succeed in a man's world—and what a man needs from a woman when love replaces all . . .

◇ ◇ ◇

ALSO BY JESSICA MARCH

Illusions
Temptations

Published by
WARNER BOOKS

OBSESSIONS

JESSICA MARCH

A Warner Communications Company

WARNER BOOKS EDITION

Cover photo by James Haefner
Hand lettering by Dave Gatti

Warner Books, Inc.
666 Fifth Avenue
New York, N.Y. 10103

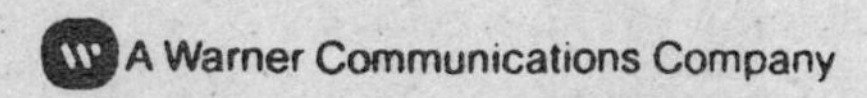

Printed in the United States of America

First Printing: July, 1990

10 9 8 7 6 5 4 3 2 1

Prologue

THE sky-blue Rolls-Royce that had been cruising at a stately pace along the wide empty road came to an abrupt stop as a dozen zebra appeared out of a thicket of palms and galloped across.

In the back seat, Niki Sandeman was pitched forward by the sudden deceleration. Her hands shot out to brace her against the lacquered mahogany sill that separated the rear compartment from the front. Even after her balance was restored, she stayed on the edge of the seat watching as the exotic black and white animals vanished again into a thicket of tall grass.

Zebra! It was hard to believe she wasn't in Africa, but on a private island only fifteen miles off the coast of North Carolina. Of course, Niki mused, it was no easier to believe she was here at all on Flamingo Island. Hadn't she been banned from the day of her birth—by unwritten law—from ever setting foot in this private paradise of the Hyland family?

Niki Sandeman couldn't resist a smile of satisfaction. Whatever the Hylands would have preferred, they had been forced to yield, not only to let her pass within their walls but to *invite* her to this meeting. What a bitter pill that must be for "Duke" Hyland, Niki gloated inwardly—though she could foresee that he would try to even the score by humbling her now that she was on his territory. Well, let him try. . . .

The chauffeur's voice broke into her thoughts. "Sorry if you got shook up, Miss Sandeman," he said as the car continued forward. A man with a face like polished ebony and a head of close-cropped snow-white hair under his uniform cap, the chauffeur had introduced himself simply as "Lazarus" when he had met her plane at the private landing strip.

"That's all right, Lazarus," said Niki, sitting back. "No harm done. It can't be easy for you to drive with all these wild animals running around." They had traveled hardly two miles from the airfield and already Niki had seen small herds of many different animals—giraffe, gazelle, okapi, water buffalo—as well as an enormous flock of the pink long-legged birds that gave the island its name, wading in a lagoon the road skirted.

The chauffeur chuckled softly. "Sure enough, Miss, it does test a man's nerves."

Niki saw the chauffeur's eyes checking her in the rear-view mirror, as though gauging how freely he could speak. Evidently the vote was in her favor. "Seems a little crazy to move these creatures so far from where God put 'em, don't it? I mean if folks can afford to do all that, why don't they just put a palace smack in the middle of the jungle?"

"I guess some folks," Niki offered, "would rather show what God could do if he had money."

The chauffeur hesitated a moment to digest the remark, then exploded into merry laughter. "Well, that is the truth, Miss. These Hyland folks do like to show what their money can do. . . ." Suddenly he stopped himself. "Not that Lazarus Baines ever had any reason to complain. Always treated me and mine right—Mister Duke and his father before him, always treated us good as can be. . . ."

Niki nodded at the brown eyes that flicked toward her in the rearview mirror, then she turned back to the window. *Good as can be*. The chauffeur's last words stuck in her mind as a bitter echo. If only they could have treated her mother right, been good as can be, then how different both their lives would have been.

Niki's throat tightened with emotion. Quickly, her hand flew up to wipe the first hint of tears from her eyes. No softness now, she commanded herself, this was no time to think of what might have been. She had to cling to the cold rage that had motivated her for so many years, the anger at what *was*. This was the fuel that had always driven her, brought her to this moment when victory over her lifelong enemies—and revenge for what they had done to Elle—was finally so close at hand.

Realizing her makeup might have smeared slightly, Niki reached inside her alligator shoulder bag for her compact and opened it to the mirror. There was no vanity in the examination she gave herself, only the practical knowledge that it would be important to look flawless for the meeting ahead. Everything about her appearance had been carefully considered and chosen to demonstrate that she had made herself their equal in taste, elegance, quality.

Certainly, nature had done its part. At thirty-three, Niki Sandeman was at the height of her uncommon beauty. Her silken smooth skin, like her thick, tawny hair, had been burnished gold from days in the sun, framing high, prominent cheekbones, a strong, determined mouth, and dark azure eyes. Gypsy eyes, Will had called them. Yes, she mused now, a gypsy is what I've been for too long, searching for a place to belong. But no more. The years of restless exile were coming to an end.

For a few minutes, Niki relaxed, letting herself take in the wondrous sights that were passing outside the window of the car—the blazing colors of thousands of exotic blooms bordering the road, the fleeting glimpses of birds with brilliant plumage perched in trees and shrubs, the herds of graceful exotic animals. She had heard so much about this place, this man-made Shangri-La. She could remember as a young child—was it her earliest memory?—being told about the place by Elle, who had mentioned it as just one part of the birthright that would someday be hers. In all of her mother's sad unfulfilled obsessions, the idea that she would someday enter—and even rule over—this paradise now seemed the saddest. For now, with her own eyes, Niki could see that the portrait her mother had painted was even paler and less magnificent than the reality. Here were ten thousand acres of man-made streams, waterfalls, game preserves, rain forest, exotic birds and fish and plants, imported from as far away as the South Pacific. From the air Niki had seen, too, a cluster of yachts berthed in a cove at one end of the crescent-shaped island, and a compound of grand houses surrounded by manicured formal gardens leading down to pristine white sand beaches. In today's world, Flamingo Island was an anachronism, a feudal fiefdom, ruled by the Hylands and served by an army of retainers who lived in small, humble cottages, much as their parents had done before them.

According to one story, the island had been won by the family patriarch, H.D. Hyland, in a high-stakes card game. But Niki knew a different truth. The huge property had been bought for a mere half-million dollars from a bankrupt stock manipulator after the market crash of '29. The maneuver was typical, Niki reflected; with their endless rivers of blood money, the Hylands were always ready to swoop down and make a killing—like vultures, picking the bones of friends and foes alike.

That, too, would change soon. Very soon.

The Rolls-Royce turned through a broad gate beneath a gilded iron archway marked with a large *H*. Far ahead, at the end of a long straight avenue of elm trees, stood a huge white mansion.

As confident as Niki had felt up to a moment ago, a current of tension ran through her body as she caught her first glimpse of Sunset House. It stood as a symbol of the family and its power in a way that their other property had not. Here generations of Hylands had entertained the most powerful politicians in America, businessmen and bankers, Hollywood stars, even European royalty. And within its walls today Niki would have to confront not just a single enemy, but an alliance. . . .

Preparing herself for the challenge, she conjured a mental picture of the three people arrayed against her. First and foremost was the family leader, Edward Hyland—"Duke"—who used a facade of Southern gentility to hide his arrogance and cruelty. Penelope Hyland would be there, too, good old "Pepper," Niki thought with a shudder, her flesh crawling with the memory of their last encounter.

Only the third member of the triumvirate evoked feelings other than hatred or contempt in Niki: "Babe"—no one ever called him William—who, in his own way, was as much a victim as Elle had been, in spite of all the privileges his wealth could buy. For Babe, Niki could still feel compassion. Indeed once, she let herself remember, she had felt something more. . . .

The car came to a stop in a circular drive fronting the soaring pillared entrance of the Greek-revival mansion. The chauffeur came around to help Niki out, then esçorted her to the massive front door and rapped a shining brass knocker a few times.

Fighting down a last surge of nervousness, Niki tugged a slight crease out of her cream linen Valentino suit and made sure the collar of her navy silk blouse was straight.

A white-jacketed black butler opened the door.

"This is Miss Sandeman," Lazarus said, "Mr. Duke is expecting her."

"Good morning, ma'am," the butler said. "Will you please follow me?"

As Niki crossed through the enormous front hall, she was confronted at once by a portrait gallery of Hylands, past and present, all looking down on her in various attitudes of repose and contemplation. As she scanned the faces of past generations she felt an oppressive tightness in her chest, a lightheadedness that bordered on vertigo. It was as if they, too, were massed against her, smug and self-satisfied, saying even now: You don't belong here and you never will.

No, you don't, she cautioned herself again and tore her eyes from the pictures. I've come too far; *nothing* can stop me. Fists clenched at her sides, she followed the butler into a spacious panelled library.

And there they were, seated comfortably on silk brocade-covered sofas and surrounded by all the trappings of their accumulated wealth—the Matisse and Renoir paintings on the wall, the priceless Hyland collection of rare books, the finest antiques money could buy.

What a charming family portrait, Niki thought, taking in the overdone makeup which was Pepper's futile attempt to keep age at bay, and Babe's worried face—and lastly Duke's expression of unbridled hatred. He's like a jungle animal, too, Niki thought—only far more dangerous than the ones he liked to import, and especially deadly when threatened.

It was Babe who rose from his seat and moved forward to greet her. A bear of a man, three inches over six feet, at the age of forty-five he still had a boyish appearance, curly blond hair and clear blue eyes, a face that showed he had never been forced to endure any physical hardship, or even make any difficult decision. Since the Southern custom of primogeniture still prevailed in the Hyland family, Babe had been frozen out of active participation in the Hyland business by his older brother. His main activity these days was racing high-powered boats which he spent millions to design and build. Though the sport was dangerous, even those strains didn't appear to have marked Babe. It occurred to Niki that perhaps Babe was oblivious to the perils because he had never valued his life very much.

"Good morning, Niki," Babe said. "It's been a long time . . ."

"Yes, it has," she returned flatly, having no taste for small politenesses.

"Sit down, Niki," Pepper Hyland instructed her in the no-nonsense tone accentuated by a husky voice acquired from years of smoking Pyramid cigarettes, the unfiltered brand made by Hyland Tobacco. At forty-seven, Pepper still had a lithe athletic body, and a narrow catlike face framed by short blond hair. Though the combination of rigid dieting and cosmetic surgery had preserved some of the illusion of youth, Niki could see that the cracks were beginning to show around the edges.

Despite Pepper's imperious tone, Niki said nothing and took a place at one end of the sofa also occupied by Babe. Let them think she was ready to oblige, to listen.

"Would you like some coffee?" Babe offered, braving his brother's displeasure.

Niki would have said no, but Duke Hyland didn't give her the opportunity.

"I don't think we have to pretend this is a pleasant morning coffee hour," he said to Babe in the lilting Southern drawl that, unlike Babe and Pepper, he had preserved and cultivated. "Niki doesn't want to eat or drink with us." He turned to her. "Do you, Niki?"

Niki stared back at Duke Hyland. The question was plainly meant as not merely a denial, but also a cruel taunt—for there had been a time when she would have given the world to sit at their table.

"No," she said coldly. "Not anymore."

"Then let's get down to business, shall we?" As rushed as he sounded, Duke paused to take one of the filtered cigarettes bunched into a golden cup on a table by his chair.

Niki went on staring at him as he took up a gold Dunhill

lighter and took the first puff on his cigarette. Once he had been one of the handsomest men she had ever seen, with oak brown hair that fell over cool gray eyes, a straight nose, and a strong chin with a slight cleft in it. The hair was gray now, the eyes looked almost bleached of color, and his face was drawn and sallow. Was it simply time or bad habits that had destroyed his looks—or was it the rottenness of his spirit that had somehow eaten them away from the inside?

"There's just one reason we called you here," Duke went on, "and that's because we're ready to make an offer. You came, I assume, because you're ready to hear it. But make no mistake, Niki, there won't be any bargaining with us. You'll get this one chance, and if you don't want it . . ." He let the unfinished thought hang in the air as a threat.

Niki simply went on staring him down.

Duke gave her a thin smile. "But since you accepted our invitation, I'll assume it's because you're ready to hear what you'll get."

"Yes," Niki said, "I'm ready to hear."

"Good. Then here it is: fifty million dollars, free and clear." He paused, to let the enormity of the figure sink in. "In return," he went on, "you will agree to end this . . . this war you've declared—and to relinquish forever any and all claims against Hyland Tobacco. You will declare in writing that you have no entitlement whatsoever."

Fifty million dollars, Niki repeated to herself. Even for the Hylands, that was a great deal of money. It told her, as nothing else could, that they were running scared.

"And how did you propose to make this payment?" she asked.

"However you want it," Pepper put in, demonstrating solidarity with Duke. "Bank check . . . gold . . . numbered deposit in a Swiss bank. You can have some of my goddamn jewelry, if you prefer."

Duke chimed in again. "Our lawyers have their instructions. The money can be moved within twenty-four hours."

"Very accommodating." Niki smiled briefly. "So in just one day, with one simple act, you propose to wipe out all the pain and misery you've caused from the day I was born—no, the day I was *conceived*." She paused, and her audience of three leaned forward, hanging on every word. "Well, it's not enough," Niki added harshly.

Babe and Pepper looked at her in stunned amazement. But it took Duke only a moment to find his voice. "Then how much do you want?" he asked. "What is your price . . . to go away, disappear forever? You've got one, Niki, I'm sure you do. Your mother could be bought, so I'd guess it would run in your blood. . . ."

She let the insult pass without comment. That would be Duke's way to defeat her, arouse her fury so she lost her cold rational determination.

"Sure, I have a price," she said calmly.

"What is it?" Babe asked, sounding surprised as much as curious.

Niki looked around at each of the three people waiting for her answer. "What I've always wanted—what *she* wanted," Niki said, referring to her mother. "I want the name and everything else that comes with it."

Both Babe and Pepper looked to their older brother. And Duke laughed. "You'll never get that, Niki. Never."

Niki stood. "Then I've wasted my time coming here." She started toward the door.

"There won't be another offer," Duke shouted after her. "And if you leave without signing the documents I've prepared, then this war you started will go on. And it will get much uglier, I promise you. We'll make you wish you were never born."

Niki stopped and turned back. "That's nothing new, Duke. You've already done that—more than once. You, and H.D., all of you. . . ."

"Niki," Babe cried pleadingly as he stood up from the sofa. "Let this end, for your sake as much as ours. Take the money. Don't you see Duke can't bend—and without him, even if I wanted—"

"Babe!" Pepper cut in before he could say anything more to indicate a break in the ranks. "It isn't just Duke. It's the *family*!" She looked to Niki. "It's H.D., too. We have to consider his . . . memory."

Niki regarded Pepper Hyland with open contempt. Did her sanctimonious reference to a respect for the dead make Pepper's position any more reasonable? H.D. Hyland had been the root of the pain and suffering that Niki was determined to avenge.

She wheeled away and continued out.

Behind her Duke roared in fury, "This is your last chance, Niki."

At the door, she stopped once more, though without looking back. "No, Duke, you've got that wrong—and you know it. This was *your* last chance."

The burst of adrenalin kept her marching down the marble corridor, across the grand entrance hall, and through the front door.

Only when she was outside did she pause for breath. She realized then that she was trembling. For all her bravado, she had to wonder if she would truly be able to prevail. The battle to claim her legitimate place as a child of H.D. Hyland had already consumed much of her life, her energy. Was it a noble crusade that must go on—to give meaning to her mother's shattered life as well as to her own—or was it a destructive obsession?

Even now, she knew, it was not too late to take the money, to abandon this quest for the last measure of respect . . . for, as the law put it, legitimacy.

The chauffeur had seen her, and was holding the door of the car open. "Are you leaving, Miss Sandeman?" he said, as she hesitated.

She paused only another second. "Yes, Lazarus," she said. "I'm leaving."

There was simply no choice, Niki understood. Whether or not it was an obsession, it was also her destiny. The course had been set long ago on a day that would have lulled any woman—as it had tragically lulled her mother—into believing in fairy tales.

☆

BOOK I

☆

One

Monaco, April 12, 1956, 6:30 A.M.

IN the harbor of his jewel-box principality, His Serene Highness Prince Rainier of Monaco boarded the royal yacht *Deo Juvante II* and set sail out to the Bay of Hercules to greet the arriving steamship *Constitution*—and to welcome his fiancée Grace Kelly to the tiny principality over which he ruled.

Jammed together on the casino terraces and the streets along the shore, twenty thousand Monegasques, journalists, tourists and curiosity seekers from around the world watched the yacht moving across the bay with Rainier standing on the bow. Ignoring the light rain, the crowds would stay for as long as it took to catch a glimpse of the gorgeous young woman who had abdicated her throne as movie queen to become a real-life princess.

On one of the higher terraces overlooking the harbor, Gabrielle Veraix braced herself against the stone balustrade and pushed back roughly against the surging mass of onlookers behind her. Elle—as Gabrielle was generally called—was a slim girl of nineteen whose lovely heart-shaped face, soft brown eyes, and short bob of silky brown hair made her appear delicate and vulnerable, even childlike. Yet there was strength in her lean frame and thin arms, both from the farm work she had done since she was eight, and the swimming her mother had made her do in mountain streams at an even earlier age. When Elle Veraix pushed, even against a crowd, the result was felt. The crushing pressure at her back eased, shifting to a point of less resistance.

Elle focused her eyes again on the royal yacht, now approaching the steamship, but it had sailed beyond the point where she could see anything of the prince but a tiny dot on the bow.

"What's happening now?" Elle said, nudging a portly man beside her who had the luxury of a pair of binoculars.

For a moment the man didn't answer. Then he erupted. "There she is—she's on the deck of the big boat . . . and she's waving to him."

The crowd, hearing the commentary, broke into delighted applause.

"And now he raises his hand . . . and he gives her a salute in return."

The crowd laughed.

But Elle made a face. A salute? What an anticlimax! A fairy-tale romance she had heard it called, this odd courtship and arranged marriage between prince and movie star. But it wasn't *her* idea of a fairy tale, Elle thought. Of course, marrying a man with a palace was fine . . . but the country he ruled was little more than a joke, and he wasn't even as wealthy as his wife's family so the rumors went—indeed, the little country needed the money that the bride's father would supply as her dowry. Now to top it off they weren't even that romantic. If ever she could live a fairy-tale romance of her own, Elle thought, she would want no mere salutes from her prince. She would want him to rush to her side, to swim from his yacht if need be, seize her in his arms—even if a hundred thousand people were watching—and kiss her hungrily, touch her everywhere, arouse her to the heights of passion that until now she only knew when she touched herself.

Her interest in the spectacle drained, Elle picked up the small cardboard valise at her feet and shoved her way out of the crowd. She began walking downhill toward the center of Monte Carlo. It was not to see the story of an American movie star unfold that she had come, after all. If she was here it was only because she realized that the story would bring others from all around the world—and among them, she was sure, would have to be the man she had spent almost all of her own days dreaming about.

To fulfill the dream, Elle had come from a small French farming village in Provence that lay only eighty kilometers from the border with Monaco. Rather than spend any of the little money she possessed on transportation, she had walked all the way, starting late yesterday so she could be here for the morning, pausing once to sleep briefly in a wayside field. So she was tired now, but she gave no thought to resting. The man she sought would certainly be here, somewhere among the crowds; she could not wait to find him.

And she had a good idea of where to start.

Making her way through the streets to the dock from which she had seen the yacht depart—and to which it would return after collecting the movie star from the steamship—Elle pushed relentlessly through the crowds until she came to a barrier guarded by colorfully uniformed Monegasque police. As if entitled to pass, she started to make her way around the barrier. A young policeman with a rakish mustache grabbed her by the arm.

"But I'm looking for someone," she explained.

"Who?"

"My father. . . ."

The policeman loosened his grip on her bare arm, though he held on. "Why would he be here?"

"He'd be with the journalists. His name is Ralph Sandeman and he takes pictures for newspapers."

"Which newspapers?"

"I don't know." The truth was out before Elle could think to stop herself.

The policeman gave her a thin, doubting smile. "So. You don't know where your own father works . . . ?"

"I—" The words dried up. How could she explain? That was the least of what she didn't know. She had never even *seen* Ralph Sandeman.

But then an idea struck. Wrenching free of the policeman, Elle dropped her flimsy suitcase, and crouched to open it. From under the tumble of clothes, she pulled a framed black and white photograph and thrust it at the *gendarme*.

"This is one of his pictures. It's famous. You must have seen it."

Puzzled, the policeman took the photograph and grazed it with his eyes. It was a striking image of a shapely young woman wearing a dark bathing suit sleek and shining as a seal's skin, her graceful body fully extended in a slight arch, her arms spread wide as if in flight, caught frozen in midair as she executed a perfect dive.

The policeman shrugged, and only then Elle realized he must be too young to have read or seen very much about the 1936 Olympics, famous as they were.

"Never mind," she snapped, grabbing the picture back and replacing it in her suitcase.

"I'm sorry, *ma petite*," the policeman said. "But you won't trick your way in here for a look at Grace with that nonsense."

"It wasn't a trick," she said softly, already starting to retreat.

But she wasn't discouraged. There would be other ways to find her father. He was here, of course—every news photographer in the world would be here—and the wedding would keep him here for days.

By evening, however, Elle was feeling the first twinges of despair. She had been to the Hermitage, and the Hotel de

Paris, and the other luxury hotels and many of the small ones . . . and none of them had a Ralph Sandeman registered among the many American guests.

She had stopped any man or woman she passed who was wearing one of the conspicuous press badges or carrying a large press camera, and asked each one if they knew Ralph Sandeman. One of the photographers, an American, had indeed shown instant recognition of the name; but from the little Elle could understand of his rapid-fire English, the cameraman didn't seem to know if Ralph Sandeman was anywhere in Monaco.

Still, for a while, Elle kept her hopes up. Ralph Sandeman took pictures of the most important and wonderful things happening in the world—as he had been there to take the picture of her mother winning her silver medal at the Olympics. Of course he must be here! Where else would he be? Wasn't this the most important and wonderful news being made in the world today?

But as the night went on, Elle's fantasy became harder to sustain. As she drifted through the crowds that were gathered everywhere, it dawned on the young woman that she had assumed too much. Perhaps Ralph Sandeman no longer took news photographs; perhaps he had been sent elsewhere. Perhaps . . . oh, she hated to think it, but it was certainly possible that he was no longer alive. He would not be so old . . . but then her mother had been even younger, and she was gone.

As the first seeds of doubt took root, then spread dark shadows through her spirit, Elle's mood swung from optimism to total despair. Foolish it had been, perhaps, but she had *counted* on finding him . . . had imagined that he would be thrilled to be united with her as she with him, would take care of all her needs, would take her back to America. . . .

And if all that had proven ridiculous, then what was left for her? Could she simply go back to Bizecque, the small village she had left yesterday? Back to where she had always been whispered about . . . mistrusted . . . looked on as an object of pity and shame? What future could she have there?

She knew very well that while many might desire her, no eligible man would marry her. The best she could hope for back in Bizecque was a widower who needed a pair of willing hands to raise his children and help farm his land. She would rather die than go back. If she had been moved to come here by an impossible dream, Elle realized now, it was only because her life had become just as impossible. She had no choice but to make a change, to build on this one hope. . . .

At ten o'clock, when a grand fireworks display was launched into the night skies over Monte Carlo to celebrate the arrival of Rainier's princess, Elle was on the quay by the central harbor. From the quay, she could also see Le Rocher, the 220-room pink stucco palace built on a rocky promontory overlooking the city. And there, on one of the many balconies, were the prince and his fiancée, watching the fireworks. How beautiful she was, Elle thought, how lucky . . . and how distant, how far above her. Seeing the beautiful princess who was on top of the world only drove home to Elle her own misfortune. As she watched the rockets streak upward and burst into gigantic blossoms of colored sparks, she could feel no exhilaration. The pyrotechnics above her seemed to be the visual symbol of her own bright hopes finally exploding, burning out, and fading away into darkness.

Hunger and fatigue were taking their toll, too, depressing her spirits even further. She had so little money, but the aroma of freshly prepared food drifting from one of the dockside restaurants pulled her nearer. It had been almost two days since she'd had a proper meal.

Standing in front of the outdoor restaurant, inhaling the hearty smells of meat cooked in garlic, hearing the music of a strolling violinist, the laughter of people enjoying food and wine and the warm sunshine of a spring day, Gabrielle realized she was starving—but not just for nourishment. For something she couldn't quite explain. Something to do with the laughter and the music and the fine clothes everyone seemed to be wearing. Though she'd been raised on frugality and thrift, Elle was pulled into the cafe.

She sat down and boldly ordered an aperitif from a passing waiter. But when he brought a menu, and Elle looked at the prices that had been raised to take advantage of the crowds, the color left her face. The cost of a meal would be *astronomical*, she realized; no matter how hungry she was, she couldn't afford to spend so much of her meager savings. She ordered a sandwich of ham thin as paper on a slice of baguette—the cheapest item on the menu—and, fighting the urge to devour it whole, took one small bite after another.

"Will there be anything else?" the waiter asked pointedly, when she had finished.

A *café filtre*, she said, hoping to buy a little more rest, a bit more comfort for her weary body and exhausted spirit.

She sipped the coffee very slowly, wanting to make it last, and closed her eyes, the better to savor its taste. The sound of the violin soothed her. Though the chair beneath her was metal, and its back dug into her cotton camisole, she relaxed into it.

The next thing she knew, Elle was being shaken awake by the irate waiter. "This is a cafe, not a hotel," he berated her hotly. "Move on."

"But I haven't finished my coffee," she protested with equal indignation.

"Well, swallow it down and leave," the waiter demanded. "We don't want your kind here—come in and order a few francs worth while you wait to pick up a customer!"

"Customer?" Elle could only attempt to stammer a defense. "How dare you! I'm not—"

"Go on, go on," the waiter said, shaking her chair now as if to dislodge some overripe fruit from a tree. "I can see well enough what you are and I don't want your kind in—"

A voice at an adjacent table cut in, a male voice, smooth except for a hint of controlled anger. "I don't think you should be speaking to the young lady that way."

Both Elle and the waiter turned instantly toward the source. Irritated by the intrusion, the waiter was preparing to launch a sharp declaration that he could handle his own business

. . . but his voice caught when he saw the young man with dark hair and pale gray eyes who had spoken. He was clearly a customer with whom it would be wiser not to tangle. The exquisite tailoring of his elegant navy blazer and gray flannel slacks, and the golden tan that bespoke a life of leisure, would have been enough to mark him as merely affluent. But there was an air about this man that the waiter was experienced enough to recognize as the absolute self-possession belonging only to the extremely wealthy.

"I think you owe the young lady an apology," the young man added forcefully, in a manner that indicated he was accustomed to being obeyed.

The waiter hesitated while Elle, too, studied her young defender. For all her own lack of sophistication, she realized he must be cultivated and experienced, for he was speaking her language quite well although he had an accent that stamped him as being either English or American. In fact, it had a sort of musical lilt that struck a chord of recognition in Elle. . . .

With a Gallic shrug, the waiter made his decision. What if the girl was a whore. She had made her score, and she would be out of here soon enough. "Pardon me, mademoiselle," he said quickly, and whisked away to another table.

"Thank you," Elle murmured shyly.

"You're welcome."

It came to her now—that special music in his accent. It reminded her of the way Clark Gable had sounded in the only American movie she had ever seen, a subtitled version of *Gone With The Wind*. The young man must be from that part of the United States where the rich had once owned slaves. What else could she say to hold his interest? Nothing came, and she retreated awkwardly into a sip of her coffee.

As she looked up from her cup she saw that he had risen from his table and was standing by hers. By reflex, her hand went to her hair, tucking away the stray wisps, regretting enormously the hasty toilette of this morning, the ravages of travel, and the crumpled condition of her dress.

"Would you like to join me?" she said, inclining her head graciously toward the chair opposite as if she had been accustomed to nothing less than good breeding all her life.

"No, thank you," he said.

Elle looked down, hiding her dismay. Was she too forward? Had he also taken her for a common—

His voice broke into her thoughts. "I don't believe this place is good enough for someone like you." A handful of coins clattered onto the table in front of her, and then Elle saw that his hand was extended toward her. She placed her palm in his and felt herself gently pulled to her feet.

"My name is Edward Hyland," he said as she gazed at him in wonder. "But you can call me Duke. I hope you don't think I'm being forward . . . but I'd be awfully pleased if you'd be my guest for dinner."

She nodded, speechless, then ducked to retrieve her suitcase from under the table.

"Here, let me carry that for you," he said. After taking the suitcase, he crooked his unused arm toward her. It took Elle a second to realize she was meant to slip her arm through his. As soon as she did, they began to walk.

"And what's your name?" he said.

"Elle," she said, embarrassed now that she hadn't the manners to introduce herself.

"Elle," he echoed curiously, since it was the same as the French pronoun for *she*. "Is that all?"

She smiled nervously. "It's Gabrielle, actually." She paused for barely an instant, as she was struck by a notion. If she was to leave her old life behind, to leave the shame of being the daughter of an unwed mother, then it couldn't hurt to take a new name—the name that *should* always have been hers. "Gabrielle Sandeman," she added.

"Mademoiselle Sandeman," the young man said, stopping to give her a courtly bow. "It's a pleasure to meet you. . . ."

"The pleasure is mine. I am lucky you were willing to save me from that awful waiter."

"Willing. Dear Elle, it was my duty as a gentleman."

As he smiled, Elle was reminded again of Clark Gable—no, Rhett Butler—and her heart quickened. Was this truly happening, or was she still asleep in the cafe? For if the dream she had come seeking remained unfulfilled, then this seemed a piece of something even better.

Two

EAT *like a lady . . . small bites*, Elle cautioned herself as she eyed the food being set in front of her, a small fragrant heap of langoustines sauteed in garlic butter, delicate *haricots verts*, and the thinnest, lightest *pommes frites* she had ever seen. No matter how hungry she was, she must remember to eat like a lady and convince this young American called Duke she was a good decent girl from a good family.

The fear clung that he might have taken her for a *putain*, had lured her here only to steal her virtue. Even if he judged her to be no more than what she was, a poor girl from the provinces, he might still be disappointed and suddenly order her to leave these wonderful surroundings.

To Elle's amazement, the young American had not taken her to a restaurant to fulfill his invitation to dinner, but instead had led her straight to the end of quay, and steered her up the gangway of one of the largest private boats berthed in the harbor. Painted in gold across the transom of the gleaming white 185-foot yacht was the name HIGHLAND FLING. Once aboard, Elle had been guided to an open rear deck, where the young man issued orders to a number of crewmen and stewards who appeared. Soon, under a green awning, a table was spread with fine linen and gold-rimmed china and sparkling crystal glasses, and chairs upholstered in soft white kidskin were pulled up. Wine was poured, dishes of cheese and pâté and fluffy breads were served, and finally the dinner materialized.

Elle did her best to keep up a conversation throughout, answering questions about herself without giving too much away—and asking idle questions about the boat, nothing her host might regard as too prying. Yet all the while she was half dazed by finding herself in these opulent surroundings, with a picture postcard panorama of Monaco stretched beyond the stern of the yacht, and food on the table more delicious than she had ever tasted before in her life.

When at last a tray of cream pastries was brought for dessert, she could no longer maintain control. Though sweets had been a rare thing in the home of cousin Jacques, a gruff farmer who had raised her after her mother's death, she'd always had a raving sweet tooth. When she bit eagerly into a sumptuous eclair and the custard squirted down her chin, Elle realized at last that her pose of gentility was at risk. She saw Duke watching her with a smile on his face that suggested he had seen through her masquerade.

She dabbed at her chin quickly with the damask napkin, then pushed away the rest of the uneaten pastries.

"Are you finished? You were enjoying them so much. . . ."

"Too much," she said defensively.

He smiled again, and to avoid his scrutiny she reached into her crocheted purse for a crumpled pack of Gauloises. As she put a cigarette to her lips, Duke produced a gold cigarette lighter. Elle leaned into the flame and inhaled deeply, affecting a sophisticated air she'd learned from Simone Simone and Danielle Darrieux and other stars of the French cinema.

He sat forward suddenly and leaned closer across the table. "Now," he said, "no more evasions. I want to know more about you. Each time I ask, though, you say as little as possible, and then you change the subject."

"You already know all there is. I come from a little town in France you've never heard of, where all they do is raise cabbages for work and drink wine for fun. I'm nineteen, and . . . I came to Monte Carlo to meet my father."

Duke nodded slowly. "I hope he won't mind that I'm keeping you out so late."

"No," she said quickly. "He knows I can take care of myself. And you?" she asked quickly. "I assume you've sailed your boat across the ocean to see the royal festivities. But then why do you sit alone in cafes, and eat your dinner with me. Someone like you should be going to all the parties. . . ."

"My father's over there right now," Duke replied, tossing a careless wave in the direction of Le Rocher. "This isn't my boat, see, it's his—all his. I just get to come along for the ride, and I'll take whatever I can get from H.D. But I didn't come because I care about being included in all that fancy royal baloney."

His tone had a bitter edge, she noticed, but she tried to keep the mood light. "Well, I would see it all if *I* had the chance," Elle said. "I'll bet the wedding will be the most beautiful sight in the world."

Duke shook his head. "No, ma'am. I'd say the most beautiful sight in the world is right in front of me. . . ."

Simultaneously alarmed and pleased by his flattery, she stared back a second, then tried to hide her blush by raising the cigarette to her mouth again.

"Shouldn't smoke those Gauloises, you know. They're too harsh, the tobacco's too strong. Try one of these. . . ." Duke jumped up, went to a cocktail table, took a fresh new pack of cigarettes from several lying in a crystal box. As he tore it open, Elle could see the brand was one of the costly

American imports. She stubbed out her Gauloise in a silver ashtray while Duke lit a fresh cigarette with his lighter, then handed it to her.

Elle took a puff. It was much milder. She could taste the smoke without having it burn her tongue.

"Isn't that much better?" Duke said.

"Yes, thank you," Elle replied. It was indeed, though she was puzzled by the intensity of the pride he seemed to take in his simple recommendation.

"Your father," she said, "is he here as a friend of the bride—or of the groom?"

Duke laughed. "Neither. It's my stepmother, Joanne, who was our ticket in this time. She went to acting school with Grace back in New York."

"Really?" Elle's brown eyes widened as she took another puff of the cigarette.

"Yeah. They shared an apartment for a while, used to raise hell together. You should hear Joanne's stories about Grace Kelly." Duke lowered his voice. "The kind that if ol' Rainier ever got wind of, he might think twice about making her the mother of his children."

"No!" Elle exclaimed, scandalized.

"Of course, all that was before Grace got noticed by Hollywood, and my mother got noticed by H.D.—that's my father. But they've kept in touch ever since. Just between us, Joanne got really ticked off when Grace didn't ask her to be in the wedding party." Duke chuckled as if his stepmother's disappointment gave him the greatest of pleasure. "She made up a story about how it was all some kind of mix-up, didn't think she could hold her head up if her friends knew she'd been snubbed. I don't know if anyone believed her, but that's just the way my wicked stepmother is."

"And your real mother," Elle asked softly, realizing she might have struck some common ground. "Is she dead?"

Duke laughed, but not in a way that seemed mirthful or pleasant. "No, though I'll bet H.D. sure wishes she was. They got divorced when I was six. I spend most of my time with her, but she sends me to H.D. for all my school vacations. Says it's for my own good, to protect my rights. She wants to make sure Pepper and Babe don't cut me out . . ."

Elle laid her cigarette in an ashtray. "Pepper . . . Babe? Who are they?"

"H.D.'s kids with Joanne. My *half* sister and *half* brother."

"They went to the party?"

Duke smiled smugly. "Nope, they're not here. Joanne wanted to bring them, but H.D. said he wasn't about to turn this cruise into a floating nursery. And that was that. When my daddy lays down the law, there's nobody who can change it."

His gaze drifted and he stared off moodily into the darkness of the outer ocean. From several of his remarks, Elle perceived that even with his handsomeness and his fine clothes and all his family's wealth, he was unhappy. He spoke about both his father and stepmother as though they were unkind to him, didn't accept him.

Impulsively, she reached out and covered Duke's hand with hers, a gesture of sympathy and understanding. Strange, she thought, that this young American prince who had rescued her seemed now very vulnerable, in need of rescue himself. And if there was one thing she knew about, it was the pain of not belonging.

His eyes came around again to look at her. As his hand turned to grasp hers, she felt the spark of true communion, felt they were speaking silently with their glances. Just as he had revealed some of his suffering to her, she felt he could sympathize with hers.

"I lied to you," she blurted out.

He smiled gently as his grip tightened slightly. "I thought so. . . ."

Shocked, she yanked her hand away. "How could you know?"

"I wasn't a hundred percent sure. But you spoke as if you'd already met up with your father—and at the same time you were still carrying your suitcase around. It didn't add up."

She blinked once, then buried her face in her hands and burst into sobs. Exposed, embarrassed, she realized now how she must look to the young man—an object of scorn and pity, just as she had always been to the people of Bizecque. And she had begun to imagine—foolish again!—that the magic of this night might not end.

Duke grabbed up a napkin and prodded it into her hands. "C'mon now, Elle, dry your eyes. I didn't say I minded. You didn't want me to know you're alone, I understand that. Guess you thought I might take advantage of you. I regard it as a compliment you were coming around to telling me the truth. . . ."

She brought her hands down from her face and studied him. He was sincere, she thought. He wasn't rushing to send her away.

"Why did you speak up for me in the cafe?" she asked. "Why did you want to bring me here?"

He shook his head slightly. "Because . . . well, because you're pretty and I was alone not having too much fun . . . and mostly I guess because you looked as lost as I felt."

Elle nodded. She had an impulse now to tell Duke the whole truth. About her name, her mother, the father she'd never seen.

But before she could start, he said exuberantly, "Seems to me this party needs some cheering up." He stood. "Why don't I go get us some champagne—just like they're drinking over there?" His arm swept toward the palace and the casino, their windows ablaze with light.

He left and she was alone; the steward who served them dinner had discreetly disappeared.

The cigarette she had put down in an ashtray had burned out. Restlessly, Elle looked around for the pack Duke had opened, but she didn't see it. Evidently he'd dropped it into a pocket. She rose and went to the crystal box which contained several other packs, all with different labels, and picked one out—a brand called Evergreen.

She was tapping out the first cigarette, when she spotted the name *Hyland* in some small print across the edge of the pack. Turning it around for a closer look, she read the whole line: "Another Fine Product of Hyland Tobacco Company." So this was the source of wealth in Duke Hyland's family. Then it must be very vast indeed.

He came striding briskly back onto the afterdeck holding a bottle of Dom Perignon and two crystal flutes. With a flourish, he popped the cork, filled the glasses, then handed one to her.

"To the happy couple," he said as he moved to the deck railing and raised his glass in the direction of Rainier's pink palace. "And may the prince never find out as much as my stepmother knows about his princess."

With a laugh, Elle imitated the gesture, and then they drank.

Leaning over the deck railing, with Duke beside her, Elle felt as if she, no less than the famous movie star, had been touched by a special destiny. A short time ago, she'd been just like all the people milling around the harbor, and now . . . here she was, on this luxurious yacht, in the company of a handsome and very wealthy young man. If only the destiny that had brought her here would show her a way to make this magic moment last.

Duke poured more champagne in her glass, then looked over at the palace again. There had been music floating across the water from that direction, but it had stopped. "I guess they'll be winding it up soon . . . H.D. will be coming back any minute."

Duke had spoken quietly, she noticed, as if to himself.

"Do you want me to go?"

"No," he said. But he didn't look at her.

Elle was confused. After the moment of intimacy at the table, then his exuberant rush to celebrate with champagne, she had thought he might grow romantic. She had begun to fantasize what could lie ahead if he did. . . . But now he seemed suddenly distant, so much quieter than before, with none of the confidence he'd shown with the cafe waiter, or in ordering the yacht's staff to serve them. Should she make a move? she wondered. If there was any chance to build on her luck in meeting him, how could she let it pass?

She eased herself along the rail until her body was pressing against his.

Suddenly, the mood was shattered. From the yacht's gangway came the sound of a woman's voice, sharp and argumentative. "I won't have it anymore, I tell you. Embarrassing me in front of my friends, saying anything you damn well please! If you can't hold your liquor like a gentleman, H.D., then you'd best hold your tongue . . ."

A man's voice boomed in return, sternly cutting off the stream of complaints. "You've got that mixed up, Joanne, honey. Seems to me you're the one who's having trouble holding her liquor. So why don't you just go sleep off all that champagne, and when you're feeling better, I'll buy you something real pretty."

"Well, you damn well better to make up for your *outrageous* comments. Because if you don't, I might find a way to pay you back. . . ."

"Now, Joanne, darlin', you don't want to be saying things you'll regret tomorrow."

A moment later, an elaborately coiffed blonde wearing a beaded gown and an ermine wrap stormed past Gabrielle, past Edward, rounded the aft deck, and disappeared in a clatter of high heels. Elle's eyes widened; to her, the woman looked like a queen, with more gems on her neck and arms than Elle had ever seen.

"That was my stepmother," Duke said. "You'll have to excuse her for not saying hello, but when Joanne gets a snootful, she does tend to forget her manners."

"She is very beautiful," Elle observed.

"If you like the type. Personally, I've always found her just a little bit . . . common."

Elle found it hard to believe that any man could fail to be impressed with such a beautiful and stylish woman, but before she could argue the point, a tall man who bore a striking resemblance to Duke appeared. He had silver-gray hair, a sportsman's weathered complexion, and steel-gray eyes. He wore his tuxedo and a shirt with glittering diamond studs in the way other men wore jeans, looking totally at home with their elegance, and he moved across the deck of the yacht as if he owned the world.

"Well, well," he drawled when he saw the young people. "I didn't know you'd be entertaining a friend, Edward." The tone was light, almost admonishing, the way an indulgent parent would talk to a very young child.

Before Elle's very eyes, Duke appeared to shrink. "There's a lot you don't know, H.D.," he said in a surly mutter which made him seem even more childish.

"Yes, Edward," the father agreed with a patronizing smile, "I'm sure there is. Now, won't you introduce me to your lovely friend?"

Duke frowned back, but then he made the introduction.

"Well, Miss Sandeman," H.D. Hyland said, "I hope my son has been showing you suitable hospitality."

It took a second for Elle to answer. Duke's father had such a commanding presence, and the way his eyes were locked on her, glittering almost as brightly as his diamond studs, made her feel oddly warm. "Yes, I've had a dinner and champagne. . . ."

"It's a pity I didn't know Edward had a friend like you. I would have arranged some tickets to one of the galas. Such a pretty young woman should be enjoying herself to the full, dressed in a gown, dancing. . . ."

As he spoke, Elle was swept up in the fantasy. She had thought this dinner on a private yacht was the height of luxury . . . but to be waltzing in a ball gown!

H.D. Hyland went on, "But since Edward told me he had no interest, I don't suppose you would, either."

Elle looked at Duke, as if he must be an alien creature from another planet—and then she looked at his father, as if he were a kind of god descended from Olympus. "But I am interested. Will you tell me about it?" she asked shyly. "Will you tell me what it was like tonight?"

"How could I refuse such a charming request?" H.D. said graciously, ignoring his son's black look. And while Elle listened raptly, he went on to describe the events of the day—a lunch at the palace at which the Philadelphia Kellys and all their friends were introduced to the Grimaldis of Monaco, followed by a private tea Grace had for her friends, and then tonight's ball, with a thousand people swirling around the huge ballroom of Le Rocher.

"What was *she* wearing, Monsieur Hyland?" Elle pleaded. "Can you describe it all . . . ?"

"Only if you call me H.D.," he said with a laugh. "But even then, I can't tell you much . . . Something in a pink—or was it beige? With lace on it, and some sort of beading. I'm sorry, my dear," he apologized, seeing that his vagueness had disappointed Elle. "But when it comes to fashion, I only pay the bills. And, of course," he added, "I appreciate the beauty of the woman who's wearing them . . ."

"And tomorrow. Where will you be going?"

"Well, they'll have the civil ceremony at the palace and a reception in the palace courtyard—"

Elle sighed and clapped her hands together. "How wonderful. And I suppose there are always dozens of photographers."

H.D. gave a bemused smile, interpreting the question as no more than a youthful measure of the glamor of an occasion. "Yes," he said, "hundreds of them."

"How I wish I could be there. Tell me more about the—"

"I've heard enough," Duke sulked. "More than enough, I'd say."

"But I wasn't talking to you, Edward. I was answering

Gabrielle's questions. If you're too tired to behave in a civil manner, I'm sure the young lady will understand . . ."

Duke glared at his father, then looked back at Elle. Choose me, he seemed to be saying silently, side with me.

Though Elle recognized the plea, she just couldn't turn away from his father. If Duke had at first seemed like a young prince, H.D. Hyland was a king, polished and confident and worldly—and clearly the master, not only of this beautiful yacht, but of everything that went with it. She stood frozen in silence.

After a minute, Duke turned on his heel, knocked into a chair. He stumbled and almost fell, but then caught himself. Flushed with embarrassment, he glanced once more at Elle and then hurried off the deck.

"You and I seem to be in the same position, my dear," said H.D. with a laugh. "We just don't seem to be very popular tonight." He picked up the champagne bottle and offered her more, and though Elle was already starting to feel tipsy, she nodded assent. She didn't want to be dismissed as a mere child by this sophisticated man, as his own son had been.

He filled her glass with a smooth, practiced movement, touching her fingers lightly, fleetingly, yet somehow with a hint of more to come. He talked for a while longer, describing all he had seen since arriving in Monaco, searching his memory for details that would satisfy her eager questions. Then he said: "Now that's enough about Grace and Rainier. Tell me about yourself, Gabrielle. Does your family live in Monaco?"

"I have no family," she replied. Her crude cousin certainly didn't count, and if Ralph Sandeman wasn't in Monaco, then perhaps he was dead after all.

"I'm sorry," H.D. said softly, and Elle could believe he meant it. He seemed to be waiting for more, and to her utter surprise, she found herself telling the story she would have told Duke if he hadn't suddenly darted off to get champagne. Not all of it, not the ugly parts—but the parts that made her proud. About her mother, Monique Veraix, an athletic girl from a small village who had shown a talent for diving, so that she was taken away and trained until she became the finest woman diver in all of France, a silver medalist at the 1936 Olympics in Munich. Elle told, too, of the American photographer who had taken pictures of her mother, beautiful pictures that made him so curious about the subject that he had sought her out. He had fallen in love with her, then, and they had spent an idyllic few weeks traveling the capitals of Europe. "It was a true love, what they had," Elle said, almost defiantly. "But then . . ." She faltered, a low sob choking off her narrative.

"Something happened," H.D. prompted gently. "Something stronger than love, perhaps?"

Elle nodded. "It was war, civil war . . . that one in Spain. My father was sent by his American newspaper to take photographs." She paused, wondering which version to tell. Sometimes, she said that her mother had married first, and that Ralph Sandeman had been killed in the fighting. It was the version her mother had told when she had first returned to Bizecque, though it had come to be disbelieved after she failed at Elle's baptism to produce documents for the priest. Elle decided to gloss over the facts, but without lying. If she were exposed as a liar, H.D. would surely want nothing to do with her. "Of course, my mother thought he would come back to her, and she went back to her home in Provence to wait. But"—here the tears spilled down Elle's cheeks—"he never came. And he never knew . . . he had a daughter. . . ."

H.D. shook his head. "You poor kid," he said, taking out a fine handkerchief and dabbing her cheeks dry.

The sympathy in his gray eyes and his soothing voice told Elle she was right to have altered the story. Better to have left out Monique's shame, when, with her infant baby already born, she had been forced from Paris to her home village merely so that they could both eat. "Later, in the war, my mother joined the Resistance," Elle went on proudly. "She was very brave, very courageous. She took great risks for her country."

"She sounds like a very special woman," H.D. said.

"She was one of their greatest heroines," Elle affirmed. There was no need to say that shame pushed Monique into taking wild, unspeakable risks, to attempt feats of daring above and beyond the call of duty to her country. "But she was captured and executed by the Gestapo."

H.D. put his arm around her, but said nothing, as if he knew that mere words would cheapen the tragedy of Monique's death.

"I was raised by a cousin," Elle concluded, "but it was very difficult—even more so after the war, when there was such hardship in France." She didn't say that during the war, everyone was united against the Boche, their common enemy. But later, after the people of the village were released from the sufferings of hunger and deprivation, they took up their narrow-minded prejudices again—and made what was left of Elle's childhood into a living hell.

They sat together in silence for a while, and Elle believed she could actually feel H.D.'s strength and understanding . . . perhaps even something more.

From over the water came the faint strains of a waltz. H.D. got up, bowed slightly, and held out his hands. The courtly gesture brought new tears to Elle's eyes as she moved into the circling shelter of his arms.

He danced beautifully. Rejecting the crude and rough gropings of the boys of her village, Elle had danced alone to the music of the radio and with partners manufactured of dreams and fantasies, but H.D. Hyland was better. Though he was very much the leader, his hand on the small of her back was gentle, his steps graceful and measured. Strange, she thought, as they glided along the deck of the yacht, that the wife of such a handsome and extraordinary man should be so quarrelsome, and his son, so childishly hostile.

When the music stopped, H.D. held her out at arm's length,

studying her face in the moonlight. It was very quiet, the stillness broken only by the lapping of the water against the sides of the yacht. A moment later, he touched her cheek, her mouth, tracing the outline of her full, sensuous lips delicately with his fingertips. His touch awoke a hunger that had never been fulfilled, a yearning to know the love and caring that had eluded her since her mother's death. When this kingly man gripped her arm lightly and pulled slightly, leading her, she followed with only the barest hesitation.

With a few steps she was through a door to a room off the deck, a long, luxuriously furnished salon where only a single lamp was dimly burning at a far end. He took her in his arms again, drawing her very close for a long, sweet kiss, she inhaled the faint aroma of tobacco smoke . . . and then something else, the scent of power and wealth, the sweetest fragrance of all. His hands were strong and sure as he caressed her, and even in her inexperience, Elle knew he was skilled in the way he touched a woman.

Giddy with champagne, with the excitement of being desired by such an extraordinary man, she offered no resistance when he began to unbutton her dress, very carefully, as if it were the finest Chanel and not just a simple provincial cotton. The way he touched her neck, the full, rounded breasts beneath her thin, frayed slip was, she thought, almost reverent. When he whispered words of endearment against her throat, she felt as though it was an incantation that had put her in a spell. She moved with him unprotesting as he prodded her gently to a silk-upholstered couch and pushed her down. When he pushed her legs apart, Elle reacted at first with alarmed glances, first toward the door they had entered, then another near the dimly burning lamp.

"No one will bother us," he whispered. "Don't worry . . . let me love you."

Love her! She relaxed again and yielded to his caress, allowing him to touch her where no man ever had before.

Patiently, he probed all the secret parts of her, watching her face, repeating what gave pleasure and retreating from what did not. Her breathing grew shallow, and the sensation of throbbing fullness grew stronger and stronger, until she felt it would sweep her away.

There was a quick, sharp pain when he entered her, as she yielded the prize she could only give once. She uttered a tiny cry, he covered her mouth with his as their bodies joined in the final, crashing surge of fulfillment.

In a minute, worried thoughts began to churn through her mind. What would happen now?

But then he said quietly, "Stay with me, Gabrielle. I'll make it better next time. I'll make everything better for you."

It was the answer to every prayer, she thought.

"Yes, I will," she whispered, holding him tighter. "Yes. Thank you."

He laughed lightly. "You needn't thank me. I want you to be happy. Make a wish."

"I have so many."

"Choose one, then, just one for now . . ."

Her mind raced, throwing up all her fondest wishes. A life of luxury and ease. Wonderful things to eat and beautiful things to wear. Plenty of money, always. And enough love to take away the taste of the sour reality she had known. Yet somehow she didn't dare utter such sweeping fantasies. "I wish," she said at last, "I wish . . . I could go to the wedding tomorrow." She looked at him expectantly, as a child might, not really believing, yet hoping all the same.

"Then you shall," he said, as if nothing could be simpler.

"*Vraiment*?" she said in an astonished whisper, her eyes glowing with renewed excitement. "You can really make that happen?"

"When you know me better, Elle, you'll never have the slightest doubt that I can do whatever I say I will." There was a hint of rebuke in his words, though as he gazed into her eyes, she saw nothing but affection. "Do you want to stay with me and learn all the things I can do?"

For the first time, she felt an edge of fear in her awe and

desire. As much as she rejected the provincial superstitions of the village people she'd grown up with, she was reminded of their tales of the devil, who would promise anything and everything in order to buy a soul. Could H.D. be the devil?

"You don't have to, of course," he went on. "But we'll be sailing in two days, right after the wedding, moving on to the Greek islands. There would be sun, and clear water, and beautiful things to see. Wouldn't you like to come along?"

She could not resist. "Yes, yes. . . . But how?" she added quickly, remembering that H.D. Hyland's wife would also be with them.

"The 'how' is simple, my dear. You are a friend of my son's . . . and as such, you are a very welcome guest."

A friend of Duke's. Now she understood. He was talking about discretion . . . the French invented discretion, had they not? Yet the mention of Duke, and remembrance of his kindness in the cafe, evoked a twinge of guilt. He had brought her aboard the yacht . . . had opened this world to her.

Yet it was her life at stake. This miraculous day had brought her the chance to leave behind Monique's shame and escape into the paradise of the wealthy. Would she ever have such a chance again? Weighed against all that, Duke's feelings seemed like a small obstacle that could be overcome. Perhaps someday they could be friends, she reasoned, but in any case, she could not give up the realization of her dreams because of a spoiled boy's wounded pride.

"Yes," she said, "I want to go with you. I want that more than anything . . ."

"Then it's settled. And now, dear girl, you'd best get a few hours of sleep."

They dressed quickly, and H.D. led the way down a short flight of steps to a lower deck. "This is my cabin, he said softly, and *that* one," he added with a meaningful glance, "that's where Mrs. Hyland sleeps. Duke is down the corridor.

We'll just put you in here, in the middle . . ." He opened the stateroom door.

Elle's breath caught in her throat when she saw the plush furnishings, the fur throw on the bed, silk curtains at the portholes, and several vases of fresh flowers. "*Magnifique*," she murmured.

"Make yourself comfortable, Elle—and ring if you need anything." He indicated a buzzer to the right of the bed. "Sweet dreams." He dropped a kiss on her lips and left.

Like a child in a toy store, Elle raced around the cabin that was now to be *hers*, touching every piece of furniture, as if to convince herself she wasn't dreaming. She jumped up and down on the mattress. Heavenly soft! And under the thick fur coverlet, there were sheets of the finest cotton embroidered with the Hyland crest. How different they were from the coarse muslin she'd slept on all her life.

She took off her dress again and hung it in the closet. Beside a silk robe that was also embroidered with the Hyland crest it looked poor and out of place. She was sure she was too excited to rest, and yet, a moment after she put her head on the luxurious down pillow, she was fast asleep.

She was awakened by a gentle tapping on the door and the fragrance of rich, dark coffee. "*Entrez*," she called.

A steward entered the stateroom, bearing a silver tray set with white monogrammed china. He set the tray on the bedside table, his expression impassive and correct. It was not his business to know who she was or what she was doing here. It was his function to serve.

"Do you require anything else, *mademoiselle*?" he asked politely.

Elle surveyed the contents of the tray, her mouth watering at the sight of enormous red strawberries, not yet in season, a plate of fragrant croissants and steaming *café au lait*. "*Merci, non*," she replied, and as soon as the door closed behind him, she tore into a croissant and began stuffing it into her mouth.

A short time later, there was another knock on the door. This time, there were two stewards, loaded down with dress bags and packages. "Mr. Hyland ordered these things to be brought to you," one of them explained.

Speechless, she stared at the two men, who stood in the doorway, waiting to hear her wishes.

"May we put your things away, *mademoiselle*?" one of them asked finally.

"Yes, of course," she answered with a composure she didn't feel. And as one gorgeous dress after another was placed in the closet, as pairs of shoes in various sizes were unpacked, along with handbags and belts and bathing suits and sports clothes, tears came to Elle's eyes. In all her life, no one had ever treated her with such kindness, such respect.

When the stewards left, Elle jumped naked from the bed and ran to the closet. She rifled through the dresses, not knowing which one to choose for the wonderful day that still lay ahead. The blue linen? The green silk? Her head was spinning with possibilities—and with the wonder of what H.D. Hyland could do while everyone else slept. Finally, she settled on a rose-colored organza, with a matching jacket and decorated with tiny, hand-sewn flowers.

She showered, lingering a long time and savoring what seemed to be an endless supply of hot water. And when she was finished, she helped herself to a dazzling array of cosmetics and toiletries, more than she had ever seen in one place. She brushed her hair, then chose a crown of pink, twisted ribbon to cover her head. Carefully, she slipped on her new dress and added a pair of matching silk pumps.

Looking into the cabin's full-length mirror, she saw a young woman she scarcely recognized, radiant and glowing—and every inch a lady.

When she walked up to the top deck, she saw that a table had been laid out. H.D. was eating a hearty breakfast of eggs and toast, but Duke, looking red-eyed and hung over, had nothing but a cup of black coffee in front of him. As H.D.

rose to greet Elle, Duke remained in his chair until his father forced him, with a silent push, to rise.

In her excitement, Elle hadn't realized she would feel quite so uncomfortable in Duke's presence, unable to escape the hurt and angry look in his eyes. Only H.D. seemed completely at ease, even when Joanne Hyland joined them at the table.

"This is Edward's very good friend, Gabrielle," he said. "I don't think you had a chance to meet properly last night. She'll be accompanying us to the wedding . . . and on our cruise to the islands."

Joanne turned coolly to Elle, taking in the new clothes before her eyes rose to inspect Elle's face. At last she said a flat "hello," and then promptly turned her attention to her breakfast.

Duke glanced from one to the other, then bolted down his coffee and left the table.

Joanne looked after him. "Don't you want to go with your friend, Gabrielle?"

Elle didn't know how to answer. But H.D. came to the rescue. "I don't see why she shouldn't finish her breakfast just because Edward isn't hungry."

Elle saw Joanne smile thinly, though she didn't bother looking up from her strawberries.

They continued eating in silence. Occasionally, Elle caught Joanne studying her, yet her expression didn't seem unfriendly, merely curious. Elle felt she had passed inspection, yet shrewdly she guessed that even if she hadn't, H.D. would have found a way to make everything all right. It was he who ruled this strange family, just like a king. And kings, in their divine right, were above the rules that bound other, lesser mortals.

She looked to him for some sort of signal, but he continued to eat his breakfast, making the kind of polite conversation he'd make if she were, indeed, Duke's "very good friend."

When they were ready to leave, he brushed up against her lightly and whispered in her ear. "Tonight," he said softly. "I'll see you later tonight."

* * *

On the morning of April nineteenth, Elle mounted the red-carpeted steps of the Cathedral of St. Nicholas, passing footmen and sentries with bayonets cocked. Walking a few steps ahead were H.D. and Joanne; at her side was Duke, silent, tight-lipped.

Through the Gothic facade of the white limestone church passed the six hundred hand-chosen guests, royalty of every kind, including the Aga Kahn, Egypt's deposed King Farouk, Ava Gardner, Aristotle Onassis, and Gloria Swanson.

Elle stared openly at the faces she had seen only in magazines and the cinema—and realized eventually that a great many people were staring back at *her*. It was a delicious feeling to be the object of such curiosity because she was part of a group so distinguished, the family of an important American millionaire.

Inside, the church was awash with flowers. The altar was covered with white lilies, lilacs, and hydrangeas surrounded by candles, and the chandeliers hung with gilded baskets of white snapdragons.

After she and Duke were seated, she attempted a whispered conversation, but he merely glowered at her. Did he know? she wondered, did he know that she and H.D. had become lovers? Or was he angry because she had been so obviously impressed by his father.

She would make him forgive her, Elle assured herself, not wanting any dark clouds to spoil this most wonderful of days.

Amidst a hush that bordered on reverence, and as thirty-eight million people watched on television, Grace emerged from the palace on the arm of her father, Jack Kelly. She was a vision of loveliness, her gown a masterpiece created from century-old rose-point lace that had been purchased from a museum, twenty-five yards of silk taffeta, a hundred yards of silk net. On the veil which framed her exquisite face were sewn thousands of tiny pearls.

As Grace walked into the church, she was followed by

four flower girls, two pages, the maid of honor, and six bridesmaids in yellow silk organza. She took her place at the altar, and a moment later, a fanfare of trumpets heralded the arrival of His Serene Highness, Prince Rainier, wearing a splendid uniform of his own design, adorned with gold epaulets and medals celebrating Monaco's history. Soon the couple was kneeling before Monsignor Gilles Barthe, Monaco's bishop.

The ceremony itself was simple, an age-old ritual much like those Elle had seen in her native village—even down to the mistakes. She smiled when the six-year-old ring bearer, Sebastian von Furstenberg, approached the altar and dropped one of the two rings he was carrying. And when Rainier had trouble slipping the ring on his bride's finger.

A short time later, the one-hour nuptial mass was over. After the last benediction, the royal couple genuflected, turned toward the congregation, and walked from the church, relaxed and smiling, and into a waiting Rolls-Royce.

They rode through the streets of Monaco, holding hands, and when they arrived at a tiny peach-colored church near the harbor—the shrine of the virgin, Saint Dévote, who brought Christianity to Monaco—Grace left her bridal bouquet there as an offering. Then at last, it was time for celebration, far more splendid than any that had gone before. Elle understood this as the Americans perhaps could not. In the eyes of Monaco's citizens, the civil ceremony had been a mere formality; there could be no real marriage without the blessing of the church.

Feeling like a princess herself, Elle tried to memorize every wonderful detail of the reception in the courtyard of Le Rocher—the music, the flowers, the feast of caviar with champagne, smoked salmon, lobsters, every delicacy imaginable. The wedding cake was magnificent—five elaborately decorated tiers—and when Rainier made the first cut with his sword, Elle imagined herself someday standing as proud and beautiful as Grace did now with her groom at her side.

But who could she marry? For the first time, she was aware that it would be a complicated road to travel before H.D. would be free to marry her.

Yet he had changed wives once before. . . .

Soon after the wedding cake was served and eaten, and a final round of toasts made and drunk, the entire wedding party left the reception to attend a soccer game at the National Stadium. Grace and Rainier changed clothes and departed on the *Deo Juvante II*, waving to the crowds as the boat moved out of the harbor, and two parachute-bearing rockets shot into the air, dropping the flags of the United States and Monaco.

So Princess Grace's honeymoon began.

And late that evening, after H.D. Hyland had come to her cabin and was gone again, Gabrielle also began a kind of honeymoon when the *Highland Fling* set sail for the Greek islands. As the yacht steamed out of the harbor, she had a fleeting moment of sadness, as if she were saying good-bye at last to the memory of the father she'd never known. But the moment passed; there was little room for regret, with the future so bright, with the promise of luxury and wealth beyond anything she'd imagined. It might be a while before she and the king who loved her could actually be married, but for the meantime she was married in any case—to a new way of life.

From the battered suitcase, she unpacked her single precious possession, the photograph of her mother in a silver frame, her arched body suspended between the sky and the water like a bird in flight, captured forever by the camera of the man who had loved her—and then abandoned her.

Snug in her luxurious cabin, her bed still warm with her lover's body, his whispered promises still fresh in her thoughts, Elle felt she had learned the lessons of the photograph well, for after her brief moment of triumph, Monique had plummeted downward, to be broken and later, to die. Elle had vowed not to repeat her mistake, to throw away everything she had to offer in the name of love. Love was not enough. Without the protection of a man's name, the comfort and respectability he could provide, a woman was defenseless against the harshness and cruelty of the world.

She had chosen wisely, she was sure of that. Yes, H.D. Hyland was married now, but that would change. Hadn't he made it clear his marriage was an unhappy one? And hadn't he explained that Joanne no longer loved him, that it was only his money she desired. Elle understood about such marriages. Even in her little village, there were couples who lived under the same roof and spoke scarcely a civil word to one another. She saw tight-lipped women in church every morning, husbands in the corner bistro every night. They didn't divorce because the church wouldn't allow it, but H.D. had no such difficulty. And now that he had found someone to love him, *anything* could happen.

With the power of his wealth, he had turned her into a lady, taken her to a royal wedding. She had no reason to doubt that he would keep the whispered promise he had made on his last visit to her bed, after they had lifted anchor to sail from Monaco: "You'll never be sorry, Gabrielle. Be good to me and I'll always take very good care of you."

Three

Willow Cross, North Carolina. August, 1963

FOR a hundred years, the air over Willow Cross had been permeated by a distinct perfume, a pungent, faintly sweet aroma—the smell of tobacco. From the auction houses where it was brought by the independent farmers to be sold for the best obtainable price, from the vast curing houses where it was carefully dried, from the factories where it was converted . . . from half the buildings in town, the smell wafted into the air so it could hardly be avoided anywhere within a radius of fifty miles.

At times, it could be cloying and somewhat objectionable—and there were some people in town who might have complained . . . if tobacco had not been at the heart of the security and ever-increasing prosperity of Willow Cross for as long as any living citizen of the place could remember.

A century ago, the geographical location of the then small river town and the climate of its surrounding region, conducive to the growth of tobacco, had made Willow Cross an appealing location for the many small companies that turned out the products which appealed to the tobacco users of the day: "plug"—dried tobacco fashioned into cakes flavored with honey and spices—and "twist"—similarly flavored leaf prepared in small rolls. Of course, at the time, tobacco was meant to be chewed. Only among the gentry were there a few men who smoked cigars or put tobacco in pipes—a custom first practiced by the American Indians. It was their encounter with the Indians, in fact, that had given the European explorers and settlers of the New World a taste for tobacco.

As competition among the tobacco manufacturers of Willow Cross increased, smaller companies were forced to consolidate; the more aggressive companies gobbled up the weaker, and finally one company overtook all the rest.

That was the beginning of Willow Cross as a company town—and the triumphant emergence of Hyland Tobacco as a giant that had grown to be one of the largest manufacturers of cigarettes and tobacco products in the world.

On hot days the inescapable smell in the air over Willow Cross could be particularly oppressive, as it was on this hot morning near the end of August in the spacious cottage shared by Gabrielle Sandeman and her six-year-old daughter, Nicolette. Though the giant attic fan moved the air around creating the illusion of a breeze, Elle had now lived through enough seasons in Willow Cross to know there would be no real relief until the tropical storms of the fall season arrived. She knew, too, that there would never be any relief from the faint but pervasive smell in the air. And she had grown to hate it more than the heat. It seemed to be the very symbol of the lure she had followed, and the disappointments she had endured.

"*Attends, chérie*, be still!" Elle snapped irritably as she finished combing her daughter's long, silky blond hair and began to arrange it into a braid.

Fairly spinning with excitement, Niki was finding it very hard to stand passively before the full-length mirror in her pink-and-white bedroom even though she knew her mother only wanted to have her look her best. Today she was being taken to register for school! For Niki, the word conjured up images from story books of happy, laughing children at play together. A very different image from the quiet cloistered existence she shared with her mother. As she shifted from one foot to the other, Niki could scarcely wait for the day to begin.

When Elle slipped a freshly ironed dress over her daughter's head, Niki began to squirm. The starched pique fabric, the elaborate embroidery scratched her tender young skin, and she rebelled against it.

"Why do I have to wear this?" Niki demanded. "Why can't I wear my blue dress? Or my red one?" She pointed to the comfortable, well-worn garments that hung neatly in her closet.

"So you won't look like just a little savage," Elle answered shrilly, her patience eroded by the heat. "You must show your quality. How many times have I told you, Niki, you aren't like the other children in this town? Someday, you are going to have a very special kind of life. You must be ready to look and act accordingly."

Niki yielded to her mother's will with a frown, though she scarcely listened to the explanation. She had been hearing such words for as long as she could remember; they had been worn thin with frequent repetition—and they had never held very much meaning for her in the first place. What did it mean to look like "quality"?

Elle caught Niki's reaction and heaved a sigh. She realized that Niki had yet to fully understand the situation. But her little girl wasn't a baby anymore, and after she started school, after she saw how other children lived there would be questions, Elle knew there would be questions she would find it increasingly hard to answer.

The indignities and hurts that Elle knew would lie ahead for Niki—as they had been part of her own life—made her wish sometimes that she had disobeyed H.D. For when she had realized she was going to have a baby, she had consulted him about terminating the pregnancy.

"I forbid it!" he had declared fiercely. "It's a violation of the most holy laws."

"But until we can be married—"

"I won't kill a child, born or unborn. I won't let you do it! We don't allow that here."

Of course, she had never raised the matter again after that. Elle could only assume it meant that H.D. would honor his obligations, every one of them, and that was all the better for her. All the better for Niki, too . . . eventually. But for the present their status remained unclarified, and Elle could only think how much easier it would have been if she had waited until she and H.D. were married before she'd had a child.

Though Elle herself had no wish to share the life of Willow Cross's poorer citizens—the employees of Hyland Tobacco—it was difficult to be satisfied with the life she had, days of boredom and exile, sweetened only by creature comforts and the promise of something better that grew more elusive with each day. The nine-room cottage H.D. had found for her was far removed from any neighbors, ten miles from the center of town, and surrounded by fifty acres of fields and forest. Once, like the adjoining properties, it had been farmed for tobacco. But during some past financial crisis, it had been foreclosed by one of the town banks, and then had passed somehow into a dusty file of the vast Hyland company portfolio. After Elle moved into the house, landscapers were sent, flowers and shrubs were planted, a field behind the house was cleared. But it was no longer farmed. Elle didn't use the land, nor even explore its boundaries. She stayed in her house, waiting for H.D. She never entertained anyone at the house but her lover—and had nothing to do with any of the townspeople other than Louise, a colored lady who cleaned the house and did the laundry and ironing, the boy who delivered the groceries she ordered by telephone, the dressmaker, and a handful of shopkeepers. As Niki had grown older, Elle was made more aware of what a lonely and barren life it was for a child, no matter how comfortable it was made by money. Elle, too, was gratified by the prospect of Niki's attendance at school, finally being absorbed into the community of other children.

Tucking a fresh linen handkerchief into Niki's pocket, Elle sent the child downstairs to wait, then returned to her own bedroom to ready herself. At a vanity, she dabbed on a liberal amount of Joy—she insisted on having the most expensive perfume, even though no one in Willow Cross sold it and it had to be shipped specially from Charleston—then paused to inspect herself carefully in the mirror. The dewy-eyed teenager was only a memory now; the impeccably groomed woman reflected in the glass was still very lovely, like a flower in full bloom. Yet a sadness in the soft brown eyes, a tightness around the mouth gave evidence of thwarted expectations and frustrated dreams.

Her excitement at being brought to America, at being provided with papers and a place to live had long since faded. Willow Cross was not the America of her fantasies; it was, in fact, no more glamorous than Bizecque, especially for a young, unmarried mother who lived on the fringe of its "respectable" society. No doubt Willow Cross was far more interesting for Joanne Hyland, Elle reflected bitterly. Joanne was the queen of the town, of the Hyland estate, the Hyland summer homes, the yachts and cars and everything else that went with being H.D. Hyland's wife—a position that Elle had expected to fill by now.

She had yet to abandon all hope, but her patience was badly frayed. For too long H.D. had teased her with the promise that a divorce was "only a matter of time"—of finding the right moment in his complicated life, of getting certain elaborate financial arrangements worked out. Something always "came up," something always made it a "bad time" to end his second marriage.

Elle patted a stray brown hair that had escaped the sleek chignon she wore these days and straightened the skirt of her creamy-white linen dress. No matter what she lacked in social standing—and no matter how high the temperature climbed—she refused to adopt the slovenly habits of this Godforsaken town, or allow her child to run around shoeless and half-naked.

As she turned to leave the bedroom, she passed the silver-framed photograph on the dresser, the picture of her mother, frozen forever in time in her one single moment of glory. As always, the image was so arresting that she stopped to stare, drawn in as though she were there, could see the graceful figure floating through space. . . . But the image no longer encouraged her, it was no longer a simple source of pride. It had become a reproach, reminding Elle not only of the tragic end to which Monique had come despite all her achievement, but also of her own bitter failures. How many times had she cursed Fate for making her a bastard? Yet now, in spite of all her efforts, she had inflicted the same fate on a child of her own. Niki did not have a name cither. Sandeman? A fiction, the name of a man who now seemed no more real than his mythical namesake who came to scatter sand in the eyes of children and send them to their sweet, impossible dreams.

"I'm sorry, Mama," Elle whispered to the picture, "I tried to do better. But how? I don't know anymore . . ." She clutched the framed picture in her hands, as if somehow it might hold an answer, a lesson she had failed to learn. But there was no revelation, no epiphany—only the urgent voice of her daughter calling her back to reality.

"*Maman*, hurry, please. I mustn't be late. . . ."

Downstairs, Niki was swinging on the screen door.

"Stop that, *chérie*!" Elle commanded, "you'll dirty your dress!" With her handkerchief, she wiped Niki's hands, then stood back once more to survey her handiwork. Her daughter already showed the promise of exceptional beauty—a beauty, Elle was gratified to think, that would surely outshine Joanne's daughter, Pepper. She would be more intelligent, too, Elle thought with some small satisfaction, judging from the gossip she heard about the Hyland girl's schoolwork and behavior. At the age of nineteen, Pepper already had the distinction of being suspended or expelled from several fine schools.

With Niki's hand in hers, Elle led the way down the winding gravel path, towards the black Buick sedan H.D. had given her as a birthday gift. As she opened the car door, the mailman was approaching.

"Mornin' Mrs. Sandeman," he said politely, tipping his cap. Since she had a child, Elle was accorded the trouble-saving title that suggested she was, or once had been married. By now, nevertheless, there were few people in Willow Cross who didn't know the facts.

"Looks like another scorcher," the mailman said affably as he dug into his pouch. "We could sure use a rain to cool things off."

Elle acknowledged the greeting with a nod and a small smile, as she had seen H.D. acknowledge his inferiors. She had taught herself to look and act like a respectable lady of wealth and breeding, that much she had accomplished. It was the reason she had chosen the black Buick sedan instead of the red convertible H.D. had originally offered. Small-minded townsfolk might gossip about her here, exactly as they had in Bizecque—but in Willow Cross there was a difference. H.D. was *king* here, and whatever his "subjects" thought about Gabrielle Sandeman, none were ever bold enough to risk affronting her directly.

"Nothing much for you today," the postman said, holding out a slender packet.

"Just leave it in the mailbox, thank you. I'll look at it later."

Elle had no curiosity about the morning mail. It was always the same. There would be circulars from stores in Charleston and Atlanta, places she shopped every few months—or more often, when H.D. was feeling generous; and bills from the local stores which, at H.D.'s instruction, she mailed in a biweekly packet to an accountant in town. And, on the first weekday of every month, regular as clockwork, there would be her allowance check for $850, drawn on the account of Hyland Tobacco's trucking division. H.D. had put her on the company payroll as an "inventory clerk," though of course he had made it very clear she was never to report for work.

Driving down the rough country road that led to her property, Elle passed mile after mile of ripening tobacco. Though she had grown to hate the sight and smell of it, as she hated everything else about Willow Cross, it was obvious that little Nicolette felt differently. Her blue eyes would survey the passing scene with an eager brightness, her nose tilted up slightly to catch the scent coming off the fields. Often, she would comment on the crop. "They'll be picking soon," she might say. Or, "Look what a pretty color it is, *Maman*."

As bitter as Elle felt, she had the wisdom and generosity of spirit not to thrust her prejudices onto her daughter. She wanted Niki's comforting illusions to last for as long as possible.

When they drove into the town, business of the day had already begun. During the summer months, everyone opened early and closed early, so as to leave a few hours' escape from the heat. The school was located just beyond the two story structure that served as town hall, fire department, and police station. As Elle parked the Buick in front, she paused to survey the exterior of the simple, gray concrete building. Distaste showed plainly on her face. None of H.D.'s other children had gone to a place like this. They had been educated by private tutors and the best of schools. Yet when she'd broached the subject of Niki's education, H.D. had seemed passive, almost disinterested. "If you want to send the child to boarding school, just let me know and I'll have my accountant take care of it." Her protest that Niki was too young to be sent away, had earned only an impatient shrug from H.D. "Well, then, what *is* it you want?" he had demanded.

Intimidated by his tone and by his displeasure, Elle had instantly backed off. In the years she'd been H.D.'s mistress, she had learned the difference between coaxing and pushing.

H.D. Hyland was a man who did exactly what he wanted, when he wanted. A mistress who ignored that reality, Elle knew, would soon become an ex-mistress. The result of the conversation was piano lessons and dancing instruction for Niki—a small enough gain, her mother felt, considering all the privileges and benefits the *others* had.

Like most public buildings in Willow Cross, James Buchanan Hyland Elementary School was named for a member of the ruling family—in this case H.D.'s uncle, who had been killed at the tender age of fourteen by a bolt of lightning as he rode his horse during a thunderstorm. Though the school was supported by public funds, the town fathers, ever mindful of the fact that without Hyland Tobacco there would be no town, readily agreed to honor the memory of young Jimmy Hyland as the family suggested.

When Elle entered the office of the school clerk holding her little girl by the hand, she perceived at once the spark of recognition that flared in the eyes of the plump thirtyish woman behind the desk. So, she would have to contend with being known, with having her little girl recognized as H.D.'s "love child"—as the Americans said. *Eh bien*, there was no help for it now. All that really mattered was that Niki should be accepted for herself, and remain oblivious and unhurt. Elle took note of the name of the clerk etched in a small plaque at the edge of the desktop, BELINDA JENNINGS. Sometimes winning people over could be no more than a matter of calling them by name, appreciating that they had an identity.

"Good morning, Miss Jennings," Elle began, compensating for being recognized by laying on her best lady-of-the-manor voice. "I would like to register my daughter for the new term."

There was a pause as the clerk's eyes rudely scanned Elle from top to bottom.

Words of rebuke formed in Elle's mind as she gave up on winning over the clerk. *Are you making pictures of me in bed with him . . . or just adding up the cost of my clothes?* She could imagine the envy a woman like this might feel for the way she looked. In addition to being overweight, the clerk had a bad complexion, and was wearing a cheap, blue shirtwaist, faded from too many washings. From a remembrance of her own past life, Elle could almost sympathize with the pain of being unattractive and ill groomed. So she held her tongue.

At last the clerk plucked a printed form from a stack at a corner of her desk. "Fill this out," she said frostily. Automatically, Elle's eyes narrowed with spite as she looked back at the woman, but she took the form and retreated wordlessly. This was no time and place to be fighting battles. Moving to a rank of chairs against the wall, she pulled Niki down next to her and began filling in blanks on the form, beginning with Niki's full name—Nicolette Monique Sandeman—and their address and telephone number.

Immediately, she arrived at a problem—a space marked "Father," and one following for "Father's place of business." She lingered over them, wondering whether to insert something—anything—rather than leave it glaringly blank. Glancing up as she pondered, she found the eyes of the clerk nakedly riveted on her. Elle realized now that the woman, who was thoroughly familiar with the form, had been anticipating the awkward problem and seemed to be relishing her embarrassment.

Almost defiantly now, she left a blank as she moved on to the next section marked "Medical History." Here she recorded all of Niki's immunizations, along with the name of Dr. Charles Boynton, the local physician who tended them both. When she came to the question of "hospitalizations," Elle shuddered, remembering that awful day when Niki had fallen from a tree, striking a sharp, protruding rock and tearing open a deep, jagged wound in her side. There had been so much blood spurting from the wound, soaking her dress . . . Elle had been terrified that Niki might die. Thank God for Dr. Boynton, she thought. He had taken care of everything, and while Elle had waited in abject terror in the small reception room of the Willow Cross Hospital, he had carefully stitched Niki's wounds and administered the blood transfusion that had saved her life. Mercifully, there had been no more accidents. Niki had been strong and healthy ever since.

After putting her signature at the bottom, Elle rose and went to the clerk.

The woman took the sheet. With scarcely a look at it, she said, "This form is incomplete. You have to provide *all* the information requested."

Elle stood frozen with humiliation and uncertainty. The first cardinal rule H.D. had laid down after Niki's birth was that he must never be named as the father. He would accept responsibility, he said, he would always support mother and child—but he would never allow any documentation to exist. At least, he amended, not until he was divorced from Joanne.

In the silence, Niki's impatience vented itself. "*Maman*, don't wait. I want to start school."

The clerk ignored the child and directed herself to Elle. "You must also supply proof of age for your child—a birth certificate. The original or a notarized copy will do. . . ."

Elle struggled for some strategy to deal with the situation. She knew that the birth records filed in the town registry said "father unknown." Gazing back at the smug face of Miss Jennings, Elle suspected that the clerk knew, too—through a friend or relative in the town offices, perhaps. Weren't almost all the families intertwined through generations of living here, serving the Hylands? It would hardly be surprising if some had an ax to grind, a score to settle for a job lost at one of the Hyland factories, a grudge nursed simply because the Hylands had it all.

"Please," Elle appealed, working hard to keep her voice steady, "enroll my child. I'll come back with the papers tomorrow." Perhaps by then she could get H.D. to agree, or just to exert pressure behind the scenes—or even forge a proper certificate. Anything to buy time.

"I'm sorry," said Belinda Jennings. "But we cannot permit any child to take a place without proper documentation.

After all, we couldn't just allow *anyone* to come in here, claiming to be one thing or another without proof, can we?"

With a tug at her mother's dress, Niki pleaded again. "I want to go to school. I don't want to play alone anymore."

For the first time the clerk examined the youngster. Elle thought she saw the woman's sour expression begin to change, and she was tempted to drop her pose, even to beg. It might tilt the balance. *All right, you know the truth, but it's not my child's fault*, she might say. *Even if you resent me or them, hate what I am, please don't make my daughter suffer. . . .*

But her pride was as much a part of Elle as her skin. She couldn't stop herself from playing it the other way. "I think the rules could be changed a little," she said with the kind of sly warning edge H.D. could use to imply his power.

"I can see why you would think rules don't matter," the clerk said, almost sneering. "But that's not the way the school is run."

Elle tried to hold her ground, to summon up a stronger protest, a threat. But she was afraid the clerk might blurt out some hurtful insult in front of Niki.

Her will broke. Grabbing Niki by the arm, she wheeled and marched her back outside to the car.

Niki was dazed. "Mama, why did we leave? Why won't the lady let me go to school?"

"Hush, *chérie*, hush," Elle said as she helped Niki into the passenger seat. "You shall go to school, I promise."

"But when?" Niki persisted. "Why didn't you tell the lady about Mr. Hyland?"

"She will be told," Elle said, her fury compounded as she heard Niki refer to the man she knew as her father in such formal terms.

Elle had argued long and hard with H.D. when he had first set down the rule that Niki must never refer to him as "Daddy" or "Papa" or even just "Father." But at last he had silenced her with his ultimatum. "Either she learns to abide by that rule—and you enforce it—or our relationship is at an end. I can't have Niki shouting out 'Daddy' if she happens to see me on the street. So it's best if she doesn't form the habit. Perhaps later . . . when things are different. . . ." Elle had carefully schooled her child in the rules, just as she had patiently told Niki how very busy "Mr. Hyland" was to explain why he did not live with them and only came to visit once in a while, though he paid for the house they lived in, the food they ate, and the clothes they wore.

But what could explain to Niki why she had been denied entrance to a school so humble that even the children of the poorest Willow Creek workers were admitted. It was beyond endurance!

Niki was still clamoring for an explanation. "Just tell me when, Mama? How long before I can be with the other children?"

Elle closed the car door with a slam, shutting off the questions. When she strode around to get behind the wheel, Niki was silent, sensing the danger of her mother's mood. Furiously, Elle shoved the shift lever into drive position and pressed down on the accelerator. The Buick shot forward, and she drove with purpose down the street and turned the first corner at such high speed that the tires squealed and the car skidded slightly.

Elle touched the brakes—and only then became aware of the destination to which she had unthinkingly headed. Her heart began to pound at the very thought of where she was going, but she gripped the wheel tightly and resumed speed.

Without being aware of the turns in the road, or the passing miles, she found herself on the road outside town that ran alongside a mile of high masonry wall ending at a great stone archway—the entrance to the estate called Highlands. As the archway appeared a quarter mile ahead, Elle kept racing forward, like a fugitive determined to break through a roadblock.

Niki, who was just big enough to peer over the dashboard, saw the arch directly ahead.

"Where are we going, Mama?" she asked, her voice tinged with fear.

"Home," Elle answered tightly.

Niki turned to her in utter confusion, but said nothing.

Elle gave the car yet a little more gas. She could bear it no more, biding her time, clinging to the illusion of better days to come—not if it meant Niki would be raised an outcast as she had been herself. She had to make H.D. acknowledge them both.

Ahead, a gateman stepped into view from under the arch. There were gates, but they had always been left open on the assumption that no one in Willow Cross would have the gall to enter the grounds of the Hyland estate unwanted or uninvited. As he saw the car bearing down, the startled gateman could only stare in disbelief.

Would he move aside? Elle wondered. Or would she have to run him down?

And no sooner did that possibility flash through her brain than she jammed her foot down on the brake, forcing the car to a screeching halt while it was still a hundred yards from the arch.

She dropped her head on the wheel then and began to cry.

Niki crawled over next to her. "Mama?" she said in a frightened hush. "*Maman*, what's wrong?"

Elle put her arms around her child and pulled her closer. "That woman . . . the school . . . I want you to go."

"But you said I would, you promised. So why should you cry?"

Elle blinked back her tears and looked at her little girl. Of course, she must get H.D. to make the school take Niki. But she could never do it by coming here, violating all his rules. That would be the end of everything.

She had to earn this favor from H.D. the way she earned everything else—in exchange for favors of her own.

Four

WHEN H.D. was in Willow Cross, rather than traveling on business or in Washington to wine and dine government people who influenced the liberal policy on tobacco price supports, he generally visited Elle on Tuesday and Friday nights. But on this Monday when she returned from the school, her part-time housekeeper, Louise, was waiting with a message.

"He said eight o'clock," Louise reported.

As usual, the indication that H.D. planned a last-minute visit took the form of simply reporting the time he would arrive. Sometimes Elle was annoyed by the necessary disruption of plans for a quiet evening, but today she was delighted; this meant Niki's enrollment could be cleared up quickly.

To divert Niki from the disappointment of the morning, Elle spent the early part of the afternoon taking her daughter to the big pool at the local YMCA for an extra session of swimming and diving. The lessons Elle had received from her own mother at an early age had provided some of their closest moments, and it had proven the same with her own daughter. Monique had been killed before any serious training could begin—and, in any case, Elle didn't have the natural talent to come up to her mother's level. But from Niki's very first exposure to the water, it was clear that she had the physical potential, and the zest for swimming and diving, to be a champion.

At three o'clock, when they returned from the pool, Charlene Palmer, one of the beauticians from Grace's salon, had already arrived in response to a call from Elle. Whenever she was to see H.D., Elle's preparations began hours before. Maintaining her appearance had become an almost religious element in her routine.

She spent two hours getting a manicure and pedicure, along with having her hair shampooed and styled. Today she also had a bikini wax. Over the years, H.D. had developed a very detailed set of instructions about how her body should look and smell and feel. He liked her body to be completely smooth of hair except for a neatly trimmed pubic triangle. He liked her nipples rouged. He liked her—sometimes—to receive him wearing certain articles of lingerie. He liked perfume applied in certain very specific places. He liked to control everything else, too. On a couple of occasions, he had even given her a handwritten script—a set of instructions he had apparently scribbled himself about how she should touch him, and things she should say while they were making love.

She did it all, of course, as she would do any sexual act he desired, in whatever way he wanted. It was the contract she had made.

At five-thirty, after the beautician had left, Elle went to the kitchen and put together the dinner she would serve tonight. She enjoyed cooking; it made her feel less like a mistress and more like a wife-in-waiting. After she'd learned that Joanne depended on servants for every aspect of homemaking and almost never set foot in the kitchen, Elle redoubled her own efforts, hoping to show H.D. how capable she would be at running a fine home.

When she was done in the kitchen, Elle went upstairs to bathe and perfume her body. By the time she was done, Louise had gone home after leaving a prepared dinner for Niki on the kitchen table. Elle put on a robe to sit with her daughter while she ate. Afterward, she took Niki up to her room and read a book to her for half an hour; they were nearly halfway through *Treasure Island*.

"I wish you could stay with me and read more," Niki said as Elle finished reading. "I wish Mr. Hyland wasn't coming tonight."

Lately, Elle didn't have to tell Niki when H.D. was coming. Niki had learned to interpret the signs for herself.

"You should be glad, *ma petite*. Because I will tell him our problem with the school, and he will solve it *un-deux-trois*. Now, remember—"

Niki broke in to show she knew the rules, too. "I know, Mama. I should come downstairs after I hear the bell, but only to say hello. Then I'll go upstairs to my room, quiet as a little mouse, and go to sleep."

Elle smiled slightly, ruffled her child's hair, then kissed her and left. She spent twenty minutes bringing the dinner further along to the point it could be finished in a few minutes.

At last, in her own bedroom, she executed the few steps that prepared her finally to go "on stage." After applying the finishing touches of *maquillage* to make her makeup glow with perfection, she put on her dress, a tangerine-red décolleté silk sheath. She was finished at a couple of minutes before eight, and then—to keep the dress absolutely fresh and wrinkle free—she stood in the middle of the room, looking at herself in the mirror . . . waiting. H.D. was almost always precisely on time.

As he was tonight. When she heard the ring of the bell, Elle pasted a broad smile on her face and hurried down the stairs to open the front door.

She could see at once that he was in a fine humor. He greeted her warmly with a giant bouquet of pink tea roses.

"How lovely," she exclaimed, knowing that such luxuries were not a part of the local florist's limited inventory or even the product of the Hyland greenhouses—and must have been flown in on one of the company planes.

"Not as lovely as you," he said with a smile, then kissed her fingertips. "It's good to be here . . . and judging from the wonderful aroma coming from your kitchen, I would say that you've outdone yourself tonight."

"It's nothing, just a simple meal," Elle demurred modestly, though H.D.'s compliments brightened her mood and buoyed up her confidence.

She put the roses into a gleaming silver vase and set them on the linen-covered dining table. Seeing Niki hovering in the kitchen doorway, Elle took her by the hand, brought her into the living room, and gave her a little push towards H.D., who was helping himself to a predinner drink.

"Good evening, Mr. Hyland," the child said, demonstrating a small curtsy.

"Good evening, Nicolette," H.D. replied. "And how are you today?"

"I'm fine, thank you . . ." Niki hesitated, as if she might say something more than the few lines she had been taught to perform. But then, glancing at her mother, she saw Elle shake her head. "Good night, Mr. Hyland," she concluded. "It was very nice to see you."

"Nice to see you, Nicolette," H.D. said. The exchange had hardly changed from the day Niki had learned to talk. Elle had given up the idea that H.D. might be touched by the child's beauty, by her manners or her intelligence. Yet, curiously, this was the one thing she didn't take personally. After all, right from the beginning she had seen him show the same kind of distance to Duke, his own firstborn son. If he wasn't fond of children, she was willing to keep Niki out of his way—as long as he did what was right someday, and gave her his name and her birthright.

She filled two slender wineglasses with the fine white Bordeaux that H.D. arranged to have sent by the case every few months. It was chilled, just the way he liked it, to accompany the poached salmon she'd prepared so carefully.

"These are wonderful, Elle," he said appreciatively, tasting the tiny new potatoes lightly touched with butter and garnished with fresh parsley from the garden.

"I'm glad you're pleased. After the long days you spend with business, you need to relax with a good meal. If it were up to me," she ventured, "I'd see to it that you were always comfortable, well fed, and happy. It would be very different from having no one but servants to look after you," she added pointedly, referring to Joanne's frequent absences from Willow Cross.

"I believe you would look after me very well," H.D. agreed.

Elle was encouraged by his tone.

"You seem to be remarkably happy tonight," she observed. "Is there a special reason?"

"A few million reasons, you might say. We've just had the test-marketing results on a new brand of filtered cigarettes with menthol—Hyland Green. Seems we have another winner on our hands. Of course, it's too soon to project exact sales figures, but my marketing people are saying that within the next five years, Hyland Green could become our biggest seller ever."

"That's wonderful," Elle said, feigning an enthusiasm she didn't feel. She raised her wineglass. "Let's drink a toast to your latest triumph—to Hyland Green . . . may it succeed beyond your greatest expectations!" Touching her glass to his, Elle sipped her wine and concealed her disappointment that cigarettes had always completely absorbed and captivated her lover more than she ever could.

H.D. smiled after his own sip. "I don't think there is a way to go beyond my greatest expectations. I want—and I expect—to have a success that continues to grow, without limit, without end."

"Do you ever think," Elle asked impulsively, "that you may want too much?"

"Why should I? I'm in a business that has always grown—and I work at it hard, give myself to it as to nothing else. . . ."

"Yes," Elle said quietly.

Her subdued tone of regret earned a tolerant smile from H.D. "I can't change the way I am, Elle. Because for me this isn't just a business, it's a way of life." He was speaking now with an animation he rarely showed. "Tobacco is a cornerstone of America's economy. Do you know that one of the issues behind our Revolution was Britain's attempt to put a tax on it? Our founding fathers weren't going to stand for *that*! And after we beat the British, they were wise enough to keep their hands off the tobacco industry. That's how it was, Elle, how it is—and how it should always be. Tobacco belongs to *us*, the families who had the vision and foresight to *build* from small beginnings. Tobacco is who and what we Hylands are."

Elle supplied an appropriate smile of admiration at the end of H.D.'s speech, then went into the kitchen to fetch a pot of strong French coffee and a large Baccarat ashtray. The right moment to raise the problem of Niki's school was at hand, she thought; H.D. had been fed a good meal, he would be enjoying his coffee and cigarette—and looking forward to his expected portion of sex.

As she returned to H.D., he was lighting up one of the cigarettes that were made solely for him with a special blend of tobaccos rolled in fine imported paper monogrammed in gold. He offered one to Elle, as he often did, but she declined, preferring her own brand—the filtered Pyramids to which Duke had introduced her. Occasionally, she had gone back to the strong Gauloises of her youth, a nostalgic taste of her origins. But they irritated her throat, and besides, H.D. scolded her whenever he saw her smoking anything but one of the family brands.

"I'd like your advice," Elle began carefully, after coffee

was poured. She noted the way H.D.'s eyes brightened. He liked it when she consulted him, affirmed his superior wisdom.

"Of course, my dear," he said. "How can I help you?"

"I took Niki into town today to register for school."

H.D. nodded, though he frowned slightly. As Elle knew, this was one area he always preferred to avoid—anything to do with Niki.

"We were turned away by a dreadful woman in the school office who insisted on having information about you."

"Me?" H.D. sat forward, clearly alarmed. "But it's agreed that my name must be kept out of—"

"I've done nothing to violate our agreement," Elle countered at once. "I don't mean that she asked about you specifically. What she insisted on having was the identity of the child's father. It's part of their regulations."

H.D. bolted up from the couch, and for a moment Elle was afraid he was simply going to walk out, close the door on this whole part of his life. But he simply began to pace.

"Naturally, I didn't wish to cause you any embarrassment," she hurried on, "so I left. But Niki must go to school. She can't spend her whole life hiding. And anyway, it seems stupid sometimes to avoid the truth. Do you imagine that people don't know about us, H.D., about Niki? You're seen coming here, your chauffeur talks to his relatives, my housekeeper talks to hers. After years of gossip, it's not possible that half the town doesn't know, if not all. Even Joanne must—"

"Quiet!" he erupted in a fierce roar and stopped pacing to glare at her.

The force of his anger not only silenced Elle, but rocked her back in her seat, as though hit by the shock wave from the eruption of a volcano.

"I don't give a shit what people say, or what they know—and that includes my goddamn wife. You know why, Elle? Because in this town, I *own* the people. I own their eyes and ears, I own their minds. They can do or say or see any damn thing they want . . . but only as long as they aren't so stupid as to go too far and make me mad. A little gossip about what they may see . . . that doesn't make me mad, because if it keeps 'em happy to talk about who I fuck, then that's just fine." He came closer to her, and leaned over. "Keepin' 'em happy," he went on, lapsing deeper into his good-old-boy drawl, "is part of keepin' 'em *mine*. You understand?"

He paused, his eyes blazing at her. And the message sank in. He was talking about her, too: as long as he gave her whatever she asked for—and she didn't have the guts to cut loose—she belonged to him, body and soul. Her head bobbed weakly in acknowledgment.

He went on: "So I don't mind if their tongues wag about us . . . 'cause that's a whole lot better than havin' 'em complain about gettin' paid too little, or workin' too long hours, or movin' on to work somewhere else. The only thing I *would* mind is givin' them something more than gossip—like some kind of proof . . . like things written down on school records or hospital records or birth certificates. Because then the folks who resent the Hylands would have real weapons; then they could do more than gossip, they could create legal problems—they could even use evidence to stir up my family, divide us against each other in a way that hurts the company, weakens our power. So I'll never let anything go down as proof about what Niki is to me . . . not unless I know it won't make problems. You clear on that, Elle? For the last time, you got that one hundred percent clear?"

She gave him another meek nod.

"Now let's go upstairs."

Elle's heart sank. She had thought she would have the strength to stand up to him on this matter, but the minute she'd seen his fury., her will failed. She saw that H.D. had no patience for dealing with any problem created by an illegitimate child. If she pushed, Elle realized, she was on the brink of losing even the support he provided.

She couldn't even bring herself to ask what solution he could suggest to the impasse at the school. All she could do, when he put out his hand, was grasp it, and yield as he pulled her toward the stairs.

On the landing, she noted as she passed Niki's door that no light showed from the slight crack above the rug. Good, she was asleep.

"Tonight," H.D. said, as soon as they crossed the threshold of the bedroom, "let's start with a fashion show. You got the package I sent last week from New York?"

"Yes."

"Put on the things that were in it."

Elle took a box from her closet and went into the adjoining bathroom. She brushed her teeth, freshened her perfume, and let down her long, silky brown hair, so that it flowed gracefully over her shoulders and down her back. Emptying the box, she began to costume herself in sheer black stockings, a red-and-black garter belt, a brassiere with the cutouts that exposed her nipples, and a gauzy G-string. She paused then to assess the effect, taking pride in the line of her still firm, youthful body. There had been a time when she reveled in the pleasure of her own youth and vigor to excite and stimulate such a powerful man; then, she hadn't minded any of H.D.'s bedtime games. But now she resented the commands that reduced her to no more than a well-fed, well-clothed slave.

Yet she endured them all for Niki's sake, and lulled herself with the lie that if she could go on satisfying him as no other woman did, someday he would want to own her even in name.

As always, when she came out of the bathroom, H.D. was already stretched out on her bed, naked, his head propped up slightly on her pillows. Elle turned on a small tape player loaded with a cassette of prechosen soft-rock music, and began to move around sinuously in the bedroom, half dancing, half strutting like a runway model.

H.D.'s gaze followed her. "Beautiful, my darling," he said softly, "It's wonderful to watch you. . . ."

She kept moving, drawing closer to the bed, but very slowly. Usually he liked to watch her until he had an erection.

But tonight it was taking a long time.

"Come here," he said at last, "beside the bed. I want to smell you."

When she was next to him, his arm looped around her, he gripped her buttocks and pulled her still nearer as he put his face in the cleft between her legs. She felt the faint warmth as he breathed deeply and then exhaled. "I love your smell," he moaned as he grew erect. "I love your taste."

"What do you want now, *chérie*?" she said. To simulate an eager desire that matched his, she dropped her voice to a husky murmur.

"I want to hear how much you need me," he said.

It was a ritual by now; she knew exactly which words to use, the rhythms in which to deliver them, how long to go on.

"I'm nothing without you, my love . . . I don't feel alive unless you're with me . . . unless I can have your big cock inside me . . . please fuck me, oh, please, don't wait. . . ."

"I don't believe you," he said.

She dropped to her knees in begging position, "Please, I'll do anything if you'll only fuck me."

"Show me what you'll do."

As though truly desperate for him, she climbed over him and began hungrily kissing his body, licking him, until she opened her mouth to take him in. She moved her head to please him until he sat up suddenly and turned her over. Then he slipped his hand through the front of the flimsy bra she had on and roughly tore it away.

"Oh yes," she moaned, writhing in a convincing simulation of heightened lust, "faster . . . don't make me wait."

As he tore at the rest of her underwear, he shifted himself so she would go on sucking him, licking his balls.

At last she was nude.

"Now," she pleaded, dropping her voice to a whisper, "Don't make me wait another minute." She tossed herself back and spread her legs as wide as she could. H.D. straddled her, but he kept himself raised on his haunches, not yet entering her.

She increased the urgency of her whisper, and put her hand on his throbbing member, to pull at him gently, "Please, oh, please . . . I want you so much, only you . . . come into me, come . . . come. . . ."

Looking down at her, he gave the same slow triumphant smile he always did, and she waited as he made his choice. Sometimes he liked to express his power by denying her—leaning back while she went on using her hand until he came in her face. Sometimes he would want her mouth again.

But tonight, finally, he plunged forward, burying himself in her. She rocked back and forth with him, keeping up the stream of desperate pleas and grateful cries, until at last she heard a low rumble in his throat followed by a hoarse cry. Then, arching her back suddenly, she echoed his sound, and relaxed beneath him.

After he had lain quietly beside her for a minute, he said, "That was worth waiting for, wasn't it, my dear?"

"Always, my darling. There is no one else like you in the whole world."

The ritual was complete. H.D. rose from the bed and started to dress.

"You won't stay all night?" Elle said, sounding sincerely disappointed. When Joanne was away, he often did; and Elle knew that H.D.'s wife was spending the dog days of August cooled by the sea breezes on the fabled Hyland summer estate at Flamingo Island. If he could wake with her, she thought, there might be a second chance to bring up Niki's schooling. . . .

"Sorry, my dear. I have an important business meeting early in the morning."

There was a silence while he went into the bathroom to wash, and comb his silver hair.

Elle got up from the bed, slipped into a peignoir, and paced the room. She could no longer stand the uncertainty. What would she do with Niki tomorrow? What could she say to explain a promise unkept? After the way she gave herself to him, wasn't she entitled to make demands?

The moment he reappeared she rounded on him. "H.D., I must have an answer about—"

He chimed in smoothly. "Give me a day to work things out, then take Niki to school again day after tomorrow. There won't be any problem."

"That woman, the school clerk, she was very firm about—"

"I don't think she'll be in the school office tomorrow," he said reassuringly. "I don't think she'll be there ever again. No one will ask you to answer any . . . unpleasant questions."

Genuinely grateful, Elle ran to put her arms around H.D. They kissed, and then she accompanied him downstairs.

At the door, he said, "Be patient in all things, my dear. It would be a shame to spoil what we have . . . especially now." He paused, allowing both the threat and the promise to sink in, then added: "My lawyers have been working on a financial plan that will protect Hyland Tobacco even after I leave Joanne."

"Really? Is it really true?" Elle asked, her eyes sparkling with excitement.

"I just said so, didn't I? Good night, my dear, sleep well." He opened the door for himself and went out.

Before getting into bed, Elle stopped by the silver-framed photograph of her mother and touched the glass surface lightly, as if for luck. She had been haunted by the idea that she might die, as her mother had, without achieving true respectability for herself and her own daughter. Now, once again, she was encouraged to believe in a better end. She would not have to go on hanging in space, falling without ever coming to earth, like the figure in the photograph.

She would finish the dive and win her prize. H.D. had promised. It was only a matter of time.

Five

NIKI walked down the hall toward the assigned classroom with slow timid steps. On the ride to school, when she had been left to sit alone while other children talked and laughed together, a hollow feeling had begun to form inside her. Now it had turned into a slight ache, as if a strong cord was tied tight around the middle of her stomach. The closer she went to the door of the room, the tighter the cord seemed to get. She had wanted so much to be with other children, to make friends, but now she saw that the rest of them had already chosen their playmates. She felt no less alone than she had through all the days of playing by herself on the big empty field behind her home.

Niki paused at the classroom door, until the teacher saw her and came over. "Hello," she said with a welcoming smile. "You must be Niki Sandeman. I'm June Farlow, your teacher. You can call me Miss June. Your desk is over there. . . ." She pointed to a rear corner of the room.

Niki sat quietly and waited until Miss June called the class to order. She stood up and saluted the flag, one hand over her heart. Then she sang "The Star-Spangled Banner." She could see that she was the only one who knew all the words, but the accomplishment gave her little satisfaction. It was just something else that set her apart.

Niki's discomfort only increased when Miss June asked her to stand up and then introduced her to the class. The other children stared, and someone even giggled at her name.

Miss June read a story aloud, and when she was finished, she asked questions about it. Eager hands shot up, voices called out answers, but Niki was silent, hunched down in her chair. With each moment, she felt more like a stranger among children who seemed, in the two days she'd been absent, to have formed a solid circle of friendships she would never penetrate.

When story period ended, the class broke up into small groups, each involved in different games. Niki sat rooted to her chair, ignored and uninvited by the others.

Miss June came over. "You've got to join in," she said. Taking Niki by the hand, the teacher walked her over to a couple of little girls by a doll house in a corner. "Kate . . . Tammy, why don't you show Niki what you're doing?"

"Yes, Miss June," the girls agreed in unison.

"We're playing house," Kate explained. She had lovely long reddish hair, freckles, and wide blue eyes. She was also too thin, Niki thought, with arms and legs almost like sticks. "The mother doll is making breakfast and the father doll is getting ready to go to work. What does your father do?" she asked.

"I don't know exactly," Niki said.

The other girls stared at her.

"You don't know?" Kate said. "But where does he go when he leaves the house after breakfast?"

Niki was mute. She had already made one mistake. How could she say that her father didn't have breakfast with them?

"Doesn't he go to the factory?" said Tammy, a tomboyish blonde.

"I . . . I think so," Niki faltered, grasping at the straw that was offered. Mr. Hyland *did* have something to do with the big factory in town, Mama had explained that.

"You *think* so?" Tammy echoed, and began to giggle. "Boy, you sure must be dumb, Niki, if you don't know where your father goes."

"I'm not!" Niki protested, her fists clenched at her side.

"Of course you aren't," said Miss June, hurrying over to referee. "And I'm sure Tammy didn't mean what she said . . . did you, Tammy?"

Tammy looked defiant for a moment, then relented in the face of authority. "No, Miss June."

"Then apologize to Niki."

Tammy faced her. "I'm sorry."

But looking into the other girl's eyes, Niki could see that she wasn't really sorry at all. In fact, she looked mad—so mad that she would never forgive Niki for getting her in trouble.

School wasn't going to be fun at all, Niki thought. It was awful. She wished she could go home right now.

The teacher was looking at her, too, but much more sympathetically. "Niki, I thought I'd paint some pictures to decorate the classroom, but it's a very big job for one person. Maybe you'd like to help me . . . ?"

Niki gratefully agreed, relieved to get away from the questions, glad to bury herself in a solitary pursuit.

All the rest of the day, Niki wondered how school could be so easy for the other children and so hard for her. There must be a secret, she thought, something they knew that she didn't about how to make friends.

But how would she ever learn it? Mama couldn't tell her, Niki was sure. For except when Mr. Hyland came to visit, Mama, too, was all alone.

At the end of the day, as she walked toward the waiting school bus, Niki noticed the long black car that was stopped across the street from the front of the school, a chauffeur visible through the open window by the driver's seat. It was Mr. Hyland's car, Niki realized, the one that always brought him when he came to the cottage. She paused, considering whether to continue toward the school bus, or go to the car. If he had come, it must be to bring her home from school. . . .

As she paused, the window of the rear compartment began to roll down. Niki glimpsed a figure in the back seat, eyes targeted in her direction. He was going to call to her, she thought . . . but she didn't even wait. She began to run to the car.

After covering only a few more yards, she could see the face of the man at the rear window, and she realized it wasn't Mr. Hyland. It was someone much younger. Niki wouldn't have known who he was, except that once when she had been walking in town with her mother, the same man had nearly bumped into them as he dashed suddenly out of a store. There had been a moment when Elle and the man gave each other a hard look before he ran off and jumped into a beautiful red convertible. The look—almost like the one Tammy had given her today—had made Niki curious, and she had asked her mother if she knew the man. "Just a little," Elle had said. "He's Mr. Hyland's son."

For a while, the answer had puzzled Niki. If she was Mr. Hyland's child, and so was the man, then weren't they brother and sister? But he was so much older . . . and certainly he wasn't Elle's son. The puzzle troubled her until she asked her mother about it a few days later and was told that Mr. Hyland had had children with three different women. Niki had also been told not to ask any more about it.

Now, as she recognized him, Niki's step hesitated. Should she get in the car? From the way Elle had talked that one time in the past, Niki had sensed that something about the man worried her mother.

But if he was Mr. Hyland's son . . . and had come in Mr. Hyland's car . . . ?

She had taken only a few more steps when the man in the rear seat settled back out of view, the window rolled up, and the long black car drove quickly up the street.

Niki looked after it in utter confusion. Why had he come?

She was jarred out of her thoughts by the blaring horn of the school bus getting ready to leave. She ran to catch it, and took a seat alone at the rear as she had that morning.

All the way home she wondered about the man.

"Did you have a nice day at school?" Elle asked, the moment Niki walked through the door.

"Yes, Mama." Niki would have liked to mention seeing Mr. Hyland's son, but hadn't she been told never to ask any more about him?

"What did you do?"

"I painted two pictures."

"Let me see," Elle said.

"Miss June hung them up, Mama. She said I could take them home next week."

"Ah . . . well, that's good. Everything's all right, then? Everyone was . . . kind to you?"

Niki paused, not wanting to say anything that would make her mother sad or unhappy. "Miss June was very kind," she answered finally.

Elle sighed with obvious relief. "That's good . . . that's very good."

The following morning, Niki woke up with a stomach ache. The cramps were so strong, so sharp that she cried out with pain. Elle was terrified that the fish she'd served for supper had been tainted.

She called Dr. Boynton immediately, and he arrived in less than twenty minutes.

A tall man who wore rumpled seersucker suits and whose graying light-brown hair always seemed in need of a cut, Dr. Boynton examined the little girl, then took Elle aside downstairs.

"What's wrong, Doctor? Could it be food poisoning?"

"Nothing that serious," he said with a gentle smile. "I'd say it's a combination of a couple of things. . . ."

Elle drew a sharp breath, but the doctor quickly went on to reassure her. "Nothing but a touch of shyness . . . coupled with an acute case of jitters. In plain English, Miss Sandeman, your child is kinda nervous about starting school."

"But she said they were kind, that she had a nice day. Niki wouldn't lie—"

"I don't think she was lying. I doubt that anything really terrible happened. It's just nerves. Give her some warm milk and cookies and let her know everyone gets scared sometimes . . . that the important thing is not to give in. I already had a little talk with her, but I'm sure it'll have a lot more weight coming from you."

Elle thanked the doctor and grabbed her purse from a table in the entrance hall. Usually, she sent doctors' bills to the office where she was supposed to work, and they were paid through the company. But she didn't want H.D. to know about this one, since he had already been bothered once by problems connected to Niki's schooling. "What do I owe you for coming out, Dr. Boynton?" she asked.

"Nothing this time," he said.

"But—"

"Please." The doctor motioned her to put away her purse.

"You're too kind."

He waved off Elle's gratitude and opened the door to leave. Then he paused, his face working as though it wasn't easy to speak. "I'm glad to see Niki's in school, Miss Sandeman. Fitting in there, I know, may take her a little extra . . . time and patience. But don't give up on it, either of you. It'll work out fine, I'm sure."

Elle was touched. It was no surprise that Boynton was among those who knew Niki's background—he had delivered her, after all. But he had never specifically told Elle he was on her side, had hinted at no moralistic judgments about her status either way. "Thank you again, Doctor," she said as Boynton went out.

She went up to her daughter's bedroom. It was a bright and sunny room. The walls were papered with pink and white flowers, the furniture painted white and decorated with tiny pink and green buds. Tucked under a white coverlet, propped against two pillows, Niki sat up, looking pale and apprehensive.

"I'm sorry, Mama," she said softly, "I didn't mean to cause you any trouble."

Elle sat down on the bed and hugged her daughter. "You didn't cause me any trouble, *chérie*. I'm just so happy you're all right."

"I'll go to school tomorrow," Niki said. "Dr. Boynton said I have to go . . . and I will."

Understanding now that everything wasn't all right at school—fearing that perhaps Niki was being isolated by children who'd been told to stay away by their parents—Elle was overcome with sorrow. After all the fine promises she'd made, she had still failed to give her child the protection of a proper family. Fine clothes, good things to eat, a comfortable home—all that was taken care of, a bounty beyond what her own mother had been able to provide. But food for the soul—confidence, self-respect, the certainty she was as good as any other child. . . . Elle shook her head sadly; in those respects her daughter was just as starved as she was herself.

The following day, Elle drove her daughter to school. "Don't forget what Dr. Boynton said, *chérie*," Elle said. "It's natural to be nervous about something new. But once you get accustomed to school and make friends, you won't have any more stomachaches."

Niki nodded dutifully, but when she kissed her mother, it was with the unwilling fervor of a soldier going off to war.

She handed the doctor's note explaining yesterday's absence to Miss June. "I'm so sorry you weren't feeling well," the teacher said with genuine sympathy. "I hope you're better today."

A snicker from one of the girls was quickly taken up by several others.

"That's enough!" Miss June snapped, her voice as cold as steel. "Do you hear me, Tammy? Keep that up and I'll have to call your mama in!"

Tammy stuck her chin out defiantly. "But it's my mama who told me. She said Niki doesn't know what her father does because she doesn't have one. Not a real father like mine."

Niki felt her stomach clench again. She hated school and she hated Tammy. She would have run home if she hadn't promised Mama and the doctor to try again.

In a gray haze of misery, Niki stumbled through the salute to the flag and "The Star-Spangled Banner." But later, when it was playtime, a miracle happened. Kate walked over to Niki's chair and held out her hand. "I choose Niki," she said clearly, so that everyone else could hear. "I choose Niki to be my partner."

Niki stared at Kate with disbelief. To be chosen by anyone would have been wonderful, but to be chosen by Kate, who looked like an angel and whose laughter tinkled like music . . . that was a true miracle. Like a devoted puppy, Niki followed Kate around, doing everything the other girl did, eager to please and grateful for her attention.

Finally, when it seemed Kate wouldn't change her mind, Niki asked why she had chosen her when no one else would.

Kate looked solemnly into Niki's azure eyes. "I'll tell you the truth. I chose you because my father told me about your tummyache. He said you needed a friend."

Niki didn't quite understand, until Kate explained that her last name was Boynton—and her father was the doctor. Niki frowned in disappointment; she didn't want someone to be her friend just because they were told to. But then Kate added, "I'm glad I did it, though. I like you, Niki. That's why I told you the truth. Because if we're going to be friends for ever and ever, we always have to tell the truth. Okay?"

Niki nodded eagerly. Friends for ever and ever? School was going to be wonderful, after all.

When Niki got home she ran into the kitchen looking for her mother. Eager to tell about her new friend, Niki stood by the sink where her mother was washing some lingerie, waiting to be asked about her day. But Elle seemed preoccupied; she was softly humming a French song with a slightly sad melody, the way she always did when she was worried or upset. Niki didn't think this was the time to impose her own happiness. "What's wrong, Mama?" she asked.

"*Rien, ma petite*," Elle replied absently, "nothing at all."

But Niki heard something in her mother's voice that said otherwise. She looked around the kitchen for a clue. On a table by an unfinished cup of coffee and an ashtray full of half-smoked cigarettes, Niki saw a newspaper open to a middle page. She went over and looked at it.

In the center was a large picture of Mr. Hyland in his fancy black clothes, beside a lady wearing a beautiful gown. That must be it, Niki thought, Mama was sad because she wanted to go to that party. Niki understood and wished with all her heart she could take the sadness away.

Kate Boynton became a regular visitor at the cottage outside of town, and Niki was welcomed in return at the Boynton home, a rambling ranch house on one level. Niki had never been inside any home except her own, and from the first she was thrilled by what she saw at the Boyntons. It was also so busy and noisy and full of comings and goings. There was a swimming pool in the backyard and a jungle gym, kept in constant use by Kate and her three brothers. The spacious kitchen was very different from Elle's tidy one; it was always spilling over with food, all kinds of things Niki had always been forbidden by her mother, like soda pop ("too sweet," Elle insisted) and bubble gum ("bad for the teeth"), and doughnuts thickly coated with sugar ("unhealthy"). Niki sighed blissfully each time she sank her teeth into one of these forbidden items, though she felt like a traitor for craving what was "worthless" over one of Elle's beautifully prepared and nourishing meals.

Niki loved the casual, relaxed way the members of the Boynton family were with each other, shouting insults, even cuffing each other with the same underlying affection. Yet it wasn't as if they were *savages*—the word Elle always used to describe the town children. As soon as Mrs. Boynton said quietly, "Mind your manners, children," the shouting would stop and even Kate's oldest brother James, who was all of fifteen, would do as he was told.

Though it seemed odd to Niki, Kate expressed the same pleasure in visiting the Sandeman cottage. She loved to hear Elle's musical accent, her use of French idioms, and best of all, to taste her cooking. She thought Niki's mother exotic, more glamorous than a movie star and endowed with the same kind of mystery. And she was enchanted by Elle's teachings on deportment and culture, preferring to hear her read than to play outside or even to watch television in her own home.

Left to their own devices, the girls made up fantasies of what life would be like in the far, far distant future, when grade school would be left behind and they would take their place in the world of adults.

"I want to be in the Peace Corps," Kate said decisively. "I want to help people who deserve it, not like the mean, old people in this town."

"I want," Niki said dreamily, trying to create a mental picture that would embody the fulfillment of all her hungers and wishes, "I want you to be my friend forever."

"Then I will. What else . . . ?"

"I want to have a family like yours when I grow up, and a real home. . . ."

"Everyone wants friends and home and family, silly. But what do you want for *yourself*?"

Niki pondered the question thoughtfully. Listing the things she *didn't* want would be so much easier. To live alone as Elle did, to cry alone at night when she thought no one was listening, to be forbidden from saying more than a few polite words to her own father. "I don't know what else," she said honestly, "I just don't know."

"But you'll be able to do whatever you want," Kate prompted.

"Why?"

"Because you'll be rich."

"Will I? How do you know?"

Amazed that she should be the source of such information, Kate stared at Niki. "My father said you will. I heard him telling my mom about it one day after you were at my house. He said Mr. Hyland would have to give you money, and I guess it would be a lot because he's very rich, isn't he? We went to a Christmas party at his house last year. It was so beautiful. There was a pony ride for the children, and a clown and a Santa Claus. . . ." Kate's narrative faltered as she saw tears form in Niki's eyes and realized the implications of what she was saying. Intending to be sympathetic she went on, "I don't understand why *you* weren't invited to the party. I mean, he must know you if he'd give you money."

Niki shook her head and blinked back her tears. How much was she allowed to say? "I think he doesn't like me very much . . ."

"But then why would he give you money?"

Niki didn't know how to answer. How much might she be permitted to say? Quickly, she suggested to Kate that it would be more fun if they went outside to play, and without waiting for an answer she ran down the stairs.

After Kate went home, Niki went straight to her mother. Slightly fearful, because it would mean revealing she had discussed her father with her friend, Niki asked, "Can we go to Mr. Hyland's next Christmas party? It's only a few months away."

Elle spun around to face her daughter. There was a hard look in her eyes that made Niki think she had made her mother very angry.

But then Elle knelt and held out her arms. Niki ran into

them. Hungry for comfort, she didn't complain even though her mother was clutching her very tightly.

"Can we go?" Niki said at last. "Kate told me it was so beautiful. Won't you ask Mr. Hyland to let me come . . . ?"

Though Elle didn't let go, Niki heard the answer whispered beside her ear with all the force of an oath. "I will, *ma petite*. I will make sure you go next time. . . ."

Elle knew that the right moment to approach H.D. with a request was always after she had satisfied him—with food, drink, and the free gift of her body in any way he wanted to use it. But she could not satisfy him unless she was with him, and so she became more frustrated and angry—and then worried—as twelve days went by without hearing from H.D. She had known he was to be away in New York for a week, but it was almost twice that long now.

Though she was under strict orders never to call his home or office, she telephoned the company headquarters. Pretending to be a journalist visiting Willow Cross, she asked if there might be any chance of a short interview with the legendary H.D. Hyland. A public relations executive told her that H.D. was unavailable, away in Washington where he might have to remain for another week. Elle felt better. The trip was not on the schedule he'd mentioned, but it was not uncommon for him to fly away at a moment's notice. Usually, though, he called every few days no matter where he was.

When another weekend passed without contact, Elle started to feel desperate, more at loose ends than at any time since she had been alone in Monte Carlo after searching fruitlessly for her father, that evening right before she had met Duke. . . .

But on the following Monday, as soon as she picked up the copy of the *Daily Signal* that was delivered to her doorstep each day, the cloud of desperation lifted. At the bottom of the local newspaper's front page—over a picture of H.D.'s wife accompanied by a porter wheeling a cart piled with luggage—a heading read: "Mrs. Hyland Plans Divorce."

At long last, it was happening, Elle exulted. H.D. would be free to marry her.

The days of not hearing from him, she realized now, must be connected to the news. Perhaps H.D. didn't want to risk complicating matters at this crucial stage by appearing with her—or even have people see him visiting her. Perhaps he wanted to come to her when things were farther along—when he could ask her to move straight into the house at Highlands. . . . She was full of dreams again, and this time they all seemed within reach.

But as another few days passed without a word from H.D., then two weeks, Elle's nerves were frayed to the point of breaking. No longer merely desperate, she was in an uncontrollable panic. Unable to face Niki half the time, she paid Louise to stay late and cook meals while she remained in her bedroom.

On weekdays, she took to calling the office regularly, adopting a variety of guises. A dressmaker who had received an order from Mr. Hyland for a surprise gift for his wife wanted to ask him what to do in view of the pending divorce. A manicurist needed to know if Mr. Hyland would be keeping his appointment for the next day. Each time there was relief when she learned that H.D. was not in Willow Cross, hadn't been for weeks. But the relief would be short-lived.

The calls stopped only when H.D.'s private secretary finally fielded one in which Elle had been about to say she was a decorator who needed to know when Mr. Hyland could discuss the new drapes. . . .

"Miss Sandeman," the secretary said bluntly, "please stop calling. I'm sure Mr. Hyland will be in touch with you soon."

Paralyzed with mortification, Elle held onto the receiver for another moment, then slammed it down without any protest or denial. Of course, it struck her now: her accent must have given her away from the very first call.

She passed one more day, driven practically insane by the conclusion that he was abandoning her. Late the next evening, a Friday, the phone rang. When she answered and heard his voice, she fought to color her voice with the right blend of charm, adoration, and eagerness.

"I've missed you so much," she said, careful not to reveal a trace of the hysteria behind it.

He was coming back to Willow Cross, he said, and he wanted to see her tomorrow night.

"Of course, my darling," she replied. "I'm here for you whenever you want me."

He hung up quickly, but it didn't bother her. Tomorrow was a Saturday! Never before had he wanted to see her on a Saturday night. Weekends had always been for Joanne, for dinners at the country club, social events with his set of local friends.

But now he was about to be divorced, and Saturday night belonged to her, too. It was almost as good as hearing his proposal.

The doorbell rang and Elle rushed to let her lover in. With the briefest of hellos, H.D. stomped into the cottage, his face dark and angry. She was surprised to see he was in business clothes and carrying a briefcase. The glow of anticipation threatened by icy fingers of fear, she led H.D. quickly to the sofa, put up his legs and removed his shoes. Then she made him a martini that was almost straight gin.

Only then did she ask, "Wasn't this a good day for you, *chéri*?"

"Rotten," he shot back. "I stayed in Washington right up to the last minute today . . . and it still didn't do any damn good. The government's going ahead with it. . . ." He picked up his briefcase from beside the coffee table, opened it, and took out a booklet.

"After all the millions I pay my people in Washington, they couldn't do a goddamn thing. I went down there to try and put my finger in the dike, but it was too damn late. The most I managed to do was get myself an advance copy of the thing . . . just so I could see for myself how those goddamn lobbyists dropped the goddamn ball!" He threw the booklet down on the coffee table.

Elle grabbed it up, impatient to understand. The document had a cover page with an official-looking seal that said "Office of the Surgeon General of the United States." She peeled back the cover and started to read.

Even without fully digesting the contents, she realized why H.D. was so angry. The report said that smoking cigarettes was a proven cause of cancer of the lung, the most common and most deadly form of the disease. She couldn't blame H.D. for being in a black mood—or, as she assumed, for being caught up for the past two weeks in dealing with the report. Obviously, it was going to be very bad for the tobacco business.

Yet she was relieved, too, that none of his troubles had anything to do with her.

"Is it true?" she asked, laying the report down again.

"'Course not," H.D. thundered. "It's a bunch of goddamn lies." As if to underline his point, he lit a cigarette. Elle did the same.

"Then you'll find a way to fight it," she offered, trying to soothe him, so that they could talk of other, more important things.

But H.D. refused to be placated. "It should never have happened in the first place, not after all the money I feed those bloodsucking parasites in Washington. I'll show those fucking bastards," he went on, "just wait till they come back to me with their slimy hands out. I'll fire the whole cocksucking lot of 'em, that's what I'll do. I'll find another team, people who can do the job they're paid for."

At this point Elle wasn't sure who H.D. was blaming. All she knew was they must have done something terrible indeed, for H.D. rarely lost his temper so completely that he raved like this, using the language of a common farmhand, retaining almost none of the composure that went with the courtly pose of a Southern gentleman.

When he had spent his litany of oaths and curses, Elle led H.D. to the dinner table and served the meal she had carefully prepared, *tournedos* of filet mignon, served with the best red wine recommended by the local merchant— ninety dollars the bottle! It was a shame he was too distracted to enjoy it properly, she thought, but there would be many, much finer meals when she became the mistress of Highland House.

For now, she would simply show H.D. how helpful and interested in his affairs she could be. "But if the report is a lie," she offered, "perhaps no one will believe it . . ."

"People have been telling lies about tobacco, saying cigarettes are bad since the first day they were made. They couldn't prove it then, and they can't prove it now. But when the lie comes out of the surgeon general's office, well, my dear, even you should be able to see that it's going to carry some weight."

Elle nodded agreeably. She made no pretense to know much about what went on in Washington, yet it still puzzled her that an important branch of the government should publish lies about such a popular product as cigarettes. However, she was not about to express any doubts to H.D. She was more anxious to get him off the subject.

By the time she served coffee and dessert, he had quieted down a bit. She led him back into the living room, brought out his favorite brandy, and made herself comfortable beside him.

"That was a fine dinner, Elle," he said belatedly. "I'm just not very good company tonight."

"You're always excellent company," she protested. "But there is something we should discuss before we go to bed."

"Oh? And what might that be?"

There was a coolness in his tone, she thought, a hint that he might be too tired or distracted to really listen. But Elle couldn't bear to wait. It was like a living thing inside her, this need she'd carried since she was a child; it was so strong now that it couldn't be denied a moment longer.

"Our wedding," she said. "I've seen the news about your

divorce. I thought we could begin to make our own plans. . . ."

H.D. stared hotly at Elle. "Good God, woman, haven't you heard a thing I said tonight?"

"Of course I heard," she said, angry now at being reproached for claiming what was hers. "All you've done since you got here was talk about business. What has that got to do with us? With all the promises you made me?"

"I told you once," he said softly, "that my business is the most important thing in my life. It's what I am—and Hyland Tobacco needs me now, more than ever. I don't have time for distractions of any kind, not when I have to fight to protect Hyland. I thought you'd be smart enough to understand."

"Understand?" she cried shrilly. "I'll tell you what I'm smart enough to understand! That you're breaking your promise! Again! And for what? *These*!" She picked up a crystal cigarette holder from the coffee table. "Little sticks of tobacco that go up in smoke. Well, I won't let my own life go up in smoke while all you talk about is—"

H.D. sat up straight. "That's enough, Elle," he cut in firmly.

But she was too far gone to stop. All the anger she'd suppressed for so long, all the disappointments she'd swallowed, all came tumbling out. "Enough? No, H.D., it isn't enough! I don't care about your damn cigarettes." She hurled away the crystal holder, and it shattered against a wall across the room. "Not if there's never going to be anything more than this for me or Niki. I'm tired of living like this. I'm tired of watching Niki suffer because it's never 'the right time.' You're going to marry me now, do you hear? As soon as your divorce is final. It's *my* time. And I won't allow Niki to be thought of as nothing more than . . . than your bastard!"

There was a silence when she finished.

H.D. went on studying her for a long moment in a way that began to make her feel more like an object than a person, as though she was a painting on a wall or a piece of sculpture that he was trying to decide if he liked.

At last, very quietly he said, "Did you say you won't allow it?" The absurdity of her threat was nakedly apparent in the mere repetition.

At once, she knew she had made a terrible mistake.

"I'm sorry, H.D. I only meant . . . well, you must realize . . . I don't know what got into me. . . ."

He rose from the sofa and pushed his feet into the shoes she had removed for him earlier.

"H.D., please. I was upset, too—as you are—by your bad news." She grabbed at his pant leg, to pull him back to her. But he walked to the chair where he had left his jacket and put it on.

She ran after him. "H.D. you can't leave . . . I've given you my life, haven't I? Of course I'll wait to marry if you want . . . I'll wait as long as you say. . . ."

He came back to the coffee table to collect his briefcase. She trailed him around the room.

"I'm sorry," she said again, her voice sinking to a plaintive whine. "Tell me how to show you I'm sorry. I'll do anything. . . ." In a final show of surrender, she knelt before him and grabbed at his pants, yanked at the zipper. "No one does for you what I do. You always told me—"

He knocked her hand away and straightened his clothes.

"Good-bye, Gabrielle," he said, looking at her coldly. "You can keep for yourself everything I've given you. Every last thing," he added with a tight smile—and she knew then that he was talking about Niki.

His cruelty overwhelmed her again, rekindling her rage. "Bastard!" she shrieked at his retreating back.

He turned to her. "Exactly," he said, and then he was gone.

She sank to her knees where she stood and went on staring at the door through which he'd disappeared. Her own final scream wouldn't stop echoing through her brain.

Six

THE days were hell, the nights were worse. She lived through the following weeks on the hope that he would relent and return to her. It would have to be his decision she realized; to call or write, to plead or explain, to intrude at all, would only thrust him farther away. She had to hope that, in the end, she meant something to him—that Niki did.

In any case, she knew that H.D. would not be easy to contact. These days he was spending little time in Willow Cross. Facing the challenge of the surgeon general's report attacking cigarettes, he had embarked on the most vigorous and comprehensive campaign of his life. The local newspaper was full of daily reports of his activities to polish up the tarnished luster of Hyland Tobacco. He was flying all over the country, meeting with the heads of other tobacco companies, with powerful Washington lobbyists, with advertising and public relations firms—personally overseeing new incentives in every corner of the United States. He increased

Hyland's sponsorship of televised sporting events and Hyland's philanthropic gifts to education and the arts. Scarcely a week went by when he wasn't pictured in some major city, presenting a check to a university president, to a museum, or rescuing, with a sizable donation, a foundering charity or good cause. Hyland money funded a clinic for handicapped children in Mississippi, a program to combat illiteracy in Arkansas, scores of Little League teams all over the country. When a small Louisiana town was all but destroyed by floods, H.D. had food and clothing airlifted to its people . . . on planes prominently bearing the Hyland crest.

Flaunting his personal contempt for the surgeon general's report, H.D. continued smoking his custom-made Hyland brand, and had himself photographed doing so when he issued public statements attacking the surgeon general's report as being based on research that was "inconclusive at best"—and damning those who would damage an industry "more uniquely American than any other—an industry that supports millions of American families and upholds the long and honorable tradition of the American free enterprise."

Meanwhile, recognizing the need to fight fire with fire, H.D. doubled the size of Hyland's research facility, hiring fresh new teams of scientists, physicians, and researchers—all with the goal of providing the kind of medical evidence that could refute or at least obscure the government's "proof" that tobacco damaged the health or shortened the lives of those who used it.

Busy as H.D. was, engaged in fighting to sustain the company that he admitted to loving more than he could any woman, Elle persuaded herself at first that it was reasonable for him to keep her waiting for a sign of forgiveness. To keep calm, she immersed herself in caring for Niki, and spent her days alone in the same kind quiet homemaking pursuits she had seen her own mother do, and, as warmer weather came, in long aimless walks exploring her property. Discovering for the first time that from one hilly prospect beyond a stand of pines, she could look across a valley and see the great mansion at the center of Highlands, she spent hours sitting under a tree, nursing the dream that it might yet be hers.

But as months passed, her hopes finally faded. She thought then of moving away, and looked into disposing of the house—only to be reminded by a local realtor that he could do nothing: the deed was still in the name of a holding company that was a subsidiary of the Hyland Tobacco Company, the property not hers to sell. Suddenly, she awakened to the bitter possibility that little of value truly belonged to her. There were a couple of smaller pieces of jewelry in her possession, an emerald ring and a gold-and-ruby bracelet, but each time H.D. had given her anything more valuable, she had accepted his advice to let him store them—in a safe-deposit box he arranged at one of his banks. She traveled up to Charleston for a day, and arranged the sale of the ring and bracelet, but when she received less than ten thousand dollars she realized it would not go far toward supporting her if she left Willow Cross.

And, though her position in town might remain precarious, as time passed it became clear that it would be better here than elsewhere. For no one ever contacted her about leaving the house, the bills that were forwarded to the office of her fictitious job continued to be paid, and men came occasionally to tend to the landscaping or fix the roof. Elle guessed that with all the machinery for maintaining her in place, and H.D. so preoccupied with business, he had simply never given the order to cut off her support. In a company with such constant large outlays as Hyland Tobacco, even the substantial funds she absorbed would probably continue to pass through unnoticed.

So she stayed.

And as she began to relax once more into a sense of security—if only the illusion of it—she began to scheme. Somehow she would make herself recognized, would find a way to give Niki her birthright. She had spent too much of herself and her child preparing to be a part of the Hyland family; it seemed unthinkable to settle for less. H.D. might be forever out of reach, but she could not forget that, at the very inception of her dream, she had been looking to a different man to make it come true.

She was at the window, waiting for the first sign of headlights slicing through the darkness on her driveway, long before the time when she had told him to come. The ritual preparations had all been done, just as in the past, her hair freshly shampooed and set, her body bathed and perfumed, a new dress worn over filmy and provocatively cut underwear. There was a dinner waiting in the kitchen, something that could be made to seem impromptu, for she had said it was only for drinks—though she intended for him to stay. Niki was spending the night at the Boyntons.

When the car pulled up outside, Elle pulled back to watch from behind a curtain as he got out. She saw at once how much he'd changed. No longer a boy, he wore the assurance of the Hyland name with complete authority, standing erect, walking with a steady gait toward the door rather than a loose, athletic lope. His thick brown hair was more conservatively styled, so that he seemed more staid and less rakish, but he was no less handsome.

It had taken Elle a long time to act on the idea of trying to rekindle Duke's interest, for she had reason to know that he despised her for rejecting him in preference to his more powerful father. Yet Elle knew something else, too—that unfulfilled longings could often be the strongest and most compelling. If she could find a way to make him understand why she'd acted as she did, if she could get him to remember how he had once wanted her, then she believed they could pick up right where they had left off.

The first signs that her hopes were not too bold had been positive. When she had called his office two days ago, he had taken the call immediately. Now he was here.

She opened the door and took instant encouragement from the way his eyes swept up and down her figure before he crossed the threshold.

She led him into the living room, and he accepted her offer of a drink, requesting bourbon and branch water—one of H.D.'s favorites. As she went to fix it at the sideboard, Elle noticed him appraising the cottage and the furnishings.

"I'm so glad you came," she said. Behind the bland opening remark, she was wondering exactly how much Duke knew about what had transpired between her and H.D.

A half-smile touched his lips. "How could I refuse? When a lady summons me, why, it would be downright ungentlemanly to refuse." He placed a faint but unmistakable emphasis on the word *lady*.

They sat down on chairs facing each other and, for a while, they made light conversation. About the way she had decorated the cottage, about the general well-being of his brother and sister. Elle was relieved that he didn't question the reason behind her call, thinking that perhaps Duke had outgrown his youthful resentment towards her. When she questioned him about his work at Hyland Tobacco, he spoke of having spent six months in each of the company's divisions. "It was the best way to learn every aspect of the business. I'm supposed to be taking over as vice-president in charge of marketing any day. . . ."

Duke would never be as elegant and imposing as his father, Elle thought as she listened, certainly not as charming as H.D. could be when he wished. But he had something else that could be no less distinct and attractive, a dark and brooding quality—born of loneliness and the futile quest for his father's love.

"I'm glad things are going so well for you," she said finally, impatience pushing her from neutral to personal ground.

Duke smiled, but gave nothing back.

"I suppose it seemed curious that I should call you after . . . after so long."

"No," he said. "I always thought you might someday."

He held up his empty glass, indicating he wanted a refill.

Another good sign, Elle thought, as she took the glass from him and went back to the sideboard. "I want to be friends again Duke," she said as she poured, working to sound casual.

"Do you?" he asked softly, his tone noncommittal. "What an interesting idea."

She brought him the drink. "I'm not forgetting that there has been . . . a great deal of misunderstanding between us. But I thought—"

He cut her off. "Do you think so? Misunderstanding?" he asked in that same soft, reasonable voice. "I've always thought we understood each other perfectly, that we even had a special bond. There was a time, Elle, though perhaps you've forgotten—"

"I haven't," she interrupted, reaching eagerly for the hope that he still desired her. "If only we hadn't met when we were both so young. We didn't have the strength, either of us, to get what we wanted, to know what was right. Now we do. . . ."

Duke sipped his drink, his eyes fixed on her over the rim of the glass. As his hand came down, he said with a smile, "I don't think so, Elle . . . I don't think there's the slightest chance that we can ever be friends. In fact, I think it's very unlikely that *you* will ever be anything to anyone in my family but what you have always been—what you were born to be."

Elle flinched as the direction he was taking became clear. But with the dying of her last hope, she hadn't the strength to defend herself, not even to avoid his continuing attack.

"Did you think for a minute you could pass yourself off as a respectable woman . . . even with all your pretensions? Why don't you give it up, Elle? You played your cards and you've lost. I didn't come here for any reason except to make sure you knew that once and for all. You're not wanted here, and you'll never belong. It's past time for you to take that brat of yours and get out of Hyland territory."

Duke's soft, lethal voice was like an echo of Elle's own inner voices, and she fought to shake it off, knowing that if she listened, if she let herself believe what he said, her life would have no meaning. None. And her daughter, her little Niki would be left with less than nothing.

Seeing his blows had had the desired effect, Duke smiled again. "But just for old time's sake . . . and because I can imagine how important weddings are to you, before you go I think you might like to attend the one forthcoming in our family. It won't be as grand as the royal wedding, of course, but I think we can manage a party that will meet even your high standards, Elle."

A wedding? The shock of ultimate defeat could not be hidden from her eyes.

"Didn't you hear?" Duke asked blandly. "Ah well, it hasn't been made public just yet—and now that I think of it, H.D. wouldn't be keeping you informed anymore, would he? But because I want you to know how well I understand you, Elle, because I know how hard you've worked to get past the front door of Highland House, it seems only right to arrange for you to be there to see for yourself what you'll never have."

She could only sit immobile, stunned by his malice, as he swallowed down his drink and rose to go. "The way things are, I suppose H.D. might not have thought of asking you. But I'm hoping he won't object to my wishes to have you there. Because you see, Elle, it's my wedding. I'm marrying Pamela Wardour . . . and if you'll come, I can't think of anyone it would give me more pleasure to have."

And with that, Duke clapped his glass down on the sideboard and took an engraved invitation from his jacket pocket. As he walked out, he tossed the invitation on a lamp table.

Elle dragged herself up from her chair and went to her bedroom where she brooded over Duke's mocking invitation to a Hyland wedding. How long he had waited to deliver such a blow, she thought, and how exquisitely perfect his timing. How he must have laughed to himself when she'd called. Blinded by her obsession, the fragile hope of a second chance, she had invited shame and ridicule into her own home.

Or was everything lost . . . ? Perhaps Duke had been blinded by his own hatred into giving her an opportunity to retrieve everything. If she went to the wedding at his invitation, perhaps H.D. might see her in a new light—not as a mistress carefully tucked out of sight, away from the family, but as someone who *could* belong at Highland House, who could, even now, be an asset to him. Joanne was gone now, there was no wife to affront or insult. And if H.D. should be annoyed by Elle's boldness, it was Duke he would have to blame for inviting her.

Once she made up her mind, Elle revived, for never did she feel so alive, so purposeful, as when she turned all her thoughts and energies towards the fulfillment of a goal.

Seven

THE day of Duke's wedding to Pamela Wardour was sunny and clear. Not even the weather dared to cross a Hyland, Elle thought, especially not in Willow Cross.

Not wanting to answer any questions about where she was going, she sent Niki to spend the day at the Boyntons. And then, feeling tense, excited, and afraid—like a Christian about to face the Roman lions—Elle began to prepare herself for the wedding.

Her dress was a cream-colored silk faille, artfully cut to show off her body, yet demure in its simplicity. Though it looked as if it cost a fortune, the dress was, in fact, Elle's own design, executed by her "little dressmaker."

Her hands were trembling on the wheel as she drove to Highland House. Just a few short miles, yet a world away, it represented the ultimate prize. How many times had she passed the place, furtively, like a thief, scheming and planning for the day she would walk through the front door as Mrs. Hyland.

She presented her invitation at the gate, her fingers still trembling, but the uniformed guard merely glanced at the gold-engraved vellum and waved her through. As she approached the sweeping tree-lined driveway, she remembered how she had once likened Duke to the elegant Southern gentlemen in *Gone With the Wind*. She had been mistaken, of course, but the great house that loomed before her now was as grand as anything she had seen in films.

As Elle turned her car over to a young black man, she heard the music of a string quartet coming from the house. There was an army of servants in livery, the old-fashioned kind, serving mimosas and hors d'oeuvres. It was as if the Old South of the movies was still very much alive at Highland House. The guests, too, were beautifully turned out, reflecting the elegance of a bygone era, rather than the trendy styles of the day. And though Elle had lived a cloistered life, she was an avid reader of the social pages (in preparation for the day when she would take her rightful place there), and she recognized at once the governor of the state and two United States senators. It was not surprising, she thought, that when it came time to marry, Duke would call upon all the royalty Hyland Tobacco could command.

Amidst the hundreds of guests, Elle imagined that she was passing unnoticed by anyone who might object to her presence. She looked around for H.D., but didn't see him. And when a rustle of activity among the servants signaled that the ceremony was soon to begin, she heard someone whisper that H.D. was going to be late, that his plane had been delayed at the airport following a meeting with the President in Washington. Leave it to H.D., she thought, forgetting for a moment her own disappointment; even at Duke's wedding, he has to remind his son that he was less important than Hyland Tobacco.

A harpist played selections from Lohengrin as the guests were seated on gilt chairs set out on the grounds behind Highland House, amidst manicured gardens of such splendor, they reminded Elle of pictures of Versailles.

As the string quartet began the traditional processional, the bride appeared on her father's arm, wearing an exquisite gown of Belgian lace that might easily have rivaled Princess Grace's in opulence. In his gray cutaway, Duke stood tall, imperial and unsmiling. Elle couldn't help wonder if there was any love in his heart this morning, if there was any room for love beside his driving ambition.

As she watched the brief and simple ceremony, Elle felt again the heavy hand of time. The boy who had desired and then hated her was now a man, beginning a family of his own, while she and Niki still lingered in limbo. And when Duke kissed his bride, Elle wondered if he knew that among the hundreds of well-wishers, there was one at his wedding who did not wish him well.

When the newlyweds joined hands and moved forward to greet their guests, a rebel yell—exultant, raucous, and wildly incongrous—launched the celebration. Soon, champagne was flowing from a six-foot fountain, and there was laughter and dancing, to the music of a Lester Lanin orchestra.

Elle kept well away from the bridal couple. She had no wish to confront Duke again, and if H.D. was not, after all, going to be here, she thought perhaps she should leave. Her fine clothes didn't change anything; she was still apart from everyone who mattered at Highland House.

"What are *you* doing here?" snapped a female voice. Elle whirled around—and was stunned to find herself face to face with Pepper Hyland, glittering with jewels and staring with undisguised hostility. Standing slightly off to one side was her younger brother Babe.

"I asked you a question," Pepper repeated, "and you'd best say something quick before I have one of the servants throw you out, like the common trash—"

"Pepper!" Babe broke in. "Be decent."

"I'd say it isn't decent to come where you're not wanted . . . and of all the people who aren't wanted here, *this* person certainly heads the list."

Elle maintained her composure. She wasn't afraid of *this*

Hyland; she knew too much about Pepper's failures—her inability to graduate from any school—to be intimidated or impressed. "I had imagined that all H.D.'s children were well-mannered and well-bred. I see I was mistaken. As it happens, I'm here at your brother Edward's invitation." She reached into her small sequined bag and brought out the vellum envelope, and, with great satisfaction, she saw that Pepper was rendered speechless.

A moment later, Pepper turned on her heel and marched away.

But Babe stayed. "You'll have to excuse my sister," he said.

Elle looked at him curiously, expecting his gentle expression and soft voice to change suddenly and reveal his own hostility. But he took her hand and went on in the same mild tone. "May I show you to a table and get you something to eat?"

Now Elle saw the admiration in the young man's eyes, even a hint of desire. "Only if you share the table with me . . ." she said with a flirtatious smile.

"I'd be delighted," Babe replied with a courtly old-fashioned bow. He led the way to a secluded table, and with a nod in a servant's direction, summoned up champagne and smoked salmon.

With Babe as her unofficial escort, Elle felt protected enough to linger a while longer. What she knew about H.D.'s younger son was that he was a good athlete, a decent polo player, that he drove fast cars, and had a taste for flashy clothes. And so she asked a few questions about his cars and horses and listened attentively as he talked—which was something she did very well.

When the bride and groom stepped forward to cut the wedding cake, there was a murmur, then a loud buzz of conversation. H.D. Hyland had finally arrived, surrounded by his personal entourage of aides and bodyguards. He shook Duke's hand, lingering long enough for the squadron of photographers to take pictures, yet there seemed to be little warmth in the gesture. When he kissed the bride, Elle noticed with a resentful pang that for a moment H.D. showed his old appreciation of a beautiful woman.

She waited until he was greeting the guests who had gathered around him, eager to shake his hand, to make themselves known. Then she said to Babe. "I'd like to say hello to your father. Will you take me over?" She hoped she could play on the penchant for chivalry that Babe had shown in defending her against his sister. With Babe on her arm, H.D. might finally see that she could fit in.

Babe seemed delighted. Together, they cut through the crowd that surrounded his father.

"Hello, H.D.," Elle said, mustering her best smile. "This is a lovely wedding. . . ."

H.D. glared at her in shock, but recovered quickly. "What are you doing here?" he said, lowering his voice, but otherwise sounding no less affronted than Pepper had.

"She's with me," Babe cut in, before Elle could reply.

It was enough of an answer. Elle simply gazed at H.D. with innocent eyes.

He responded with a burning look, and for a moment it seemed he might explode, heedless of disrupting the wedding. But then he shrugged, and the gesture was more eloquent than words in declaring that Elle wasn't worth any more consideration. He walked away, leaving a murmur of speculation in his wake.

Elle's brief triumph turned to ashes. She retreated from the stares of the other guests. "I should have known it would be like this," she said heavily.

Babe walked with her. "Then why did you come?" he asked, with real curiosity rather than malice.

Elle paused, wondering how frank she could be with this young man who was, after all, Joanne's son. "Duke invited me," she said finally. "He meant it as a kind of cruel joke. But then I thought, why shouldn't I 'come out of the closet,' as you Americans say."

Babe nodded approvingly. "It took guts, Elle. I can admire that. H.D. and Duke don't always think too much of me, either. They don't think I can handle the business the way they do. But the one thing I've shown 'em is that I'm not afraid. It's the only way to get anywhere with them sometimes. Duke can be such a mean damn sonofabitch, meaner than H.D. I'm glad you didn't let him get the better of you."

She shook her head. "It was a stupid idea. I think I'd better leave." Looking into Babe's eyes, she ventured: "I'm grateful to you, though. I'm glad you don't hate me the way everyone else in your family seems to."

"I couldn't hate you, Elle. In fact, I've always been curious about you. I was always hearing things, you know, you always seemed so . . . mysterious. I saw you on the street a couple of times," he admitted. "I thought you were awfully pretty and . . . and I could see why my father . . . why . . ." Babe's apparent sophistication evaporated, and he began to blush.

Elle smiled tolerantly. "That's very gallant, Babe." She had heard that Babe was often seen with "older" women, and she could guess the reason. Living as he did in H.D.'s shadow, under the dominant force of Duke's hunger for power, his own value must have been constantly called into question. It was only natural, she thought, that he'd turn to older women for reassurance and kindness. "I'm glad you're not like your brother," she said. "It must be terrible to be so unhappy, so filled with anger and hate."

Babe's blue eyes clouded for a moment, as though recollecting his encounters with Duke. But a moment later, his sunny nature reasserted itself. "Maybe Duke's new wife will straighten him out. She's a swell gal, a really good sport. Maybe she can make him a little more human."

The music began to play, and Babe asked her to dance. It was a slow, sedate fox trot, as if the band were just coming out of a deep sleep. Babe led her around the dance floor with the polish and ease of a much older man, humming the melody in her ear.

"Did you go to dancing school?" she asked. "You dance very well . . ."

Babe grinned. "Hell, no. My mother taught me when I was eight or nine. She said it was never too early for a gentleman to acquire the basic social skills."

After they had danced a few slow numbers, Babe spoke to the orchestra leader, who soon obliged with a recognizable version of the Peppermint Twist. A few guests began to move to the rhythm of the popular dance, but many looked puzzled or simply sat down.

"Let's put a little life into this party," Babe said with a boyish laugh, as he signaled for Elle to follow his lead. She kicked off her shoes, thinking there was nothing left to lose. As she twisted and turned to the music, she made herself and Babe the center of attention—for once, not caring about the stares and whispers that followed her every movement.

"I couldn't resist," Babe admitted mischievously, when they sat down to catch their breath. "I'll bet H.D. splits a gut . . . but who cares if he does. I swear, that old boy wouldn't know a good time if it came up and bit him on the nose."

Elle laughed along with him, feeling as if she and Babe had suddenly become partners in something.

"Have you ever been to the Peppermint Lounge in New York?" he asked.

She shook her head.

"Great music . . . not like the stiff stuff *this* band plays. You should go sometime. I like the clubs up in New York. . . ."

Elle was silent, remembering back many years ago when H.D. would promise that someday he would take her to places far from Willow Cross. But she had never been anywhere.

Babe broke into her reverie. "Hey, maybe you'd like to go sometime."

Had he been reading her thoughts? "I would love to go," she said, a bit wistfully, already thinking it would never happen.

Babe grinned, and Elle could see just how devastatingly handsome this boy with the twinkling blue eyes and curly blond hair would be. Like a Greek god, she thought, that's what he'll look like before long.

Elle was already charmed by his easy manner, his boyish ways. It was easy to like Babe Hyland, she thought, to appreciate his sunny good nature. Of all the Hyland men, he was the only one who didn't seem obsessed with Hyland Tobacco, choosing instead simply to enjoy the wealth and privilege it gave him.

When he offered to see her home, she agreed at once, asking only that something be done about her car.

"No problem, Elle. I'll have one of the servants bring it round to you in the morning."

He drove her home at high speed in the most dashing car that Elle had ever seen, a Jaguar twelve-cylinder painted bright red, with all the chrome replaced by polished brass fittings.

Like his brother, Babe was openly curious about Elle's home, and so she made light of what might have been awkward when he accepted her invitation to come in.

"*Voilà*!" she said, laying on the French accent, "Welcome to the lair of the scarlet woman!"

But Babe didn't laugh. After scanning the living room, he looked at her earnestly. "If I ask you something, will you tell me the truth?"

As tall as he was, there was a certain innocent intensity in Babe's face that made Elle think of a little boy. She had to fight back a smile. "I will do my very best," she said.

"It's about H.D. I was wondering . . . do you still miss him?"

"No," she said softly. Gazing up into his eyes, she realized at once what his motive was in asking. "No," she said quietly, "not at all."

He stared at her. Then he bent slightly lower. "Miss Gabrielle . . . would you mind . . . ?"

She didn't wait for him to stumble through the rest of the

question, but reached up to put her hand lightly on the back of his neck.

His lips came down onto hers, a kiss so sweet and tentative that she was reminded of the timid awe of love she had once felt and had left so far behind.

"I've always wanted you," he whispered passionately as their lips parted. "Always thought it was crazy for you to be with him. . . ."

Of course, she knew, what Babe wanted had nothing very much to do with who she was—nothing beyond the fact that she had once belonged to H.D., and this son of his had a need to measure himself against his father.

But that didn't matter, Elle thought. She was alone—and he was sweet, and he was vulnerable, and he was a Hyland. And Niki still needed the name.

In the weeks that followed Elle and Babe became playmates, lovers, and friends. After the complexity of H.D., and in contrast to the dark, smoldering Duke, Babe was refreshingly simple and open, giving Elle what she had never known: the gift of childhood. Eager to have fun, he was the perfect companion; together they drove to secluded roadhouses, drank too much and danced until dawn. If Elle couldn't arrange for Niki to be away at Kate's or watched by Louise, she would have Babe at the house. And after Niki played a game with them—for Babe could enter right into the spirit of hide and seek—Elle and Babe would have a party in the living room of the cottage, singing bawdy songs, drinking champagne until they were too giddy for anything but making love. They gossiped together about "them"—congratulating each other on deceiving Babe's family, on sharing a secret they both knew would drive H.D. mad with anger.

Knowing the Hylands as she did, Elle was the perfect audience for Babe's repertoire of family stories. Babe never attacked directly, he simply told stories, funny, on-target stories that made Duke appear foolish, and H.D. seem pompous and old.

Though Elle believed at first that Babe's interest in her was only a symptom of his damaged relationship with his father, with the sheer ebullience of his sunny nature, he helped her put doubts aside and enjoy what he brought into her life. After the long, lonely months of exile, it was a blessed relief to laugh again and to feel wanted.

Babe was even kind to Niki, in ways H.D. never had been. Though scarcely past his own childhood, he was in turn curious and delighted with his half sister. Seeming not to care that she was the living proof of his father's infidelity, he took an indulgent uncle's stance, engaging Niki in conversation, asking about school, looking with real interest at her lessons, telling childish jokes—and always remembering to bring a small gift for her when he came to call.

How different he was, Elle thought, this son of H.D.'s second marriage, how much more human and generous than Duke. He was truly capable of love, she thought. Even if the liaison between them had been born out of their weaknesses—her desperation, his need for some kind of affirmation—they had gone beyond that. Lying in Babe's arms, Elle believed that she had finally found the haven she'd been seeking. Though they had both been wounded, even damaged by the other Hylands, together she and Babe almost seemed to be whole, and capable of surviving.

Eight

NIKI sat up in bed, the reflex of cold terror that had invaded her sleep already causing her to grip the blankets tight against her chest.

A nightmare? She had no memory of a bad dream. But then why was she shivering? The night was hot and sultry.

It must have been thunder. Somewhere at the corners of her mind, she believed she could still hear the echo of a loud boom dying away. Yet when she looked toward the open window, she saw no rain falling, heard no pattering drops. She remembered then that sometimes thunder and lightning came without a shower—an electrical storm.

She became aware now of the music. Very loud, the jazzy records that Mama liked to play when Uncle Babe was here. Thump, thump, thump, the music had a good solid beat behind it. Though Niki thought it wasn't just the drums that were thumping against the floor. The other sound must be their feet. Dancing.

The noise that Mama made with Babe had awakened her

before, but she didn't complain. She liked having Uncle Babe in the house. He was so much fun. Niki loved to ride in his car, to hear him and Mama laughing and joking. He had promised they'd all take a long trip on his boat soon.

Niki lay down and burrowed under the covers to dampen the sound of the music. No, she mustn't complain. She didn't want to do anything that would make Mama unhappy, or cause Babe to go away and not come back the way Mr. Hyland had.

But the music seemed to get louder. And even though she told herself it was only a party, and reminded herself—as Mama had told her—that thunder couldn't hurt her . . . for some reason she couldn't stop feeling very frightened. She imagined that an evil monster had come in through the open window while she slept.

Her heart started to pound faster, until she could no longer bear to stay alone in her room.

At the same time, she knew it would be bad to bother Mama and Uncle Babe. She had been well trained by all the years of being sent to bed early, all the warnings to stay in her room whenever Mr. Hyland came to visit.

Niki got out of bed very quietly, tiptoed barefoot across her room, and then started down the stairs. She didn't have to talk to Mama, it would be enough to see that she was there, dancing with Uncle Babe. As long as she stayed hidden, Niki thought, they couldn't be mad at her.

As she descended toward the soft glow coming through the portal from the dimly lit living room, Niki realized that, while the music was still blaring, the thumping sound had stopped. At the bottom of the steps, she leaned forward very slowly and carefully to peer into the living room. Her view expanded to take in the windows . . . the fireplace, where a few logs were crackling . . . then the long couch beside the fire. And now, her mother's face came in sight, looking straight at the door, as she reclined on the sofa.

Niki started to shy back, but then she saw her mother was asleep, her eyes closed. She dared to peek in just a bit farther, and saw in the shadows, the figure of a man kneeling, blocking off all of Elle's body except for one arm, sheathed in pale pink silk, that was stretched out across the floor. The man's back was to the door, but Niki could tell by his movements that he was doing something with his hands.

She almost let out a gasp as she realized that he was fiddling with Mama's silk robe. Uncle Babe was undressing her!

She mustn't watch another second, Niki told herself. Yet she was riveted to the sight as the kneeling figure rose to his feet, and Niki realized it couldn't be Uncle Babe because he was much taller and broader than this man. Again, Niki stifled a gasp this time by damming her hand against her mouth. Even without seeing the man's face, she knew it must be Mr. Hyland . . . and part of her was possessed by an urge to run to him, so that he wouldn't leave again because when he had left the last time Mama had been miserable for so long. . . .

But it was Babe that Niki liked. Why wasn't *he* here? Why had Mama let Mr. Hyland come back instead, and why was he touching her while playing that music so loud—the music Uncle Babe liked?

The figure at the couch began to move, as if to turn, and Niki retreated instantly, scampering back up the stairs. She couldn't bear to watch, anyway, couldn't stand thinking about things that made no sense.

She jumped into bed again and pulled the covers up. Suddenly, the music stopped. It was so quiet. . . .

Faintly, just after her eyelids began to droop, Niki heard the kind of tinkly sound icicles made when they grew so big and heavy they fell from the edge of the roof onto the hard ground.

But just before she fell asleep, she remembered it wasn't winter.

When she opened her eyes again it was morning, and she wasn't sure what had really happened. Had she gotten up to go downstairs in the middle of the night? Had Mr. Hyland really been there? Or was it only a dream?

She jumped up and ran to find Elle. The bed in her mother's

room was already made, so Niki ran downstairs knowing Elle would be in the kitchen.

As she hopped off the last step to the floor, Niki glanced into the living room and then froze.

"Mama!" she cried, seeing Elle still asleep, but not on the sofa anymore. She was lying near a window in her pink silk robe, and there was broken glass glittering all around her. Niki ran across the room to shake her. A little splinter of glass pricked her foot, but she hardly noticed. "Mama, wake up!"

Niki started shaking her mother more vigorously, calling to her louder and louder until her cries had become hysterical screams.

It hadn't been a dream, she knew now. While she was sleeping a monster had come in through the window. . . .

"Niki, please talk to me," said the man who was wearing a holstered gun on his belt, and a pocket watch on a gold chain that hung across his large stomach. "I know this is very hard for you, but all we want is to help you—and I can give you the most help if you tell me whatever you remember about last night. . . ."

Niki said nothing. She didn't want to talk about that. If she talked about it, then it would be real . . . if she didn't then it might not. Monsters weren't real, after all. Mama had told her so many, many times—whenever she woke up from a nightmare. If she just waited long enough—and didn't talk about it—then she would surely wake up from this one. How much longer could it last? Running down the road from the house, her bare feet scraped and cut from stones on the road . . . the telephone repair truck stopping . . . the men who listened to her choked account of what she had seen . . . the ride to the police station . . . and then waiting in this room until this man and some others came in. . . . It had already been such a long nightmare. It couldn't go on forever.

Suddenly, a door in the room opened and a man in a uniform entered. He was carrying a container of milk and a cupcake. He offered them to Niki, but she shook her head silently. There was a cold, hard knot in her stomach and a giant lump in her throat, and she knew that if she tried to eat, she would only throw up.

"We're all very sorry about what happened to your mother," the pocket-watch man said, "and we're going to do everything we can to catch whoever broke in . . . and hurt her so terribly . . ."

The knot in Niki's stomach exploded into an agonized wail. Her shoulders shook and she sobbed uncontrollably. It was real, she thought, it wasn't going to end. Mama had gone away and she was never coming back.

The policeman patted her head awkwardly, murmuring sounds of consolation. "There, there, Niki, you have to be brave now . . . for your mama's sake."

But she remained mute, torn by grief and paralyzed with fear.

The pocket-watch man cleared his throat. "Little girl," he said, in a softer tone. "I wouldn't mind waiting until you feel a lot better to get this done. But the sooner you talk to me, the sooner we might find out how to . . . to punish the person who did this bad thing. You've got to tell me, honey—anything you heard or saw, and if you have any idea what time it might have happened. . . ."

Niki stared at the pocket-watch man. She recognized him now—from a visit her class had made to the police station. He had been in uniform then, and Miss June had introduced him as Chief of Police Haynes. "The police are here to uphold the law and protect us from harm," Miss June had said, smiling brightly as the class had stood at attention. But the police hadn't protected Mama from harm, and because they were keeping her here, Niki felt a little like she was the one who had done something wrong. She wanted to go home, and run in the door, and find her mother waiting . . . but they wouldn't let her leave. The police wouldn't let the nightmare end.

"Niki," the chief said again, as patiently as he could, "it

looks like a man broke into your house and your mother caught him. Did you hear any struggle, any sound of glass breaking?"

Very quietly, she said, "Music, that's all I heard. . . ."

"Music," the chief repeated. "You woke up because —"

The door opened again, banging back on its hinges this time, and a stranger strode in briskly. He was very tall, with gray hair and a small, neatly trimmed white beard and mustache. He looked very angry. "You know better than this, Bill," he snapped at the chief. "You should have waited until I arrived before questioning this child. You had no business—"

"It's police business," Chief Haynes protested mildly. "I was only doing my duty . . ."

"You know where your duty is," the tall man cut in sharply, "and if you've forgotten, I'll be happy to remind you come next election. Now leave us alone."

The stranger gave the chief a long hard look. He shuffled in place for a moment—and then left the room.

The tall man approached Niki and smiled as he stooped over in front of her. His voice was soft when he spoke. "I'm so sorry, child, I came as soon as I could. I wanted to spare you all this." He made a gesture that took in the grim, green interrogation room. "I'm a good friend of your mother's, and I'm here to look after you now . . . the way I know she'd want me to."

Niki's eyes formed the question: but I've never seen you.

"My name is Sterling Weatherby," he said gently, "and though we've never met, I've been taking care of your mama's legal affairs for a long time. And now, I'm here to take care of you. But I need your cooperation. Do you understand, Nicolette?"

Niki felt as if she had no choice. This man said he was a friend of Mama's. "Do you think it was Mr. Hyland who hurt my mother?" she asked in a ragged whisper.

There was an electric silence before the lawyer said, "Why would I think that?"

"He was there."

Sterling Weatherby shook his head and smiled. "But he couldn't have been, child—and he certainly wouldn't have hurt your mother. It was Mr. Hyland who called and instructed me to help you—and he called from Washington, where he's been for the past three days."

"Really?"

"Niki, I hope you'd never mention to anyone else that you think Mr. Hyland was there. It's not possible, and it would just mix everyone up. You wouldn't want to do that. The police know a lot about what happened. . . ."

"I told them about the music," she said.

Weatherby paused and gave Niki a sidelong glance, then flashed another dismissive smile. "They know," he went on, "that someone broke in—a burglar, who wanted to steal things—and your mother tried to stop him, and . . . the burglar fought with her."

"I didn't hear any of that."

"You slept through it . . . ?"

Niki nodded.

"And that's what you told the police?"

"I didn't tell them anything yet, not even about Mr. Hyland."

"But he wasn't there, Niki. That can be proved."

She thought she had seen him, but now she was all mixed up. Maybe that part had been a dream, and the real things had only started to happen this morning.

Weatherby suddenly seemed to become aware that she was sitting in her nightgown and robe. "Are you cold, child?" he asked solicitously. "Do you need a blanket?"

Niki shook her head. She was too numb for either cold or heat.

Mr. Weatherby pulled over another chair and sat down across from her. "Nicolette, I'm sure you want to be able to leave this place very soon. You can do that as soon as you tell the police what you've just told me—that you were asleep the whole time. But it would be wrong to say anything unless you're sure it's absolutely one hundred percent true. Do you understand, child?"

Niki wasn't sure she did, but Weatherby's words seemed to make sense, and somehow she had no desire to displease him.

"If you do exactly as I've told you," he said, "you won't have to worry about the police anymore. In a little while, this will all be over, and you'll be well cared for . . . Mr. Hyland will see to that. You should be grateful, Nicolette, that Mr. Hyland is so concerned about you."

Because there was nothing else to do and nowhere else to go, Niki obediently spoke to the police and said exactly what Mr. Weatherby had told her to say, and then followed him out when he said they were going to his house, "until this terrible business is cleared up."

He lived in a large white house right near the center of Willow Cross. There didn't seem to be anyone else who lived there except his housekeeper, an elderly black woman named Martha. Her eyes showed some surprise when she saw Niki, but she didn't say anything when Mr. Weatherby told her that Niki would be staying a while.

"Give the child a bath and put her to bed, Martha," he said. "I'll send someone over to fetch her clothes later."

Martha did as she was told. Though Niki couldn't imagine attempting sleep, somehow the touch of the housekeeper's gentle hands and the warm, soothing bath made Niki drowsy and tired. And when she was taken to bed in a small guest room, she soon dozed off.

She spent the next two days sleeping at Mr. Weatherby's house, and being taken out for meals and to go to the police station. She was bored and scared and lonely all at the same time, and at times when she remembered she was never going to see Mama again it was almost unbearable.

The Boyntons came and visited, but she didn't even feel like talking to Kate, and went up to her room. When they were leaving, Niki heard Mr. Weatherby arguing with the

Boyntons downstairs—something about his "obligation" to keep her in his custody.

On the third morning, Martha woke Niki, gave her a new black dress and coat to wear, and said she was going to her mother's funeral.

Sitting in church and staring at the white coffin, a ride to the cemetery, the casket going down into the deep hole in the earth—more of the unending nightmare. Throughout the services, there were very few people around her that she knew. Louise, and some of the people who ran shops Mama had used a lot, and Mr. Weatherby, and some of the policemen. But that was all. Not Mr. Hyland . . . not even Babe.

The evening after the funeral, while she was listening to the big radio downstairs in Mr. Weatherby's house, she heard his voice from a nearby room as he argued with someone on the telephone.

"I won't allow it. . . . Because there's no damn need for her to appear, that's why, and it would just upset her. You've got all the evidence you need for an inquest. The child has answered enough questions."

But the next morning, after Martha had given her a bowl of farina with honey, Mr. Weatherby sat down at the breakfast table and said he was taking her out to see a judge who wanted to ask her some questions.

"But I heard you say I'd answered enough," Niki protested. "Why do we have to see a judge now?"

"It's part of deciding about your future, Nicolette, about where you should live."

The explanation seemed ominous and frightening, as did the prospect of facing a judge. Niki knew she couldn't stay at Mr. Weatherby's house forever, but where else could she go?

"Don't be afraid, Niki," Mr. Weatherby said, as though he knew what she was thinking. "I promised to look after you, and I will. I'll find a good place, a place where you'll be happy."

No, Niki thought, that wasn't possible. She couldn't ever be happy again.

When Niki entered the room at the county courthouse where Mr. Weatherby had taken her, she saw Mr. Hyland in a row of seats at the back. It made her wonder if he'd come to take her with him. Had he changed his mind about not liking her, after the terrible thing that had happened to Mama? She thought about asking Mr. Weatherby, but the serious expression on his face told her to be quiet.

When the judge came into the courtroom and took his place on the bench, Mr. Weatherby got up and walked towards him.

"Who are you?" the judge asked.

Mr. Weatherby cleared his throat. "Sterling Weatherby, your honor. I represent the child."

The judge glanced across the room, to where Mr. Hyland sat.

"Very well," he said. "The court will recognize and hear you."

"Your honor," he said, "in the matter of the minor child, Nicolette Sandeman, recently orphaned . . . we understand that normally, she would be taken under the jurisdiction of the court and made a ward of the state. However, since the deceased, Miss Gabrielle Sandeman, was an employee of Hyland Tobacco, we have taken a special interest in the child's welfare. Therefore, I petition the court to appoint me guardian of the minor child and executor of her mother's estate."

"Is there anyone here who objects to Mr. Weatherby's request?" the judge asked.

No one spoke.

"Very well," he said, "your request is granted, and the court appoints you guardian of the child, Nicolette Sandeman, until she reaches her majority."

Everything was happening so quickly. No one told Niki anything, yet suddenly her bag was packed and she was told to get ready.

"But where am I going?" she asked Mr. Weatherby fearfully, as he ushered her out of his house to his waiting car.

"To school, Niki," he said finally. "A very fine school, I might add, with girls your own age. You'll like it."

Niki was silent. What did it matter what she liked? The packed suitcase told her she was going, no matter what she said.

She got into the car feeling like a prisoner, with no hope of escape. Suddenly she sat up straight, remembering something, something *important*.

"I can't go away yet," she said. "I have to go back, I have to go back to the house, to *my* house Mr. Weatherby. Please."

"Nonsense," he said, obviously annoyed. "You can't go back there. It's—"

"I have to," she cried, and tugged at the car door, as if she meant to jump out.

But Weatherby's strong arm restrained her.

"What is it?" he asked. "What is it you want to do?"

"I have to get something . . . I'll die without it, I know I will."

Weatherby studied her a moment, and then shrugged. "It's not far out of the way. I suppose we can stop. But only if you promise me there won't be any more problems."

"I promise."

"Good." Weatherby started the car. "You ought to be grateful instead of making problems. Do you know how fortunate you are to be sent off to a fine school, not a state orphanage? Remember that, Niki. You're a lucky girl there's someone still willing to take care of you. . . ."

Someone taking care of her? She didn't feel as if anyone was, or ever would again. She certainly didn't feel lucky. The only person who had ever really loved and wanted her was gone forever.

The door of the cottage had an orange sticker pasted on the door with some big words printed on it. Niki got as far as reading the word CRIME . . . printed right at the top before she tried the knob and, finding the door unlocked the way it always was in the morning, ran inside and straight up the stairs to her mother's room.

She paused for only a second to look around. Nothing had changed. Nothing and everything. Looking at the empty bedroom made her heart feel as if it was tearing in two.

A blast from the car horn came through the window.

From the top of her mother's dresser Niki grabbed what she had come for, the framed photograph of a young woman flying—her grandmother. Many times she had seen her mother holding it, talking to it in the way that people in fairy tales Niki had read would talk to magic rings or bottles or rubbed magic lamps to have their wishes granted. Had any of Elle's wishes come true? Some, Niki thought . . . for a little while.

Niki stared at the picture. She understood why her mother had believed. As bad as the world was, there had to be magic in it somewhere if a woman could fly like that.

The horn sounded again, a longer blast than before.

Clutching the picture to her chest like a shield against evil, Niki ran from the room, determined to find the magic.

BOOK II

Nine

Virginia, September 1971

BALANCE.

Balance is everything, Niki told herself for the millionth time. Though the message didn't even have to form in her brain anymore. Without being articulated, it was there in her nerves, her bones and sinews, always there, as soon as she stepped to the edge of the board and prepared for the dive.

She took a few deep breaths, then closed her eyes. Like a primitive hunter listening in the darkness for the almost imperceptible sound of the shewdest prey, or a blind musician homing in on a single pure note, she waited within herself for the moment when she was sure she had found what she was seeking—the perfect balance.

It came—and it was the trigger. Arms were set in fluid motion, legs bent to spring, muscles throughout her body flexed in practiced synchrony . . . until, without any real thought or decision, she was catapulted off the springboard into space. Tumbling, twisting, then unfolding again, arms straight—the image of her grandmother that she always carried somewhere in her mind come to life—and at last the sudden fresh chill against her skin as she knifed cleanly into the water.

Niki swam to the edge of the pool and threw her arm over the side to rest. Okay, she thought . . . just okay. A hair short of full extension at entry, hands not quite together, toes pointed up maybe a few degrees off the perfect angle. She glanced to the clock on the wall at the far end of the pool. Almost six o'clock. Still time for a few more. Niki climbed out, walked back to the board, and went on with the drill.

At the age of fifteen, she had a fine body for a diver, long legged, slim and tall, well developed and strong without being bulky. Her participation on the swim and diving team at the Blue Mountain School had been the principal reason for its success in interschool, and more recently intrastate, championships. But now she had her eyes on a bigger prize, a place on the Olympic team for the games in the summer of 1972. There would be a special sweetness in going to these games because they would be held for the first time in thirty-six years in the same city where her grandmother, Monique, had won her silver medal. Munich.

Niki knew her chance of joining the U.S. women's team was only marginal. As good as she was, there were enough who were better. But all through the summer break she had worked, three-hour sessions twice a day even when the coach couldn't make it, longer sometimes. If she kept practicing, questing, devoting herself to the search for perfection, maybe. . . .

She checked the clock again. A half-hour had gone by! Now she would be late for dinner—not good, tonight especially. Vale House, the dorm where Niki would be spending sophomore year, was getting a new housemother; a notice announcing the arrival of Mrs. Helen Czardas had been pinned on the dorm bulletin board for several days, along with the detail that she would also be teaching elementary biology. Mrs. Czardas had probably arrived while Niki was here, and she would be waiting with dinner at the regular time, six-thirty.

Niki hurried to the empty locker room, dashed in and out of the shower, and threw on jeans and sweatshirt, not even taking time for underwear. Without stopping to dry the blond hair she kept long under her swim cap, she left the pool building, locking up with the key she'd been given by the coach.

It was still warm outside, the low sun of evening slanting through the big old oaks onto the red brick classroom buildings. Though not in the first rank of boarding schools for girls, Blue Mountain Preparatory School for Young Women was known for the natural beauty and tranquility of its campus. Niki was not in so much of a hurry that she had to run. She preferred to stroll, to savor the evening and appreciate the signs that a new school term was near. Classes didn't begin until after the weekend, but a few students had already begun to arrive. In the driveways outside a couple of the white-frame colonial houses which served as dorms, big new cars stood with their trunk lids open, as luggage was unloaded by a chauffeur or a single parent. At Blue Mountain, almost all the parents were divorced; a mother and father almost never appeared together except at graduation. The school had a reputation for taking problem children, special cases who would not be admitted elsewhere.

Passing not far from a mother and daughter saying goodbye, Niki caught the glances that switched in her direction as the girl lowered her voice to an excited whisper. Niki wasn't unaware that she had gained some notoriety on the campus. Partly, it was the celebrity status that came with often having her picture in the school newspaper—or even sports pages of city papers—receiving a trophy. But, of course, that was not the only reason the girls talked about her. Because she didn't leave the school at holidays or summer recesses, because it had become her only home, because she almost never received mail, there had always been talk. Whether or not her schoolmates had their facts right these days, Niki couldn't be sure. But in the past—she knew from the times when other girls would dare to ask if the stories were true—there had been many different rumors. That her parents had been killed in a plane crash. That her mother and father had been spies, executed by the Russians. At first, when she was little, she would correct them with the truth: her mother had been murdered by a burglar, her father was a rich man whose name she wasn't ever allowed to tell or he would let her starve. But no one had believed that either. In defense, she had taken to humor. Now when anyone asked, she would say deadpan that she had been dropped at the school by a passing stork. It was only one of the devices that Niki used to keep people from getting closer and asking too many questions. The intensity with which she pursued her diving, the emanations she gave off of preferring her privacy, had earned her the reputation of being a habitual loner.

She had come to Blue Mountain three years ago straight from the elementary boarding school in Arkansas where she had been sent as a girl. As before, the choice was made for her. Mr. Weatherby had shown up in the spring to say that as soon as she graduated, she would move to Blue Mountain. It was all arranged, the necessary letters sent to explain Niki's tragic history, the bills paid by the Hyland Tobacco Company as part of a special scholarship given the orphan of an employee. Without having to ask, Niki knew that whatever school had been chosen would also have made provision for her to live there beyond the regular term. It had always been that way. For nine years, she had been a kind of constant student. No visitors except, very infrequently, Mr. Weatherby. Babe had sent Christmas and birthday cards to her the very first year or two she'd been away, but they'd soon tapered off. Niki had been looked after by a succession of dormitory housemothers, pleasant women but none that she'd grown close to—none she wanted anything from. Her heart remained locked against any substitute for her real mother.

Vale House was, like all the other dorms at Blue Mountain, a large, white center-hall colonial with varnished wide-board pine floors, and flowered wallpaper everywhere. Niki pushed the door open and headed straight for the stairs. At dinnertime, the code called for skirt and blouse or a dress—no jeans, *ever*. She was inspired to hurry by the aroma hovering in the air—the smell of a stew, Niki thought. Whatever else might be said about the new house mother, she seemed to be a much better cook than most.

"Young lady . . . come down here!"

Niki was halfway up the stairs when the firm demand arrested her. She turned.

At the bottom of the steps stood a hefty woman with gray hair gathered and pinned back rather carelessly, eyes of a dark chocolate brown that made them seem to flash all the more brightly, and strong yet not unpleasant features.

Niki started to descend, talking as she went. "I just lost track of time. I'm really sorry, Mrs.—" She stopped dead, not certain of how to pronounce the name and fearful of offending the woman further.

"Czardas," the woman said, with a *ch* sound at the beginning, and a *ssh* sound at the end. "Helen Czardas." She put out her hand, and Niki shook it as she stepped to the floor. Having grown over the summer, Niki found that for the first time she was a couple of inches taller than a housemother.

"Pleased to meet you," Niki said. "I'm Nicolette Sandeman." By reflex, she made the very slight little dip that Miss Neimeyer, the last housemother, had liked the girls to do. It felt incongrous in her jeans. She thought of retracting her hand, but found that Mrs. Czardas went on grasping it.

"Of course, I know who you are," Mrs. Czardas said, as her dark eyes scanned Niki's face. "I'll bet I even know why you're late. You were practicing your dives at the pool, am I right?"

Niki nodded, and studied Helen Czardas curiously. She could hear now that the woman spoke with an accent, though it was faint and Niki couldn't pin down its origins.

Mrs. Czardas smiled. "It would be hard not to know a few things about the most famous resident in Vale House."

Being noticed and set apart made Niki uncomfortable. It reminded her of all the other things a housemother would know from her file. She started to pull away. "If I'm still permitted to have dinner, Mrs. Czardas, I'd better change. . . ."

"Niki," the house mother said quickly, "you are called Niki, aren't you . . . ?" Niki nodded, and Mrs. Czardas went on. "None of the other Vale girls have arrived yet. I've looked forward to having dinner alone with you, because . . . I think it's very important for us to be well acquainted, and this is a good chance. So of course, you should come to the table. And you needn't bother to change." She smiled again.

Niki was impressed with the warmth the smile projected, yet she hesitated. Housemothers had almost always made her wear a dress to dinner, even in the summer when there were no other girls. Perhaps this new one didn't yet know all the rules. "Mrs. Czardas, the code is very clear about—"

"I know the code," Mrs. Czardas said. "Rules are a necessity for giving a sense of order to a community like ours. But rules are made to serve us, not enslave us. Remember that, Niki: we must never be slaves to the rules." She swept a hand toward the dining room in an inviting gesture, and walked away.

Niki took a moment to follow. Had Mrs. Czardas just told her that rules could be broken? This woman was definitely not like any housemother Niki had met before.

During dinner, they did indeed become better acquainted—Niki, at least, learned a great deal more about the woman she was told to call "Helen." She learned, first, that Helen was not simply an adequate cook, not merely a good one . . . but fabulous. A hearty split-pea soup with bits of smoked ham was followed with a thick and delicious goulash accompanied by tangy whipped turnips, and the only string beans Niki had eaten in nine years that weren't institutionally limp and overcooked. Hungry from the avid training that burned up so much of her energy, Niki ploughed through first and second helpings of everything.

"Don't expect to eat like this all the time," Helen warned with a laugh. "I made some extra effort tonight. I will always try, though, to see that you have the kind of diet that helps with your training, even if it means some extra cooking."

Once school began, the main meals would be handled largely by a rotation of students who lived in the dorm; a housemother had only to supervise and make special desserts whenever she pleased. So Niki was usually able to provide for her own special needs. But she appreciated Helen's offer, nevertheless; it was the first time a housemother had ever volunteered to take that kind of extra trouble.

Though she was shy about asking personal questions, Niki hoped she could spark Helen to reveal how and why she had come to Blue Mountain. Other housemothers had always struck Niki as being somewhat lost and lonely, in need of the position of authority and the instant "family" that came with the job. Helen seemed so much more independent.

"The way you cook," Niki said, "it's hard for me to understand why you'd want to be here instead of running a restaurant."

The remark was answered with a shrewd glance. Helen perceived she'd been fishing, Niki thought.

"It shouldn't be hard to understand. I believe there's nothing more worthwhile than teaching. And this is such a nice place to do it—with nice rooms to live in as part of the bargain."

"You may not think it's so nice when all the girls are here."

Helen laughed with a gusto Niki had never heard from *any* woman, much less a housemother. "Not *quite* as nice, perhaps. But I believe I will enjoy having a house full of noise, and shouting, and girls growing up." She paused before saying softly. "I've been alone too much, Niki . . . as I believe you have. . . ."

Niki looked away. She didn't mind hearing somebody else's personal history, but she hated delving into her own.

As if Helen understood, she went on talking about herself, an explanation of the twists and turns in her life that had brought her finally to Blue Mountain. Niki sat and listened in fascination. Though Helen Czardas talked about her life modestly, the way it added up made her seem to Niki like a heroine from a novel.

She had been born in Hungary, in the capital city of Budapest, and had still lived there in 1956, when an uprising against Russian control of their country was led by university students. By then she was married to a man who taught economics at a university, and she was herself a practicing doctor, hoping to become one of the few woman surgeons in her country. After the brief revolution was crushed by massive Soviet military intervention, Helen's husband, Georgi, was among the intellectual group accused of being instigators, and he was sent to prison. As his wife, Helen was made to suffer, too—stripped of the right to practice medicine, forced instead to take a job as a laundress in the same hospital where she had dreamed of performing surgery.

For the next five years her life had remained grim. Then her husband had been released from prison, and they had begun petitioning the communist government for the right to emigrate. When three more years went by, they had organized an escape, risking death to cross through the heavily guarded border into Austria. Once in the West, they had found their way to America.

"After a while, my husband was able to teach again—not college, but at a boys' preparatory school in New England. While we were there, I studied and began to teach, too. Georgi died two years ago—only a young man, just fifty-one. But his health was broken in prison, and he had always been a heavy smoker, which made it harder for him to recover. I couldn't stay at the boys' school on my own. Last year, I studied to get a special teaching degree so I could improve my position. Then I found this job."

Tentatively, Niki asked, "But why didn't you go back to being a doctor?"

Helen looked down. "We can't always do exactly what we want. Too much time had gone by to start over. Georgi needed me more. There were many reasons. . . ."

For the first time, Helen sounded sad. Niki was sorry she'd asked the question. It was better not to talk about things that brought on sadness. That was the beauty of being so totally involved with diving. Emotions could be left out of it.

As though to bury her own emotions in physical activity, Helen rose abruptly to clear the table. Niki helped, but was told to sit down again before the desserts were brought in—a creamy hazelnut-flavored cheesecake, a bowl of grapes, and a plate of cheeses.

Niki couldn't stop eating, and Helen looked on with pleasure. At last, Niki pushed herself away from the table. "This is awful, Helen. . . ."

"Awful?"

"No, I mean wonderful. But it's awful for me. I have to keep my weight down, and this makes it hard. I have an Olympic tryout soon, for God's sake."

"I'm sorry, Niki, I should have thought of that. I just couldn't resist cooking. There's such a nice kitchen here. And," she added ingenuously, "I guess I wanted to impress you. . . ."

"Don't worry, I'm impressed. I haven't known anybody who could cook such delicious things since my mo—"

Suddenly, Niki's tongue turned to stone in her mouth. She sat paralyzed in her chair, staring at the woman across the table. Her words had poured out in unthinking reply. For Helen to say she wanted to impress her, was to say she *cared* . . . and Niki had risen to the bait, had almost confessed she could care in return—by making a comparison with her mother.

But no one could take Mama's place. Not in any way. Never.

Helen paused for only a second, waiting to see if Niki

would add anything. Then she said, "I appreciate the compliment, Niki."

Niki stared back. Her feelings were suddenly in turmoil for reasons she couldn't comprehend. She hadn't finished what she was going to say, so how could Helen thank her? Doing that made Niki angry for some reason . . . made Niki so furious that she wanted to show this woman immediately that she couldn't be taken for granted, her compliments—her *caring* assumed. Niki's arm shot out and swiped all the plates within reach onto the floor. China shattered. Cheesecake, fruits, and cheeses scattered in a mess.

"Niki!" Helen Czardas cried out, more in amazement than reproach.

Niki didn't answer. She had already bolted from the table and was running up to her room.

Once inside, she threw herself on the bed and cried as she hadn't since she was little . . . since the day she'd found Elle dead. Niki let the tears come until she was exhausted . . . and then listened for a little while to a Judy Collins album, one of the records she bought with the small allowance that came every two months from Mr. Weatherby's office.

As she thought back to the look on Helen's face when the plates broke, Niki began to feel ashamed. And then amazed, too, that Helen hadn't come straight after her, announced some punishment. Any housemother would do that. In fact, Niki believed that she deserved to be punished. What had gotten into her?

Yet she was left alone.

Later, just after she had turned out the lamp by her bed, Niki heard light footsteps approach her door. She waited for a knock—or for Helen to burst in suddenly, the way Mrs. Neimeyer used to raid the rooms when she thought one of the girls was smoking. But the footsteps padded away after a minute.

She lay awake for a long time in the dark trying to understand why she'd flown into such a rage. All Helen had done was make her a delicious meal, food as good as any Elle had ever cooked.

For that matter, maybe even better. . . .

Throughout the next day, other students began to arrive. To avoid the embarrassment of facing the new housemother, Niki went to the pool at daybreak and stayed there for the morning. For lunch, she went to the student center and bought crackers and soda from a vending machine. Then she went to the library and looked at the syllabus for her new courses.

When she came back to Vale, more girls had moved in. A couple were maneuvering a trunk up the stairs while three others sat in the lounge catching up on summer adventures. Niki saw no new faces. She was acquainted with all the girls, but friends with none. They nodded at her, or said subdued hellos, and she continued up the stairs.

As she came to the landing, Helen Czardas emerged from a room at the end of the corridor holding a light bulb she had evidently replaced. She smiled at Niki as she approached, then continued past her. Niki took only another step, before her will broke.

"You ought to punish me," she blurted, running back to catch Helen.

"Should I? For what?"

"You know—making a mess, being rude. What are you waiting for?"

"Nothing, Niki. I don't see any point in punishing you. My guess is you're already sorry, and nothing I do will make you any sorrier."

Niki gazed at her for a second. "I want to apologize, Mrs. Czardas."

"Helen," the housemother reminded her quietly before saying a polite "thank-you."

"I don't know why I was . . . such a geek," Niki said then. "I . . . I really liked the dinner so much. . . ."

Before Helen could answer, a couple of girls from the

lounge came running up the stairs. She waited until they had vanished into a room.

"Perhaps," Helen suggested then, "it hurt to be reminded of things it's been easier to avoid thinking about. . . ."

Niki looked back silently, a film of tears forming suddenly in her eyes. "Yes," she said, mustering only a whisper. "Yes, it hurts." It was the most honest thing she'd said to anyone in almost ten years.

Helen moved closer and put her arm around Niki's waist. "Do you want to talk some more about it?"

Niki looked at the floor and shook her head.

"Whenever you do," Helen said, "you know I'm here." She lifted Niki's face and carefully brushed away a spilled tear. Then she added perkily, "Right now, I think you might like to meet your new roommate. Her name is Blake Underwood. She's in there unpacking. . . ."

Niki looked bleakly toward her room. She had yet to like any of her roommates, and always regretted the end of summer when she had to give up her treasured solitude. But there was no choice.

Helen put an arm around her shoulder, gently urging her along the corridor. Niki broke away, partly to escape from the feel of Helen's arm around her. The casual touch had almost the same confusing effect as the delicious food. Simultaneously, Niki loved it and loathed it, wanted more of it—and hated herself for wanting it. Only her mother should be able to touch her like that. . . .

Turning into her room, she saw the new arrival dumping a leather suitcase full of clothes onto the still unmade bed. A mound of other clothes was already heaped on the mattress, several previously emptied suitcases lay open on the floor. Niki had seen enough privileged roommates come and go to recognize the luggage as Vuitton, the kind that cost thousands of dollars for a set. Still unpacked in the middle of the room was something Niki hadn't seen before—a Vuitton duffle bag.

At a glance, even without a full view of Blake Underwood's

face, Niki knew she could never like her. Blake didn't even look like a teenager. Though petite, her body was shapely, and clad in the sort of outfit Niki associated only with full-grown career women—a close-fitting red suit with a black velvet collar, sheer nylon stockings, and high heels. Her dark hair was cut and styled as only a hairdresser could have done it. She was wearing lipstick and eyeliner, and to top it off, the stockings had stylish black clocks running up the back. Around her wrist was a gold bangle bracelet that must have cost more than all the luggage, the duffle bag included.

Niki wavered between telling the girl she wasn't going to be able to go on wearing the same clothes and makeup—and running back to plead with Helen for a change of roommate.

But now the other girl noticed her and spoke first. "Hi," she said, and started to open the duffle bag. "Will you give me a hand to dump this out? Damn thing is heavier than a gorilla's dick."

Shocked, Niki mutely complied, helping the girl hold up the duffle and shake its contents onto the clothes heap.

"Thanks. You're Nicolette, I suppose. . . ." The girl nodded toward the name card on the door.

Niki nodded.

"I'm Blake Underwood." She went on pushing clothes around the bed, not bothering to shake hands. "So . . . is that what I have to call you? Nic-oh-lette?" Blake glanced over with a wince. "A little hoity-toity, dontcha think . . . ?"

Softly, helplessly intimidated, she answered "I use Niki. . . ."

"That's more like it." Blake paused to look her over. "Christ, just what I need: an inferiority complex."

"What?"

Blake gathered up an armload of clothes. "Well, you're so fucking blond and beautiful . . . and tall, too. And what's this I hear about you being some sort of star athlete? Jesus, Niki, how the fuck do you expect me to feel?"

Niki was nonplussed. Could she apologize for how she looked? She didn't think she could ever get used to the language Blake used, either. "Listen . . . um . . . maybe you'd rather change rooms. . . ."

"Are you kidding? If you're a star around here, I can't think of a better friend to have."

Niki thought of explaining that she didn't have friends, not even her roommates ever got close—that no matter what she looked like, or how many trophies she won, the other girls had figured out that she liked to be left alone.

But she had only to ponder a second, before Blake was talking again. "So where do I put my shit, huh? Which drawers are mine?" She started toward the long, high dresser.

"The bottom three."

"You only use the one on top? That's not half—"

"I don't have so many clothes."

"Yeah, I guess all you ever wear are bathing suits. . . ."

Niki watched as Blake went to the dresser and stuffed her clothes in without sorting anything. In ten seconds, the job was done.

As Blake straightened up, she stopped to examine the few personal articles that Niki had neatly arranged on top of the dresser. She looked for a long moment at the photograph in the silver frame.

"You know," Blake said at last, "I think I've seen this picture somewhere. . . ."

"It's kind of famous. Every now and then, some magazine will print it again. It's from the Olympics—the one where Adolph Hitler—"

"No, no," Blake broke in. "I don't mean I saw it in a magazine. I mean, I saw *this* one." Blake whirled around. "I think we went to school together!"

"We—? Where?"

"How should I know? I've been to twelve goddamn schools before this one. Where'd you go before?"

"Only one other place, Brightpoint School in—"

"Holy shit!" Blake screamed. "That's it! Arkansas! Dinky little place. I was there when I was . . . eight, I think. Second place I was sent. Lasted a year, that was my average in those days. Then they canceled me. Wet my bed too much, or stole something, I forget. But I think you were in a room down the hall. I went in there a few times. You roomed with . . ." Blake hunted in her memory.

Niki thought back to her first year away. "Alicia Benson," she murmured.

"Yeah. Little Alicia—pigtails, wore those thick glasses, real little twerp. But her mom used to send these big boxes of chocolates . . . and I'd go in and take a piece every now and then. I can't remember you at all, though. Liked to keep yourself, sort of invisible, didn't you hide out a lot? But that's how I saw your picture, when I went looking for candy. You kept it in a drawer then. . . ."

Niki nodded. It was still her habit to tuck it away except when she had the room to herself.

Blake kept shaking her head and smiling. "What a crazy world, huh? Though I suppose it figures—I've been through so many schools, I was bound to meet someone I knew. . . ." Suddenly her smile faded. "But there was something else about you . . . all the girls used to talk about it." She searched her memory again. "You're an orphan, right? Your folks were run over by a train, or had a suicide pact, something like that . . ."

Niki took a few seconds deciding how to answer. "My mother was murdered. My father pays for my school, but he never married my mother and I'm forbidden to talk about him. If I ever do, and he finds out, he'll stop paying and I'll have to leave."

Blake stared at Niki. "Rough," she said quietly, and shook her head again.

Niki went to the dresser, took the photograph in the silver frame, and put it in the top drawer.

Blake latched her suitcases and stacked them in the corridor outside. A caretaker would move them later to the basement. Returning to the room, Blake closed the door.

Niki lay down on her bed and looked at the ceiling. It surprised her that she had told Blake the truth—especially about her mother never marrying.

Blake had gone on arranging her things. "Niki," she said, "I'm loud and I've got a dirty mouth, and a lot of other bad habits, and I could tell right off that . . . well, I'm not your type. But, if you don't mind, I'd really like to try and . . . be the right roommate for you. Okay?"

"Sure," Niki said. In an odd way it mattered a lot for her, too, that they had known each other—sort of—a long time ago. It was only the flimsiest thread of a shared past, yet it was as close as Niki had ever come to having something like a sister.

Niki was distracted suddenly by the smell of smoke. She looked over to see that Blake had lit a cigarette. Niki bolted up. "Hey, you can't do that. You'll get suspended if you get caught—maybe even expelled."

Blake took another casual puff, and blew the smoke into the air. "I doubt it, toots. My daddy gave the school an extra fifty thousand bucks to take me and promise him that this time I'd go all the way and graduate."

"Put it out, anyway," Niki said crossly. "And don't ever do it again. I'm in training. It isn't good for me."

Blake lowered the cigarette very slowly, held it a few more seconds, then opened the window and tamped it out on the ledge.

"All right?" she said.

"Yeah," Niki said. "Thanks."

Blake went back to settling into the room.

Niki lay down again and suppressed a sigh. Between Blake Underwood for a roommate, and Helen Czardas as her housemother, she thought, it looked like she was in for an interesting year. But, of course, nothing could really make too much difference. Whatever the problems, she had learned how to survive, how to stay cool and untroubled and ready for anything—how to keep her balance.

Balance was everything.

Ten

"LAST chance, toots," Blake called across the room to Niki. "Are you in or out?"

Niki was at her desk studying. "Out!" she shot back, trying to sound insulted—how could Blake even think she might be interested in such a game!—but laughing in spite of herself.

"Okay, ladies," Blake said to the other Vale girls clustered everywhere around her bed, seated on her desk, the windowsill, the floor. "That makes a total of nine participants. May I have your money for the envelope, puh-leeze. . . ."

The others each handed Blake a ten-dollar bill which she slipped into an envelope. The betting pool had been her idea, of course, the sort of mischievous gimmick she was forever dreaming up. The girls had been comparing notes on their periods, and somebody had mentioned having an exceptionally heavy flow, then another girl claimed hers was heavier—and in no time Blake had conceived the contest, winner take all. Anyone who wanted to enter could come to Blake with a tampon from their self-estimated peak time, and she would weigh it, to the nearest ten-thousandth of a gram, on an electronic scale "borrowed" from the science lab.

Licking the envelope, Blake said, "Thirty days from now—or maybe just twenty-eight—we ought to be able to announce a winner. Now skedaddle, everyone. I've got a bio test *mañana*, and Chardy's just itching for an excuse to give me the old flunk-ola."

The other girls dispersed. Blake sat down at her desk, put the envelope in a drawer, and dutifully opened her biology text.

Niki had given up telling Blake she was disgusted by some of her tricks weeks ago. It was only a waste of breath. Blake would express heartfelt regret for offending her . . . then go right ahead doing as she wished.

But there was never anything malicious about her pranks, Niki had learned. That was Blake's saving grace. She might admit to having stolen chocolates in her childhood, but Niki had never seen Blake take anything from anyone at Blue Mountain. Whatever Blake did was meant only to amuse, or stimulate, or share, or dare, or sometimes even to teach. But never to hurt.

In fact, Niki did more than merely tolerate Blake. Although she didn't say it or demonstrate it very openly, she had come to like her outrageous roommate. The antics that made Blake a popular center of attention, keeping the room busy at all hours with visits from other girls, games, rap sessions, had left no choice for Niki but to become more sociable. She didn't come completely out of her shell, but she had shed the protective coloration of seeming to be cynical and untouchable. Her fondness for privacy earned respect now rather than suspicion. The Vale crowd had begun coming en masse to swim meets to root for Niki. Not that girls from the school had never come before. But in the past, Niki's performances would be observed in awed silence; she would be studied more than watched. Now the girls from Vale—and lately from other dorms—would shout and cheer: "Let's go, Niki . . . do it, Niki. . . ."

She was accepted. And she appreciated Blake for making it happen.

Blake was generous, too, and had helped Niki to develop a sense of fashion. From her vast trove of clothes that was constantly—needlessly—being expanded with shipments from her wealthy father, Blake offered Niki anything she wanted. Anticipating the difference in sizes, Blake had already sent a note to her father—the owner of a large chain of Midwest department stores—saying that she'd had a growth spurt, and the latest trend was also to wear things large and droopy.

"But when he sees you," Niki protested after Blake confessed the ruse, "he'll be mad."

"He'll never look at me long enough to know if I've grown or not," Blake said. "Anyway, he just tells the shipping department to pick out a few things . . . anything where the inventory is overloaded. Daddy-o doesn't even know what they send me."

Even for girls with a real father, Niki realized, there was plenty of pain. Her heart went out to Blake.

For Helen, too, Niki's affection continued to grow. One Sunday in late October, when Niki spent a night in the infirmary because she had a slight cough and was running a fever, Helen had arrived after dinner bearing a tray with a teapot, and a strip of the cherry strudel which had become her most popular dessert. "I didn't want you to miss out on this," she said.

Because Niki was sick in bed, being given special loving attention brought memories of her mother rising up again. But this time Niki didn't block them. She told Helen how she was reminded of when she had chickenpox and Elle had brought an extra-special chocolate mousse . . . and then she cried in Helen's arms, and lamented the years of being sent away among strangers almost as if she had committed some crime herself. At last Niki loosed a torrent of rage against all the faceless, nameless people who had looked down on her mother and her because they were both—the word came hard, but Niki did manage to spit it out—bastards.

"It's a stupid word," Helen said, sitting by the infirmary bed. "But only a word. It doesn't define who you are, Niki. The communists put my husband in jail; they called Georgi —what was the word then?—a *revanchist*. Another stupid made-up word . . . for those who wanted to fight against the dictators, the injustices. And for me, they took away a word: I could no longer be called *Doctor*.

"But it didn't change the people we were." Helen gestured to a bottle of cough syrup on a shelf. "Take the label off that bottle, Niki, you are still left with the bottle and whatever is inside. The only difference is people will have to taste for themselves to find out if it's bitter medicine . . . or honey." Helen gripped her hand. "You mustn't worry about those who simply read a label and walk away. They will miss the greater truth of what's in the bottle. And whoever discovers for herself—or himself—what is inside you, dear Niki, will never care about the label. They will know they have found something special, something both very sweet and very strong all at once. . . ."

Since that visit to the infirmary, Niki would have tea with Helen in her rooms at least twice a week, sometimes in the afternoon, sometimes in the evening. There were other girls who received similar caring attention—Patsy Kellogg who had been forced into incest with her father . . . Jenna Forrester whose arms and legs had been slashed in a crazed murder attempt by her mother before the woman was diagnosed as schizophrenic and put away. Helen was a haven and confessor for anyone who needed her. But Niki knew that a special bond had developed between them. After one tea, Helen had told her that "if Georgi and I could have had a daughter, I would have wanted her to be exactly like you."

Niki's outward reply was no more than a sincere "Thank-you," as if for any compliment. But inside, she felt her heart being swept by an emotional wave that had been absent since her mother's last embrace.

When Thanksgiving break came, Niki felt none of the forlorn desolation that had always gripped her in the past as she watched other girls going off to spend the holiday with family—even a piece of a family—somewhere else. A few other students would be staying, too, but no one else in Vale. Niki was pleased to think of having time alone with Helen.

"Sorry I can't take you with me, kiddo," Blake said. She was going alone by train to Washington where her father's private jet would pick her up to fly her for the weekend to some exclusive Caribbean island. "But it wouldn't be doing you a favor, would it? Who wants to eat fucking coconuts with all the trimmings for Thanksgiving? You're *lucky* you can stay and have Chardy's turkey and pumpkin pie."

"Yes," Niki said, truly feeling it, "I am lucky."

The weather over the Thanksgiving break was perfect. Crisp and sunny, an Indian summer had come very late. While Helen spent her free hours looking through biology texts for her courses, and making some new curtains for the downstairs lounge, Niki devoted herself to extra training. Tryouts for alternate positions on the Olympic diving team would be held in two weeks at the state university. In addition, a regular place had opened up because one of the best girls on the springboard—Niki's event—had recently withdrawn after a nondiving accident.

As hard as Niki trained, however, there was ample opportunity to grow closer to Helen. For the holiday feast on Thursday, Helen told Niki, she had invited several friends to come and join them. But on the two evenings preceding Thanksgiving Day, they were alone for supper, and each night they prepared the meal together. Helen taught Niki to make *palaczinta*, a kind of Hungarian crepe and, the second night, her cherry strudel. Standing in the homey, old-fashioned kitchen of Vale House, her hands covered with flour, Niki recalled a moment from a vanished past.

". . . Niki?"

She'd been lost in the memory. "Yes . . . ?"

"Didn't you hear me? I said you've rolled that dough enough. Too much, and it won't be flaky."

Niki transferred the dough to the baking pan. "I was thinking about my mother . . . making cookies with her. I must have been only five or six. . . ." It was no longer difficult to talk about it with Helen; even the tears came only rarely.

"I have some good cookie recipes, too," Helen said. "We can try them for our Thanksgiving feast."

Niki smiled at her. "I'd like that." Helen's quick offer to re-create a part of the old memories would have seemed threatening once, competition for the ghost of her mother. No longer.

As she spread cherries on the pastry dough, Niki said suddenly, "I love you, Helen." To underplay the confession, she kept working over the strudel. "Like I loved my mother," she added.

There was no answer. When Niki turned around, she saw Helen standing motionless over her own baking sheet. "Helen . . . ?"

Niki went to her. For all her own tears, it was the first time she had ever seen Helen crying. Niki put her arms around her, and Helen squeezed her back. They stood hugging each other for five minutes. Then Helen eased herself away. A smile came to her face as she looked up at Niki.

"You are so lovely, my girl, so beautifully grown up. How I wish Georgi could see you. . . ."

It was, thought Niki, almost as if Georgi was being included in their new family—a father for Niki, even if he was only a memory, too.

Helen's friends started to arrive at a little before noon. Niki heard the first car drive up, and looked out a front window. Outside stood a battered Volkswagen painted a shade of lime green that could only have been concocted by its owner. A short rotund man with a bush of light-brown hair flaring from his head got out from behind the wheel, holding a package. From the other side came a pixyish blonde wearing a jacket that seemed to be made of monkey fur, a pink miniskirt, and red boots. They linked arms as they came up the path.

When the bell rang, Helen shouted from the kitchen. "Will you greet the guests, Niki. I'm basting. . . ."

Niki took a breath. She couldn't imagine making conversation with this couple.

As soon as she opened the door, the man bounced inside, seized her and held her at arms length for an inspection. "An angel!" he exclaimed. "Helen said you looked like an angel, and so you do! Niki, right? I'm Lotchy . . . this is Karyn," he waved to the blond pixy who had sidled in at his shoulder.

Niki recognized a thicker version of Helen's accent. Bowled over, she replied with only a restrained smile.

Suddenly, Lotchy lifted his nose in the air. "The sorceress is already working her magic. I must follow the scent. . . ." And off he went to the kitchen.

Karyn smiled self-consciously. Niki offered to take her coat. Under the monkey fur was a red-and-white peasant blouse cut exceedingly low. She led Karyn into the living room where Helen had set up a bar liberally stocked with beer, vodka, and wine.

This Thanksgiving dinner, thought Niki—in terms she'd picked up from Blake—was going to be an absolute riot.

And so it was. When all of Helen's friends were assembled, a total of eight, Vale House was kept rocking with boisterous laughter, loud discussion, good-natured argument, fragments of nostalgic native song, and moments of sad recollection, sometimes conducted in the Hungarian language. With one exception all the guests were Hungarians, too, refugees of the 1956 uprising. "Lotchy"—Helen introduced him more formally as Ladjos Palgyar, Georgi's favorite cousin—edited a small journal of Hungarian writing, not only that of other refugees, but smuggled out from dissident authors still in their native country, most in jail. Karyn, his considerably younger wife, was the daughter of a poet who was still a political prisoner in Budapest. She had visions of making a success as a member of an emigre rock band called Savage Protest.

There was also a man named Tibor—Niki gave up on trying to remember or pronounce last names—who had been a teaching colleague of Georgi's in the old days and was now a professor of political science at Dartmouth College. And Ferenc and Anna, a lovely older couple who bought and sold rare books, and their daughter, Gertusz—"Gertie"—who worked for the Voice of America. There was a middle-aged man named Viktor, messily dressed in a plaid vest and stained paisley tie, who was introduced as a sculptor—though he worked for a dry cleaner and smelled faintly of the cleaning solvent. Viktor showed endless good nature in the face of kidding from the others about having spent the past twelve years on a single massive marble of a hunter killing a bear—an allegory of the revolution, he called it.

Finally, there was the exception: a tall Russian, thin to the point of emaciation, named Dmitri Ivanov. He had long black hair streaked gray, and slightly slanted coal-black eyes—mongol eyes—that burned like beacons above cheekbones so prominent they seemed about to pierce his pale translucent skin. Dmitri was a theater director, successful in his own country, who had sought "artistic freedom" eight years ago by defecting during a cultural exchange. Gertie had met him through her work at VOA, where Dmitri was occasionally brought in to help with broadcasts of Russian language dramatizations. She had brought him for Thanksgiving because he would otherwise be alone. He was substantially older than her, and their liaison did not strike Niki as being romantic—though they took incessant ribbing about the possibility from the others.

That was only one of the many subjects that inspired banter all through the sumptuous traditional feast Helen had prepared. Niki sat listening in awe. She had never been in the midst of such a colorful, amusing group.

Gradually, with some prompting from Helen, the others

made efforts to include Niki, and drew her into separate conversations. Tibor suggested that she think of Dartmouth for college, and told her about the famous Winter Carnival. Gertie invited her to spend a weekend in Washington and think of working in government. Karyn promised to keep her informed of her rock group's upcoming singing engagements so Niki could come, and bring her friends. . . .

And the Russian actor kept eyeing her, and getting more and more drunk on straight vodka. "You must meet my son," he said at last, pausing over his pumpkin pie. "You're such a beauty, you two could make the most exquisite children."

"Dmitri," Helen put in quickly, "the girl isn't thinking about children."

"Why not? A beauty like this was made for breeding. Look at her. Where I was born, the women were on their second or third child by Niki's age—"

"Where you were born," Lotchy said, "they are still just peasants, running everything as if it's nothing but a gigantic farm full of animals. So of course they make babies all the time. What else can they do? The farmer in the Kremlin makes all the decisions, and tosses out a little chicken feed, while no one else is allowed to do anything but eat, drink, and fuck."

"Lotchy," Helen scolded sharply, with a glance toward Niki. "That language is unacceptable."

"Forgive me," Lotchy said to Niki. "Poetic license."

So it went. Though, as Dmitri got drunker and drunker on vodka, his eyes kept wandering back to Niki, always provoking a fresh mention of his son.

"He has such an eye for the women, and I know you'd like him. . . ."

"His son again!" Lotchy chided him. "Where is this famous son? We're forever hearing about him, and every Thanksgiving here you are bitching that he's somewhere else. Bring him."

"He goes off always to the home of some American school friend," Dmitri explained. "Alexei says to me 'it's an American holiday, father, it's important to see exactly how they do it. . . .' "

"Can anyone cook a better American turkey than our Helen?" said Ferenc, patting his thoroughly satisfied stomach.

Instantly, the small group broke into an ovation.

"You are right," Dmitri said, banging the table with a fist. "Hungarians you may be . . . but you are almost as smart as Russians. Alexei should be with his father. Next year he comes." Then, again, he ogled Niki. "And you will see, Nikuschka—he is the man you will want to make your children."

Helen's objection was not so mild this time. "Dmitri, stop it. Niki hasn't the least interest in what you're talking about. Right now, she has different goals." Earlier, when Niki did not stuff herself like the others, there had been mention of her strict regimen of training for the Olympic tryouts.

"Ah yes," Dmitri said. "Well, my dear, I shall hope you get to make your dives at the Olympics—and *drown* every filthy communist in the splash you make!" He drank down the rest of the vodka in his glass. "And then, you can come home and make babies with my Alexei."

When the last car drove away, it was almost midnight. There had been hours of talk after the feast was finished . . . and then leftovers heated up, and a lively gathering at the table all over again. By the end, Karyn had coaxed Niki into learning a few lines of a Hungarian folk song, and joining in. With these people, Niki no longer felt restrained or uninteresting. She loved them all, and hugged each one as they left. She had found a family.

With the others departed, Niki was prepared to do some cleaning up. But the ever-efficient Helen went straight from the door to plop down on the couch like a limp doll. Niki wasn't surprised. As the evening went on, a different Helen than the always wise and sedate housemother had been revealed. Having taken a glass of vodka before the main meal, and steadily sipped wine from then on, Helen soon grew tipsy. She became as endearingly boisterous as the rest.

"No, leave it. . . ." she said when Niki started to gather empty glasses and coffee cups. "Leave it for the mice to do." Then Helen giggled.

Niki paused. She had been so involved with the group that this was her first opportunity to look more closely at Helen's intoxication. She wasn't sure she liked it. Helen was supposed to be taking care of her. Helen was supposed to be someone she could rely on. . . .

"C'mon," Niki said. I'll help you get to bed." The cross edge in her voice came through.

Helen returned a wary glance, but then raised her arms to let Niki pull her up, and they weaved along to her rooms on the main floor.

"I'll be all right now," Helen said as she opened her door. They looked at each other, then Niki kissed her on the cheek.

"Good night," Niki said.

Helen caught her hand. "You seemed to have a wonderful time today. . . ."

"I did," Niki said.

"So did I. But I surprised you, eh? Perhaps you think I had too much of a wonderful time . . . ?"

"Well," Niki replied slowly, "I'm seeing a new side of you."

"A side I'm letting you see—something besides . . . the perfect 'housemother.' It bothers you, eh?"

"Yes."

Helen put her hand to Niki's cheek. "Labels, dear girl . . . watch out for labels . . ." She slipped into her room and closed the door.

A smile spread slowly across Niki's lips as she sauntered toward the stairs.

She had never trained with such single-minded fervor as she did in the span of days following the holiday and leading up to the Olympic tryouts. Mornings and evenings at the pool with Miss Steadman, the swimming coach; classes, study, and meals carefully scheduled in between. Up at five A.M., in bed by nine P.M., on a strict diet of brans and salads and fruits designed to provide an exact scientific ratio of protein, carbohydrates and fats. Niki even cut her hair short, in case it might make a difference to the Olympic scouts.

Unable to fit her own irrepressible activities into Niki's demanding schedule, Blake cooperated by moving out of the room—a *temporary* move, she was careful to stipulate. "No way I'm changing roomies now. You're going to be an Olympic hero, baby . . . and I intend to bask in your reflected glory."

Blake began organizing a cheering section for the tryouts. All the girls in Vale would travel by bus to the state university.

Though she didn't know how to tell Blake, Niki wasn't happy about it. She didn't need anything that would put more pressure on her to deliver. She planned on having Helen drive her.

"Of course, I will," Helen agreed. "It will be more relaxed for you that way than going in by bus. But must you discourage the other girls from coming?"

"Helen, this is serious. Nothing else has ever meant as much. Do I have to let Blake make a party out of everything?"

"A party? Niki, Blake wants this for you as much as you do yourself. All the girls do. Don't you understand—they feel connected. If you earn this honor, they'll be so proud. They feel, in a way, they belong with you, encouraging you. And you belong to them. . . ."

Belong. She did understand, then. Of course, Blake had to come. Everyone. Doing it for them as well as herself would only make it easier.

Late on the last afternoon before the day of the tryouts, Niki packed all her suits and other swimming gear. She intended to go to sleep at six, then leave with Helen at four A.M. for the drive to the state university. A light snow had begun to fall, and though it was expected to stop, the trip might take a little longer than usual. Still, if they left early, there would be time for Niki to try out the board she'd be using.

She was about to start getting ready for bed when Helen came into the room. Her face wore an expression of grave concern.

"Niki . . . Mr. Weatherby is downstairs in the writing room."

"Why is he here?" Niki asked anxiously. The writing room was a small lounge with doors at a rear corner of Vale. It was the place that was used whenever sensitive conversations were to be held between students and visitors, as for example, when someone came to tell a girl her parent had died unexpectedly.

"I don't know, dear. All he said was it's important to talk with you in private." Though Helen had not met Weatherby before today, she had received a number of letters from him in his role as Niki's court-appointed guardian. Having been told by Niki about H.D. Hyland, Helen was fully aware of the power the lawyer exercised over Niki's life, and of its ramifications.

Niki went down to the writing room. Sterling Weatherby was standing by a window, looking out at the campus, trees and pathways with their white dusting of fresh snow. Niki noticed a newly lit log fire just beginning to take hold in the fireplace. Helen had apparently started it to make the room cozier for this meeting.

"It's lovely here, isn't it?" Weatherby said when Niki entered, his gaze lingering on the view.

"Yes," she answered warily.

He turned to her at last. Dressed in a dark-blue suit, with a silver-gray bow tie, he was a reminder of that formal yet genteel world which she had left behind. A world run by Southern gentlemen with a soft tongue—and a will of iron.

Weatherby's eyes widened as he took in the changes in Niki since the last time they had been face to face, almost a year ago. He had come then with some papers to be signed for tax purposes, a declaration that Niki knew the money spent on her behalf was part of a charitable contribution, not to be taken as proof that the party from which it came had any personal interest or responsibility for providing support.

"Well, Niki," he said, not hiding his approval, "you've developed into an extraordinarily beautiful young woman. I must say, though, that I liked your hair much better when you wore it longer." With a gesture, he indicated they should take chairs by the fire. "But I imagine you cut it as part of your swimming regimen. . . ."

"That's right," she said quietly. She was fighting hard against a fear that had gripped her from the moment Helen announced Weatherby's arrival. It was exceedingly rare for the lawyer to drop into her life at all, but even when he did it had always been planned, he would prepare her with a call a week or two ahead. Why this sudden invasion?

He sat, and she took the chair opposite. For another few moments, his eyes roamed over her body. "I can see, too," he said, "that you're in the peak of physical condition."

"I've been training. In fact, Mr. Weatherby, just as you came I was planning to get to sleep. You see, tomorrow—"

"I know about tomorrow, Niki," Mr. Weatherby said. "I came because I know about tomorrow." He smiled.

For a fraction of a second, she was relieved. He must have come to wish her well—why else? But then she saw, along with the rightness of his smile, the hard glint in his eyes.

"Do you know," he continued, "that it costs a great deal of money for our nation to send its best athletes to the Olympics?"

Niki nodded. Why was he raising this?

Weatherby went on. "A lot of the money comes from corporate donations. As it happens, the Hyland Company—and the Hyland family—have been generous contributors since the 1950s. Of course, they don't blow their horn too loudly; some people might think it's self-serving to give money to help those who believe in attaining the peak of physical excellence—while selling cigarettes. But the Olympic committee knows and appreciates the financial commitment, that's the main thing. . . ."

Niki's alarm grew as she sorted through the possibilities. Was Weatherby saying the Hylands had influence with the committee and would try to use it on her behalf? That would be disastrous, she was sure.

"The reason I'm giving you this background," Weatherby said, "is so you'll understand how a contributor like Mr. Hyland manages to keep abreast of Olympic activities. If he expresses an interest in some phases of development, the committee obliges with reports. And he's been interested for some time in knowing if you intended to aim for a place among the divers. He remembers that your mother was very proud of her mother before her, of what she'd done at the Olympics . . . so he suspected you might be inspired to distinguish yourself in a similar fashion. That's why he's been keeping a watch on the reports . . . and how he noticed your name among the young women who would be vying for a place as an alternate in tomorrow's tryouts. . . ."

She couldn't keep silent any longer. "My chances of being chosen are very small, Mr. Weatherby. I'm not counting on it. But no matter how much influence Mr. Hyland might have, you can understand I wouldn't want any . . . help."

He gave her the sort of sidelong glance which seemed to indicate that he didn't understand her position at all. But then suddenly he tossed his head back, as though comprehension had struck with an almost tangible force. "Help? Oh, you needn't worry, Niki. But the fact of the matter is, small chance or no, Mr. Hyland is concerned that there should be absolutely no doubt about the final outcome. That's why he sent me here today. He wants to make certain that you do *not* win a place on the team. . . ."

"Not win," Niki said in a shocked murmur.

"Well, it's insurance, you see. Once you were on the team, then suppose you distinguished yourself? You might actually be chosen to represent our country in some event at the games.

You do seem to be a young woman of extraordinary character and determination, you really could win the chance to represent us. And then what? Billions of eyes around the world focused on you, newspaper stories printed all across this nation. Of course, the papers would be bound to play up the angle of an American girl trying to replay the high point of her French grandmother's life. Even if you didn't win a medal, there would be so much attention paid . . . such an exquisite young woman, I dare say you'd be the nation's sweetheart in no time. The public would be hungry for all the details, and journalists would stop at nothing to dig them up, every single one. How did your family come to America . . . who are your parents? Well, you see the problem, Niki—you see why Mr. Hyland has to take preemptive measures. He doesn't want it revealed that you—''

Her response started as a whimpering plea. ''Please, oh, please Mr. Weatherby. Don't do this to me. I won't hurt Mr. Hyland. I'd make him proud—no, no, I'm sorry, I don't mean that I'd let anyone know about him . . . I wouldn't, not if he didn't want that. But let me try, it's so important to me, always has—''

''Niki, please. You have to look at it from Mr. Hyland's point of view. He can't take even the smallest chance on having every newspaper in the world—''

''Please. . . .'' She was begging now, propped forward on her seat at the point of falling to her knees if she had to.

But Mr. Weatherby shook his head in a way that made it perfectly clear the most abject appeal would be useless.

On the brink of having sacrificed her pride, Niki grabbed it back, all the more fiercely determined never again to come so close to losing it. Rising from her chair, she advanced toward Weatherby's chair. ''Get out of here. You slimy heartless . . . bastard. You can't make me do this. I don't care what court put you in charge, you can't take away everything I care about.''

''Oh, but I can,'' Weatherby replied, calmly looking up at her. ''Do you like it here, Niki? Do you want to keep going to school—and then go on to college, and after that have some small support to count on while you try to establish yourself at whatever you choose to do for a living? Or do you want it all to end tomorrow?''

''Let Mr. Hyland keep his filthy money,'' Niki exploded. ''I'll do what I please, and manage without him.''

''Will you . . . ?'' Weatherby rose to his feet. But not to leave. He picked up the poker from a set of fire irons, and then prodded the burning logs. ''How, Niki? Do you think this school will keep you without receiving tuition payments—much less the extra board that takes care of holidays, summers, gives you a home you might not otherwise have?''

Helen, she thought. Helen would find a way to keep her here; she was part of the faculty, after all. . . .

But Weatherby had no trouble imagining the drift of her thoughts, and correcting her assumptions. ''I suppose you'd have a champion in Mrs. Czardas . . . but I don't think the school would be quick to do her any favors, either. And circumstances could be hard for a woman like that once she's discharged from one job. Could be hard for any refugee. . . .'' He turned holding the poker. ''Indeed, Niki, if you defied Mr. Hyland's wishes, there are many lives beside your own that might swerve from their comfortable path onto . . . a much bumpier route. . . .''

He held the poker for another second, as if wanting her to see it as a symbol of the power he could wield—through H.D. Hyland—to smash absolutely anything he wished.

She was not the only potential victim, Niki realized, but Helen . . . and even her friends. She sank back into her chair.

Weatherby put the poker back in its stand, and went to pick up the overcoat, muffler, and hat he'd left on a chair in the corner. ''Given your cooperation, Niki, you can count on everything to go on as before.'' He slipped into his coat, then reached into his inside jacket pocket and pulled out an envelope. ''Oh, I almost forgot . . . there's a check here for your allowance, a little extra this time. Treat yourself to . . .

well, maybe a good meal at a restaurant. You won't have to worry so much about counting your calories anymore.'' He put the envelope on a table.

She was too numb to respond to the cruelty of the lawyer's last words. When he said, ''Good-bye, Niki,'' and went out, she didn't even respond.

She heard the faint sound of the front door closing, a few seconds later Helen came into the writing room. She saw Niki staring disconsolately into the fire.

''Niki . . . what's wrong? What did he tell you?''

Niki looked up. The shock was evident in her eyes. Helen rushed to her, knelt by the chair.

''What is it, child?''

''They won't let me. . . .''

''Let you what?''

''I can't dive.''

''—can't?'' Helen's eyes remained clouded for only another instant. Then comprehension broke in a wave. ''Oh, no . . . no, they can't do that. No!'' She jumped to her feet. ''Sons-of-bitches. Always the same. Think they can crush the people who try for something more. . . .'' She ran from the room.

Niki was roused from shock by the sound of Helen's footsteps running away along the pine-board corridor, then the front door opening and closing again. She sprang up and raced after her.

When Niki caught up, Helen had already run halfway along the path from Vale to the parking area where Weatherby was climbing into a black limousine. Helen began to scream an agitated mixture of English and Hungarian just before Niki grabbed her and held her back.

''No, Helen, no . . . he'll hurt you, too.''

Helen struggled furiously to break away. ''He can't hurt me! Before they thought they could crush me—and they had tanks, Niki, they had guns, soldiers. But I'm here, Niki. And you will be here, too, you will not be destroyed. Let me go! We must fight them, *fight*! You will survive.''

"No! *no*, Helen!" Niki shrieked. "It isn't worth fighting this. I want the other things so much more. I want to stay here. I want you to keep your job. . . ."

"My job?"

"And I want Lotchy and Tibor and all your friends to be left alone. Don't you want that?"

Helen stopped resisting and turned bleak searching eyes on Niki's face. "They would . . . go that far?"

Niki nodded.

Helen went on staring at Niki for a long moment, then looked away along the winding road that led across the campus to the exit. Through the trees, the black limousine could still be seen just turning out through the gate.

"They are no different, are they?" Helen said. "Just different kinds of tyrant." She turned to Niki. "And you are just another kind of refugee." She put her arm around Niki, and they went back along the path to Vale.

Before they went in, Helen stopped and embraced Niki. "There will be other dreams, my girl. They murdered this one . . . but you will have others they will not be able to kill. It will happen for all of us . . . and we must all live for that day. Do you believe me?"

"I believe you," Niki said.

"Come in now, child. It's cold out here."

They went in. But even after Niki was in bed, beneath warm covers vainly seeking the refuge of sleep, it was hours before she could stop shivering.

Eleven

NIKI survived the murder of a dream, just as she had survived the murder of her mother. Whatever her losses, over the next year and a half she felt more than compensated by her gains: friends, people who loved her; allies who shared her griefs and furies, boosters who encouraged the formation of new dreams.

Most important, of course, was Helen. She gave Niki every bit of the extra emotional support required to see her through any rough patch. She was also the inspiration for Niki's new, and no less involving goal: to become a doctor. The closer Niki grew to Helen, the more she thought of fulfilling the career that had been denied her surrogate mother.

Helen herself did not actually encourage the ambition. She was gratified by Niki's choice as a signal of devotion, but she sensed, too, that medicine was not necessarily the best choice for Niki. It became a sensitive subject between them. Niki would bridle defensively at Helen's occasional suggestions that she ought to consider other careers.

"You think I wouldn't make a good doctor . . . ?"

"I think you'll succeed at whatever you do," was Helen's reply. "But I think of you as someone who needs sunlight, being outside and active. You don't want to spend your life in dingy hallways and operating rooms."

"It was good enough for you."

The competitive edge that marked their exchanges on the subject, Helen realized, was similar to what would occur between any real mother and daughter.

Niki moved much closer to Blake, too. Their friendship had been based initially on an amicable camaraderie. Blake amused Niki, and Niki's even-tempered good nature provided the perfect complement to Blake's frenetic overdrive. They were able to share the same space without getting in each other's way. But they both had well-developed defenses which, at first, kept them from becoming too trusting and intimate.

So when Niki was forced to change her Olympic plans abruptly, she didn't want Blake—or anyone else—to know the true reasons. She swore Helen to secrecy, and answered the avalanche of questions from all the other girls by saying that, on the eve of the tryouts, she'd had a failure of nerve, a realization that she wasn't capable of handling the extraordinary pressure of Olympic competition. As if to reinforce the story, she gave up diving completely—though that was more because she no longer saw the point of spending so much time at it if she couldn't go on reaching for new pinnacles.

Blake seemed to accept the explanation. But then came a night late in May when a bat flew into their room and swooped around, waking them both and scaring Blake witless . . . until the creature landed on a wall, and Niki quickly but gently trapped it in her hands and let it out the window again.

Back in bed, as they lay waiting for sleep to return, Blake said quietly, "It had nothing to do with nerves, did it?"

Niki knew instantly what she was talking about. "No," she answered, and then told Blake the truth.

"Oh Christ, baby," Blake said when Niki was done. During the story, she had turned on the light, then moved to sit on the edge of Niki's bed. "Why didn't you tell me back then? I wouldn't have let that happen to you. I'd have gotten support somehow. Maybe just split with you everything my old man gives me—like with the clothes. He'd never have known the difference."

"He would when it came to paying school bills."

"Then I'd get him to adopt you."

Niki laughed. "Thanks. But he's got a full inventory of daughters." Niki knew by now that Blake was Mr. Underwood's daughter by the second of four marriages; his collective output of children so far numbered four girls and two boys.

After Niki told Blake about Weatherby's visit, an extraordinary trust developed between them. There was nothing they wouldn't do for each other, or say to each other. As with Helen, Niki could talk freely about her mother and the Hylands. Knowing all of Niki's history led Blake to raise an interesting question one night. She and Niki had spent part of the evening watching TV in the lounge, and they had seen an episode of Perry Mason in which a woman had murdered her husband.

When they were back in their room studying, Blake said, "Do you ever think maybe your father did it?"

"Did what?"

"Murdered your mother."

At first, Niki dismissed the question as the product of Blake's love of melodramatic fantasy. Yet once the idea was planted, it took root. In classes, or lying awake in the small hours, she found herself thinking back to things she had seen that night nine years ago. The images in her memory were murky . . . but hadn't Mr. Hyland been there . . . ?

But why would H. D. have killed Elle? Certainly not to escape from the responsibility of supporting her. He could easily afford to give financial support—and, in any case, he had gone on paying the bills for Niki ever since.

So was he jealous about the romance with Babe?

Or did he have to be? Niki wondered. Hadn't she seen H. D. undressing Elle that night—being accepted again as her lover?

Also, when she'd found the body, Elle was dressed in a silk robe . . . lying by a broken window. . . .

Each time Niki started thinking about it, the questions would spin through her brain until, to give herself rest, she told herself that the judgment reached at the coroner's inquest was probably the truth. It certainly wasn't unlikely that a burglar would have been drawn to the cottage. Elle was known to be a rich man's ex-mistress; she could be expected to have valuables on hand—and to be alone and unprotected. Perhaps the thief wasn't even a professional, merely someone in town in need of money . . . someone who had panicked when Elle heard the window break and went to investigate. Yes, the official police version wasn't improbable. . . .

Then again and again, Niki would recall the blunt and effective way Sterling Weatherby had delivered the message of the Hyland's power. So whatever evidence and opinions had been presented and certified by the police and the judges and the citizens of Willow Cross, she knew, they would have been no different even if H.D. Hyland was the actual murderer.

At last, at one of their afternoon teas, Niki raised the possibility with Helen.

"I don't think you'd be wise to have the case opened again," Helen said, "unless some significant new evidence came to light. Poking around in general, making accusations that might prove groundless, wouldn't be in your own best interest. H.D. Hyland is your benefactor, Niki. You don't want to provoke him into withdrawing his support."

"But how can I take anything from him if he's my mother's killer? Suppose that's the very reason he's paid for me all these years—to put me in his debt, keep me silent."

Helen took a long sip of her tea. "Unless you know that he's guilty, unless you have proof, you'll only hurt yourself by reopening the matter. It's better to give him the benefit of the doubt." She put her cup down. "He is, after all, your father. . . ."

Calmed by Helen's advice, Niki stopped rerunning the old memories of that night. As she moved into her senior year, she was preoccupied with visits to Ivy League campuses, choosing a college with good premed courses, keeping her grades up, going to admissions interviews. If suspicions of H.D. surfaced at all, she shut them out quickly. As she looked ahead to next year, she saw that his support was only becoming more crucial.

Then, on an exceptionally cold January night not long after Christmas vacation, an incident at the school jolted Niki into a different perspective. She and Blake were together in the room studying, and Blake was smoking a cigarette—an infraction which Niki had begun to allow on occasion, especially since she had given up diving. By now Blake was a habitual smoker, and whenever Niki forbade her to smoke in the room, she simply went outside the dorm to have a cigarette. Niki was reluctant to send her out on such a cold night.

But this time Blake's smouldering butt end started a small fire in a wastebasket—and that led to Helen conducting an inquiry. Because the cause was a cigarette, she placed both Blake and Niki on suspension. Later, Niki went back to Helen to protest: she ought not receive the same punishment as Blake; she had not been smoking, too. "It won't matter that much to Blake," Niki said in her appeal. "But my record is clean otherwise, and this might affect my acceptance at some of the best schools. . . ."

Helen would not be budged. "I'm sorry, Niki, I can't help that. You were there with Blake . . . you allowed her to do it. In one sense, your guilt may be less—yet your responsibility may be even greater. Blake is in the grip of a habit, an addiction, and that weakens her judgment. But you could have stopped her—*should* have. Good heavens, you talk about wanting to become a doctor, and you let your friend do something that ruins her health."

Niki left in an unforgiving fury. Having loved Helen—believing she was loved in return—Niki could not understand how Helen could be so strict, do something that stood even the smallest chance of damaging her future. She knew that Helen was always tough where the rules against cigarettes were concerned; there was an element of personal vendetta against smoking because the habit had contributed to her husband's death. But the rules could be broken in special circumstances, Helen herself had said so.

Feeling alienated from Helen, Niki decided that she had been foolish to expect special treatment—the kind of transcendent forgiveness that only a mother would always summon for her child. Helen was *not* her mother. Her one and only mother had been Elle . . . who had been murdered.

Enraged by that loss, convinced that she had put her faith in an unworthy substitute, Niki suddenly resolved to throw caution to the winds. She would take steps to get the case reopened. The murderer must be punished. Even if it was H.D. and he cut off support, what did it matter? The way Niki felt now, she didn't care if she became a doctor.

She spent the week of suspension writing down her recollections of the night Elle had been murdered, getting them clear in her mind so she could present them as an affidavit. Since her petition to have the files reexamined would have to include a suggestion that the police in Willow Cross might have been involved in a coverup, she planned to send her notes to the state authorities in North Carolina.

She got them ready to mail, an envelope all sealed and addressed . . . and then she hesitated. The envelope stayed propped against the mirror on her dresser for a week.

At last, on a Saturday morning near the end of January, she put the envelope in the pocket of her parka and headed downstairs to walk to the mail drop.

Helen caught her as she was going out the door. The timing was so perfect that it was obvious Helen had been watching for her. "Niki," she said quietly, "will you please come into the writing room?"

Niki followed, her heart thudding in her chest. Weatherby, again. Somehow he must have gotten wind of what she was planning. But how? A spy—someone who'd sneaked a look at the pages in her desk—?

When they reached the writing room, there was no one else. Niki looked questioningly toward Helen, who nodded at the coffee table in front of the sofa. A couple of local newspapers lay unfolded on the table, also a *New York Times*. Niki picked up the *Times*. The picture of H.D. Hyland was in the lower left corner, next to the first column of his obituary, and beneath a headline reading: "Tobacco Industry Giant Succumbs at 69."

She tossed the paper back on the coffee table. She didn't have any appetite to read the details of his life. His death, she felt, had cheated her of a chance to be sure that justice was done. But she absorbed the news without suffering any shock, nor even very much surprise. It seemed only fitting, since he had also cheated her of what she deserved while he was alive.

"Are you all right?" Helen asked. It had been cool between them since the suspension.

"Yes. You haven't heard anything from Mr. Weatherby yet?"

"No."

"I need to know if I can continue here. . . ."

"You don't have to wonder about that, Niki. No matter what happens, I'll see that all your needs are met."

Niki turned away, ashamed now of the petty hostility she'd been harboring toward Helen. Of course, there had never been anyone she could count on so completely. "I'm sorry," she whispered, her eyes cast down.

Then she felt Helen's arms around her. "Let's just put it behind us," she said. "It's your future we have to think about."

Niki returned the embrace, joyous at being reconciled. Then she said, "You might be able to keep me here, Helen . . . but afterwards, the expenses will be enormous. . . ."

"Somehow, it will be managed. Lotchy and the others might help."

Through a succession of holidays, Helen's group of friends had continued to become more and more like close relatives of Niki's. Yet even the closest of poor relations, she thought, should not be saddled with obligations they had never expected. The continuing expense of college and then medical school would probably be out of reach.

Niki said nothing, however, happy for the spirit behind Helen's kindness, whether or not she could ever accept the deed.

Three weeks later, a letter finally came from Sterling Weatherby, written on the letterhead of his Willow Cross law offices. Addressing her as "Dear Ms. Sandeman"—as he always did in writing—he followed with only a couple of succinct lines:

> You will no doubt be happy to learn that provisions have been made for you to continue your education under the sponsorship of the Hyland Tobacco Company.
>
> Kindest regards,

Nothing more, no details, nothing to indicate she had any entitlement to such "provisions." But Niki did not contact Weatherby to request more details. She had the only answer she really cared about now. The question of H.D.'s guilt in Elle's death would remain unresolved; even if punishment was deserved it would never be meted out. But the man—the veritable stranger—who was her father had acknowledged some small justice, at least, by maintaining her lifeline of financial support.

Some months later, another letter came from Weatherby to inform Niki that "in the spirit of magnanimity for which he was well known," H.D. Hyland had also arranged to deed over to Elle Sandeman's sole heir, the house and property in which she had lived. Understanding that Niki could not occupy the property alone, a long-term lease had been arranged. The money from that lease would provide supplementary funds for Niki's tuition—indeed, that had been the purpose of H.D.'s bequest.

Niki dreamed of the house that night, dreamed of being in it, of living there with her mother. But the few happy images that rose into her self-consciousness flowed into a dark terrifying memory of a little girl wandering down a stairway that seemed almost endless, until she looked through a doorway and saw a vampire leaning over her mother, undressing her. . . .

Waking from the nightmare, she couldn't imagine ever returning to the house willed to her by H.D. Hyland. Leaving it to her seemed no less cruel than kind, and she wondered if he had done it only as another way of purging his guilt, washing the blood from his hands.

Twelve

Beverly Hills, November 1974

PENELOPE—"Pepper"—Hyland rose slowly to consciousness out of a deep, Valium-induced sleep. For the first moments, she wasn't sure which house she was in, on which coast of the United States—whether she was even in a bed, or lying on somebody's floor. She had a sense of being lost.

But when she opened her eyes and looked around, she recognized the familiar, sleekly modern custom decor of the master bedroom in her Beverly Hills "bungalow" (the term favored by local realtors for a house with only two or three bedrooms that nevertheless managed to sell for four million dollars). Pepper remembered then why she was feeling disoriented. She had arrived only last night on a red-eye flight from Atlanta, the departure hub for the small charter plane that had brought her from Willow Cross. Throughout the two preceding days, she had spent every waking hour in a conference room at the Hyland Company headquarters, dealing with a team of family lawyers—and being harangued by Duke as to why she had "no choice" but to sign the pile of documents that would allow the estate of H.D. Hyland to be distributed to its heirs now that government inheritance taxes had been settled. Babe, who did not want to forfeit his entry in a boat race in Bimini, had left his sister with a power of attorney to act for both of them. Though she had stalled, asking the lawyers to go over H.D.'s stipulations again and again, forcing Duke to explain the tax advantages of accepting H.D.'s elaborate construction of trusts and time-linked disbursements, Pepper had realized right from the beginning that her threats to fight the will were empty, and she would ultimately have to yield. H.D.'s bequests to her and Babe were not equal to Duke's, but the will had been strictly drawn and recorded, and H.D. had died too young to support a claim that he hadn't been in his right mind when he gave his instructions.

So, Pepper and Babe would each have to accept stock and assets worth slightly more than a hundred million dollars—while Duke's inheritance might be worth three or four times as much. In addition, Duke had been given the right to inhabit the best of the Hyland real estate—Highlands and Flamingo Island. Though they were to be considered joint property for purposes of distributing revenue from any future sale, Duke was obligated to let Pepper and Babe inhabit the houses with him for no more than thirty-six days out of every year. Finally, control of a majority share of Hyland stock rested with Duke.

As large as her own inheritance was, Pepper resented the superior position that had been given to her older half brother. At first, it surprised her, too. Unlike herself and Babe, children of H.D.'s later marriage, the offspring of his first had spent much of his early life apart from the family patriarch. On the rare occasions when Duke was together with H.D., there had always seemed to be terrible friction between them. Accordingly, Pepper had always regarded Duke as the outsider among the Hylands. In recent years, though, he was the one who had shown the most talent for the business—

and in the end that had been what made him H.D.'s favorite. Pepper sensed, too, that H.D. felt he had some sort of special debt to Duke—perhaps as compensation for his childhood. But the main reason Duke had been given the lion's share of the fortune, she realized, was that he was the one who could best be trusted to preserve it and make it grow.

Fair enough, perhaps. The two husbands who'd come and gone before Pepper was twenty-eight had each cost her a couple of million dollars out of the fifteen million-dollar trust she'd come into at twenty-one. A few million more had fluttered away on homes, yachts, art, antiques—a catalogue of acquisitions she was often too lazy to use or too drunk to appreciate. So a fresh hundred million would certainly come in handy. Nor would Babe complain: his share was enough to support his lifestyle, aimless except for his love of boat racing. Yes, the money would do—for now. But if a time came when she wanted to fight Duke on his own ground—give up her hedonistic pursuits in exchange for the kind of dull responsible duties that Duke willingly undertook—then perhaps she would increase her share. Already she had an idea that might someday pay dividends. . . .

Pepper kicked off the covers and stretched. Looking up at the mirrored ceiling, she pursed her lips playfully at the slim woman floating overhead, then smiled, admiring her own tanned body and the provocative feline face framed by golden hair in a feathered cut. In spite of the reckless pace at which Pepper lived, she remained in reasonably good condition with regular stays at expensive spas, daily visits at home from fitness trainers, a diet of health foods between the occasional binging and also—the best beauty secret, she firmly believed—a steady diet of athletic sex in all its variations. The sex was good for her mind, too, Pepper thought; it cleared her head. She couldn't think straight when she was horny. Like now. In fact, the trip to Willow Cross had caused an unaccustomed interruption in her usual habits. So as not to inflame Duke, she had made a point of being on good behavior, staying away from the roadhouses where she could always pick up some tobacco farmer's brawny son. She'd had no sex for five days.

Pepper rolled onto her side and took a hundred-dollar bill from the loose sheaf that was lying in a drawer of her night table. Then she pushed a button at the head of the bed.

An attractive young Mexican girl in her late teens wearing a beige maid's uniform entered the bedroom a minute later.

Pepper had covered herself again with a sheet. "I want breakfast, Dorinda."

The maid nodded, and waited for further instructions.

"Come here," Pepper said.

An apprehensive look came over the maid's face as she approached the bed.

"I want you to have breakfast, too." Pepper peeled back the covering sheet. "Doesn't that give you an appetite? I've been away for so many days. . . ."

The maid looked at the hundred-dollar bill which was folded into the cleft in the neatly shaved triangle of wiry blond hair between Pepper's legs. Then she started to climb onto the bed.

"Not yet," Pepper said. "The uniform. . . ."

The maid quickly slipped the uniform over her head, took off her underwear, then clambered up onto Pepper. She bent over, picked up the paper money in her teeth, and spat it out next to the bed. Then she put her mouth on Pepper again, and began furiously working with her tongue.

The orgasm came after only a few minutes. The maid sat back on her haunches, waiting for any further instructions.

With a sigh, Pepper reached again into her night table for another hundred-dollar bill. The maid, still on her knees, started to slide up along Pepper's body.

"No, no, Dorinda," Pepper said impatiently. "I don't want you to, not this morning. The extra money is just because that was good, damn good. If you could only iron a silk blouse as well as you do that," she added tartly while the maid began to dress, "you'd be an absolute treasure. Now bring me some fresh orange juice, a bowl of oat flakes, and decaf."

The maid finished dressing, gathered up her payment, and was gone in another ten seconds.

Pepper got up and went to the shower in her enormous bathroom. She felt much better now. She knew exactly where she was . . . and her head was clear. She could remember exactly how pissed off she'd felt sitting with Duke and all those damn lawyers who were no doubt in his pocket. She could remember how hard she'd concentrated on everything being said—hoping to learn something, pick up some little morsel of information that might be turned to advantage. And she remembered what she'd overheard as she was on her way out of the meeting, and Duke was pulled into a corner by one of the lawyers:

"Are you sure that does it?" the lawyer asked. "You don't expect the girl to come in with any claims against the estate?"

"She wouldn't dare," Duke said.

"There are some loose ends you may want to clean up to be certain. . . ."

"I will," Duke muttered. "Don't worry about the girl. . . ."

The girl. In the context of a possible claim, Pepper knew the reference could only be to H.D.'s bastard, the daughter he'd had by that French woman. Pepper had known about the girl since she'd been twelve, and had heard her mother raging about the affair in a screaming argument with H.D. Since the marriage had survived another few years, anyway, Pepper had assumed the whole mess was simply painted over with a transfer of money. She vaguely recalled some of the other gossip—the woman had been killed by a burglar years after her father had stopped seeing her—and the child had been sent away from Willow Cross.

But this latest reference to "the girl" signaled Pepper that her illegitimate half sister continued to be a factor in family matters. An extremely minor factor, perhaps—yet obviously enough of one to merit Duke's concern. There were loose ends he intended to clean up. . . .

To find out what they were, Pepper realized, was of the highest priority. Because there was just a chance that those loose ends would provide her someday with the means to keep her older, and none-too-beloved half brother tied up in knots.

Niki stopped at her mailbox in the lobby of Centennial Hall, the freshman dorm at Barnard College, on her way to her chemistry lab. Crossing the large quadrangle area in front of the Lowe Library, she began to flip through the small handful of mail. A note from her English professor asking for a conference. A letter from Gertie, who had become a regular correspondent. And a postcard with an amusing photograph of quite an old woman peddling a bicycle with a towering bundle of French breads behind the seat. Niki knew without reading the message that the card was from Blake. Her old roommate was spending this year in Paris where her father had arranged for her to do some inconsequential job in one of the smaller design houses. Blake's only means of correspondence was postcards, but she sent three or four every month, always with a quirky picture. Niki laughed out loud when she read the two lines on the other side. "Doesn't this look like a pain in the ass? (*Pain* is the frog word for bread in case you forgot. . . .)"

Then she turned to the last piece of mail. As soon as she saw the return address, the smile vanished from her lips. Niki sat down on the library's stone steps and tore open the envelope. Inside was an airline ticket for a round trip to California and a letter. Niki pored over the page of surprisingly childish handwriting.

Afterwards, she skipped the chemistry lab and went straight to a telephone to call Helen.

* * *

The letter, Niki said, extended an invitation to visit California at Thanksgiving as Pepper Hyland's guest. "She says she wants to get to know me. . . ."

"Then you should accept, of course," Helen said.

"But I've always had Thanksgiving with you," Niki countered. "Anyway, this is so . . . so weird. None of them have ever wanted a thing to do with me. Why now?"

"That's what you need to find out," Helen said. "Listen, my dear, don't rule out the possibility that there are simply good intentions at work. Mr. Hyland may have kept you locked out of the family. But he's gone now. His children —at least one beside yourself, if not all—might be cut from different cloth. This daughter, Penelope, may want to heal any wounds caused by her father. There are things you'd like to know, too, aren't there? Things maybe she can tell you. . . ."

Niki still hesitated. "All right, I'll call her. But I'll suggest coming to see her another time."

"Niki, you only have holidays free. If you don't go now —then it would be Christmas. I'd rather have you with me then."

"But I'd hate to miss this Thanksgiving. Dmitri absolutely swore—"

Helen laughed. "I know. But he swears to it every year. Go to California, Niki. You'll be missing nothing. . . ."

Niki agreed she would go, and sent a brief note back to Pepper Hyland thanking her for the invitation and the ticket, and giving a planned time of arrival.

As Thanksgiving approached, however, Niki wondered less about why she'd been invited to meet Pepper than she did about whether this, at long last, would be the year when Dmitri finally managed to show up with the famous Alexei.

So far, it had been nothing more than a running joke that never stopped gathering momentum. Dmitri would always promise to bring the handsome son with whom, he insisted, Niki was destined to make the most beautiful little *malchiki*.

But he had yet to materialize. "He's staying at school this year," Dmitri would say. "He is studying to make sure he gets the very best grade." Another time Dmitri had said the boy was having his turkey with the parents of a new girlfriend.

Lotchy and the others mocked him mercilessly. "There is no such person as this Alexei . . . he is an invention of the K.G.B."

"You think so?" Dmitri roared back. "Well, you will see. Next year he will be here, without fail."

But each year the holiday gatherings came and went without Dmitri's son. Helen had finally told Niki the true story she'd heard from Gertie: Dmitri was separated from his wife who had custody of the boy; wife and son had supposedly never forgiven the Russian director because they had been left behind in Moscow at the time of his defection—he had not even warned them of what he planned to do—and they had been forced to arrange their own emigration, which had been denied for years. Embarrassed by the story, Dmitri preferred to pretend that he remained on good terms with his son.

Lately, though, it had seemed to be less of a pretense. At last year's Thanksgiving, Dmitri had silenced the others' usual jibes by producing a photograph of himself standing with a young man who was exceedingly handsome—a young Cossack with silky black hair and intense dark eyes. "There," Dmitri said. "Isn't he everything I've said? But you'll see for yourselves *next* year. He will come, I know. At last, he has truly forgiven me. . . ." Dmitri's willingness to impart a piece of the truth also seemed to signal a change.

After the many years of hearing about Alexei Ivanov, Niki had become curious to meet him. Of course, the talk of being paired off with him was worse than embarrassing, it was ridiculous. Her interest was on exactly the same level as Helen's or Lotchy's or any of the others'. Though, she reflected privately, the young man in the picture was certainly unusually handsome. . . .

Each time Niki expressed even the slightest interest in changing her travel plans, however, Helen would insist that it would be a mistake.

"For better or worse, Niki, a door is being held open. You must not slam it shut."

Two days before Thanksgiving she flew to California. At the arrivals gate, she searched the waiting crowd for any woman who might be Pepper Hyland—and saw instead a chauffeur holding up a signboard with "Nicolette" on it. The chauffeur took Niki's valise and escorted her outside the terminal to a silver Bentley convertible.

She rode in the front passenger seat and tried at first to make conversation. But the chauffeur, who was quite young and looked very dashing in his tailored black uniform, apparently spoke only Spanish. Niki settled into watching the passing scene, so different than anything she was used to. Palm trees, low buildings, broad boulevards, the rim of hills on a distant horizon, and the huge beautiful houses lining the wide streets of Beverly Hills.

The car turned at last into a short curving driveway and came to a stop in front of a large house in the style of a hacienda, with stuccoed walls and arches and a red tile roof. Its pleasant, informal look encouraged Niki to believe she might get along well with Pepper Hyland.

A maid opened the door and gave Niki a welcoming smile. "Miss Hyland is wait for you at the pool," she said, starting to guide Niki along a wide corridor with a view of a large garden at the far end.

Niki had glimpses of immense rooms at each side of the corridor filled with art and beautiful furniture before she passed through sliding glass doors onto a tiled patio that surrounded an enormous swimming pool. The maid pointed across the pool to a row of chaises. On one chaise Pepper Hyland lay stretched out, wearing nothing but a minimal bikini bottom, her eyes closed against the bright sun.

Niki paused, uncertain about disturbing her hostess while she lay half-nude. But the maid had said she was waiting. Niki walked around the pool.

"Miss Hyland . . . ?"

Pepper opened her eyes and shaded them with her hand as she looked up. "Nicolette?"

"I'm called Niki . . ."

"And I'm Pepper." She sat up and extended her hand.

Niki shook it as she sat down on the end of the adjacent chaise.

Pepper took her sunglasses from a side table and slipped them on. "Well, you're a dynamite looker, I'll say that. . . ."

Niki didn't know how to answer. Pepper was certainly attractive, too, but a reciprocal compliment might seem fawning now. They spent a long awkward moment examining each other.

"So. . . ." Pepper said. "You came. I'm glad."

Niki wavered between all the polite choices of small talk —the beauty of the house and pool, the change in the weather, the details of the flight—and decided to speak exactly what was on her mind.

"Why are you glad?" she said. "What difference does it make to you . . . ?"

"Well," Pepper said with an approving lilt, "spunky little sister, aren't you? Cards on the table, get it all right out in the open. . . ."

"What else should we do? Tiptoe around each other for a week, pretend this is just a normal family get-together?"

"That would never do, would it?" Pepper agreed. "Well, then. Why did I reach out? First, because I was plain damn curious. You know, Niki, you and your mother weren't exactly a deep dark secret. The sort of man my father was—" Pepper cut herself off pointedly, before going on. "I mean *our* father was . . . well, nobody could ever tell him what to do or how to do it. He made his own rules, and he could always afford to pay the freight to get things done his way.

So he didn't much care who knew about you—as long as it was never made 'official,' nothing in writing that he might regret. But as much talk as there was, I never saw you, and I couldn't help wondering how you turned out. . . ."

Niki felt anger rising. She didn't like the idea that she'd been invited just on a whim—to be put under a microscope. But she reined herself in. The ground rules were hers, after all; she had called for honesty.

Now Pepper swung her legs off the chaise onto the ground, so that she was facing Niki directly. "But that's not all. I always felt you got a raw deal—being kept on the outside looking in. Familywise, maybe the only real difference between you and me is that my mother was more of a hard-ass. She might have let H.D. take her to bed before he gave her the ring, but it was only to catch his pecker in a trap, and then she hung on until she got everything she wanted." She laid her hands over Niki's. "You get it, kid? Your mom gave it away on a wish and a prayer, so H.D. left her hanging—along with you. But he's gone . . . and I decided maybe it's time we let you into the club."

Niki took another long look at Pepper Hyland. There was no doubt that they weren't kindred spirits; but their differences might be no less or no greater if they had been raised together as true siblings.

Pepper smiled slightly as if she understood the result of Niki's appraisal. "Why don't you go and unpack? Get comfortable, then I'll show you some of the sights. Okay, Sis?"

"Yeah," Niki said. "Sounds good. Except for one thing. . . ."

"I know," Pepper said. "You don't want to be called 'Sis.' "

Niki had to smile.

The maid, who had been hovering in the background, led Niki to an immense guest room furnished as if for a Spanish princess. At the center was an antique wrought-iron canopy bed, with elaborate scrollwork. Nearby was a massive armoire decorated with cupids and a silk-covered chaise. Curtains of exquisite gossamer lace hung at the windows and around the bed canopy. Niki could see a huge green marble bathroom through a partly open door. It was nicer than any room she'd ever slept in before.

Her valise was standing against a wall, and she picked it up to unpack, only to find that it was empty. All her things had been distributed to the drawers, closets, and bathroom shelves.

So this was what it was like to be rich, she thought. No ugliness, no menial tasks, surroundings of beauty. She felt a flash of hate for the Hylands—who had prevented her from having these things. . . .

But, in the wake of that single concentrated flaring of emotion, all the anger and bitterness seemed to burn itself out. Would she want to change places with Pepper Hyland? To be indolent and spoiled, without any ambition? Niki liked being herself. And what was the point of hate? Especially now, when the first steps toward reconciliation had been taken.

Even if she and Pepper could never be close, Niki realized, perhaps it wasn't impossible that they would find some common ground.

They went out together in the Bentley convertible, Pepper driving, modishly dressed in a Day-Glo orange parachute suit. As they rode through Beverly Hills, Pepper pointed out the homes of various stars past and present, then they headed to Rodeo Drive for a tour of the shops.

Mainly because Pepper seemed honest about who she was and what she wanted, Niki found her easy to be with. On the ride through Beverly hills, Pepper confessed that neither she nor Babe was especially fond of Duke—and they were both smarting over the result of H.D.'s will which had treated their half brother very favorably.

"But who are we to complain?" Pepper said, with a glance at Niki. "You didn't get anything, right?"

At first, Niki wanted to change the subject. Given her own situation, she felt that Pepper's complaints were crude and insensitive. But then she reminded herself that one of the reasons she had come was to learn whatever she could. "I never expected anything from the will. What I get now is enough. I just hope that doesn't stop."

"So you *are* getting something . . . ?"

Niki explained the payments that came via Hyland Tobacco for tuition and basic expenses.

Pepper took it in and became thoughtful.

A dark shadow of doubt flitted through Niki's mind. Had it been wrong to tell Pepper any details of the provisions that had been made for her? Wrong even to come . . . ?

But then the shopping tour began, and as they moved through the gilded, perfumed boutiques of Rodeo Drive, Niki was overwhelmed by Pepper's generosity. No matter how much she protested, expensive dresses and blouses and belts and other accessories were bestowed on her. And, in fact, Niki enjoyed getting these new clothes, the sort of chic but *outre* things she would never have bought for herself. Leaving one shop in a new suede skirt and fringed cowboy shirt, she felt that she'd come out of herself, adopted some of the fearless confidence that Pepper demonstrated. Was this what she would feel like if she had been brought up with all the money that Pepper had?

When they returned to the house, Pepper told Niki they'd rest for a while, then go out later for dinner.

"Can I try the pool?" Niki asked.

"Sure. Make yourself at home."

Niki went to her room, put on one of her standard tank suits, and returned outside. Pepper had disappeared, the garden was empty.

Niki swam a few laps, and then started practicing dives off the springboard. She didn't miss competition—had turned down approaches from the coach to join her college team—yet she liked to keep her dives sharp.

She worked for twenty minutes and had just broken to the surface after executing a near perfect one-and-a-half with a twist when she heard the sound of someone clapping. Looking around the edge of the pool, Niki saw a very pretty young woman with light-blond hair leaning against one of the stucco pillars that supported a shaded porch.

"Nice diving," the blonde said, sashaying closer to the pool. She was wearing a scoop-necked white sun dress, "You must be Niki, the long-lost relative Pepper's been talking about. I'm Terry Dyer. . . ."

Niki cleared the water from her eyes and took a second look. She didn't go to the movies often, but she recalled having seen the blonde playing leads in a couple of the more popular films of the last few years.

"How do you do," Niki said.

"You're beautiful to watch, Niki. Let's see that last one again."

"I was about to stop. Pepper wants to go out to dinner."

"Don't worry about what Pepper wants. I'm having dinner with you, too. C'mon . . . just one more."

Niki obliged, and earned another expression of admiration from Terry Dyer. As she picked up her towel and rubbed her hair, Niki said, "How do you know Pepper?"

"We met at a party. There's a lot of parties in this town, and between me and Pepper we don't miss too many, so it had to happen." Niki nodded. Then Terry added, "Afterwards, we found out we'd been involved with half a dozen of the same guys. That made us feel like soul sisters."

"Hey, what're you telling her?" The shout came from Pepper.

Niki turned to see her striding out onto the patio. She had changed into a dress of sheer spring-green chiffon that floated on the breeze as she walked. Niki gave her a puzzled look. Pepper's shouted question seemed to have a sharp, suspicious edge.

"Nothing bad, baby," Terry said. "Just that we've shared a few guys. . . ."

"Well, knock it off," Pepper said, a bit more softly. "She's just a kid—and I'm supposed to take care of her."

"Okay, okay," Terry said, backing off slightly.

"Go and get dressed, Niki. Put on one of those new things."

Niki didn't have to be told to wear something from the wardrobe Pepper had bought for her. She had no other clothes to match the way the other two women were dressed.

As she went into the house, Niki glanced back for a moment. She saw Pepper and Terry Dyer standing very close, talking intently, as though arguing. Niki still couldn't understand what Terry could have done to annoy Pepper so much.

Niki didn't notice the name of the restaurant, but it was obviously one of the most popular places in Los Angeles because there was a line of people waiting inside—which Pepper and Terry led her quickly past—and when the *maître d'hôtel* led them straight into the room, Niki had to stop herself from staring at all the celebrities she recognized at other tables. Carol Burnett . . . Warren Beatty with Jack Nicholson . . . Jimmy Stewart . . . Dean Martin . . . Jane Fonda. . . . Equally impressive were the number who obviously knew Terry and Pepper, and waved to them, or called out a few words. This was another kind of family, Niki thought, a kinship of fame and wealth. Here, tonight, it looked like a wonderful family to belong to. Niki liked the sensation of being invited in. She liked the feeling of glamor that came with wearing the multicolored, backless silk print Pepper had given her . . . of having famous faces looking her way, wondering who she was to be in their midst.

When the waiter came to take orders for drinks soon after they were seated, Niki was going to decline. But Pepper ordered a bottle of champagne for the table. "We've got a reunion to celebrate," she said to Niki.

Except for a sip or two of wine urged on her at Helen's

holiday dinners, Niki never drank anything alcoholic. But she accepted the champagne and drank when Pepper proposed a toast "to my little sister . . . and many happy returns of the day." Since she found the taste of the effervescent wine pleasant and refreshing, Niki didn't count the glasses, and was already beginning to feel lightheaded by the time she realized the stuff had a powerful effect and refused any more.

She sat through dinner with a feeling that she was not quite anchored to her seat but floating an inch or two above it, watching the famous people around her—who sometimes caught her glance and smiled back—and answering questions from Terry and Pepper, but not remembering a word of the answers she gave. She did know, however, that whatever she ate wasn't as good as Helen's cooking and that she laughed a lot—couldn't stop the giggles, in fact, after Warren Beatty caught her staring and winked at her, then stopped by the table on his way out to introduce himself and ask her name. The rest was a blur until they were back at Pepper's house.

Though her head was clearing a little, she walked to the guest room leaning on Pepper, and started giggling again when she thought of telling Warren Beatty her name. "I said Sticky Candyman, didn't I . . . ?"

"No, kid. What you said was 'Sickie Madman.' " Pepper eased Niki down onto the bed. "I don't think it put Warren off, though. He still wants to fuck every beautiful girl who ever lived, and right now he's in between affairs, so he'll probably be calling here for days, starting tomorrow. Should I tell the maids to say you went back home to Timbuktu . . . or would you like to sleep with Warren?"

"Why would I want to sleep with him?"

Pepper put her chin in her palm and gave Niki a droll look. "Shit, imagine that," she said.

"What?"

"You're still a virgin, aren't you?"

"Sure."

"How old are you?"

"Nineteen."

"Nice," Pepper said, and hesitated a moment. "Well, I'll leave you to undress yourself. Good night, Niki."

Before she turned through the door, Niki called out, "Pepper . . ."

Pepper stopped and looked back.

"Thanks," Niki said. "I had a great time."

Pepper smiled. "My pleasure, kid." She paused and leaned on the door. "You know, I wasn't sure I could like you—but you're okay. Sweet dreams." She went out, closing the door.

A fog of pleasant impressions rolled through Niki's mind for just a moment before she lost consciousness.

There were hands all over her skin—it felt like a thousand hands—and she could see them, when she looked down, on the skin of her leg. Then she realized that she wasn't looking at her own skin, the leg belonged to another woman . . . and then she realized it was Elle's. There weren't a thousand hands, really, there was just one hand, sliding over her mother's body, peeling back some fabric that could have been a dress or a blanket . . . and beneath it, her mother was as blue-white as a statue. Dead. But then she gave a moan of pain, and the man whose hand had undressed her came up to cover her mouth while she bent low to whisper something in her ear. Niki saw the man's face then—the face of H.D. Hyland. He looked around suddenly, and seeing that his crime had been witnessed, his features darkened. He was ready to do murder again. . . .

Niki jolted awake, her heart pounding, her body drenched in sweat, the dim blue light of the swimming pool lights casting soft shadows over a strange room. It took a second to remember where she was.

As she lay awake calming herself, waiting for her heart to

slow down, she heard a sound from somewhere not too far away—a sound like a woman's moaning, then a sharp cry.

Was Pepper having a bad dream, too? Or perhaps, Niki thought as she drifted back into sleep, it had been nothing more than the mewing and the yowl of a stray cat.

Thirteen

WAKING to bright morning sun, Niki looked out at the pool beside her room and felt the need to purge the achy wooziness left over from last night. A swim would also exorcise the ghosts of her dream. She put on her bathing suit and ran out through the glass doors to plunge directly into the pool.

She had been practicing dives for half an hour when she saw Terry Dyer emerge from one of the sliding glass doors around the patio. The robe worn by the movie star hung open, unbelted, and beneath it she was naked. Running her hands through her hair and rubbing her neck, she moved unsteadily to one of the patio chairs and slumped down. Terry had apparently been so drunk, Niki thought, that Pepper had not let her drive home.

"Oooh," Terry murmured, "that splashing sounds as loud as tidal waves. How can you stand it?"

"I didn't have as much champagne as you did."

"Champagne's not the half of it, baby-doll."

Niki got out of the pool and dried off. "Pepper still asleep?"

Terry nodded. "She's positively wasted. She won't get up for hours. If you were going to do any sightseeing, better do it on your own. I'd keep you company, but I'm supposed to have lunch with my agent. . . ."

Niki left Terry soaking up some curative sun while she went to shower and dress. If Pepper was going to sleep away the day, she certainly didn't want to waste it herself.

As she emerged from her room, one of the maids appeared to announce that breakfast was waiting. She guided Niki to a poolside sun room where a lavish display of fresh fruits, cheeses, pitchers of juice, cold cereals, and smoked fish was set out on a sideboard. Except that the round marble table was laid with a single place-setting of crystal, silver, and china, Niki would have thought twelve people were expected for breakfast. The maid stood by and asked Niki if there were any cereals or hot dishes she wanted to order.

"No, thank you," Niki said. Seeing such an abundance of food with no one to eat it but herself had the effect of dampening rather than enhancing her appetite. She took some canteloupe while a man servant she hadn't seen before appeared to pour coffee.

As she finished eating, the chauffeur who had driven her yesterday came into the dining room. "Ms. Hyland left orders I should drive you everyplace you want."

His English was heavily accented, but obviously not as limited as she had thought yesterday. "That's all right," Niki said, "I'll get around on my own."

"Pardon, *Señorita*, but is difficult. In Los Angeles you must have car."

"Okay, then," she relented. It would also help, she realized, to have someone who knew the landscape and might suggest places of interest.

The chauffeur introduced himself as "Pancho," then asked if she preferred to be driven in the open car he had used yesterday, in a closed limousine, or the Ferrari in the garage.

Niki laughed at the idea of such choices. "I like the sun, Pancho. Just bring out the same old car from yesterday. . . ."

As they drove away from the house in the Bentley convertible, Niki explained that she knew nothing about Los Angeles, and that she'd like to be taken on a tour of the same sights the chauffeur might show his own sister. He drove her past some of the movie lots, old and new . . . and through the UCLA campus . . . and to the La Brea tar pits where the fossils of dinosaurs had been found . . . and then out along the beach to Malibu, past the homes of movie stars.

Finally, when it was around lunch time, the chauffeur suggested driving down to Venice. "Is where young people like yourself like to be . . . and many artists, and little shops—but no expensive like in Beverly Hills."

"Sounds just right," Niki agreed.

As they headed back down the coast, Pancho finally allowed himself to be more talkative with Niki. He told her about his upbringing in the poverty of a Mexican village, how he had crossed the border illegally into California a few years ago, how he had come to work for Pepper. "I was working as a dish-washer then, but I hear from a girl I know about Miss Pepper . . . how she pay very well, and how she like good-looking people to work for her. So I came. Is true, she pay very good, and the job is easy. I don't mind all the extra stuff she want sometime. . . ."

"Extra stuff?" Niki said. "What do you mean?"

As the Bentley sped down the freeway, the chauffeur had been talking quickly, unthinkingly, even telling Niki about being an illegal alien. But now he paused to glance over at her. Then instead of providing a simple reply, he said, "Miss Pepper has call you sister. But you are so unlike . . . I can no believe."

"We had different mothers, and we grew up apart. This is the first time I've met Pepper."

"She is nice woman," Pancho said. "I am happy to have job with her." The chauffeur turned on the radio. "What kind music you like?"

"Anything," Niki said distractedly. She wasn't sure what had happened. Pancho didn't want to talk about his job anymore, that much was clear. But why? What sort of "extra stuff" did Pepper require him to do? Niki couldn't imagine.

When they drove into Venice, Niki saw immediately that it would be fun to explore. There was no mystery about the reason it had been named after the famous Italian city: winding canals traversed by small bridges ran through the center of the community. Historic old stucco buildings and arcades lined a broad white-sand beach.

She didn't object at all when Pancho pulled over within view of a beachside boardwalk and suggested she might like to walk around on her own for a while. "I'll come back and pick you up here in a couple of hours. . . ."

Niki had the feeling that the chauffeur had a few errands of his own to run. She agreed, and they arranged to meet again in three hours. Delighted for the chance to explore on foot, Niki strolled the beach where hordes of beautiful young men and women played volleyball, and worked out with weights, or just lay tanning themselves. She meandered along the boardwalk, surrounded by roller skaters in bikinis, watercolor artists who had set up their easels to face the sea. She stopped at a small kiosk and bought some postcards to send Helen and Blake and Lotchy and Gertie. Then she chose some souvenirs: for Helen, a big seashell painted in Day-Glo colors—as wildly improbable as California itself—and for Blake, a T-shirt emblazoned with the slogan: "Life is a Beach."

As she strolled along the arcade, her eye was caught by an enormous, dramatic black-and-white photograph in the window of a gallery. The picture showed a man, wearing the dramatic black uniform of a Nazi SS officer, gently holding an adorable infant girl while watching a family with two children being herded into a truck by German soldiers. A caption beneath the picture read "Berlin, 1937." Niki was drawn inside.

The small art gallery was filled with more black-and-white photographs, as vividly dramatic as the period they portrayed. They told of a country moving from defeat towards aggression—in the smokestacks of the factories, in the twisted cross symbol, superimposed on the chiseled faces of young men and women of "Aryan" birth. Niki's pulse quickened when she saw first one picture and then another of the 1936 Olympics—of a discus thrower's rippling muscles, of a runner caught in the last agonizing effort to win. When she came to the pictures of the swimmers, the hair on the back of her neck stood up, and she began to shiver, though the day was quite warm.

There in front of her was a picture of a woman poised at the end of a board in the moment of balance in the instant before taking her dive. The face of the diver was the same as in the picture Niki still kept close at hand wherever she was, just as Elle had done. The diver was her grandmother, Monique Veraix.

With a pounding heart, Niki asked the young man in jeans, who was tending the gallery, for more information about the pictures.

"Do you like them?" he said. "They were taken by one of our local photographers."

"Who is he?" Niki asked quickly.

The young man nodded to a wall where the photographer's name had been stenciled in large letters.

Niki stared at the eight letters: SANDEMAN.

It was as if time had stopped.

"His full name," she asked in a tremulous voice, "is it Ralph Sandeman?"

"Yes. He took those when he was quite a young man, on assignment to cover the Olympics in—"

Niki couldn't remember leaving the gallery, yet she found herself sitting on the beach, staring at the ocean, trying to absorb the shock of what had just happened. The story of her grandmother, of the faded photograph—they were parts of a fairy tale, but one without the traditional happy ending. She had never seen her grandmother, Monique, nor the man who had been responsible for loving—and leaving—her. In Niki's mind, the past that went as far back as her grandmother had almost assumed the character of fiction. She had been prepared to close the book, leave that part of her story unfinished. What was to be gained if she dared to seek out Ralph Sandeman now? It would be unbearable, she knew, if he turned her away, denied her as H.D. Hyland had done. And could she count on any other result? It was this man—this unknown grandfather—who had started the cycle of denial and rejection that repeated itself in her own mother's tragic life. He had declared his wishes by deserting Monique Veraix almost four decades ago.

Yet she was here—within minutes of being able to see him. She had come, Niki reminded herself, because Helen had urged her to learn about her history. And more than that advice must have been at work, Niki thought. There was fate and destiny in having come to this place . . . seen that picture. . . .

She picked herself up from the sand and went back to the gallery. When she entered, the young man looked surprised.

"Are you all right? The way you ran out of here—"

"I need the address of the man who took these pictures."

He studied her for a moment, then went to a small office at the rear and returned with a piece of paper.

Following the directions given to her by the man at the gallery, Niki found herself wandering down a street that bordered a canal. Referring to an address number tacked to a wooden gate, she stopped in front of a rustic, frame cottage, the last in a row of similar cottages, set on a tiny piece of land. The shrubs behind the gate were neatly trimmed, and there was a small patch of wildflowers.

She went through the gate and knocked on the door. There was no answer. Maybe after all her agonizing, he wasn't at home, she thought in a panic. She knocked harder, then went to the back door and tried again. There was a sound from within, then a voice, slightly raspy. An old man's voice, she thought. "Keep your shirt on, I'm coming . . ."

The door was opened by a man of medium height, in his late sixties or early seventies, with a full head of straight white hair cut very short, almost G.I. fashion. He was wearing khaki shorts and a short-sleeved white shirt. Niki stared at him, all her questions frozen in her chest.

He smiled encouragingly and finally she found her voice. "You're Ralph Sandeman, aren't you?"

"Guilty," he said, "but I have to warn you . . . I don't buy magazine subscriptions, and if you've come to save my soul, you'd best not waste your time."

"I . . . I'm not selling anything," she said, her voice quavering. "I . . . I think you . . . well, my name is Niki Sandeman . . ."

She waited for a sign of acceptance, but Ralph merely looked suspicious. "Sandeman?" he echoed. "Young lady, I only had a sister in Baltimore, and her two kids are—"

"Nicolette Sandeman," she said. "My grandmother was Monique Veraix."

"My God," he whispered as his face changed before her eyes. It was as if the years dropped away for a brief moment, and Niki could almost imagine the young man he had been. As he stared at her, the light of recognition burned brightly in his eyes, even joyously. Niki knew at that moment that he wouldn't deny her.

"Come inside," he said, his voice hoarse with emotion. As he led the way into a small living room that was filled with souvenirs—masses of photographs, weapons of previous wars, and a collection of medals and insignias—Niki could see that he limped badly, as if one leg were much shorter than the other.

Evidently taking time to adjust, he offered Niki coffee, then spent ten minutes alone in the kitchen making it. At last he brought Niki a cup of steaming, bitter coffee with milk and one for himself.

"Sandeman," he murmured, gazing at her. "You were given my name. . . ." The twin notes of shock and bewilderment rang in his voice.

"My mother was your child. She took the name when she came to America. And kept it . . . because she never married."

The bewilderment only seemed to grow. He shook his head, then stood up and walked around the edges of the room. Suddenly, Niki understood a part of the story she had never been told—that her own mother might not have known.

"But didn't you know," Niki asked, "that Monique gave birth to *your* child?" It was more than a question; it was a plea—for him to erase the heritage of rejection and abandonment.

"Of course I never knew!" Ralph Sandeman declared. "I loved your grandmother, Niki! God, how I loved her. She was so beautiful, so graceful, so full of life . . ." He stood by a window, looking out as if the past was part of the view.

"She was killed in the war," Niki cut in, wanting him to feel responsible. She went on with the bitter postscript to Monique's great love—the story of her shame, of her isolation in the small French village, of the desperate daring that had delivered her into the hands of the Gestapo. And though it had all happened a long time ago, Niki told it with passion—because it was a story that had been lived and relived, from one generation to the next.

When she was done, Ralph Sandeman was sobbing unashamedly, still looking out at the sun while tears coursed down his lined face. Niki believed it was true that he'd loved Monique, yet that knowledge didn't satisfy her. What good was the kind of love that left you wounded and crippled?

Finally, Ralph Sandeman walked back to his chair and sat down. Then, in a slow, halting voice, he began to tell his own story. "We were so in love and we were so young . . . we didn't imagine anything could happen. We lived as if we had all the tomorrows in the world. I thought covering the civil war in Spain would be a great adventure. And it was

. . . until I was wounded. I was in the hospital for over a year . . . in a coma for the first two months. After I started to recover, I just didn't imagine Monique would still be interested in me. I had no idea she was pregnant when I left. We'd had a magical few weeks together, but I figured she'd go back to France and marry someone from there. I guess I could have taken a disability pension and gone to find her again, but I had to go back to the war. The bad things that were happening in the world seemed more real and more important than the little bit of perfect time we'd shared. And I had to prove to myself that I wasn't afraid. I went to the South Pacific and I was wounded again." He gestured to his crippled leg. "I was shipped straight back to a hospital in the States. Later, everything else seemed so unreal, so far away. I went to work for the movie studios, taking publicity shots on location—nothing to compare with the 'real thing' . . ." He paused and studied Niki's face, as if searching for a resemblance. "How did you find me after all these years?" he asked.

"I was visiting . . . a relative in California. I went sightseeing and saw your pictures in a gallery here in Venice. That was it. . . ."

His face brightened. "I'm glad you saw the exhibition," he said shyly. "It's some of the best work I've ever done. The very best was that picture I took of your grandmother. It helps to remember I was that good once—especially lately. I've been working for advertising agencies, taking pictures of ice cubes floating in vodka, that kind of thing. I never did get married," he added, as though he felt that might please Niki.

He paused again and looked down, wringing his hands, evidently struggling to find the next words to ask. "You said you were visiting a relative," he said softly. "Your mother . . . is she with you? Because if she is . . . and she's willing, I'd like . . . if she'll understand . . ."

"My mother's dead, too," Niki said flatly, and saw the color drain from Ralph Sandeman's face. She didn't mean to be cruel now, except that the facts were cruel—and he had to take his share of responsibility. "She was murdered when I was very young."

"Who did it?"

For a second, Niki contemplated revealing all that she suspected. But it would open up so many other wounds. Ralph Sandeman seemed to be a decent man whose desertion of Monique Veraix had come not out of heartless malice, but out of the pitiless circumstances of war. "It's never been solved," she said.

Ralph Sandeman nodded slowly. His lips moved, but Niki heard no words come forth. Then he bowed his head and began to weep again, dry, racking sobs for the child he had never known and never would.

At last he regained control and looked up at her. "You've had a terrible time, haven't you?"

"I've managed," Niki said. Whatever she wanted from him, it was not pity.

He smiled through his tears. "You've got her spirit . . . she was like that . . . Monique was a fighter. Tell me more about you," Ralph urged. "Where you live . . . where you go to school. . . ."

She told him she was at Barnard in New York.

"Transfer," he said abruptly. "Come to UCLA. You're alone, aren't you? So am I. That would give us a chance to get acquainted . . ."

"It's an idea," Niki said only to be polite.

Ralph caught her tone. He took a breath. "I know," he said. "I don't really deserve to know you, do I, Niki? You've got my name, my blood, but things went wrong somehow way back when. . . . History came along like a runaway train, and some of us who were standing in the way got caught by surprise. Pieces of life—loves we would have liked to have kept, children we wanted to know—they got . . . cut off. But Niki, I swear I'll. . . ." Once more, he was overcome with emotion.

This time she was moved. She walked to his chair and

knelt in front of him. "I'm glad I could meet you . . . glad to know you're the kind of man you are. But I don't know if it can change anything, Ralph. . . ."

He looked at her and mustered a smile. "For me it already has, Niki. I hope you can forgive me, so that I can . . . be a family for you."

"There's nothing to forgive," she said. She believed that he had never known Monique Veraix was left with his child. But hearing his request to become a part of her life only made her more conscious of the fact that they were strangers, perhaps even less real to one another than she and Pepper. Ironically, though she had come fearing Ralph Sandeman's rejection, she was now uncertain whether to accept the complication of keeping him in her life.

"I have to go now," she said. "I'm . . . meeting someone."

He was gracious about her sudden departure.

"Can I write to you at Barnard?" he asked as he took her to the door.

"Yes, of course. Maybe we can arrange to . . ." she shrugged.

He understood. "Maybe. . . ."

As he stood holding the door for her, she saw the look of anticipation in his eyes. Yielding to his unspoken wish, she leaned forward and kissed him gently as she said good-bye.

Niki turned back once as she walked away, and saw him standing at the window of his living room. She wasn't sure if she would ever come back or what she would do about this grandfather who had suddenly become a person instead of a legend. Though Niki was glad he had really cared for her grandmother, what difference did it make now to Monique? Or to Elle, who had once told Niki she'd dreamed long and hard of finding him?

It had happened too late.

When she returned to the house, preparations for a large party were in full swing—Pepper's way of celebrating

Thanksgiving eve, apparently. A tent had been set up at one end of the patio, caterers were arriving with food, flowers were being delivered and arranged.

In the middle of it all, busy supervising, stood Pepper. She took no notice of Niki's thoughtful mood, but simply announced that the festivities would begin at eight, and Niki should make a point of looking her best.

Niki went to her room, pulled the curtains across the glass doors, and stayed there in the gloom, still trying to digest the discoveries of the day, her mind running endlessly through fantasies of all that would have been different if Ralph Sandeman had not gone to photograph the Spanish Civil War . . . had come back to Monique . . . had known about the daughter he conceived.

The hours passed like minutes, and then she heard the music of a small orchestra drifting into her room. She peeked around the edge of the curtain and saw guests starting to arrive. Strangers, she thought—she was surrounded by strangers. Was Pepper really family . . . or even Ralph? She thought of fleeing, returning to Helen.

But it was Helen who said she must come. . . .

Twenty minutes later Niki appeared at the poolside wearing the swirling, white pleated chiffon dress that Pepper had bought for her yesterday.

Pepper saw her and winked, but kept talking to a tall, sleekly tanned man who looked familiar. Though Niki couldn't connect the face with a name, she thought he was the movie actor who had once been linked to one of Lyndon Johnson's daughters.

Left on her own, Niki accepted an invitation to dance from a good-looking man who said he was an actor and model. He asked Niki a lot of questions, and then she realized he wanted to know how she was related to Pepper and what branch of the Hyland family tree she sprang from. When she said "I'm just a poor relation," he excused himself to get a drink and didn't return.

She wasn't having a great time, but Niki dutifully pretended she was, nibbling hors d'oeuvres from a buffet, taking an occasional glass of champagne from the tray of a passing waiter, moving among the guests and smiling at anyone who talked to her. She was beginning to think of going to her room and trying to shut out the noise, when she heard a shout and then a loud splash from the swimming pool. By the time she turned around, the first splash had been followed by several others, and she saw that several guests were in the pool, fully clothed. Then one of the women pulled off her dress to the accompaniment of approving shouts and applause. Not to be outdone, her escort took off all his clothes, and soon the pool was filled with naked people.

Niki had had enough. She looked around for Pepper, wanting to say good night before she retired, but couldn't find her. She went inside and along the corridor toward the wing where Pepper slept. Nearing the door of Pepper's room, Niki heard voices—angry and quarrelsome. A moment later, the door opened, and Pepper came tearing out, so angry that she didn't notice Niki as she stormed past.

Just as she was about to retreat to her own room, Niki heard a stream of curses, the shattering of glass, and then, the sound of crying. She peeked inside Pepper's bedroom and saw Terry, face down on the bed, her fists pounding the mattress. Niki stepped inside the room. "Is something wrong?" she asked, feeling shy about intruding, yet wanting to help if Terry and Pepper had been fighting.

Terry sat up. She smiled when she saw Niki and patted a spot beside her.

As Niki took the invitation to sit, she noticed the overpowering smell of liquor that surrounded Terry. "What were you and Pepper arguing about?" she asked.

"Nothing much. Pepper can just be a real bitch sometimes, especially when she's around her V-list friends." Terry was slurring her words, and when Niki looked closely and saw the ring of white powder around her nostrils, she realized that the movie star was suffering the effects of more than alcohol.

"V-List?" Niki said.

"Yeah," Terry replied with a childlike leer. "Her vice list . . . the types she can't have around when her society friends are here. If you ask me, Pepper likes those lowlifes a lot better than she'd like to admit. She forgets her *real* friends . . ."

"I'm sure she didn't mean to do that," Niki said, seeing what looked like real hurt on Terry's face. "Don't you think you can straighten things out tomorrow?"

"Don't know if I want to," Terry said. Her hand closed over Niki's. "But you're awfully sweet to care. Pepper told me you were special," she said softly, stroking Niki's arm now.

Niki smiled. "You're special, too. And maybe you ought to try to get some rest now . . ."

Terry's hand moved upward, stealing past Niki's shoulder, dropping suddenly to her breast. Niki tried to shift, to dislodge the hand without causing a fuss. Terry must be so drunk she didn't realize what she was doing; there was no need to embarrass her.

"Relax," Terry crooned, her hand more insistent now. "Just relax and let ol' Terry make you feel good. I know how to do it, too, just ask big sister Pepper if you don't believe me."

And then, to Niki's horror, Terry's mouth was on hers, her tongue probing as her hands wandered downward, pushing their way past her dress, searching for the soft pink flesh hidden by her underclothes.

Niki struggled. But drunk or sober, Terry was stronger than she looked—and Niki's writhing movements only seemed to excite her. "You like me, baby," she murmured, "I can tell you really do. . . ."

Feeling as if she was about to throw up, Niki gave a desperate shove that sent Terry sprawling against the headboard. "Hey!" she complained, "what's the big idea?"

"I'm sorry," Niki said, "really. But I'm not . . . I'm not like that."

"Like what?" Terry asked, her beautiful face sullen and angry.

Niki flushed with embarrassment. "I mean, I don't do . . . those things . . ."

Terry's eyes narrowed. "Who do you think you are to turn *me* down?" she spat out, her face wrought with rage. "You've got some nerve putting on airs and acting like you're so all-fired righteous. I know all about you, Niki-baby! Pepper told me, gave me a good laugh. How your mother was a real whore, selling herself for Hyland money! So what makes you think you're any better? Why the hell do you think Pepper brought you here, anyway? 'Cause she can't wait to make things up with you . . . ?" Terry erupted in an ugly, raucous laugh. "She told me all about it. She's just looking for some handle to get back at her brother. Thinks it might just piss him to high heaven if she makes friends with you. What else did you think? That she's so nice and sweet and she wants to adopt you?"

Niki fled the room, her ears ringing with Terry's ugly revelations, and her cruel taunting words. Desperate to escape unseen and unnoticed, she ran to the guest room she'd occupied, tore off the dress she was wearing, dressed in her old clothes and stuffed only the things she'd brought with her into her suitcase. She telephoned a taxi and asked it to stop outside the security gate, grateful she hadn't spent all her monthly allowance, glad to be able to pay her way out of this place.

Though she told the dispatcher it was an emergency, the cab seemed to take forever. Niki sat in the chill darkness of a California November night, shivering in spite of her jacket—and hoping none of Pepper's V-list friends would come out and see her.

When the taxi finally arrived, she hurled herself into the back seat, bag and baggage, and told the driver to "step on it."

Niki spent eight hours in the airport terminal before she

could get a flight, but she scarcely noticed the discomfort, so eager was she to leave California. All through the night, she brooded, her sense of betrayal reviving old angers and hurts. The Hylands had treated her mother like dirt, and now, after pretending to care, Pepper had managed to make her feel like dirt. She swore to herself that she'd remember this night, so that she would never, ever forget what the Hylands were like—and never allow them to fool her again.

Fourteen

WITH the coming of the new year, Niki sank back gratefully into her studies. It was pleasant to have predictability in her life—a set schedule of classes, the steady demands of learning facts from books, the system of grades, rewards for doing well on her examinations. There was a kind of security in such absolutes, and so little else in her life had ever seemed built on solid ground.

With the passing of time, Niki found it easy to put Pepper Hyland out of her mind. No communication came from California, no call to find out the reason for Niki's abrupt departure, no letter of apology or explanation. Pepper evidently shared a willingness to write off their few days together as a failed experiment.

It was very different with Ralph Sandeman. He began to correspond regularly, short handwritten letters without any terribly significant content. He told her about the work he was doing, the few sales he'd had as a result of his exhibition, the small events of his days—"planted a new azalea bush out front and the neighbor's dog dug it right up.'' His letters struck Niki as exactly the kind she would have received from a grandfather who had always been part of her life. No doubt, he had chosen to give them that quality. Niki responded to it, sending back a short newsy note of her own every three or four weeks.

About ten days before the Easter holiday, Niki received a postcard from Blake inviting her to visit Paris, all expenses paid. ''Wine . . . delicious food . . . gorgeous guys . . . and the most romantic city in the world,'' Blake tempted Niki in her customary telegraphese. ''P.S. Are you still a virgin?''

Even in her room, with no one watching, Niki blushed. And she realized then that, even if she could obtain a passport in time, she wouldn't make the trip. It was all too obvious that the focus of her time in Paris would be getting paired off with some attractive Frenchman whom Blake had selected to provide a sexual adventure. There was no doubt that Blake was very active sexually—at Blue Mountain after every school vacation she would regale Niki with tales of her latest exploits, including the friends of her father's whose propositions she sometimes accepted—and she was always telling Niki it was past time, as Blake put it, ''to let the walls of Jericho come a-tumbling down.'' Niki didn't want to be under that kind of pressure, even though there was ample opportunity, since Barnard was the women's college of Columbia University. In fact, she had worked hard enough at avoiding entanglements at school with any of the numerous men who were always asking her out—whether they were moderately acquainted from sharing a class with her, or had simply spotted her walking across the campus and been swept away by her stunning beauty. She knew all too well the result of romance. The lives of both her mother and grandmother had been destroyed by it.

Yet even Helen had begun suggesting that it wasn't completely reasonable for a beautiful young woman to isolate herself so much from contact with the opposite gender. The subject had come up prominently during Christmas vacation in a conversation that had revolved, at first, around Alexei Ivanov. By now, Dmitri's son had achieved almost legendary status, but no longer because he was suspected to be non-existent. For he had finally put in his long-awaited appearance—on the one Thanksgiving at Helen's when Niki was absent in California.

According to Helen, Alexei Ivanov was everything that his proud father had boasted. From the time she reported that Dmitri's son had materialized to eat her turkey dinner, Helen did not stop singing Alexei's praises. "An absolutely charming young man . . . so handsome . . . those Cossack eyes and a devastating smile . . . such a nice sense of humor . . . and well brought up. Imagine, he wants to be a doctor, too! I must ask Dmitri if he can come and visit us over your next holiday. . . ."

At Christmas, Niki had traveled back to Blue Mountain feeling a mixture of curiosity and discomfort at the prospect of being thrust into the company of the famous and adored Alexei.

But at the Christmas Eve gathering of the usual group of Helen's friends, neither Dmitri nor his son appeared. It dawned on Niki, after seeing the way Gertie moped during the evening, that Dmitri had probably been her lover, after all. This was confirmed later when the guests had gone and Helen and Niki were having tea together from a tray on her bed, just as they had in the old days when their relationship was student and housemother.

Helen remarked that Dmitri had stayed away because he had given up Gertie for someone new. "I told him to come anyway, because I was so anxious for you to meet Alexei. But Dmitri said he was too busy directing a show for off-Broadway in New York and Alexei has other plans, too. It's true that Dmitri is beginning to do well as a director . . . but I'm sure the real reason he's not here is that he couldn't face Gertusz. It's a shame. . . ."

"A shame she ever loved him," Niki said.

Helen gave Niki a sharp glance before saying softly, "No,

I meant a shame you didn't get to meet Alexei—and perhaps, now, never will."

"I don't think of it as a loss. What can he be like—the son of such a father? Dmitri is charming, too, but obviously an unreliable man, bound to make a woman unhappy. The way he defected—just went off, leaving his family behind. . . ."

"His family got out of Russia eventually. You might not judge him so harshly if you were a passionate artist who lived in tyranny, and had to make a sudden choice of one passion over the other—your heart . . . or your art."

"Why are you defending him, Helen? Even his own son found it hard to forgive."

"But not impossible. In the end he did forgive him." Helen pushed the tea tray between them to one side so she could move closer to Niki. "My dear, you talk as if you think all women must be abandoned in the end by the men they love. I know what happened in your own family made a wound in your spirit that's hard to heal. But the only cure will lie in opening your heart—letting yourself be loved, so that you discover how good it can be, that there are men who will *not* leave. Loves like the one I had. . . ."

"You ended up alone, too," Niki observed.

Helen smiled. "Is that what you think? That Georgi left me?" She shook her head, then tapped her breast. "He's still with me . . . in here. That's what love can be."

"Well," Niki grumbled, "you were the one who used to tell Dmitri not to go on yammering at me about making babies with his son. Are you changing your tune?"

Helen laughed lightly and gave Niki a hug. "Darling girl, I want you to live your own life however you wish. I'm not trying to get you married off. I just . . . don't want you to be afraid of any part of living, any experience that can give you joy or pleasure."

"I won't have an experience like that with Alexei Ivanov," Niki said breaking away. "So stop talking about him."

But when Niki arrived at Blue Mountain to spend Easter with Helen, the first words that Helen said after greeting her were, "Guess what?"

The twinkle in Helen's eye—and the fact that holidays traditionally meant gatherings of her friends—made the guessing easy. "The Ivanovs are coming," Niki said.

Helen nodded, and Niki found herself wishing she had chosen Paris with Blake.

"Easter is such an important holiday for the Russians. I wanted to make it special for them. And Gertie is through moping over Dmitri."

Niki sighed, and settled for extracting a promise from Helen that she would allow any friendship to develop naturally, and not play the part of "mother hen," herding the young people together.

"When you meet him," Helen said, "I don't think any extra encouragement from me will be necessary."

On Easter Sunday, Helen prepared a meal that was more from Russian cuisine than Hungarian—hot borscht, chicken Kiev, and dumplings filled with meat and potato. It was plainly done to curry favor with the Ivanovs.

Yet half an hour after all the Hungarians in Helen's circle were gathered and waiting to sit down to lunch in the dining room of Vale House, the Ivanovs had still not arrived.

"Aha—what did I tell you," Lotchy said. "Dmitri Ivanov is actually a Russian spy and this is another K.G.B. torture. He tricks you into cooking all these tempting things . . . and then leaves us here smelling their irresistible aromas, but unable to eat."

"We won't wait any longer," Helen said at last.

They had just sat down to dinner when Dmitri barged alone through the unlocked front door and charged into the dining room. "A thousand pardons to all," he bellowed theatrically, "but I was delayed by the totalitarian procedures of this imperialist police state. . . ."

The crowd around the table stared curiously at Dmitri, who was suddenly talking as if he had readopted the communist party line.

"Listen to the ingrate!" Gertie said. "America takes him in . . . and then he calls it a police state."

"He meant the state police," said a fresh voice coming from behind Dmitri. "They detained us to serve me with a speeding summons on the way here. . . ."

Niki couldn't help staring at the young man who entered the dining room. He was indeed extraordinarily handsome. Like his father, Alexei Ivanov was tall and had the same sculpted face, the same pale taut skin; but where it made Dmitri seem slightly too gaunt, on the much younger man it gave him an exquisite ascetic air. His silky black hair fell rakishly across his forehead, and he had flashing black eyes—Cossack eyes, as Helen had said. He was wearing dark-gray slacks and a black turtleneck that accentuated his long neck and straight aristocratic bearing, yet he was saved from looking severe by the brightness of the smile he showed everyone in greeting, and the humorous glint in his eye.

"I apologize most humbly for keeping you all waiting," he said, though by now he had turned to Niki, and his eyes rested on hers, and it seemed he was talking to no one but her. "Of course you are responsible. I was racing to get here—going far too fast—rather than lose a moment of the chance to be together."

The room had gone quiet. Everyone was looking at Niki and Alexei as they looked at each other.

Helen broke the silence. "Niki, this is Alexei. . . ."

The absurdity of the formality brought laughter from the others.

"And who else would she think it is?" Dmitri said as he took one of the two vacant seats. "The king of France?"

They were still looking at each other. "How do you do," Niki murmured.

He smiled back and took the other seat, which was at the far end of the table away from her.

The rest of the meal was the usual turbulent gale of rowdy repartee and political argument. But Niki wasn't aware of a thing that was said. When she wasn't staring into her plate, avoiding the open gaze and charming smiles that came her way from Alexei, she was trying furtively to look at him without being seen. She observed that Alexei participated actively in the conversation, that his words often created laughter, but she couldn't concentrate enough to listen.

After the dessert of *palaczinta* flamed with apricot brandy, everyone got up from the table to move into the living room for after-dinner drinks. Niki started to clear the table.

"Leave that," Helen said. "It's such a beautiful day. Why don't you show Alexei around the school. It was raining when he came on Thanksgiving and he didn't get to see it. . . ."

Niki sent a hot glance Helen's way. Wanting an opportunity to be alone with Alexei only made her more annoyed at Helen for departing from the pledge of neutrality. To Alexei, Niki said, "You don't really have any interest in seeing the school, do you?"

"Not the slightest," he replied with a lilt. "But there is nothing I'd like so much as to take a walk with you."

No spring day at Blue Mountain had ever seemed quite so lovely to Niki as this one. Had she been unhappy in this place once? She couldn't remember. Possessed by a feeling of well-being, she walked quietly beside Alexei Ivanov along the pathways between the ivy-covered brick buildings. She was full of questions—yet oddly certain that there was no rush to ask any of them, they would all be answered eventually.

He spoke first. "Helen told me that you're taking premed courses. I'm already an intern."

"I know."

"Helen told me, too, how you came here . . . how she regards you as a daughter. . . ."

Niki looked at him and saw sympathy in his expression. She supposed he was telling her right up front that he knew all the details of her background.

"I've heard you had a difficult time, too," she said. "The way your father left you behind when he defected. . . ."

He smiled. "So . . . are we to have no surprises about each other? Have we each been told so much . . . ?" The question was asked lightly, and she smiled back. But then he stopped walking to look deeply into her eyes. He touched her cheek fleetingly with his fingers. "Niki. It seems I've known you for such a long time. . . ."

It frightened Niki to think of saying the words that came at once into her mind, but she could not hold them back. "I feel the same. . . ." Then, as if to belittle the depth of feeling behind the admission, she added, "Of course, you became a legend here. Your father was always talking about you. When you didn't come, year after year, we began to wonder if you really existed."

He put his hands lightly on her arms. "Now you see," he said quietly. "Do I exist?"

The way he asked seemed to demand an answer. "You exist," she replied, able to summon no more than a whisper.

They kept looking at each other for another second.

Suddenly, the current of fear in Niki intensified. This was how it began, she realized . . . it must have been the same for Monique, for Elle, for every woman who ever gave her heart too quickly.

She turned from Alexei and continued walking, more briskly, not meandering.

He didn't seem put off by her change of pace. He stayed alongside as he said, "What made you think of becoming a doctor?"

"Why do you ask?" Her defenses were up now.

Alexei shrugged. "I ask everyone who chooses the profession. I suppose it's because I think being a doctor is a very odd thing to do—even though I want to do it myself. Some doctors, I have discovered, don't have an answer."

Did she have one? Niki wondered suddenly. Only one, and she told him. "I know it will make Helen happy—give her some sense of reviving her own dream. And there's nothing else I'd rather do. . . ."

He eyed her with concern. "Is that your reason? To make someone else happy?"

"There's no one who means more to me than—"

"But Niki—what about making yourself happy?"

"Of course. That's part of it. . . ." His probing made her uncomfortable. She turned it back at him. "What's your reason?"

"The thing I like about medicine," he answered easily, "is that it doesn't have any boundaries, its language is the same all over the world. It's like belonging to a very big family, a family dedicated to healing. I need those things . . . because once I was kept behind boundaries, and being kept there broke my other family apart."

Niki glanced at Alexei. Until now, she had thought of the burdens of her background as being unique, and certainly greater than those of anyone who'd been born with united parents. But listening to Alexei, she realized that the burdens of his past were as heavy as hers. With that revelation, she felt instantly less alone than she ever had before.

He broke into her thoughtful silence. "You're at Barnard College, aren't you?"

"Yes. And you are at NYU Medical Center."

He laughed. "Perhaps we should simply have Helen and my father prepare our dossiers. We will exchange them, and check off what we already know about each other. Then we can start to learn all the things we don't know." He took her hand in his. "Which are, of course, all the most interesting things."

The palm of her hand felt as if it were burning. A wonderful terrible sensation. Niki stopped and looked at him, then yanked her hand away. "Alexei, I . . . I think we should go back. . . ."

He paused to look at her closely like a doctor making a difficult diagnosis, and Niki could imagine from the sympathetic cast of his eyes that he would be excellent at the profession he had chosen, a natural.

He nodded, clearly recognizing her panic. "Of course."

They turned around. "Niki," he said when they were half-way back to Vale House, "I would like very much to see you again in New York. Please do not refuse me."

She looked down as she said, "I'm not sure. . . ."

"Because you are frightened by your feelings," he said. "Am I correct?"

"Alexei . . . the things that have happened to women in my family—"

"I understand," he put in earnestly. "But you can trust me. I would never hurt you. I swear."

She gazed back at him. His oath seemed as solid and real as he did. "Please call me," she said. "My dorm is Centennial Hall."

The gathering had moved to Helen's private rooms. Helen smiled as the young people entered the room. Niki went shyly to sit at one side of the room, Alexei to the other. They smiled at each other once or twice, but did not talk privately again before Alexei said it was a long drive back to New York, and persuaded Dmitri it was time to leave.

When they were finally alone together, cleaning up the kitchen, Helen said, "So you see . . . it can be a good feeling to meet a young man you like. . . ."

"I hate it," Niki said, and stopped drying a handful of silverware. "I've been standing here thinking about him—as if there's nothing else to think about. I have an actual crush! Like a stupid little schoolgirl. And I don't want to . . . to be possessed like that. I don't want to lose control . . . lose *myself*."

Helen smiled. "You won't, Niki. You'll just find a new part of yourself."

"I hate this feeling," Niki said again, and dumped the silver into a drawer.

Helen passed another handful from the sink. "Then perhaps

you shouldn't see Alexei Ivanov at all. Not ever again. I will explain to Dmitri that—"

"Don't you dare!" Niki erupted with genuine fury.

Helen shook her head and began to laugh, and at once Niki's anger dissipated and she was laughing, too.

"I hate it," Niki repeated. "I can't stand it." But she was laughing all the time, and she didn't know how she would manage to survive until the next time she was with Alexei, filled with the unbearable, incomparable feeling of being touched by him.

Fifteen

A BLOODCURDLING shriek ruptured the silence. Then another, followed by the sound of weeping.

Niki held her breath. Except for a couple of experimental college productions, she hadn't taken time to go to the theater. She had little basis for comparing the off-Broadway production of *Medea* directed by Dmitri Ivanov with anything more grand and full-blown. Here the theater was small, the sets consisted of merely a few scattered columns made of painted cardboard, many of the actors were young—even those playing the parts of old men or women—appearing for the first time on a stage in New York. Yet it was enough to hold Niki in a spell, capture her mind and pull her back to ancient Greece, where a princess enraged by losing the love of her warrior husband was being driven to seek the most terrible revenge.

"Ah wretch! Ah lost in my sufferings!" came a woman's lament from offstage. "I wish I might die."

A gray-haired nurse leading two small boys scurried across

the stage. "Run quickly, dear children," she said in an urgent hush. "And keep well out of sight. Your mother frets her heart to anger. Be careful of the wildness and bitter nature of that proud mind. . . ."

When the final curtain fell on the remorseless Medea, who had broken her faithless husband by murdering not only her rival in love but her own two children, Niki sat stunned by the power of the play.

Alexei gave her a nudge. "For heaven's sake, Niki," he whispered in the dark, "clap . . . or you shall be forced to answer to my father. He's back there right now, peeking through the curtain and planning his own revenge on those who do not applaud his genius."

Niki laughed and joined in the applause. As the houselights went up Alexei took her hand, and they went backstage to pay their respects to the director.

This was their fourth date in the three weeks since they had met. He had called right away, but Niki had put him off until the next weekend, pleading the necessity to study for a couple of exams. She was still warring within herself. On the one hand, she was eager to see him. On the other, she was apprehensive, aware that the more they saw each other, the more certainty there had to be that he would expect more than handholding . . . then more than a kiss.

On their previous dates, they had eaten together at inexpensive restaurants on upper Broadway, near Barnard, had seen a movie together . . . and had studied together. But each time, Niki had declined with feigned regret when Alexei spoke of bringing her back to the apartment near Washington Square. It had been easy enough to make excuses when going to his apartment meant riding all the way downtown.

But when she had accepted Alexei's invitation to see his father's production, she hadn't looked ahead to realize that it was playing at an off-Broadway theater very near where Alexei lived. If he made the suggestion of going to his apartment, she would only be able to refuse by frankly admitting that, no matter how attracted she was, she would never take the slightest risk of putting herself in a position to be seduced. She wondered if that would be the end of his interest.

The theater's backstage area was a warren of tiny dressing rooms along a narrow corridor. Squeezing past other well-wishers and actors with their makeup half removed, Alexei led Niki to a door marked IVANOV. He tapped lightly and walked in.

Dmitri was sitting in a chair staring into a three-paneled mirror illuminated by a strip of light bulbs. In a stream of excited Russian, he was lecturing his own reflection in the mirror, but stopped abruptly when he saw his son enter.

"Niki just wanted to tell you how much she enjoyed the play," Alexei said, prodding her forward.

Dmitri shook his shaggy gray mane. "It was not a superior performance," he said sadly. "I have just been reproaching myself. It's a director's duty to notice when his actors are getting stale and tired."

"But I liked it very much," Niki said. "It didn't seem stale to me at all."

Dmitri sighed. "You liked it?" Then he leaned forward, his voice harsher. "But did it make you think you must leap to the stage and defend those two innocent children. Did it raise your passions . . . ?"

Even if Niki could have found an answer, Dmitri was evidently uninterested in hearing it. He had swiveled back to the mirror to fix his reflection in a baleful stare. "No, it did not move the audience enough. You failed, Ivanov. You are accused of committing serious crimes against the theater, perpetrating the deadly sins of carelessness, indifference, pride, sloth. . . ." And then he was back into Russian again, shaking his finger at himself as the lecture went on.

Leaning over between Dmitri and the reflected image, Alexei interrupted the tirade to wish his father good-bye. "I'll see you when you return." To Niki, Alexei explained that Dmitri had been honored with an invitation to go to a repertory company in the Midwest and direct a production of Chekhov's *The Sea Gull*. "His reputation is spreading, you see."

"Hah!" Dmitri said mockingly. "Where I'm going they probably think *The Sea Gull* is a sweet little play for children, and I'm the only one they could get to do it."

"Father. You are an artist, don't run yourself down."

"After what I allowed on a stage tonight, am I an artist? I should be shot." And he was off again into shouting at his image in the mirror. "You should be exiled to Siberia . . . !" On it went.

Alexei put a finger to his lips and pulled Niki out of the room. She hesitated but a moment, afraid to be rude, yet Dmitri did seem to be thoroughly absorbed in remonstrating with himself.

"Does he do that often?" she asked as they went down the corridor.

"Talk to himself? All the time," Alexei laughed. "My father usually prefers his own company—and his own criticism—to anyone else's. He's the only theater person I know who really and truly doesn't give a damn what critics say about him." They stepped through an exit door into an alleyway. "Maybe they know it, too—because they rarely say bad things. The worst he's been called is 'eccentric' or 'volatile' . . . and he'd be the first to agree with those opinions."

"It must be wonderful to care so much about something," Niki remarked wistfully. They were strolling slowly along one of the streets in Greenwich Village, the night mild and clear.

Alexei thought for a moment. "I don't think it has to do with caring," he said. "When Dmitri starts a new play, it's more like . . . an obsession, really. It's all he eats, drinks, and sleeps. Nothing can save him from it—except another play. Why do you think he left Russia? Because they wouldn't let him direct exactly as he wanted. I think his devotion can be . . . a kind of curse—like the obsession Medea had to destroy Jason, even if it meant killing her own children. The love my father has for the theater will destroy him someday. As it destroyed my family. . . ."

"Still," she insisted, "to be so completely involved, so passionate." Her yearning and admiration came through.

"Have you never felt passionate about anything, Niki?"

"One thing, perhaps. I wanted very much to dive," she said. "To be as good as my grandmother."

"Then why didn't you?"

As much as she had enjoyed being with Alexei, Niki had done nothing that would move her from safe ground—had trusted him with no secrets, expected no emotional investment. But she took a first step toward intimacy now by sharing with him the full story of why she had stopped diving.

At the end of it, his arm was around her and he was holding her close to him as they walked. "If I had been in your life then," he said, "it wouldn't have happened. I would have done anything to keep you from being hurt, from losing anything you cared about. . . ."

Looking at Alexei, she believed him. The shared pain she saw in his expression seemed so great that all she wanted to do was soothe *his* disappointment. "It doesn't really matter," she said. "Looking back, I can see that there really wasn't a chance for me to make the grade as a diver."

"You can't be sure now. You'll never know." Then, obviously determined to cheer her, his tone brightened. "But now let me share one of my passions with you." When he saw her hesitate, Alexei added, "I promise it's not too sinful."

He guided them eastward, and after walking briskly for several blocks they reached a neighborhood that had been settled at the turn of the century by immigrants from the Ukraine. There were still a number of small storefront cafes that served Russian food, and Alexei steered Niki into one that seemed to be the smallest and least pretentious.

An old woman with hair dyed a flaming red rushed forward and greeted Alexei, smothering him with hugs and kisses and chattering rapidly in Russian. When Alexei could extricate himself from her arms, he introduced her to Niki as Madame Komorevski, the proprietor.

They were ushered by the Madame to a table in a tiny private alcove lit by a single candle. In the background, a recording of balalaika music played softly. Soon a procession of dishes began to arrive at the table—blinis with caviar, tiny dumplings filled with ground meat and spices called *pelmeni*, and shashlik. A small carafe of vodka was brought, too, encased in a block of ice that kept it so cold that it was the consistency of syrup.

As good a cook as Helen was, the Russian dishes she had made never tasted nearly as good to Niki as these.

"My father brought me here," Alexei said, "soon after I began speaking to him again. Until then, I had stayed with my mother. She lives in Hartford, Connecticut, and supports herself writing Russian translations for publishers—and she still refuses to forgive Dmitri. But I could not stay angry. I never felt he rejected me as much as he simply followed his passion for theater. And I knew for sure how much we had in common when he brought me to Madame K's little bistro. For food is a passion of mine, Niki, and this is the best of its kind anywhere outside of Russia. Madame K's grandmother worked in the czar's kitchen. As she tells it, the recipes were handed down to her mother and then to her."

The mention of such family legacies made Niki thoughtful, sparking memories of cooking with her own mother—memories that seemed to be fading like ancient photographs. Once, she had felt that all the love had faded from her life along with those memories. But with Alexei beside her she was beginning to feel that wasn't true.

For the first time, she was the one to reach out, make the move to take his hand in hers. His black eyes, shining in the candlelight, told her that he knew she was letting him cross a boundary that had been closed until now.

There were pastries, and then strong black coffee, and then *slivovitz*, a strong plum brandy that made Niki feel that her insides were glowing.

"You liked it here?" Alexei asked when all the dishes were cleaned, the glasses and cups emptied.

"It's the best meal I'll ever have," she said.

"No, Niki, we'll have many more. We'll share this passion of mine."

He paid the bill and, after another exuberant exchange of Russian with Madame Komorevski, they left. Niki leaned on Alexei, just the slightest bit unsteady, so that she felt she was gliding more than walking.

A taxi came by, and Alexei hailed it. When they were inside he told the driver to take them uptown to Barnard College.

"No," she said. "I want to stay with you." He glanced at her uncertainly, and she smiled. "To share more of your passion," she added.

Alexei's apartment consisted of a single room in a three-story walk-up on a short street near Washington Square called Minetta Lane. He turned on a single small lamp as they entered, and she stood by the door taking it in. At the center was a large desk that served for dining as well as studying, a double bed with a massive wood frame was against a wall. Two old-fashioned deck chairs, the sort that might have sailed on a vanished ocean liner, were covered with blankets and placed in opposite corners. Covering the floor was a Persian rug that seemed to be of excellent quality, the colors of the weaving still vivid though it was worn through in places. Like Alexei, his room managed with only a few touches to convey a distinctive style. Niki found it easy to feel at home.

"Can I give you a drink?" he said. "I put champagne in my refrigerator just for us. . . ."

"You knew I'd come tonight?"

He smiled and came to her. "I hoped you'd come *someday*. I put that bottle in there four weeks ago—the day after we met. A prayer, you see, a kind of offering to the gods. . . ."

She smiled back, and their arms went around each other. "Do you mind if I don't have any? I've had so much vodka . . . and brandy."

"Why should I mind? My prayer has already been answered."

He lowered his mouth to hers, and their lips met in a flurry of quick eager kisses. He whispered her name as his hands moved over her body and loosened her blouse and skirt. She closed her eyes, drinking in only what she could feel. His hands caressing her skin so gently. His kisses, the warmth of his mouth moving along her neck to her shoulders. He had opened her blouse and bra, and her bare flesh tingled from the touch of his fingers. She gasped as she felt the moist warmth of his mouth close over her nipples, and then a long, deep sigh escaped. A sigh of surrender. And freedom, dizzying exultant freedom, as she felt herself released from the prison of fears that had kept her unloved.

She was lifted in his arms, and then they were on the bed. As he finished undressing her, slowly and tenderly, she looked up to see his handsome face floating over her, his dark eyes glittering with passion. "You are beautiful," she said.

He laughed lightly. "And you are stealing my lines, Nikuschka."

She reached up and drew him close again, and now his nakedness lay against hers. The tingling of her flesh became like fingers of painless flame licking at her body. His lips, his hands were everywhere, exploring and probing, uncovering sensations she didn't know existed. He raised himself up for a moment and looked at her, his eyes scanning along her length, and though she had never been seen naked by a man before she was not ashamed or embarrassed. She looked at him, too, and it felt perfectly natural to touch him everywhere, to feel his hard throbbing penis in her hand. Then she pulled him close again.

When he entered her, she moaned as the heat rippled from her very center, ravaging thought, leaving only feeling. The moment of pain as he entered her seemed oddly like part of a ceremony, a sacrament that bonded them, and as it faded Niki felt herself rising up on a wave of thrills that lifted her higher and higher. Clinging to him, her hands pressing against his strong back as he rose and fell inside her, she felt herself arriving at the brink of completion—and hovered there, vaguely conscious that it was something like standing at the edge of the board, waiting for the perfect moment of balance . . . and then she was flying, but not alone now, she was soaring and spinning and diving with him, until gravity pulled her down. But not into the cold reality of a pool. This time she ended surrounded by warmth and light, secure in his arms.

It was all so natural. In a while, she wanted him again, and they made love again more slowly, and took time to look at each other. At one point, she felt thirsty and left the bed to go to the sink in a corner—his "kitchen." As she walked back to him, his eyes followed her.

"Show me a dive," he said. "I want to see how you looked then. . . ."

She shook her head, laughing, and climbed back on the bed.

"Please," he said. "Show me."

So she stood on her toes on the springy surface of the bed as though it was the board, and she balanced over him. Then just before she might have sprung, he reached up and seized her hips, and kissed her thighs and put his mouth between her legs.

As she came, she heard herself calling his name. And when she lay down again, he said, "I love you, Niki."

At last they slept.

She woke with sunlight on her face, and when she looked around the room it seemed like a strange place. Then she saw Alexei asleep beside her . . . and the memories of the dark hours flooded back.

Yet she felt none of the warmth and certainty that had made it so easy to be with him. She could only think that there must have been nights like this for Monique, for Elle . . . passion, soon followed by loneliness and desperation. She was horrified by what she had allowed him to do.

His promise of love—did that make any difference? All women who had ever fallen, she was sure, had been won with words, given promises. Asleep, with the light of the sun on his face, beautiful Alexei looked so content . . . but Niki saw it as the smug satisfaction of conquest.

She slipped out of bed and hurried around the room, gathering up her scattered clothes.

"Niki . . . where are you going . . . ?"

She didn't stop at the sound of his voice. "I . . . I have a class. . . ."

"It's Saturday."

"A special seminar," she lied.

He got out of bed. As she dressed, she averted her eyes from his nakedness. He saw her embarrassment and grabbed a pair of pants. "Why?" he pleaded. "Niki, it was wonderful. Don't—"

"I was stupid to come here," she said, hasty fingers fumbling with the buttons of her blouse. "This is how my mother's life was ruined . . . my grandmother's. Being fooled by feelings, giving up the rest of their lives for a few moments of—"

He grabbed her and pulled her around, forcing her to look at him. "Niki, don't be foolish. I'm not going to let that happen to you. I want to be with you forever, I—"

"Don't make me promises!" she broke in harshly as she tore from his grasp and prowled for her shoes. "Please. They had promises, too, and it meant nothing. . . ."

Alexei shook his head in utter confusion. "But then . . . how do I prove you can trust me? How do we go on?"

She stopped for this moment to face him squarely. "I don't know, Alexei. I don't know if I can." She ran to open the door.

He appeared dumbfounded. "But . . . don't you care about me . . . ?"

Stopping in the open doorway, keeping her back to him, she answered, "I'm sure of only one thing: last night was a mistake."

As she ran down the stairs, she heard him calling. "Forgive me, Niki. The way we felt . . . I wanted you so much. . . ."

In the dorm, she took a shower, running the hot water over her skin until it was pink and raw. Yet she couldn't erase the memory of his touch, his kisses everywhere—a memory of madness.

She sat in her room then, agonized by the questions that tumbled through her brain. Suppose it happened to her, too—as it had to her mother—suppose she became pregnant? Would he stay with her?

He wanted to be a doctor, to belong to the world of medicine. *That* was his family, he had said. Why would he burden himself with obligations that would make it harder to achieve his goals?

Or was it her own fault? A weakness in the genes that was destined to tempt all the women of her blood into loving too quickly, too fiercely . . . and losing themselves, their futures. . . .

No. If he had truly loved her, he wouldn't have pushed her so quickly into this kind of torment and doubt.

Throughout the day and evening, other women knocked on her door to tell her there was a caller for her on the dorm's common phone. Niki sent them all away to say that she wouldn't speak to him. Later, she stopped replying to the knocks, pretending that she wasn't in her room. Shortly after midnight, she was told once more that a man named Alexei was on the phone.

"Tell him not to bother me anymore. It's no use. . . ."

And the next day, he didn't call. Not at all. Her fears seemed confirmed. He would have persisted if he truly cared.

The weekday brought classes, and she was able to immerse herself again in work. When she returned to the dorm, she half dreaded and half hoped she would find a message slip in her mail box. For a day none came. The next day there were a few. "Urgent," said one, and there was a long number to call back that she didn't recognize. Long distance, she thought. So much for caring. He had gone away . . . as Ralph had left her grandmother. She tore up the message slips and threw them away.

But by the end of the week, when she plucked a message slip out of the box, she had decided to reward his persistence. She went to the phone, referred to the hasty scrawl of whoever had taken the message: "Call today. Very Imptnt," and dialed the string of numbers.

"Weatherby, Farrington and Blaine," said the answering voice.

Not Alexei, after all. Niki almost hung up. Mr. Weatherby never brought good news. But she knew from experience that there was no avoiding him. She gave her name and asked to speak with him.

"I'm glad you finally called back," Weatherby said as soon as he came on the line.

Niki realized then that some of the earlier messages must have been from him, too.

"I suspect you would have thought me unkind if I simply sent off a letter to report the developments in regard to your financial support."

"What developments?" Niki asked. But as Weatherby began to talk, she wasn't fully concentrating, more involved in wondering how many of the earlier calls had come from Alexei—or whether he had called at all.

"I'm sorry. But these things are out of my hands. The company has provided a great deal of help, but under their financial reorganization all special endowment funds paid directly by Hyland are being discontinued. There will be others set up through a special foundation, and you may wish to apply, but until then—"

His words finally penetrated. "Are you saying, I've been cut off? That I'll have nothing to pay for my studies here —?"

"Not nothing," Weatherby replied blandly. "Remember there's the house that H. D. Hyland was good enough to give you. The lease ended, but you might be able to get something by selling it. I could take care of that for you. . . ."

Niki was silent. Parting with the one tangible souvenir of the few happy years she had shared with her mother wasn't easy to accept. "How much would I get for it?" she asked.

"Not a great deal, I'm afraid. The tenants ran the property down . . . and there are some tax liens that have piled up. . . ."

"You haven't been paying the taxes?"

"Nicolette, I was trying to let as much money as possible flow through to you. There were some oversights . . ."

She could guess that nothing Mr. Weatherby had done was to serve her interests, only the Hylands. The taxes had not been paid so she would lose the house. But she reined in her rage. She had to think clearly.

"How much would be left if I could sell it?"

"A few thousand."

It wasn't enough, she knew. "Why are you doing this?" she asked. "Why can't you leave me alone—leave me with just the little bit I had?"

"It isn't me, Niki. It's the company. It's just a question of their reorganizing—"

"You know that's not true."

He droned on, his level voice devoid of sympathy. "I know it's a shock. But it's not the end of the world. You're made of good stuff, Niki. Part of you, anyway. So you'll survive, you'll—"

She hung up and walked back to her room in a daze.

Why now? In her troubled, guilty state, she was half ready to believe that it was connected somehow to the episode with Alexei. The punishment of fate for having gone beyond the limits, dared to dream of love.

But then Niki remembered telling Pepper Hyland about the money that came to her from Hyland Tobacco. Perhaps it was Pepper who had arranged to have it stopped . . . or had, at least, brought it to the attention of her half brother who was now running the company. But weren't they enemies, too?

All she could know for sure was that more distance was deliberately being put between herself and the Hylands.

In her room, she pondered her alternatives. Helen would help, of course. Yet as Niki thought of taking Helen's money to finance her extended education, the answer came to a question she had been asking herself ever since Alexei had raised it: why did she want to become a doctor? For Helen, Niki realized, only for Helen, a way to express love to her surrogate mother. She hadn't always been confident of being able to express that love in other ways. But now she was.

Now Niki became aware that she was not actually disappointed at the prospect of not going on to med school. For Helen, it might be a disappointment. Yet hadn't Helen always encouraged Niki to seek her own happiness in whatever way was best for her?

So what was best? Was there any way to find happiness or fulfillment?

Suddenly, it came to her. Happiness might be forever out of reach, but she had a chance at least of finding satisfaction. What the Hylands wanted was to put more distance between her and them . . . but they had been able to have things exactly the way they wanted for too long. Well, she'd be damned if she'd move farther away. She was going to get closer, so close they might find it unbearable.

She was going back to Willow Cross. Going—for want of a better word—home.

☆

BOOK III

Sixteen

NIKI drove her rented car to a motel just outside Willow Cross and deposited her valise in a room that was nondescript but clean. She took a few moments to freshen up, then went back to the car, strangely eager to be on her way.

The sky was streaked with wispy sheets of clouds; the details of the landscape looked almost gray in the pale, filtered sunlight of the late afternoon. She remembered now the filmy quality the air around Willow Cross often had, as smoke from the vast curing houses hovered over the broad valley. Watching the country scene that rolled past, dotted here and there with billboards advertising farm equipment and used cars, Niki inhaled deeply, vaguely conscious of seeking out the familiar perfume of tobacco.

She drove at top speed, pushing the posted limit, until she reached the boundaries of the property, the only remnant of her mother's existence. Then she slowed the car, almost to a crawl, giving herself a moment to prepare for a look at the house where she had known the happiness of her early childhood—and the nightmare of its abrupt end.

Yet sadness rather than fear was her first feeling when she saw the house. How derelict it was, how miserable and lonely it looked, silhouetted against the hazy sky, the garden overgrown with weeds, the spacious grounds neglected and unkempt. How unhappy Elle would be to see this ruin! All the loving care she'd lavished on the house had been wiped away; only the tax collector showed an interest in its future. Even the once-neat white picket fence had broken down, the pieces lying by the roadside like grave markers.

Niki got out of the car and pushed through the high grass that covered the pathway. The door to the house was padlocked. She almost smiled at the absurdity of such a measure. A memory from childhood sent her to the back. The window to the downstairs bathroom was caked with dust and grime. She jiggled it. A little more effort—and it moved. No one had ever replaced the broken lock. Niki opened the window and squeezed herself through its narrow opening.

There was an ugly smell of mildew and neglect. The bathroom sink that had once been so pretty was cracked nearly in half and covered with dirt. The tile floor that once had shone was disgustingly stained. What kind of people had lived here? Niki wondered as she walked slowly through the house, taking in the rips in the sofa, the gouges in the furniture, the thick layers of grime that covered every surface.

She threw open a window to let in some air and clean away the stink of decay. As she went from room to room, she half expected ghosts to leap from every corner. Yet all she found was something in herself—a feeling of protectiveness, even territoriality. Dammit, this had been Elle's house—her *own* now—the only element of a settled life that H.D. had ever been willing to bestow in exchange for the loyalty Elle had given to him.

Niki's indignation grew when she went upstairs to her mother's bedroom. Of all Elle's lovely things, nothing but the bed remained. The rest had either been sold or stolen or irretrievably broken. The bedroom that had once been Niki's was now just a storeroom, crowded with cartons and old newspapers, a broken-down sewing machine, and a dress-maker's dummy.

She went back downstairs to the kitchen—the place where all the laughter in Niki's memories of time spent with her mother seemed to originate. The blackened wall around the stove told of a grease fire, but the rest, the cabinets and floor, weren't as bad as the rest of the house. She felt some gratitude for that.

Finally, she went to stand by the portal looking into the living room. Her heart began to pound as though it was that night when she had crept down the stairs. She saw the man standing by the sofa, undressing her mother as she lay on the sofa . . . then that last fleeting glimpse of her mother in life was replaced by the horror of the next morning, when she had come down to find her mother lying dead by the broken window.

Niki felt suddenly as though she was suffocating, and ran to the bathroom to climb again through the window like an escaping thief. Seeking the refuge of her car, she drove away quickly, but not to leave. She steered down the narrow, rutted dirt road that ran across the whole property, fifty acres.

There was not a single soul in sight, not a hint of human activity. Even in the fading light, the land, still covered with the dead and rotting remnants of an unharvested tobacco crop, seemed rich and strangely beautiful. At the far edge of the property, she stopped the car and got out again and walked to the top of a high knoll—a place she remembered visiting once with Elle, a vantage point from which the great mansion at Highlands could be seen in the distance.

This was *their* territory, Niki reminded herself, the Hy-lands' sacred fiefdom. They had banished her, intending never to see her again. Did she dare to come back?

Yes, damn it, she had as much right to be here as they

did. Her eyes burning with angry determination, she stared at the distant mansion and vowed that she would never leave again except on her own terms.

"*Never*!" she bellowed impulsively across the broad undulating carpet of treetops sweeping down to the vast property of her enemies. "You hear me? Your *bastard* is back!"

The town of Willow Cross seemed smaller than she remembered. There were some new stores on Main Street, a fancy bakery, a place that sold only athletic shoes, but otherwise it had changed little. It was still bucolic, quiet, a little beaten down.

Sterling Weatherby's office was on the first floor of a relatively new three-story brick building; the other two shingles belonged to a dentist and a veterinarian.

Niki charged in, startling the elderly receptionist who sat at a danish modern desk in the waiting area. Leaning combatively over the front of the desk, she announced, "I'm here to see Mr. Weatherby."

"Who are you young lady?"

"My name is Sandeman, Niki Sandeman."

The woman nodded passively, and Niki realized then that she'd expected a more dramatic reaction. Could it be that the name Sandeman no longer evoked scorn or contempt from the people of Willow Cross?

"I'm sorry, Miss," the receptionist said. "But Mr. Weatherby has left for the day."

"Where did he go? Home?"

The receptionist hesitated.

"Look, if you don't tell me," Niki declared, "it won't matter a hell of a lot. I'm still going to find him. But I'll be in a better mood if I don't have to hunt so long."

The receptionist smiled slightly, as though admiring Niki's spirit. "He's gone over to the hotel for a drink."

The hotel had always meant the Hyland Hotel in the center of town. "Thank you." Niki said and started out.

The door wasn't even closed behind her when she heard the receptionist grab up a phone. Niki lingered as the call went through, wondering if Weatherby was going to be warned to stay out of her way.

Then she heard the receptionist speaking: "That you Lucette . . . ? You'll never guess who just walked in here . . . H.D.'s love child. . . . Cross my heart. . . . Mmm-hmmm, bright as brass and tough as nails. She's chasing after Weatherby . . . gonna be some fireworks, I'd say. . . ."

Niki smiled ruefully to herself, rather pleased at the way she'd been described. Let them all talk. She wasn't going to pretend she couldn't hear them, as Elle had done. She was going to listen . . . and, pretty soon, start talking back.

The Hyland Hotel had been established at the center of Main Street as a small inn at the turn of the century, the time the Hylands were just beginning to put together their cigarette manufacturing business. During the years that Niki was being raised in Willow Cross, the hotel had still been a relatively small, stylish hostelry. Now, as she parked her car outside, Niki saw that it had grown to a size that could compete reasonably with a luxury hotel in most major cities. A modern annex of ten stories had been added, and the broad, expanded lobby into which Niki entered offered a choice of several restaurants and bars, all named in some way connected to the industry that supported Willow Cross—The Curing Room, The Golden Leaf, The Plug 'n Twist.

Niki poked her head into the different bars, and when she tried The Curing Room—where the chosen decor of wood paneling and plaid upholstered chairs was meant to re-create the atmosphere of a small men's club—she spotted Weatherby at once sitting with another man at a table near the door. She headed toward him.

The moment he saw Niki, too, Weatherby rose and came forward to intercept her.

"Nicolette," he said, attempting to sound cordial, though

his smile was obviously forced. "What a surprise. . . ." He took her arm and tried to steer her around to leave the bar with him.

She resisted. "I'm sure it is," she said. "An unpleasant one, perhaps. But I've had a nasty surprise myself, seeing the way you've allowed my mother's house to be run down. . . ." She let her voice rise.

"Please, Niki, don't make a scene." Cupping her elbow in his hand, the lawyer tried more forcibly to maneuver her into a less conspicuous place.

She didn't resist this time. It suited her—for the moment—to let Weatherby think he held sway.

They went out to a corner of the lobby. "I understand that you're distressed. But I took what tenants I could get—a tobacco farmer and his family. Unfortunately, he wasn't reliable, he was a drinker . . . the rent went unpaid . . . and he didn't take care of things very well. . . ."

"Mr. Weatherby, what's the amount of tax owed on my property?"

"I don't know the exact amount—but it's been adding up for a while. I'd guess, it's up around ten or fifteen thousand dollars."

"And if those taxes aren't paid," Niki asked, "what happens to the property?"

"Well . . . it gets sold at auction to settle the bill."

An auction, Niki thought, at which the high bidder would no doubt be Duke Hyland. For she could perceive now the outlines of a strategy that had probably been unfolding since H.D.'s death. The patriarch of the Hyland family had bestowed one kindness on Niki—and perhaps an inadvertent one, really motivated less by generosity than by wanting to dispose of the house where he had committed murder. Still, his principal heir could not stomach it, wanted to wrest that last piece of territory in Willow Cross away from Niki, to erase any possible connection.

Had Pepper also been working to undermine her—in league with Duke? Perhaps.

"Mr. Weatherby," Niki said, "Tomorrow morning, I want to see all the papers pertaining to that house—leases, tax liens, running expenses, everything you've got. I have to know exactly what I'm up against . . . because I intend to get those taxes paid and keep the house and land."

He stared at her in astonishment. "But why would you?"

"Because it's my home," she said. "It's where I'm going to live."

He was silent for a moment. "I may have some trouble laying my hands on all those papers at such short notice. I have the tax bills, of course, but the lease. . . ."

"By tomorrow morning," she said firmly. "Everything."

He seemed to understand that if he failed to deliver, she would find a way to exact some odious penalty—if only to track him again to his nightly drink, and make a much more embarrassing scene the next time.

"I'll do my best," he said.

"Let's hope that's good enough," Niki answered, striding away.

Back in her car, she had a failure of nerve. Did she really want to move back in with the lions? Her mother had stayed past the point when she should have gone—and had been destroyed. Perhaps it would be best to cut the last tie, take whatever she could get for the house and leave.

But there was the whisper of a ghost in her ear asking for justice—and vengeance.

As if it might help her decide, Niki found herself heading back to see the one old friend she remembered as part of her childhood. In a few minutes, she brought the car to a stop in front of the house that had been a second home to her. But as she approached the mailbox of the sprawling ranch, she noticed that the name on it was not "Boynton" but "Stevens."

Seeing a station wagon in the driveway, she rang the doorbell. A middle-aged woman Niki didn't recognize opened the door. When Niki inquired about Dr. Boynton, she was told that he had passed away last year, and that his widow had gone to live with a son in Richmond.

"I don't suppose you know anything about his daughter, Kate," Niki ventured.

"Matter of fact, I do. She married a fella named Forest or Forester or some such—not from round here. They run a day-care center in town."

Ten minutes later, Niki was climbing the steps to the Magic Rainbow Day-Care Center, a small two-story frame structure, painted yellow with white trim. A posted sign gave the hours as seven to five, and it was past six, but Niki tried the door and found it unlocked.

The spacious room that comprised the whole first floor was filled with cribs and playpens, tiny desks and chairs. Chests of drawers and cupboards were painted in bright, primary colors. In one corner was a partitioned stainless-steel kitchenette. The walls were hung with pictures, some made by children, others cut out from books, and the floors were strewn with toys.

Seeing a flight of stairs outside, in the rear of the building, Niki climbed them and rapped on the door. It was opened by a young woman with soft brown hair and gentle eyes behind wireless granny glasses. She wore a shapeless calico dress that evoked images of the bygone peace-and-love era.

"Kate? Is that you?" Niki asked tentatively.

The gentle eyes grew wide with wonder and recognition. "Niki!" Throwing her arms around her old friend, Kate murmured, "I thought I'd never see you again."

"That's what I thought, too. But here I am," she said, laughing to ease the lump in her throat. "I guess the bad pennies always turn up again."

"Don't say that, Niki, not even as a joke. Come on inside, let me make you a cup of tea—or dinner if you're not busy."

She followed Kate into an apartment that seemed to match the day-care center in comfort and livability. The furnishings were made of sturdy oak; the hardwood floor was bare, except for a woven rug of a primitive design.

Kate made herb tea in an earthenware pot and set out two matching mugs on an antique table that had been stripped and refinished. "Now," she said, sounding like a teacher, "tell me all about yourself. We have a lot of catching up to do."

"You first," Niki said. "I thought you were going to join the Peace Corps. I didn't really expect to find you here."

"I did join the Peace Corps. I was in Nigeria for two years. That's were I met Tim, my husband. I guess I always knew I'd marry someone like dear old Dad," she said with gentle affection, "and when I met that guy, I wasn't about to let him get away. Tim wasn't sure marriage was the way to go, but I dragged him to the American consulate and made an honest man of him before he could say 'free love' . . ." As she spoke of her husband, Kate's face seemed to glow. Niki felt a pang of envy, not because Kate was married, but because she had made a plan for her life and followed it.

"Hang around and you'll meet him," Kate went on. "He works in town—opened up a small craft shop—while I run this place."

"No kids yet?" Niki said.

Kate's eyes grew sad. "I can't have any of my own," she explained in a voice free of self-pity.

"I'm so sorry," Niki said, feeling tactless.

Kate nodded. "Me, too. But there are plenty of kids to love in my day-care center. And Tim and I are talking about adopting."

"What made you come back here?" Niki asked. "If I remember right, you always talked about living somewhere else."

"I changed my mind when Dad died. Tim and I came back for his funeral. Hundreds and hundreds of people turned out for it, Niki, so many we didn't even know who came over to tell us how sorry they were to lose him. I always knew he was a good guy, but that's when I really understood how much he'd done for Willow Cross—and how much he'd be missed. Suddenly, it seemed kind of dumb to be running around saving the world when there were so many needs right here. Besides, Tim fell in love with the town—and when I tried to see it through his eyes, I realized that the people here were just like people anywhere else. So here we are . . ."

"And you're happy?" Niki asked wistfully, as if she needed to know that such a thing was possible.

"You're still asking the wrong questions. I'm doing what I need to do. Now quit stalling and tell me about you. . . ."

Niki felt that her own story was pitifully meager compared to Kate's. She told it briefly, every part except her romance with Alexei. "All I've really done is go to school," she summed up apologetically. "Now it seems the money is about to run out. So I came back here to see if there was a way to save Mama's property."

"Maybe it's time you did," Kate said gently. "It sounds to me like you've been doing most of your living inside your own head, Niki. Maybe it's time you stopped being satisfied with just surviving things that other people do. Maybe you need to start making some choices of your own."

Niki nodded. Shyly, she reached for Kate's hand and held it, just the way she did as a child.

Kate seemed to be remembering, too. "Now that I've found you again," she said, "I hope you're not planning to just drop out of my life."

"Drop out?" Niki said quizzically. "It's funny, you know, I always thought it was the other way around."

"That's because you were a mixed-up kid, Niki Sandeman. I wrote to you a lot your first couple of years away. Don't you remember? You just never answered. I figured you'd met some new friends and didn't care about me anymore, just wanted to forget me, right along with all those bad memories."

"You were never a bad memory," Niki said, her voice breaking as she recalled a younger Kate, rescuing her from the torment of a friendless childhood. "You were the best thing that happened to me. You . . . made a big difference in my life."

"I can't believe it . . ."

"It's the truth, Kate."

"Then you owed me better." Kate's declaration was gently reproachful. "I never gave you any reason to think I didn't want to be your friend anymore. If you believed anything else, it came out of your own head, Niki. Maybe you had a tougher life than I did . . . hell, I'll admit you did. But that doesn't give you license to shut out somebody who really cared about you."

"I'm sorry," Niki whispered, then sat silent in the face of Kate's rebuke.

"Apology accepted," Kate said with a smile. "I just had to get that off my chest. For you, not just for me."

Niki nodded with understanding and acceptance. And then her mind drifted away. If she'd been wrong about Kate, then how many other things had she been wrong about? Alexei—had she thrust him away too quickly? Yet how much could he have cared if he gave up so fast?

Suddenly, there was the clatter of footsteps on the stairs. A man's voice called out: "I'm home, sweet thing. Come and give your old man a great big kiss!"

Kate ran to the door to meet her husband, blushing like an adolescent. They came together for a long kiss, oblivious to anyone else. As Niki studied them, she couldn't help but smile—for Tim looked so much like Kate, right down to the rimless glasses. Finally Kate pulled away. "Honey, there's someone here I want you to meet. My old friend, Niki Sandeman. Niki, this is my husband, Tim Forester."

"Glad to know you, Niki," Tim said, endowing the time-worn words with unusual sincerity. "Kate's told me a lot about you."

"You're a very lucky man, Tim Forester. Kate's a very special person."

"Don't I know it," he agreed with a sweet smile, stroking Kate's hair with a touch so gentle, Niki could feel the love that flowed between them.

"I'm the lucky one," Kate insisted. "I've found me one

of the truly liberated men in this world. And he's a great cook, too! Stay for supper, Niki, see for yourself."

"I will, if you let me help."

Tim plucked an apron from a hook on the door and handed it to Niki. "This one's mine," he said, "but since you're such a good friend of Kate's, I'll let you borrow it."

They worked companionably in the cheerful kitchen, surrounded by tiny clay pots of herbs, shiny copper pots, and assorted memorabilia of the Peace Corps days in Nigeria. There was such warmth, such caring in everything Tim and Kate did for each other.

"This is a real home," she said, as they sat down to a light supper of homemade vegetable soup and whole-grain bread. "It reminds me so much of the way Kate's house used to be, when we were kids. It's . . . it's a place you don't want to leave."

Tim and Kate smiled at one another. Then Kate turned to her friend. "It's easier to do something when you've been taught how. But Niki . . . it's never too late to learn."

Seventeen

IGNORING the sweat that bathed her body and drenched her work shirt, Niki stubbornly battled Nature's own bastard children—weeds—the wild uncontrolled growth that had made a veritable jungle of what had once been Elle's garden. It was slow and monotonous work, and though she felt herself in excellent physical condition, the repetition of bending and pulling made her back ache and her legs cramp. As the morning sun climbed higher in the sky, warming the muggy air and dissipating the last wisps of cloud, Niki found herself stopping more and more often to take a drink of cool water from a nearby thermos. Still, as she filled one trash bag after another with the withered and rotting remains left by the departed tenants, Niki felt an exhilarating satisfaction in reclaiming what was rightfully hers.

Straightening up, she stretched her arms upward, rotating her neck to relieve the cramping. She pushed a stray hair from her face, smudging her cheek with the heavy gardening gloves she'd learned to wear only after a harvest of blisters had demonstrated all too painfully that her hands weren't suited to this kind of work. How would her mother react, Niki wondered, if she could see her daughter now? She would probably be shocked at first; Elle had disdained physical labor, had chosen to follow the lure first dangled by H.D. Hyland because she was so desperate to escape from the peasant life of physical labor she had known in her native village.

Yet in the end, Niki was sure, her mother would approve the decision to struggle, no matter how hard, to save all that was left of the legacy for which Elle had sold her soul.

But could it be done? There was a growing list of supplies needed to restore the house, and the time was coming when it would be impossible to continue without paying for some help. Scarcely a day went by that Niki didn't study the documents Weatherby had so reluctantly provided, trying to figure out how she could meet the taxes except by selling the property.

She worked another hour pulling weeds, until the pathway to the house was cleared. Then she dragged the heavy plastic bags to the side of the road where the local carting service she'd hired would pick them up along with the broken furniture, and the torn and stained mattresses she'd piled up in the back of the house. In throwing out those broken and irreparably damaged pieces, she had left herself with little more than the barest essentials.

She filled a bucket with hot water and ammonia, set a rickety ladder against the side of the house, and attacked the layers of grime on the second-floor windows. As she scrubbed and wiped, Niki hummed an old French folk song Elle used to sing when she was feeling homesick or sad, as if to remind herself that the task she'd undertaken had meaning and purpose.

Midway through the afternoon, the sky darkened suddenly; a few moments later, a shower sent Niki scurrying inside. Quickly, she dumped the filthy water from her bucket and set it in the middle of what used to be Elle's room to catch the water that would soon come leaking through the roof.

Am I crazy? she asked herself for the hundredth time since she'd arrived in Willow Cross. I must be, she told herself each time she laid out some precious dollars—to turn on the electricity, to install a telephone, to change the locks on the doors, an act that felt symbolically right, if not absolutely necessary.

Perhaps she would have retreated from the drift toward settling into the house, but encouragement to continue came from a surprising source. Whereas Niki had imagined that Helen would be disapproving of plans to give up her education and any ambitions to become a doctor, Helen had, in fact, insisted it was the right choice—the only choice—for now, at least.

In a phone call right after Niki had arrived in Willow Cross, while she was still daunted by the prospect of restoring Elle's house, Helen had urged her to stay. "It's something I believe you need to do, Niki," she said. "It has always seemed to me your own growth stopped in a way when your mother ceased to live. Your emotional growth, I mean. You were left so frightened and alone, you instinctively shut out anything that might threaten your survival. For so long, you had yourself to count on, and no one else. You couldn't let yourself take a chance of relying on anyone, letting anyone into your heart."

"But I've let you in," Niki said.

"I know, my dear. But perhaps there's a deeper level you are still protecting." She paused. "Alexei called me. He said he was very anxious to speak with you. Apparently, you ran from him and then refused—"

The mere mention of Alexei touched a nerve. "I don't want to talk about him, Helen."

"But there's something you should know. He told me —"

"There's nothing I *want* to know!" Niki broke in. "Promise me, Helen, promise me you won't ever talk about Alexei to me. I know you'll go on being his father's friend, and you may see him. But that's not part of my life now. My life is going to be here—especially if you think it's right."

Helen sighed. "I do. Because I think you must rediscover yourself in order to grow—and you can best do it where you are."

With obvious reluctance, Helen did promise that she would say nothing further about Alexei Ivanov—and subsequent to the phone conversation she sent Niki a check for a thousand dollars to be used for repairing the leaky roof. Aware that Niki had avoided taking money from her, Helen said to consider it "a loan."

But Niki put the check aside, anyway, unwilling to pursue her plans that were still uncertain on borrowed money. So the roof still leaked, and once she had put the bucket in Elle's room, Niki had to commandeer two cooking pots for similar duty in her own room.

With the cottage protected against the rain, Niki went into the kitchen to fix herself a belated lunch. Here, at least, she had managed to create a semblance of normalcy. She had scrubbed and scraped until her knuckles were raw, trying to revive the luster of Elle's treasured cooking utensils, to erase the residue of neglect from the floor and cabinets. A row of potted herbs just like the ones Elle had always kept now stood along the windowsill. Nearby were all the housewarming gifts Blake had sent—or, rather, had arranged to have sent from one of her father's department stores—everything from an electronic coffee maker to a portable color television set. And though their gleam and sparkle seemed incongruous in a room that still desperately needed a coat of paint and a new refrigerator, they were like a ray of sunshine, a glimmer of hope that somehow Niki could succeed in reclaiming her home.

She ate her peanut-butter sandwich and sipped a glass of milk slowly, to make them last, and promised herself one glorious, indulgent feast on the day—if ever—she paid off the taxes and had made this house whole again.

After her simple meal, Niki went back to work. As she began the slow and tedious task of removing the rotted wallpaper from her bedroom walls, the telephone rang. Perhaps it was Weatherby; she had asked to meet with him, to see if he would offer any help in delaying land tax payments due, or make some attempt to recover uncollected back rents.

The caller turned out to be Kate. "Were you expecting someone else?" she asked, noting that Niki sounded surprised to hear her voice.

"I was," Niki admitted, "but I'd rather talk to you."

"Good. How about coming to dinner tonight? Tim's promised to make the vegetable lasagna you liked so much. And we have some great homemade ice cream in the freezer. . . ."

Niki smiled. It was almost like old times, the way Kate and Tim had adopted her. "Sounds wonderful," she said, "but I don't think I can. There's so much work to do, and by the time I quit, I'll be too tired to do anything but sleep."

"Relax, Niki," Kate urged. "Leave some of the work for the weekend, and Tim and I will come out again and give you a hand."

"But you've already done so much," Niki protested—weakly, however, since her friends' help and their company always made the work seem easier and happier.

"Tim loves to putter," Kate insisted. "And I'm ready to do anything to keep you here."

Yet in spite of Kate's steadfast reinforcement and her own commitment, Niki came to feel that each time she turned a corner, she was likely to find another setback lurking there.

The day after she finished painting the kitchen, with more than a little help from her friends, Niki's refrigerator died. When she attempted to buy a new one on credit, the manager of the Willow Cross General Store turned down her application. No credit history, no collateral, he said, refusing to change his mind even after Kate and Tim offered to provide references and co-sign the application. It wasn't simply a matter of credit, Niki realized; it was a matter of being an outsider. In the end, she cashed Helen's check and then made do with a secondhand refrigerator from the town's thrift shop, giving up eighty dollars from the money that would now be all she had to meet every need.

When she was ready to paint her bedroom, Niki finally called in a roofer to patch the leaks above. It couldn't be done, he insisted; the roof was beyond repair and needed replacing, to the tune of three thousand dollars. In the end, Tim climbed up on Niki's creaky ladder and covered the leaks with tar paper. "It won't hold for long," he warned, "especially if we get any bad storms." When Niki tried to have Elle's old Buick repaired, she was told that it would cost at least a thousand dollars. Somehow that disappointment bothered Niki more than the rest, for to her, Elle's car represented more than just transportation. It was, like the house, a symbol of what she had bartered her life for.

Desperate for money, Niki called Weatherby's secretary again, threatening to camp on the lawyer's doorstep if he didn't respond to her request for help. He was her court-appointed guardian, after all; if her affairs were in disarray, he was partly to blame. He should have kept a closer eye on her property. And couldn't he use his influence in town, and with the Hylands, to get the tobacco company to reconsider granting the payments they had made to her over the years?

Weatherby's response to Niki's threat arrived on a sunny morning a few days later while she was outside putting a few nails into some of the loose siding. The mailman who made rural deliveries honked the horn of his truck as he came by, summoning Niki to sign for a manila envelope that came by registered mail. Inside, Niki found a sheaf of papers clipped beneath a letter from Weatherby.

In keeping with the impersonal, almost anonymous manner with which he had always treated her, the lawyer wrote, "A final check to your account has recently come through from the Hyland Company, but as you see it falls somewhat short of covering my bill for services rendered and expenses incurred. In view of your expressed difficulties, I have decided to forego the balance." Enclosed was a copy of a deposit slip for $3,500 to the account managed by Weatherby in his role as her guardian; this was money that might have gone toward tuition—if she were staying in school. Now it could have gone to pay the expenses. However, along with the proof of deposit, came a bill for legal and management services rendered during the past year—drawing a lease renewal, for example—and expenses such as filing fees, document transfers, even the cost of making copies, that amounted to something over $3,800. And there was a copy of a check that Weatherby had written to himself—closing out the guardian's escrow of Niki's funds—in payment of the legal bill.

The array of documents stunned Niki more than the confirmation that she could expect no help to relieve her financial burdens. How could Weatherby deny her the few thousand dollars that had come to her as the final bit of largesse from the Hylands? Stuffing the contents of the letter into her handbag, she drove straight to Weatherby's office, pushed her way past the receptionist and threw the papers on the lawyer's desk.

"How the hell do you expect to get away with this?" she demanded.

Weatherby remained calm in the face of her anger. It was almost as if he were expecting her. " 'Get away with . . . ?' Are you suggesting, Miss Sandeman, that there's something improper about my conduct?"

"Damn right. There never was any love lost between us, Mr. Weatherby. The court appointed you my guardian at a time when I had nothing to say about it—and since this was your territory more than mine it seemed like a good enough idea to leave you in place. But I didn't know that you were using your position to undermine me, letting the only thing of value I own get ruined, giving my property away without ever bothering to collect rent—"

"Well, that is most regrettable, Miss Sandeman. But you see," he gave her his genteel smile, and when he continued his accent seemed to be laid on just a bit thicker, "this is the South, and we have certain ways of doin' things. Now, bein' the daughter of a . . . a foreign person yourself, and not havin' spent time here in a long while, you may not understand our customs. But we don't always hold with the impersonal way they do things up North. If we let a man take on a house and land, we try to trust him to do his best, and—"

"Trust!" Niki exploded. "I can't even buy a new refrigerator on credit here, and you let people *destroy* my mother's house, let them take her things without—"

"Is there a point to this outburst?" he put in with forced politeness. "I do have other work. . . ."

"You bet there's a point, Weatherby. You brought me a message once from the Hylands—warned me that they'd do anything to keep me from embarrassing them in front of the world—and it's been pretty clear ever since that you're just their errand boy. Now the message you're passing along is that I can't make it here, shouldn't even try." She advanced on the desk where he still sat regarding her calmly. "Well, that just makes me more determined. And maybe the first thing I'll do to show that I have big plans of my own is get another lawyer to go after you—look over everything you've done as my guardian and see what a court has to say about whether you were guilty of mismanagement—and gross conflicts of interest, paying yourself to serve—"

The mask of politeness slipped as Weatherby rose from his leather chair. As he came around the desk, his eyes narrowed and his voice took on a cutting edge. "I wouldn't make threats if I were you, Miss Sandeman. It isn't an unknown practice to receive a fee for looking after affairs such as yours. Any court in this town, county, or state is certainly not going to find it unreasonable. So if you want to engage another lawyer—and throw away whatever money you may have left on a useless legal action, why you just go right ahead. I think you'll find that if you challenge *my* integrity in *this* town, you'll learn just what people make of your own—and your mother's, the most famous mistress we ever had in Willow Cross." He folded his arms as he held her in his stoney gaze.

Niki's hand clenched at her side. She wanted to smash Weatherby with her fist, but it was all she could do to stare him down. There was something in his manner—in this moment—that made her feel as if she were ten years old again, frightened and alone, completely dependent on the goodwill of others. If she had any chance of surviving in Willow Cross, it was true that she could not afford to waste time, energy, and money on a prominent citizen—one who also had the backing of the Hylands.

Hastily grabbing up the papers she had flung on Weatherby's desk, Niki ran from the office without another word. As she passed through the waiting area, the receptionist gave her a smug smile, and Niki's mind began to buzz with the gossip that she imagined would soon start burning up the telephone lines of Willow Cross.

Still shaky and vulnerable, she drove over to Kate's day-care center in need of her friend's advice and encouragement. She found Tim there, too, since his craft store was open only at odd hours. While it was the children's nap time, Niki sat down with Tim and Kate at a small table in the day-care center's kitchen and showed them Weatherby's final accounting. They were no less shocked.

"He's your guardian," Kate said. "He should have been preserving your assets—whatever they are."

"And that bill!" Tim objected. "Even in New York, I wonder if lawyers charge that kind of fee. . . ."

"What am I going to do now?" Niki asked. "He knows I can't afford to sue him. But he's left me with nothing!"

Tim looked at his wife, who nodded, as if they had already discussed Niki's future.

"Niki," Tim said, "I think you're sitting right on top of the answer. A way you can get that property of yours to pay for itself and maybe have a little left over—"

"No, Tim. It won't sell for much in its present condition.

Anyway, I can't bring myself to let it go. It's all I have of—''

''Who's talking about selling?'' Kate chimed in. ''What we had in mind was that you might. . .'' She glanced to Tim, as though it was something that would be taken more seriously coming from him.

''Well . . . what?'' Niki demanded.

''Grow tobacco.'' Tim said.

''Tobacco . . . ?'' Niki echoed softly. Tobacco was the foundation of the business that had enriched her enemies. Did she want any part of that?

Kate leaned over the table, talking very quietly because she had seen some of the napping children stir beyond the partition. ''It'd be a shame to let your land go fallow, Niki. Fifty acres is enough to give you a decent living. Lots of small farmers around here get by on less.''

''But I don't know the first thing about farming,'' Niki said. ''And even if I did, I don't think I have enough start-up money.''

''Hire some help,'' Kate suggested, ''and learn as you go. Use the money Helen sent you, and when that runs out Tim and I will help.''

''No, I can't—''

''Niki, I told you once how much it hurt to be cut off. Well, this is the same. When you don't let people help, it's another way of cutting them off—showing you're afraid to let them be part of your life.''

Niki looked down, hiding the tears that came to her eyes. Kate got up and came around to hug her, while Tim reached over and took her hand.

''Be a part of us, Niki,'' Kate said. ''It's the best thing you can do now. You've always wanted to belong somewhere. Well, this is tobacco country where you've come to live. Be a part of that, too. Unless you do something, and soon, you're going to lose what you came back here to save.''

She left Kate and Tim promising only to think about what they'd said. Yes, it made sense. But she was still scared—

not because it meant trying something new, but because this particular endeavor would take her into an area that the Hylands controlled with a grip no less strong and sure than that with which they had controlled the rest of her life, and her mother's.

Yet when Niki returned home, she looked out across the fields and imagined them filled with growing plants instead of rotted and decaying stalks. She savored the irony of entering—even at the fringes—the business that belonged to her enemies. Would they try to keep her out?

She thought it over all through the next day as she worked on the house, and was not convinced she should take the risk. Even experienced farmers could lose a crop. Suppose she spent Helen's money, and Tim and Kate's, and came up with nothing.

That night, she lay awake tormented by the same doubts. Then, at a little after three in the morning, she thought she heard the crunch of gravel that might come from a car rolling slowly up the unpaved drive that led to the cottage. Niki got up and looked out the window of her bedroom.

The land was bathed in the soft glow of a half moon, but the driveway was a lane of black shadows between rows of tall elms. Niki peered into the darkness. Was a car parked in the shadows? She wasn't sure.

But then she saw a figure step into the moonlight. A man. As she watched, he lifted his hand . . . and then Niki saw the end of a cigarette glow in the dark as the visitor took a puff.

Who could it be? Weatherby? Someone sent to harm her?

Niki thought of calling out, then decided against it. Better just to observe. Within the darkness of her room, the intruder couldn't see her standing at the window. He would probably think she was asleep. If he approached the house, tried to break in, she would have time to sneak away out of danger.

But the man didn't move. For a long time, he just stood looking at the house, taking an occasional puff on his cigarette. At last, he threw down the butt and ground it out under his shoe. Then he retreated back into the shadows. Niki heard the motor of the car start, saw the parking lights go on as the vehicle reversed slowly and quietly along the drive. Then it was gone.

Who had it been . . . who had come with no greater purpose than to look at the house, to dream in the moonlight? A man who'd been kept lying awake—like herself—and who had found his way here seeking some kind of answer? Was it someone who wanted her to go away—to be *frightened* away.

Was it, indeed, any man she knew? Or a man who had known only her mother?

Waking to the light of a bright sunny morning, Niki could hardly be sure that she hadn't dreamed the mysterious visitor in the moonlight. As soon as she was dressed, she went outside to the spot where she had seen the shadowy figure standing. A flattened cigarette butt lay in the grass.

The questions of the night circled in her brain again, but she could find no answer. She thought it possible, however, that someone had meant to disturb and bedevil her with this very uncertainty. There was an implied threat in a visit from a man who stood below her window and silently watched.

And in thinking this she found at last the only answer that really seemed to matter. She would stay, because it was the only way to answer all the other riddles of her life. Was there only one silent watcher, after all? No, she was surrounded by them as her mother had been. Niki vowed to show every last one she could not be frightened away, to show them that Gabrielle Sandeman's daughter belonged right here.

Eighteen

AT a small Baptist church a few miles out of town, the monthly meeting of the Willow Cross Tobacco Cooperative was soon to begin. Niki wore jeans and a plaid shirt, her idea of what a farmer of either sex should look like. But when she arrived, she saw at once that she had guessed wrong. Men, women, and children alike were turned out in their Sunday best. "Why didn't you tell me?" she hissed at Kate. "Why didn't you warn me that what I was wearing was all wrong?"

Kate, in her all-purpose flower-child dress, smiled. "I told you, Niki, it's time you learned some things for yourself. Besides, this isn't a fashion show. Our farmers may be kind of . . . provincial—but unless you turn out in sequins and feathers, your clothes aren't going to make or break you either way."

"Thanks a lot. And here I thought you came along to keep me from making a fool of myself."

"I'm here to help you get acquainted. People around here are kind of funny about strangers."

Niki gave Kate a sharp glance.

"Hey, don't look at me that way. Doesn't matter whether or not you were born in town, as far as the farming community is concerned you're still a stranger."

As she'd done in grade school years before, Kate took Niki by the hand and led her around the church hall. "Mrs. Clay," she said to a large, heavily corseted woman in black, "I want you to meet my old friend, Niki Sandeman. She's living out at the Martin place."

Niki gave a start at hearing Elle's cottage identified by Kate only by the name of the tenants who had been there, the tobacco farmer and his family who had treated it so badly. She almost said something, but Kate gave her hand a quick squeeze, and Niki realized then that it would smooth the way in this gathering.

"How do," said the woman. "Are you kin to the Martins?" she asked, her eyes asparkle with curiosity.

"No, no I'm not," Niki replied.

"Nice people," Mrs. Clay volunteered. "Darn shame, the way they had to leave so sudden. Anyway," she said, shifting quickly, "I wish you the best of luck, Mrs. . . ."

"Sandeman," Niki supplied, searching for any telltale hint of recognition in the woman's face. But there was none; there were places around Willow Cross, she supposed, where Elle Sandeman had not been so notorious, or at least had been forgotten.

"I hope you don't mind," Kate said quickly after the woman walked away, "but the Martins lived in your house a good part of the time you were away, so they're identified with the place as far as these people are concerned. Besides, you were talking about making a fresh start. I thought I'd leave it up to you to say whatever you wanted about the past."

Niki nodded. She understood and appreciated Kate's motives, yet she felt uneasy about denying her true kinship, as though it meant confessing to being ashamed of her own mother.

Kate made a few more introductions. Pleasantries and small talk were exchanged, and if the people Niki met were curious, they were too polite to ask more than she was able to answer.

Promptly at seven o'clock, a wiry older man took the podium and asked everyone to be seated. "That's Thomas Clay, the minister," Kate said, as she and Niki took two empty seats near the rear of the hall.

The minister announced the birth of twins to Mary and Jack Conway, then cleared his throat. "Some sad news too," he said. "Kenny Tucker's mama passed away last night. Funeral will be here at the church Saturday morning. We'll be needing pallbearers, so all you special friends of Kenny's, come by and see me after this meeting. Now I'll turn the meeting over to Will Rivers."

A chorus of whistles and foot stomping welcomed a tall man who emerged out of the crowd to climb rather slowly up the stairs to the platform, as though slightly unwilling to take charge and embarrassed by the ovation. It wasn't shyness, though, Niki thought as she watched him, just the kind of modesty that disliked being singled out and invested with power. As he held up his large, strong-looking hands to silence the applause, Niki took in the details of his appearance. His clothes were simple, similar to hers, and he had straight, thick, dark brown hair that had been left to grow too long. Heavy, expressive eyebrows accentuated eyes that showed hazel, almost golden, under the lights aimed at the stage, and he had a straight, narrow nose—what would have been called an aristocratic nose on anyone but a farmer—and a sensuous mouth. His face was weathered from an outdoor life, and, though he was young, there were deep creases in his cheeks that showed as he gave the crowd an acknowledging smile. Even from the back of the hall, Niki could feel the spell Will Rivers cast over his neighbors.

"Who is he?" Niki whispered.

"Just pay attention and you'll find out," Kate whispered back.

"Reverend Clay has asked for one kind of help just now. I've got to ask for even more. Most of you already know about Luke Carson's accident," he said. "Doctors say it isn't likely he'll have the use of his legs, at least not any time soon. I'm looking for volunteers to help out Carson's wife and boys with this year's planting. If you can't spare a whole day, you know even a half-day will make a difference to Miz Carson."

There was a collective murmur of sympathy, then a rumble of conversation as the farmers began to talk among themselves. In a community like this one, Kate explained, people took care of their own. "It works, Niki," she said, "it works better than welfare or insurance or anything else that city people have invented. And it's a heck of a lot more personal."

Will held up his hand again. "I've already talked to some of the big-hearted ladies here . . . you know who you are," he said with a smile that set off a chorus of feminine giggles. "We'll be running a benefit dance and raffle for the Carson family. Four weeks from tonight. I don't know what kind of prizes the ladies will round up, but I'm already pledged to buy five books of tickets—so they'd better be the cat's pajamas!" There was another burst of laughter. "Hope you'll all give whatever you can," Will urged. His amiable smile faded and his hazel eyes settled down to serious business. "Now I got some more serious business. I'll try to say it simple. None of us expect tobacco farming to be easy, never has been, never will be. We've got more than our share of natural enemies. Got the black root rot, fusarium wilt, bacterial leaf spot, downy mildew, blue mold and black shank," he singsonged, as if reciting a nursery rhyme. "Got the sucker bugs and grasshoppers, flea beetles and cutworms, burdworms and aphids. Hell, we've got more different plagues here than they had in the Bible! No offense intended, Reverend Clay," Will added, with a nod towards the minister.

"That's always been part of what us leaf growers expect. We live with the natural enemies, and we pray for a good year, just the way our daddies and granddaddies did. . . ."

Will Rivers strode closer to the edge of the stage and stuck his palms down inside his waistband. "But sometimes we have to worry about something else. Our *friends*, the folks who buy our crops, who make the cigarettes and chew—why, every so often, they start acting not so friendly. Seems sometimes *they've* got more money than God—forgive me again, Reverend—but it never seems to be enough. They figure if we're looking for a decent return on honest work, looking to put away an extra dollar or two for a rainy day, then we're taking money out of their pockets. . . ."

Niki listened with fascination to the way Will Rivers held the crowd with the quiet eloquence of his words. He could be a politician, an evangelist, or even an actor—indeed, he seemed to be a bit of all three. But even more interesting, Will seemed to be mounting an attack on her own natural enemies.

"I know you all like to plan on going to the annual Hyland picnic," he said in the next breath. "You like to eat their barbecue and drink their whiskey—thinkin' we're just all good ol' boys together. But folks, it just ain't so. . . ."

A farmer in the audience spoke up. "Listen, Will, we all know you got a head on your shoulders—and we respect what you have to say. But I don't think we want to be pickin' this time to have a fight with the tobacco company. We need them as much as they need us. They're the ones with the cash and the clout. They're the ones who stick up for us in Washington to make sure we keep our subsidies."

Again there were rumbles of agreement.

Will nodded his head. "I hear what you're saying, Hank. Maybe sometimes it looks like we're just one big family—but we've got us a greedy bunch of relatives that don't mind gobbling up everything that's on the table. If they can get away with it."

Niki's interest was growing by the minute. She had her

reasons for mistrusting the Hylands, and now it seemed that others did, too.

"History is what I'm talking about," Will continued, "the kind my granddaddy and my daddy lived through, the kind that can happen again if we don't watch out. Back in 1900, there was a tobacco trust, just like there was for oil and steel. Premium leaf was selling for seven to nine cents a pound, but the trust offered my granddaddy just *three* cents a pound. Well, my granddaddy said he'd just as soon leave it. He and some other growers got together, started something like what we got here today. Know what the trust did? Broke 'em apart—by offering the scabs *twelve cents a pound*! Think of it, Hank," he continued, pounding the podium for emphasis, "those bastards paid the highest prices in history—just to show the growers who was the boss!

"Well, Hank," he said, still addressing the same farmer (who by now had wilted into his seat), "the Supreme Court busted the tobacco trust, just the way the trust busted the association. But that didn't change the way the companies think—or the way they do business.

"Back during the depression, my daddy had to sell off acreage to keep from going under, just like a lot of other farmers did. But the companies were doing fine. Hell, folks may have been hungry, but they didn't stop smoking, no sir, they didn't. Then Roosevelt gave us price support—though the companies tried their damndest to stop it. Price support's taken care of your family and mine. We've been getting along, even while the banks have been foreclosing on farms all over the country. But if we're not careful, folks, I see hard times ahead—and I'll tell you why." He paused, like a storyteller, to heighten the drama of his tale. "No matter what happened to prices, we were always safe on one count. American cigarettes were always made of American tobacco. We grew the best, and we still do." The pride in his voice was obvious. "But now the companies are starting to bring in tobacco from places like Brazil and Zimbabwe—and what

I'm hearing is that the leaf is a whole lot better than it ever used to be."

He paused again, to let the impact of this revelation sink in. "Well, the honest truth is that we just *can't* beat—or even match up to that kind of competition. Not when a lot of foreign tobacco is grown under slave-labor conditions, not when the oil companies have driven up the price of gasoline for our machinery and fertilizer for our crops. We have to stop it—now!"

Voices rose from different corners of the audience. "How?" "What do we do about it?" "What's your answer, Will?"

"Glad you asked," Will replied with an easy smile. "The thing we've got to do is start making some noise before the problem gets worse. Get some petitions going, talk to the politicians in Washington. The companies own most of 'em, but there are a couple who fight for the farmers. We'll talk to the newspapers and the television people, get them to do some stories about *why* foreign tobacco is cheaper than ours."

"Sounds like trouble," one of the older farmers grumbled. "Sounds like you're looking to stir up a hornets' nest, Will Rivers, and I don't see it'll do us a damn bit of good."

Will faced the man squarely. "John, I can't promise there won't be trouble," he said solemnly, "or that we can beat the manufacturers on this. But I'd like to remind you that 'way back when, a very smart man said: 'We'd better hang together—or we'll sure as hell hang separately.' That was Benjamin Franklin, folks, and he was talking to a couple of other fellas who were a little bit scared about signing the Declaration of Independence. Well, we all know what happened when those folks decided to stick together. I'm asking you to do the same . . . and get this protest goin'."

As Will stepped down from the podium, Niki noticed that the applause was more reserved than it had been before, but that didn't seem to trouble him. He began moving among the farmers, shaking hands and obviously trying to gather support for his position.

Niki knew very little about the history Will had spoken of, but she was fascinated by it—and more than ready to believe that the Hylands had always been unscrupulous in business as they were in their personal lives.

A short time later, Mrs. Clay announced that refreshments were being served. Already, people had started to gather around a makeshift trestle table covered with a bright-red homespun cloth. On it was a bowl of fruit punch, a coffee urn, and a dazzling variety of homemade cakes and pies. Will Rivers was just beginning to draw himself a cup of coffee as Niki and Kate approached. Niki was anxious to talk with him, to get more information about the position of the farmers.

But then a trio of women descended on Will Rivers, each carrying a plate of baked goods, each urging him to try a bite of pie or a morsel of cake.

"You asked who he is," Kate said. "Are you beginning to get an idea? Will is a lot of things to a lot of people—but to the single ladies of Willow Cross, he's just about the most eligible bachelor around. Are you interested?"

"Not that way," Niki answered quickly. "But he seems to be the one to tell me if I'm making a mistake to get involved in farming right now. . . ."

"You're going to have a hard time getting him alone for that kind of discussion," Kate observed, "unless you bake him something extra special."

As they helped themselves to cake and punch, Niki watched from the corner of her eye and saw Will gallantly sampling each and every item that was offered him—rewarding each woman with a compliment and a boyish grin.

Suddenly, Will broke away from his circle of admirers and walked towards them. "Kate," he said, holding out his hand, "it's great to see you again. I've been meaning to thank you for taking the Clifton baby while her mama was in the hospital. I see you've brought our newest neighbor along with you."

"The human telegraph works fast around here," Kate laughed, and introduced them to each other. "Niki wants to try her hand at tobacco farming, Will. I thought you might be the one to help her find some experienced hands."

"Always glad to be neighborly," Will agreed. "But maybe I ought to have a look at the place myself—just so I can see what's needed."

"Niki would really appreciate that, wouldn't you?" Kate volunteered, as if she didn't trust her friend to give the right answer.

"Sure," Niki said. There was a momentary pause while she and Will examined each other. He showed no more outward reaction than she did.

"I can come out tomorrow," he said finally, "but it'll have to be first thing in the morning."

"Okay," Niki agreed. "I'll see you about nine o'clock."

Will burst out laughing. "Not hard to see you're new to farming. First thing in the morning around here usually means when the sun cracks the horizon about half-past five. But since you're a tenderfoot, I'll make it a little later. Think you can pull yourself away from your beauty sleep by . . . seven?"

"I'll meet you anytime you say, Mr. Rivers," Niki replied shortly. She meant it to sound like an answer to a challenge—and then regretted that it sounded more like she was simply getting on line with all the other women who pined for Will's attention.

Will smiled at her. "My daddy was the one they called Mr. Rivers. I generally answer to Will." He offered his hand.

Niki accepted it. "Will it is then." His handshake was firm and strong, she noticed, making no concession to the fact that she was a woman.

They were interrupted then by a group of men who looked as though they'd formed a separate delegation to argue with Will. He gave his attention to them, and Kate pulled Niki away.

"You're all set," Kate said. "Will's the salt of the earth—and he's been farming tobacco since he was a kid. If he looks after you, you'll get along just fine."

"I don't need anyone to 'look after me,' " Niki countered. "I just need a little good advice."

"Well," Kate said, eyes twinkling behind her granny glasses, "it's up to you if that's all you want. But I'd say you made quite an impression on our Will, and he'd go more than a country mile to help you out."

"How could you tell?" Niki asked casually, trying to sound as if the question was an afterthought.

"That little gift he gave you," Kate said. "An extra hour and a half of—well, you heard what he called it—beauty sleep."

When the alarm clock jarred Niki awake at six o'clock in the morning, she was still telling herself she didn't particularly care what Will Rivers thought of her as long as he provided plenty of good advice about growing tobacco.

Yet she covered the kitchen table with one of the few remaining cloths that wasn't torn or poorly mended, and then set about baking some of the fragrant, smoothly textured *brioche* from Elle's recipe.

Well, I have to eat breakfast, too, she muttered to herself as she brewed a fresh pot of coffee and the smell from the oven filled the kitchen. And when she was finished, she dressed with care, choosing a soft, blue lamb's-wool sweater to go with her jeans, and applying just a bit of matching shadow on her eyelids.

She heard wheels rolling up the drive at almost seven o'clock sharp, and looked out the window to see a pickup truck sliding to a sharp stop.

In the daylight, Will looked even better than he had the night before. His dark-brown hair showed reddish highlights in the sun, his golden eyes sparkled with vitality, and he exuded a kind of raw energy when he moved. He was, Niki thought, the most *masculine* man she'd ever met.

He accepted her invitation to talk over breakfast, and sat down at the kitchen table.

"You should try the *brioche*," Niki said as she poured him a cup of coffee. "It's a French kind of muffin."

"Is it?" Will said excitedly. "Well, let's see now . . . French—does that mean it's from France?" As he went on, he opened the linen napkin Niki had put at his place and tucked it under his chin like a bib. "Why, ma'am, I've never had such hospitality. Imagine you having these little—brushes didja call 'em?—sent all the way from way over near Russia."

"I *made* them," Niki said as she poured his coffee. "And France isn't anywhere near . . ." Suddenly, as Niki paused to study the tilt of his smile and the glint in his eye, she realized how stupid she'd been. "Sorry," she said. "I didn't mean to be patronizing."

"That's okay, Niki." Will pulled the napkin from under his chin and spread it conventionally on his lap. "I just wanted to deliver the message—before maybe you do give some offense in the wrong quarters—that tobacco farmers don't all live up tobacco road. Happens I spent some time living in France, after college a few years back. I dunked a few brioche in my time right on the Left Bank."

Embarrassed by her gaffe, Niki fell silent, remembering how Kate scolded her for making decisions about people without knowing the facts.

Will picked up the slack easily, his manner pleasant, though businesslike. "There are some things I need to know to help you plan your planting. Do you know, for a start, if Judd Martin's allotment covered all your acreage?" he asked.

"Allotment?" she asked. "For what?"

In the midst of dunking a piece of brioche in his coffee, he stopped to stare at her, as though unable to believe what he was hearing. "For the price support program," he said finally. "You mean to say you don't know anything about that?"

For a moment, Niki withered under the weight of his incredulity. "No, I don't," she said at last. "In fact, when it comes to farming, I don't know anything about anything. That's why I asked you here. To see if you could make a dent in my colossal unequaled ignorance."

He grinned, "Okay, my turn to apologize for coming on a little too strong. I'm not used to being a teacher, though. We just don't get many Yankees down here looking to farm tobacco. Especially pretty ones who look like they'd be more at home on a magazine cover."

"I'm not a Yankee," she said stiffly, "I was born here."

"That a fact?" he said. "Well, that's a start. Maybe you got some of the know-how in your blood. And I don't mind filling in a little country know-how. Least I can do for a brush—or was that a *brioche*?—this good. . . ." He winked at her, and she allowed a small smile in return.

She knew that she was working too hard at keeping up her defenses, yet Will Rivers was attractive and charming and humorous, and he seemed so secure in an awareness of his own attributes. Niki was determined not to be just one more of the local "belles" who wanted him. And beyond that, she had to insure herself against the fate that had befallen both her mother and grandmother.

Will pushed aside his coffee cup and got down to business. "Here's how we'll start," he said. "I'll look up your allotment, and I'll get you some pamphlets from the Department of Agriculture that educate you about the federal program. Meantime, here's what you need to know in a nutshell. Every tobacco farmer who wants into the program gets an allotment of acreage. You can farm it yourself or rent it. Then, if you can't sell your crop within one percent of the set price at auction, the tobacco cooperative takes the leaf and warehouses it—good leaf can keep for anywhere between five and ten years—until it can be sold for the right price. Meantime, you're paid out of government loans—they're called "nonrecourse" loans, which means they don't have to be paid back. Do you understand—or would you like me to go over it again?"

"I understand," she said. "I'm inexperienced, but not dumb."

"Never said you were, Niki." Will hesitated a moment,

then asked, "Mind if I give you some neighborly advice . . . and this ain't about farming?"

Niki nodded reluctantly.

"Seems to me you've got some kind of chip on your shoulder. Be careful, Niki, that could get in your way. Now let me ask you a serious question. . . ."

Niki tensed, certain he was about to get personal—perhaps to probe her past.

"Are you sure you want to farm this place?" Will went on, "After what you heard me say last night, maybe you have some second thoughts. A lot of young people are leaving family farms these days to take jobs in factories. It isn't an easy life, Niki, not even when you're used to it, not even when times are good."

"I'm sure," Niki said flatly. "I'm damn sure I want to try."

Will got up from the table, taking his cup to the sink and rinsing it out. I wonder who taught him to do that, Niki thought.

"Okay, that's settled," he said. "So let's have a look around. That'll give me a better idea of what you need to get set up."

They went outside, Niki trailing half a step behind as Will strode to his pickup truck. He held the door open and Niki slid into the passenger seat, resolving not to do or say anything more to make her appear foolish or ignorant in Will's eyes.

As they drove the roads that crossed Niki's land, Will looked out at the fields, grunting now and then as he formed some silent opinion. But he said nothing, taking his cue from Niki's silence.

When his inspection of the farm was completed, Will drove Niki back to the house. They sat down in the kitchen again.

"It's not too bad," he said, "considering the crop was left to rot. You've lost the chance of harvesting your own crop this year, but you can get ready to plant. That means there's a lot of clearing to be done before you can burn out the fields."

Though this advice had no meaning for her, Niki refused to ask for an explanation.

Seeing the look on her face, Will smiled and supplied one. "You've got to kind of sterilize your land before you plant. To kill all those bad things you heard me mention last night. You can use steam or chemicals, but most of the farmers around here just fire the fields after harvest."

Niki nodded.

"I never did understand why Judd Martin left in such a hurry," Will said. "I don't suppose you know anything about that?"

There was almost an accusation in the question, and Niki's voice was edgy when she replied: "It was my understanding that they couldn't pay their rent, so they just cleared out. What they did to the land was nothing compared to the way they left the house."

Will frowned. "That's funny. I would have bet my bottom dollar that Judd paid his debts. Of course, the Martins did have a bad patch a couple of years back. But last I heard, they were doing okay. Then, bingo, they up and went. Somebody said that Judd's daughter was in trouble up in Baltimore, but I don't pay much attention to rumors." Apparently satisfied that Niki had no more information about the Martins, he asked, "So how did you come to rent the place?"

Niki hesitated for just a split second—and chose truth. Kate's evasion was well meaning, but it didn't sit well with Niki. She had made a commitment to Gabrielle Sandeman, and she wasn't about to start off by denying her name or her memory.

"I didn't rent," she said. "I own the place. It belonged to my mother." She waited for Will's response, not realizing she was holding her breath.

Will's brow creased as he searched his memory. "Wait a minute," he said finally, "I *did* hear something about this place. Wasn't there a . . . ?"

"Yes," Niki cut in, "my mother was murdered here. And yes, she was H.D. Hyland's mistress!"

Will's hazel eyes flickered. "Like I said before, it looks to me like you have a chip on your shoulder. Maybe there's good reason for it. That's still no excuse for judging people you don't know. I'm sorry about your mama's death. As for the other part, I figure that was her business."

"That's not how the other people around here saw it! They made her feel like a . . ." Niki couldn't make herself say the ugly word, not to a man she scarcely knew. "Rubbed off on me, too. A lot of folks treated us like dirt."

Will looked down, almost as though accepting a portion of the shame himself. "Well, nobody ever accused us of being liberal-minded down here." He glanced up again. "But why did you want to come back if you had such a bad time of it here?"

"Because I wasn't ready to let the tax collector take my mother's house. Raising tobacco seems to be the only way to keep it."

"Sounds like there might be a little more to the story," Will suggested, waiting for a moment. "But okay . . . if it's none of my business . . ." He leaned across the table. "I'm not just being nosy, Niki. I figured maybe you could use a friend, someone to talk to—being a kind of stranger here."

"I'm used to being a stranger," she said quietly.

"Maybe that was your first mistake."

Niki wasn't about to take personal advice from the local lothario, so she changed the subject. "I'm going to need some help here. Kate said you might be able to get me the hands I need. Can you help?"

"Tobacco's a demanding crop, Niki. I guess you could say it's a feminine kind of crop," he explained with a smile. "It needs some kind of attention every single day. If you let it alone, you're likely to be sorry."

Niki looked away, letting her impatience show. She needed help, names of people she could hire, not a lecture.

Will went on steadily, "The point is, Niki, you've got to make a big commitment—and keep it—otherwise, you can kiss any investment you make a fast good-bye."

"I'm here to stay," she declared. "I've made the commitment."

"Only part of it. What I'm telling you is that if you want someone to work here and care about the crop, you've got to give him a stake in it, a share of the profits, not just a wage."

"I don't care how it's done. As long as I can make enough to keep my . . . my home."

Will nodded. "All right. Matthew Parker might be available, I'll ask him. And Lem Hansen's boy needs work. Bo's kind of simple, but as long as there's someone else to direct him, he'll give you more than a dollar's worth." He paused heavily, eyeing her from under heavy brows.

Niki sensed he was weighing whether or not to provide one more suggestion. At last, he said, "There's a man named Jim Dark who'd make you a good foreman."

It sounded to Niki like there was a "but" coming. She waited . . . and it came.

"Jim got out of jail a couple of weeks ago. He's been doing odd jobs here and there. I promised I'd try to help him out. How do you feel about hiring a man who's been in prison?"

Niki started to shake her head. But then she remembered Helen's teaching about "labels," and thought of how she'd been judged herself—and Elle, too—how they'd also been kept in a kind of prison.

"What was Jim Dark's crime?" Niki asked.

Will looked her straight in the eye. "He killed a man."

Niki's mouth fell open. "You want me to hire a murderer?"

"Jim's no murderer. The law took it to be manslaughter, the judge let Jim plead to aggravated assault. I took it to be a man defending himself when somebody attacked him. If the fight hadn't have happened in a bar, Jim would have gotten off altogether." Will shrugged. "I figured you could be more open-minded than most. Guess maybe I was wrong. . . ."

Niki resented the way he put her on the spot, the way he was trying to make her feel guilty just because she had reservations about hiring a convicted criminal. She lived here alone, for goodness' sake. Was he being dense—or was he testing her in some way? "Will, I live here alone. . . ."

"I can understand your reservations," Will said. He pushed back his chair, preparing to leave.

"You think he's the only man I can get for foreman . . . ?"

"Nope. But I think Jim is the best man to help you. There's nothing about farming tobacco that he doesn't know. He's smart and hard-working and he can think on his feet. He joined the AA when he was in jail, and he's been sober for at least a year now."

"He wouldn't have had much choice in prison."

Will smiled. "People always have choices—even there."

"Okay," she conceded. "But what if he starts drinking again?"

"Human beings don't come with guarantees, Niki. But I've known Jim a long, long time, and I don't think he'll disappoint you. But why don't you meet him and see for yourself? If you're still not sure, give him a few days' work clearing your fields. No obligation. Nothing to lose. If you decide to take him on, you can count on me to keep an eye on things."

"You seem to have an answer for everything."

"Nope. Not everything. For instance, I don't know if you're coming to the dance to raise money for the Carson family—and I would like an answer to that."

"I haven't made up my mind."

"That wasn't the answer I wanted. But if you decide to come, I'll be glad to see you there. And now I'd better get back to work." He walked Niki to her door and left with a jaunty wave and a promise to arrange a meeting with Jim Dark.

What nerve, she thought, as she marched into the house. What conceit, she thought, as she gathered up the breakfast things, slamming them into the sink with such force that she cracked a saucer in half. He didn't even invite her to the Carson benefit like a normal man would. No, he just wanted to keep his dance card free for the benefit of *all* the cooperative's single women. Not that she would have accepted—no chance of that. But his casual assumption that she'd be pleased to be a member of his fan club . . . that was just too much.

Still, she would be in Will's debt for helping her get the farm going—assuming, of course, that she didn't get murdered by the man he had proposed as foreman.

Nineteen

THE building that housed the executive offices of the Hyland Tobacco Company had been conceived in 1952 by Henry David Hyland. At fourteen stories, it was by far the tallest in Willow Cross. In keeping with his policy of buying the best, H.D. had first engaged Frank Lloyd Wright as his architect. "I want the finest building in the South," he had told Wright, "but I don't want it to look new. I want people to see history when they look at Hyland Tobacco. I want them to see something . . . everlasting." Long before the foundation was laid for Hyland's tobacco temple, Wright had resigned the commission, unable to accept H.D.'s clear intention of making the project completely his own, constantly demanding revisions in the blueprints, regardless of the effect on architectural integrity. Wright was replaced by a Southern architect—and then another, as attempts to satisfy H.D.'s vision fell by the wayside.

The final result was an odd kind of hybrid. Neither a cathedral nor a museum; neither an antebellum reconstruction nor a contemporary adaptation, the headquarters of Hyland Tobacco that emerged was not necessarily in the best of taste, esthetically speaking. But H.D. Hyland was satisfied that it expressed the message he wished to convey: his family's tobacco company represented history, continuity, and power, all tempered by Southern feudal paternalism at its benevolent best.

The entire lobby floor was devoted to a historical representation of the tobacco industry, a kind of miniature world's fair of tobacco, open seven days a week to the public. The first exhibit depicted the plantation of Captain John Rolfe, Pocahontas's husband and the first major grower of American tobacco. Next came a patriotic representation of the tobacco growers' protest against the British Crown's prohibition against direct foreign sales of their crops. It was titled: "Tobacco Leads the Fight for America's Freedom and Independence."

Then came a working model of the original nineteenth-century Hyland factory, showing the manufacture of "plug" and "twist." A five-minute recording explained how the hogsheads of tobacco were hoisted by a pulley system up to the second floor of the factory, where they were opened and steamed. The midrib of the leaf was removed and the leaves loaded into a furnace-heated drying room, where they were dehydrated. Next the leaves were dipped into a bubbling vat containing licorice or sugar. Then they were hauled up to the roof to dry in the sun. If there was rain, said the recorded voice, all hands rushed to bring the precious leaf inside.

"When Nature finished her work," the voice continued, "the leaf went into a drying room, kept at well over one hundred degrees Fahrenheit, to remove every last trace of moisture. Then the leaves were sprinkled with rum or other flavorings, to impart the unique Hyland taste enjoyed by so many Americans." Now the worker known as a "lumper" shaped the leaves into a cube. Nearby a "stemmer" removed stems from the leaves used to wrap the lump. Lumps that resembled cakes were known as "plug"; those that were rolled out were called "twist." The finishing process came after the lumps were hand shaped and subjected to pressure. They were packed in sycamore cases, placed into wooden billies reinforced with iron bands—franked with a tax stamp and shipped by railroad.

The exhibit moved on to show the first mechanized cigarette rolling machines of the early 1900s, proceeding in a straight line to a scale model of the present-day Hyland factory—a cluster of modern, well-equipped buildings where a racially integrated employee force worked in harmony with the sophisticated machines that did everything from redrying the leaves and removing the stems, to shredding the leaves and mixing the blended tobaccos in a "merry-go-round" just before the cigarettes were made.

At the far end of the exhibit, a trio of attractive young women handed out free samples of Hyland cigarettes and escorted visitors through a pictorial representation of the company's good works. Under the title "First in War" were photographs of battle-weary G.I.s. receiving specially marked "We Care" packages of Hyland products. There was a framed commendation from President Franklin Delano Roosevelt, lauding Hyland's support of the war effort by matching every employee purchase of war bonds.

The "First in Peace" section offered a dazzling display of Hyland's good citizenship, with poster-size photographs showing the company's participation in dozens of philanthropies, as well as its sponsorship of major sporting events.

Upstairs, occupying the entire penthouse floor, were the offices of the chief executive officer, which had passed from H.D. Hyland to his firstborn son, Edward. It, too, was a kind of museum, housing the memorabilia that accompanied the family's rise from the middle class into the rarefied domains of the very, very rich. But where the public exhibition conveyed a message of public service, here the tone was set by H.D. Hyland's personal code of ethics, engraved in gold on a plaque behind the executive desk.

BE THE LION, NOT THE LAMB
BE SILENT. THE EMPTY WALNUT MAKES THE MOST NOISE
BE QUICK—OR BE DEAD
FIGHT YOUR ENEMY WITH HIS OWN WEAKNESS
REWARD YOUR FRIEND WHEN NECESSARY

In the years that Duke had ruled Hyland, his own unwritten amendments to the code had come to be well understood among all his subordinates: There are no friends, only allies. A well-placed noise can mask the sound of danger. Remember a favor . . . but never forget an insult.

On this winter Friday morning, Duke entered the private elevator reserved for his personal use and acknowledged with a nod the operator's greeting. Where the doors slid open on the top floor, Duke's secretary, Nancy Butterfield, was waiting on the other side—having been alerted to his arrival by a signal from the security guard downstairs.

Like an old plantation servant, she trailed a half step behind her employer as he marched through the reception area, past the enormous conference room, and into his office. Following her usual ritual, Miss Butterfield listed the calls that had come in his absence—knowing that the written memos on Duke's desk would be swept into the wastebasket, unread. She waited a moment, and when there were no instructions forthcoming, Miss Butterfield prepared a fresh pot of coffee, poured it into a silver thermos, and left.

Duke rubbed his eyes as if to erase the merciless hangover that had wakened him at dawn. Waves of nausea had emptied his stomach; a throbbing headache had nearly blinded him with pain. From the top drawer of his desk, he took two small bottles—one containing a prescription painkiller, the other, a special blend of vitamins and minerals. He half filled a porcelain mug with coffee, added a generous shot of bourbon, and washed down the pills in two scalding gulps. Closing his eyes, he leaned back in his luxuriously upholstered glove-leather chair and waited for relief, silently damning the incompetence of the personal physician he had just fired. "I pay you to keep me healthy," Duke had told Dr. Joseph Kendrick, the latest in a long line of Hyland doctors, "and you're doing a lousy job of it. I don't see any reason to keep on paying when I don't like the results."

"The responsibility for results is yours, Mr. Hyland," Dr. Kendrick replied. "Time and again, I have given you good advice and treated your excesses. If you continue to disregard my advice, if you refuse to cut down your drinking, to change your diet and alter your way of living, there's not much I can do to keep your body from wearing itself out." The doctor no longer dared to tell H.D. that his smoking was the habit most likely to kill him.

Duke thought it was all bullshit. A doctor was a mechanic like any other on the Hyland payroll. It was his job to keep the machinery working, not to dish out warnings and excuses.

When he was feeling a little better, Duke buzzed Miss Butterfield to admit Josiah Mayfield, his personal barber. Mayfield was a light-skinned black man who made the trip from town once a week, just as his father had done before him.

After offering his usual " 'Morning, Mr. Duke," Mayfield noted his employer's pallor and bloodshot eyes—and refrained from further conversation. Silently he opened a worn leather bag and laid out the tools of his trade on Duke's desk. With a flourish, he unfurled a spotless linen cloth and deftly fastened it around Duke's neck.

"Nothing off the top," Duke muttered.

"Yes, sir," Mayfield agreed, though in fact no instructions were necessary. After six years, the barber knew exactly how and when to trim the thick brown hair, which had recently begun to gray. Comb in one hand, scissors in the other, Mayfield worked slowly, precisely, gathering up the fallen hairs as he cut, so as not to leave any trace of his labors.

Giving himself over to the barber's silent ministrations, Duke lit up a cigarette and pondered the week's balance sheet of successes and frustrations. On the plus side, he had beaten out Regal Tobacco in a bid to purchase Birmingham Brothers, a small company that manufactured snuff and chew. Though the firm was financially healthy, it was the century-old name that Duke wanted to acquire—as well as the pleasure of outmaneuvering Regal.

But his satisfaction had been marred by another of Pepper's public escapades. Turning on his television to watch the evening news, Duke was treated to a filmed account of his half sister's arrest on charges of disturbing the peace and assaulting an officer. It seemed that Pepper and her worthless friends had decided to liven up one of their drunken parties with a fireworks display. After several neighbors, nervous about possible terrorist activity, had reported the explosions, a police car had been dispatched to investigate. When she found a policeman at her door, Pepper invited him to join the fun. He had declined, and Pepper had flown into a drunken rage, screaming obscenities as she slapped and kicked the officer.

Duke grimaced with distaste as he contemplated the rash of scandal sheet articles that would soon appear, once again dragging the Hyland name through the mud. Joanne's offspring were a constant thorn in his side, now even more than when they were children.

The barber finished his work, dusted Duke's neck lightly with English talcum, removed the white linen cloth, and disappeared with a murmured "See you next week, sir."

Duke rose from his chair and walked to the glass-enclosed cabinet that held his father's priceless collection of royal souvenirs. Everything in the cabinet had a royal pedigree, from the Faberge eggs that had belonged to the last Russian czar to the diamond-studded snuff box that had been the property of the French king Louis XIV.

Duke unlocked the glass door and removed the crown jewel of the collection, a magnificent gold goblet encrusted with rubies. According to legend, it had been commissioned by Henry VIII, king of England—and endowed with special powers by his court magician. H.D. christened it the *Henry Cup*—in his own honor—and claimed that a drink from the cup before every important business endeavor assured him of luck and success.

Duke poured a shot of bourbon into the jeweled goblet and raised it to the portrait of his father, mocking H.D.'s memory and his pretensions as he swallowed the whiskey.

As a kid, Duke had been intimidated by his mythical father. But after coming into his own as an adult, he had been able to cut H.D. Hyland down to human dimensions, surrounding himself with reminders of H.D.'s failures and limitations.

Duke raised his glass again and drank to a huge uncut emerald that sat on a brass pedestal. *Hyland's folly*, Duke called it, recalling how his father had bought a worthless Brazilian mine on the strength of this single stone and a fast-talking group of con men who pretended to be disgruntled civil servants.

He made a final toast to the model of a steamship, the *Hyland Queen*, supposedly the first of a shipping line known as Hyland Overseas. After being burned by the Brazilians, H.D. abandoned the venture, resolving to stick to the only business he cared about—the business of tobacco. "Stupid," Duke muttered, draining the last of his whiskey, "that was damn stupid." By foregoing the chance to buy all the government surplus ships that were being sold at giveaway prices after World War II, H.D. had thrown away the chance of a lifetime. Leaving his son to play catch-up with companies who understood early the value of diversification.

Another of H.D.'s mistakes. Just like the wives that had come back like bloodsucking vampires after his death, trying to squeeze an extra million or two out of his estate.

Duke smiled. He had shown the bitches—and he included his own mother—that their ride on the gravy train was over. Just the way he showed his own ex-wives what they could expect if they pushed the limits of his generosity.

His smile broadened as he recalled his second wife's petulant demand for an extra fifty thousand dollars to pay for her spiritual reclamation by some half-assed New Mexico guru. "You owe me, Duke," she whined. "Brother Singh says you wounded my psyche and it's gonna take *years* to mend it. The least you can do is pay for the damage."

Duke had disposed of that demand in one terse sentence, telling the bitch just what would happen to her psyche and her worthless ass if she didn't get herself out of his life.

The desk intercom buzzed. "Are you ready to see your brother now, Mr. Hyland?" his secretary asked.

Duke glanced at his appointment book. By his reckoning, Babe would have been waiting at least a half-hour. "Send him in," Duke said.

The door to the office was opened slowly, tentatively, to reveal a man whose appearance had changed very little over the years. Years of exposure to the sun had given Babe Hyland's skin a perennial tan, etching a network of fine lines on his boyish face. Failure and disappointment had dimmed the light in his pale eyes, but he was still strikingly handsome. As a concession to his brother, Babe wore a conservative gray suit, rather than the more casual yachting clothes he favored.

"Come in, little brother," Duke called out expansively, "come on in and rest yourself. You must be tired after all that flying."

"I am jet-lagged," Babe admitted, "but it's nothing a good night's sleep can't fix."

"I'm sure. Can I offer you some coffee?" he asked solicitously, indicating the silver thermos on his desk; Duke knew very well what kind of liquid refreshment his brother wanted—needed.

"No . . . no, thanks," Babe declined, casting a longing look at the mahogany bar, past the doors that had been left tantalizingly open, revealing a glistening array of glasses and bottles. He glanced at his watch, as if to determine when he might appropriately request a drink.

Seeing all this, Duke made the opening move in a game he enjoyed, a game he would relish even more if it weren't always so easy to win. He picked up a sheaf of papers on his desk. "I've read your report, little brother. I must say," he paused, watching Babe lean forward in his seat—still taking the hook even after all these years, "I am surprised. Disappointed," he said, watching Babe sag into his chair. "I asked you for a comprehensive report on our farms in Brazil and Zimbabwe. I asked you for projections on the yield-per-acre of the new strains of tobacco we're developing. You didn't tell me that such a report was beyond your abilities, little brother." Duke's voice was gentle. It gave him such enormous pleasure to punish Babe for simply existing. Especially when there was no cost whatever. No risk. Duke *counted* on Babe to screw up, so he always had someone working behind him, doing the job right.

Babe paled beneath his sportsman's tan. He had dreaded this moment. "The new strains are growing fine," he said. "I put that in my report."

"Then what's all this other *crap*, little brother?"

"It's my honest opinion of what we should do."

"Your honest opinion," Duke repeated, his voice laden with sarcasm. "What makes you think you're qualified to have an opinion? Have you spent enough time on *anything* in your whole misbegotten life to *earn* an opinion?"

"There's no need to talk to me like that," Babe said quietly, struggling to maintain his dignity.

"I think there's every need when you bring back a report that's damaging to the very future of Hyland Tobacco. Do I have to tell you what could happen if some nosy reporter got hold of this?" he demanded, rattling the papers for emphasis. "Did you think for a minute what kind of ammunition you were gathering for our enemies? Or is thinking too difficult for—"

"I think we'd be damaging Hyland Tobacco if we went on with this venture," Babe cut in. "If you could see for yourself, Duke, if you could only see the conditions I saw. The farmers who work for us in Brazil are dirt poor. They're barefoot and undernourished, they plow their fields with oxen, Duke—in this day and age! For transportation, they use wooden carts that look like they came from the Stone Age. They live in crude huts that aren't fit for livestock. The stench of raw sewage . . . I can't begin to describe it. Or the children, Duke, their bodies covered with festering sores. It's . . . it's like a leper colony out of the Bible!''

''But we're giving these people something very valuable for the future, little brother,'' Duke said with exaggerated patience. ''We're giving them our own Hyland-trained agronomists, to teach them how to grow high-quality tobacco on their miserable land. We're making an investment in time and effort, Babe . . . it's only right that these people give something back. Meanwhile,'' he added with a smile, ''we're able to buy their tobacco for less than half of what we pay for domestic crops.''

''It's worse in Zimbabwe,'' Babe pressed on. ''Hundreds of workers living in a tiny compound, all using one broken toilet. No water for washing, no medical facility for more than a hundred miles. Nobody can live on what we pay these people. It's less than twenty dollars a month. It's worse than slavery.''

Duke shook his head. ''You poor fool,'' he said, ''you poor, ignorant fool. You don't know a damn thing about business and you never will.''

Humiliation burned Babe's face, but the shameful conditions he'd seen had so touched him that he felt compelled to speak out. ''If that kind of suffering is what good business is about, then, yes, I guess I am ignorant.''

''I'm glad you finally realized that,'' Duke said with a satisfied smile. ''And since you're obviously not suited to work with our foreign import division, I see I'll have to find someone less . . . sentimental for the job. But don't get discouraged, little brother—we can talk again soon. I'm sure that if we both keep trying, we'll find *something* suited to your talents and abilities . . .''

Babe half rose from his chair, but Duke wasn't yet finished with him. ''There's something else. I don't like what I've been hearing about your personal life. If you *still* haven't learned to drink like a gentleman, maybe it's time for a refresher course at Woodland Hills . . ."

Babe shuddered at the mere mention of the institution to which Duke had shipped him shortly after H.D.'s death, as if somehow to demonstrate that absolute power was now his. For thirty nightmarish days, Babe had been subjected to what the doctors called "aversion therapy," an excruciating torture that had him begging for the merciful release of death. That dreadful memory gave Babe the courage to speak now. "The old man's been gone for years," he said quietly. "Do you still have to resent me so much?"

Babe feared an explosion of temper, but Duke was amused by the question. Yes, he thought, the old man was long gone and there was no one to stop him from treating his half brother any way he damn well pleased. "What makes you think I resent you?" he asked softly. "Do you think I have reasons to feel that way?"

"I . . . I don't know," Babe stammered, instantly regretting the Pandora's box he'd opened.

"Let me see," Duke said, enjoying himself more by the minute. "Could it be that I resented you because H.D. dumped my mother to marry Joanne?"

Babe was silent.

"Could it be that I resented you because the old man forgot I was alive? Because he made me earn my lousy allowance while he spoiled you rotten? Because he gave you every goddamn thing you ever asked for? Let you play with Hyland railroad cars? *Gave* you a goddamn string of polo ponies because you said you *might* enjoy the game? Never said a word when you got tired of that?"

Babe sat perfectly still, not daring to interrupt Duke's litany of recriminations. He looked longingly at the model of the *Hyland Queen*. If only H.D. had built the shipping company he'd started, then maybe Babe would have had a place to belong. A place where he could fit.

When Duke paused for breath, Babe made an effort to bring the invective to an end. "But H.D. loved you in his way," he said. "No matter what he did for me, he made you his heir."

"Love," Duke mused, "now what do you suppose that commodity is fetching on the exchanges these days? No, little brother, H.D. made me his heir because I was born first. Because the old man was a traditionalist. You and I both know what his love counts for." With an impatient wave of his hand, Duke signaled that the conversation was over.

Released at last, Babe got up and left. Weary as he was, it never occurred to Babe to argue with his brother. Like an obedient son, he allowed Duke to dominate him. Babe attempted one job after another, trying to do his best, even after it became very clear that Duke would see only failure and incompetence in his efforts. Babe's only relief, his only opportunity for winning, came during his periods of "unemployment," when he was free to race his beloved power boats.

Satisfied that he had put Babe in his place, Duke congratulated himself on having had the foresight to make sure there would be no children in either of his marriages. People assumed that was a grave disappointment to him. Yet when a *Time* reporter once asked how he felt about not having a son and heir, Duke had given him an honest answer. "Did Napoleon have an heir? Did Alexander the Great have an heir? No, sir, I put it to you that a man who creates his own greatness is better off without children." Then he had smiled, leaving it to the reporter to interpret his meaning. If he had spelled it out, Edward "Duke" Hyland would have said that he had no desire to have a son like the weak, worthless sot who had just left his office. Even less would he wish to have a son like himself—a man-child hovering in the background, waiting for him to die, ready to claim what he had spent his life in building.

No, Duke thought, his dream of immortality lay in his vision of Hyland's future—a vision that exceeded anything his father had imagined. H.D. had but one love in his life, the company. That love, that obsession, had narrowed his perspective, made his thinking parochial rather than global.

On a conference table was a part of Duke's vision for the future—a miniature greenhouse. Under a protective plastic cover were living samples of the new strains of *nicotiana rustica*, especially bred to grow with weedlike rapidity in the climates of Brazil and selected locations in Africa.

In spite of Babe's sniveling complaints, the project was already a success, and in the years to come it would provide Hyland with tons of cheap tobacco.

But control of cheap foreign tobacco was just one element in Duke's three-pronged plan for the future. The *trinity play*, as he liked to call it, also called for the kind of diversification his father had never understood and the intense development of foreign markets for Hyland products. With vast profits to invest, Duke knew there was just so much that could be accomplished with modernization. Already he had ordered machinery and additives that could produce cigarettes using 25 percent less tobacco. Yet in a growing national health consciousness that Duke blamed on California crazies and the goddamn hippies, domestic cigarette sales weren't as strong as they once had been—while Hyland sales abroad were like the seedlings in his greenhouse, growing rapidly and showing greater promise every day.

Everything Duke touched seemed destined for glory. With the success of his plan for the future, Duke fully expected Hyland tobacco to become the richest, most powerful tobacco-based empire in the world. Already he had begun recruiting the smartest, toughest young executives he could find. Using a team of headhunters, but relying always on his own shrewd instincts, he chose men who, like himself, recognized that the business climate they lived in was ruled by Greed. Men who would carry out his will—yet who could bring to the company creative resources of their own. A delicate balance, he had to admit, and one not without risks.

Duke pressed the buzzer on his desk, signaling Miss Butterfield that he was ready for his next appointment. Glancing at his appointment book, Duke reckoned that this man had been kept waiting even longer than Babe, at least an hour. A moment later, Sterling Weatherby entered the office and approached Duke's desk.

Not bothering with pleasantries, Duke didn't invite the lawyer to sit. "Well," he said, "did you take care of that matter we spoke of?"

The lawyer fumbled with his hat and shifted awkwardly on his feet. "I did everything we discussed."

"But she's still here," Duke observed. He was a study in rage about to explode. But he controlled his temper as Weatherby stumbled through his excuses.

"She must have other funds, Mr. Hyland," he said. "I swear to you, I did everything I could. Haven't I kept her away all these years, done everything else—"

"And you've been paid very handsomely," Duke said. "Now, if you can't complete your job—"

"It's only a matter of time, Mr. Hyland," the lawyer cut in. "I can assure you, it's only a matter of time."

"Can you now?" Duke said softly. "Well, then, if it's time that's going to do the job, I won't be needing you, Weatherby, will I?"

The lawyer stared at the man who had written his annual retainer check for more than a dozen years. "You can't mean that," he protested, his voice faltering.

"Oh, but I do. Consider yourself retired, Weatherby. Without pension. Now get out."

Weatherby stared at Duke Hyland in disbelief. Of course, the retainer he had received was not the whole of his income. But as soon as it became known that he no longer had the patronage of the Hylands, all the rest of his business was bound to slip away. Yet if he fought, what was to be gained? He could only hope that Duke would need him again and change his mind. Weatherby shuffled out of the office looking years older than when he had entered.

Damn her, Duke thought, damn that daughter of a whore.

It was intolerable to think of her still there in that house. As long as she was, she would be a reminder of her mother—the woman H.D. had stolen from him—a reminder of so many things in the past he wanted only to purge from his memory forever.

Twenty

THE day that her fifty acres were cleared of the dead weight of an aborted crop, Niki felt as if she, too, had shed a heavy burden. Perhaps it was the lifeless weight of a dead past, she mused, or even the crippling confusion of a shadowed identity.

Now she had a new life. She was a tobacco farmer, a landowner—part of a uniquely American tradition, as old and venerable as the land itself. Working shoulder to shoulder with her hired help, it no longer seemed the slightest bit odd to Niki that her foreman was a convicted felon, that he in turn relied on a grown man with the mind of a child. Or even that her adviser was apparently the local Romeo of Willow Cross.

The day that her fields were to be burned, Will showed up with two of his own workers. "Just in case," he said, not putting into words the danger of a shift in the wind. "But I don't want you to worry . . . Jim knows what he's doing."

As the easternmost section of Niki's fifty acres was set aflame, a column of smoke rose upward, a sharp acrid smell filled the air. Shading her eyes with her hand, she tried to follow the direction of the flames. "Don't worry," Will repeated, "it smells bad and it looks scary, but the weather forecast is with us."

To Niki, cleansing the land seemed a symbolic ritual, destroying not only weed seeds, nematodes, insects and diseases—but also purifying the spirit of the farm and restoring it to her. Will's passion for farming made her feel he'd understand, yet Niki kept her thoughts to herself. A new life didn't necessarily mean new habits.

"I want to thank you for all your help," she said. "I know how busy you are. I just wish I knew how to repay you. . . ."

"It's nothing more than I would have done for any good neighbor," Will said quickly, as if her gratitude embarrassed him.

Niki hoped that was true, though Will's generosity was beyond any kind of neighborly courtesy she'd ever known. Not only had he walked her through every step she'd taken, he had also helped her apply for a loan through the cooperative, making it possible for Niki to live in some small comfort until she sold her first crop.

"As for paying me back," he added, "you've already done that. By giving Jim and Bo a chance."

"It wasn't as much of a chance as you made me think. They're decent men. You didn't have to . . . to scare me the way you—"

"Didn't I?" Will put in. "Suppose I hadn't mentioned Jim's prison record. Suppose you heard about it from someone else who didn't care about Jim the way I do?"

"Jim told me himself. The first day he came here. I never would have guessed," Niki admitted, recalling her first impression of the man. Jim Dark looked more like a rural preacher than a barroom brawler. He was slightly built, neatly dressed, and had a small Bible tucked into his shirt pocket.

After he'd introduced himself, he said: "Whatever bad things you heard about me, they're true. Sober, I work harder than any man alive. Drunk, I'm like the devil himself. I'm swearing to you here and now, I been sober for three years. That's all I can say. I'll do my best for you, Miss Sandeman. I hope that's good enough."

So far, Jim's best had been more than Niki could ask of anyone.

"About Bo Hansen," she asked Will, "is he really retarded?"

"Around here, we say 'simple.' Why do you ask?"

"I don't know," Niki said slowly. "It does seem to take Bo a while to grasp directions, but when he does understand what's needed, he's so quick and capable. And his eyes, Will . . . they're so bright and alert."

"Well, Bo's always been slow to learn. But who can say what that comes from? His folks love him, but they've got six other kids to feed and a piece of land that's been nothing but bad luck as long as I can remember. When Bo had trouble in school, his folks just accepted it as the Lord's will. They took him out when he was twelve. . . ."

"And nobody stopped them?" Niki asked incredulously.

"There was talk of sending him to a special school over in Raleigh, but Bo's folks didn't want to send him away."

Niki was about to argue the case for trying again—until she remembered how it felt to be sent away, to be alone in a strange place. "At least he's with people who love him," she murmured. "That counts for a lot."

"Sure does," Will agreed. "And even if he isn't good at learning, Bo knows how to love people back. That counts for a lot, too."

Niki said nothing. If Will was talking about her, she had no intention of explaining that she knew how to love the people she could trust. And if that didn't happen to include a man right at the moment, that was none of his business.

When the day's work was finished, Niki invited Will to stay for supper. She had prepared an enormous stew the night before, and now she planned to feed Jim and Bo and whoever else cared to stay.

"Thank you, ma'am," Will said, "but I'll have to be getting home. My mama's alone in the house, and she needs looking after."

"Then take some of this stew with you—unless your mother would be insulted—"

"Whoa, there, whoa! I'll be happy to take whatever you're offering—and thank you very much. My mama *is* a great cook, but that doesn't make a kindness any less."

Now Niki felt silly, as if she'd been caught trying to impress, when all she wanted was to show her appreciation.

"Hey, Niki," he said, chucking her under the chin, as a big brother might. "You know you don't have to try so hard. You'll do fine here. Just be yourself."

Easy for you to say, was her first reaction. After all, Will Rivers was practically the undeclared king of the Willow Cross Cooperative. Not that he didn't deserve it, she had to admit. Yet after she'd given him some of Elle's *pot au feu* in a covered plastic container, along with one of the loaves of French bread she'd baked, he hugged her warmly—again as a brother might—and she realized how deeply grateful she was for his easygoing way of trying to help her fit in.

He arrived back at the house unannounced, a few days later, at eight in the morning. "Throw on your jacket," he said, "there's something I want you to see."

Niki did as she was told. Twenty minutes later, they pulled up in front of Johnson's Warehouse. "What's going on?" she asked. "Why are all these people here?"

"Welcome to the Carolina Farmer Tobacco Show," Will said. "Even though you'll be buying all your supplies through the cooperative, I figured you ought to be here. Just to get the feel of things. Besides," he added as they passed inside, "this is where you'll be auctioning off your crop."

The warehouse was cavernous. "Wow," Niki exclaimed, her eyes widening.

"Four acres under one roof," Will explained.

It resembled a county fair brought indoors. Colorful, banner-laden booths displayed everything that would interest the tobacco farmer: tractors, irrigation devices, fertilizers, seedbed covers, pesticides, as well as pamphlets from the U.S. Department of Agriculture.

Though Will had a long shopping list of his own, he took the time to educate Niki as they walked between the booths, pointing out the merits of one kind of fertilizer over another, explaining that rising prices had made it more necessary than ever to choose wisely and buy well.

They stopped by a display of flue-curing equipment. "After you harvest your leaf," he explained, "it'll have to be cured. We do what's called flue curing here; it's efficient and it only takes from four to six days to do the job. You need barns that are small and tightly constructed. The furnaces inside burn wood, coal, oil, or liquid petroleum. They're equipped with special ventilators called flues that extend from the furnace around the floor of the barn. Are you getting all this, Niki, or am I going too fast?"

Niki no longer took offense at Will's teasing. "Getting it all just fine, sir."

"Good," he grinned. "Then we'll finish up this lesson with a mention of aircuring, which is done indoors, in buildings equipped with different kinds of ventilators—and maybe some artificial heat. And you should also know that curing can be done with wood fires, which is almost the same as aircuring—except that the smoke gives the leaf the aroma of creosote."

"Thanks very much," she said with a smile. "I think that's enough for today."

Beyond the equipment display was a Hyland Tobacco booth, with the motto "We Take Care of Our Own" emblazoned on a bright-green banner. The booth was decorated with pictures showing the benefits Hyland provided for its workers—the enormous cafeteria serving free hot lunches, the spotless infirmary staffed by a team of physicians and nurses, the distribution of free turkeys at Thanksgiving, the lavish Christmas parties and summer picnics. Niki paused for a long time before a picture of a costumed Santa Claus in a sleigh, being pulled by eight reindeer (actually horses with papiermâché antlers attached to their heads) onto the snow-covered lawn of Highlands. She could remember the hurt of being excluded from that event. . . .

"Look at this," Will said, calling her out of the painful reverie. He was looking at a display of sepia photographs dating back to the Depression era and titled "Work for the Unemployed." The first showed scores of ragged, sad-looking men milling around aimlessly. The rest pictured them being put to work on various Hyland projects, planting trees around the family estate, cutting new roads on Flamingo Island, painting and refurbishing the old Hyland Tobacco factory.

"You don't see the rest of the story here," Will observed quietly. "Nothing about why these men had no work, why they lost their farms in the first place, or why Hyland could afford to hire them when nobody else could."

"Sounds like you have a grudge against Hyland," Niki said.

"I think they bear watching. 'Cause anytime it suits 'em, they'll give us the shaft." He put an arm around her shoulder in that brotherly way he had. "Now that you're one of us, maybe you'd like to help me convince some of the other farmers that Hyland isn't looking out for our interests."

"I might," she said, enjoying the idea of fellowship as much as she enjoyed the prospect of helping Will keep the Hylands in their place. "Yes, I just might do that."

At that moment, a very attractive young woman appeared, wearing a rustic costume that was part Betty Crocker, part Playboy bunny. "I have a gift for you," she said, offering Will a shopping bag filled with packages of different brands of Hyland cigarettes.

Will stopped to smile at the girl and openly appreciate the "samples" displayed in her very low-cut costume.

"No thanks," Niki said, and grabbed Will's arm to steer him away.

Will laughed. "Hey, wait a minute, I promised the boys I'd bring home as many samples as I could carry. . . ."

Niki was startled to realize she had acted on feminine reflex, pulling Will away from the temptation of the seductive model. Yet she didn't release him. "You want samples," she said, "then get them from here." She pushed Will towards another booth, where a motherly woman with blue-gray hair was handing out packages of snuff and chewing tobacco. A small sign said "You must be 21" but Niki saw parents grabbing the free samples and handing them out to their youngsters, some of whom looked to be no more than eleven or twelve years old. When Will made a request on behalf of his workers, the motherly woman turned coquette, smiling flirtatiously as she filled two bags with her products.

"You sure have a way with women," Niki said dryly.

"That's what comes of growing up with two sisters," Will replied.

Niki hoped Will might open up more about himself, but when he didn't she refused to ask. Once again, she didn't want to simply fall in line.

When they tired of walking, they stopped to rest at one of the many refreshment booths that were sponsored by various manufacturers and suppliers. Sandwiches, fried chicken, beer and soft drinks were given out free, along with buttons and baseball caps bearing the sponsor's name.

Shortly before noon, Will looked at his watch. "Got some business that needs lookin' after," he said. "But I won't be more than a half-hour, so don't go away."

Niki agreed to wait and Will moved off. A few minutes later, she saw a flurry of activity around the raised stage that stood in the center of the vast warehouse. A chubby man wearing a polka-dot shirt and old-fashioned armbands took the stage, followed by a trio of musicians in country garb. There was the loud hum of an amplifier being adjusted as the man spoke into a microphone. "Welcome, welcome," he said, "I hope you folks have been having a good old time for yourselves. Now I'm here to tell you, it's gonna get a whole lot better. I want you all to give a warm Carolina welcome to our own . . . Will Rivers!"

Niki gazed at the stage in astonishment. Why hadn't Will said he was going to make a speech here?

A moment later, he ran up to the stage, waving to the cheering crowd. To his faded blue jeans and white T-shirt, he'd added a fringed leather vest and a matching bandanna, and his long brown hair was half hidden under a large beige Stetson tipped back on his head. Where had the hat come from? Now Niki remembered half noticing some cases in the back of his truck when he'd come to pick her up. One of the boxes must have also contained the highly polished wooden guitar that Will was holding.

Will strummed a few chords on the guitar and the crowd grew quiet. "Howdy all," he said, "thank you kindly for that welcome. Sure is a pleasure to be here, and see you all again. I'd like to start with a new number, something I wrote when I was thinkin' back to when my daddy died. I call it 'Some Rivers Run Deep.' Hope you like it." He nodded to the band behind him, they played a few bars of introduction . . . and Will began to sing. "Lookin' across to where the sun is settin', I see the shadow of a man that's comin' home . . ."

Will's voice was a husky baritone. Like Will himself, it was too rugged to be pretty, and sometimes it cracked when he reached for a feeling, yet he had a way with a lyric that made it seem pure and true. As he sang of the father who never spoke of love but gave it when he could in a life filled with hard work, a hush fell over the crowd. When Will reached a point in the song that told of his father's death, Niki's eyes filled with tears.

There was a long moment of stillness as Will strummed the last chord and his voice died away, then thunderous applause erupted.

Will acknowledged it with a nod and moved into his next

number, a plaintive ballad titled "Forever's Not What It Used to Be." Hearing him sing of love's sweetness and pain, Niki found herself wondering how much of the lyric came from Will's poetic imagination, and how much from experience.

He finished his set with a rousing, thumping number called "Farmer Brown." The crowd clapped and whistled as Will sang of a tobacco farmer's life—the work that never got done, the small triumphs, and heartrending losses.

"More," the crowd chanted as he concluded the final chorus, and so he started again, this time with everyone singing along.

At last, he begged off. "That's all I have for you today," he said, holding up his hands for quiet. "Besides, the Country Cousins have been waiting here to entertain you. You folks give them the same fine welcome you gave me."

Then he tipped the big Stetson to Niki—and suddenly a hundred pairs of eyes were staring at her.

"I didn't know you were a singer, too," she said when Will had finally made his way through a gauntlet of backslapping and handshakes. "And here I thought you were just a good old country farmer."

"Farming's what my family's always done. After my daddy died, there was nobody left to run the farm but me. But singing's what I love."

"I thought you said you had sisters. Why don't they run the farm. Unless you think a woman just can't do it . . ."

"You won't catch me on that one, Niki," Will said, knowing she was testing as much as teasing. "I wouldn't mind handing it on to my sisters, but they've got families and husbands. 'Course, if my mama were twenty years younger, and in good health, hell, she could drive any six men into the ground." He paused and looked at Niki, as if seeing her for the first time. "You know," he said, "I think it's about time you came out to the farm and met Mama."

Niki was startled by the suggestion. The look on her face must have told Will what she was thinking for he laughed aloud.

"Don't look so scared Niki. I'm not havin' you looked over for a bride. She's just curious, that's all, doesn't get out much anymore. She gets all her news from the other ladies who come by to visit—but it isn't the same as seeing with her own eyes."

"Sure, I'll come," Niki said.

"Good. How about right now?" he asked.

"Right now?" she repeated.

Will had the grace to blush. "I sort of promised her . . . well, I figured you wouldn't mind . . . ."

"You've never thought of selling the farm and making a career of singing?" Niki asked as they drove away from Johnson's Warehouse.

"Never," Will answered. "I guess for the same reason you didn't want to sell your mama's place, Niki. It's like family. Tobacco farming's a way of life around these parts. Has been for almost four hundred years. Know what they call the red clay soil that stretches from Virginia to Georgia?"

"What?"

"Tobacco Road. Nothing takes to that land so well as the golden leaf. Or to the blistering dry summers. And when it's good, Niki, when it's good, it's like *real* gold. Just one acre of top-grade leaf, why that can bring in a profit of a thousand dollars."

Listening to Will, hearing his pride and excitement, made her feel glad to be part of the same endeavor.

Niki expected the Rivers farm house to be rustic and homespun, a natural environment to raise the kind of man Will was. What confronted her instead was a sublime evocation of the Old South, a stately centuries-old mansion with a graceful portico and beautiful Palladian windows. "It's magnificent," she said as they drove up the sweeping driveway, even though she could see that it was in need of many repairs.

"It's a white elephant," Will grumbled. Still, there was a pride in his voice that belied his words. "That house eats money faster than I can earn it. But Mama's attached to the place. There's been a man from my family living in that house since Ethan Rivers built it, back in the first days of Independence. Ethan started right in to farm tobacco. In fact, he had more than two thousand acres under cultivation."

"But you don't have that much . . ." Niki said. She had heard Will refer to his five hundred acres.

"No. I guess you could say the family history runs true to its name," Will explained with a smile. "Our fortunes move like the rivers, up in rain and down in drought. Old Winston Rivers, my great-great-granddaddy, he was a true son of the South. He sold off five hundred acres to save the Confederacy. His gold bought arms for a whole battalion. Made him a popular man, but that didn't mean too much after the war, when things got really bad. Back in the depression—I mean the one in 1897—Jefferson Rivers had to sell off more land just to pay off his debts."

"Your roots must go back even before the Hylands," Niki said.

"Oh sure, they were just upstarts back a hundred years ago. But don't be too impressed. Not all the Rivers men were such upstanding citizens. We've got a couple of black sheep with stories that could make the white sheep turn red."

"You'll have to tell me about them," Niki said.

"Another time. Mama said not to drag my feet. She's expecting us for coffee and cake. That's her favorite time of day."

"And you always do what your mama says?" Niki teased.

"Always."

Like everything else about the Rivers family, Will's mother proved to be a surprise. Charmaine Rivers was a small woman with a manner of speaking that was only vaguely "country." Her blond hair was carefully arranged in soft waves, complementing skin that was very smooth and fair, as if it hadn't seen much of the sun. Her makeup had also been skillfully applied, Niki saw, though not so well that it concealed deep lines that came from worry or pain. That there was a measure of pain in her life there could be no doubt, for as she made her way across the foyer of her house to greet Niki, Charmaine Rivers needed to use a metal walker.

Whatever her difficulties, however, it was not reflected in the genuinely welcoming smile that accompanied her greeting. After telling Niki that she'd been hearing a lot about her from her son, Will's mother suggested they all go to the kitchen to sit down.

For all her difficulty in moving, Charmaine Rivers maintained a spotless kitchen, and didn't stint on cooking. The round oak table was laden with muffins of various kinds and what looked like a homemade coffee cake.

"Will tells me you have no family here," Mrs. Rivers said when they were all seated.

"Yes ma'am," Niki replied, unconsciously copying Will's folksy ways.

"You must be pretty brave. Or pretty independent to live alone on a farm. It's a good life, but it can be mighty lonely."

"I do have an old friend in Willow Cross," Niki offered. "Kate Forester. She used to be—"

"Charles Boynton's girl. Charles was a fine doctor. I don't have much use for the one who took over his practice."

"That's because he lets you push him around," Will teased, but with obvious affection. "Charles knew better than to let you get away with anything."

Mrs. Rivers returned her son's affectionate glance. Suddenly, as she opened her mouth to speak, she began to gasp for breath.

Will reacted immediately. He rushed to the sink and poured out some medication from a nearby bottle. Quickly, he returned to his mother's side and helped her sip the liquid, wiping the side of her mouth with a handkerchief. Then he stroked her head tenderly, waiting until her breathing evened out and her muscles relaxed.

"Is there anything I can do?" Niki asked.

Will shook his head. Gently, he lifted his mother into his arms and carried her upstairs. When he came back, his face was dark with concern.

"Is she all right?" Niki asked.

"For now," Will dropped heavily into a chair. "It's rheumatoid arthritis. She's had it since my sister Ellie was born. By now, she's suffered as much from the therapy as the disease. Six operations. Joint replacements. Gold treatments, cortisone. It kills me to see her in such pain, but there's only so much the doctors can do for her."

"I'm sorry," Niki said.

"When she first got sick, I used to dream about being so rich that I could make it go away. . . ."

Again it seemed that Will might be inclined to share more of his personal thoughts. But then he shifted gears abruptly. "Come on," he said, springing out of his seat, "I'll show you around the house."

Though the rooms Niki saw were all beautifully proportioned, with such details as marble mantels and ornately carved moldings, more than half of them were empty, making her suspect that some furnishings, like the land, had been sold off in hard times.

"We only really use five or six rooms," Will explained apologetically, "so we keep the rest closed off. Mama says she wants to restore the house when the Rivers fortunes are running high again. I promised her it would happen. Though I'll be damned if I've figured out how to do it."

He stopped and opened a door to a room where a small piano, piled high with sheet music, stood in the middle of the floor, and a couple of banjos and a guitar were propped against the walls. "Here's a room that gets plenty of use. When I'm not too sleepy, I do my composing at night. I do it down here, so I don't bother Mama when she's trying to rest."

Niki noticed something framed on the wall. Stepping closer, she saw that it was a diploma from the University of North Carolina naming Willis Ethan Rivers dated June 5, 1972. She wondered, how much of Will's "country boy" manner was actually an act? Which was the real Will Rivers, the man who'd been brought up in a huge plantation house, the tobacco farmer, the eligible bachelor, or the beguiling singer of country-and-western songs? Could the real Will possibly be all of those things?

Even if he was, Niki told herself, he still wasn't her type.

Twenty-one

ON the day the planting was to begin, Niki rose before dawn, and when Jim and Bo arrived, she was waiting with strong coffee and a platter of scrambled eggs and ham. Too excited to consume more than a cup of coffee herself, she watched the two men eat, taking pleasure in their hearty appetites. Then they went out to the field.

In his gentle preacher's way, Jim showed Niki how to prepare a tobacco seedbed. "You take a half ounce of seed—about this much—for every hundred square yards. Next you sprinkle some of this fertilizer on the seed and mix it with a little wood ash and a little white sand. . . ."

It took her and the crew two days to prepare the seedbeds, working from sunup, stopping only for a half-hour lunch at noon. When they were finished, they covered the beds with a thin cloth as protection from sudden changes in temperature, destruction from wild animals, and hungry insects. According to the pamphlets Will had given her, Niki knew she could expect anywhere from fifteen thousand to twenty-five thousand plants from each hundred square yards of seedbed—though Jim had added his own proviso that she could expect a good crop only "if and when the Lord is willin'." There were so many insects, weeds and diseases that preyed on the tobacco almost from the day it was planted, through the three to four months of growth—and even beyond the harvest—that Niki could imagine how it might take divine assistance to bring in a maximum crop.

For the next two weeks, they worked the soil of the burnt-out fields, clearing what remained of the old plants, turning the earth in preparation for transplanting. As she worked, Niki felt like an expectant parent, preparing a nursery for children yet to come. For the first time in her life, she was doing real work, beginning something that was uniquely her own—instead of feeling like an actor in a story written by other people.

Eight weeks later, the seedlings were ready. Will had promised the use of his equipment. But after two days of heavy rain had soaked the earth, Jim gave Niki the bad news. Because the soil was so wet, it was necessary to do the job by hand. When he saw her expression of dismay, he touched the small Bible in his shirt pocket and said: "The Lord always does things for a reason, ma'am. It sure is harder to do the work this way, but I like to think that there's a harvest ahead for all of us."

"I hope so, Jim," she said ruefully, as she contemplated the cost in time and in additional back-breaking effort. "God, I do hope so."

The transplanting took more than two weeks, but no one complained, and in that time of daily camaraderie, Niki came to know the true worth of her hired hands. She observed Jim's patience with the childlike Bo, and when she complimented him on his kindness, he once again responded with a Biblical quote—about how the Lord had said to suffer the little children unto him.

Niki noticed that whenever she added a few broad gestures

to her communications with Bo Hansen, two things happened: understanding came more quickly and the teenager seemed to relax. One afternoon, she came upon him in the onetime gardener's shed where Elle's defunct Buick was stored. Bo was sitting behind the wheel of the car, pretending to drive. Niki told him that the car was broken and couldn't be used, or she would take him for a drive. Bo got out of the car then, lifted the hood and pointed to the engine, then to himself. She understood that Bo was indicating a desire to repair the car, and she decided there was nothing to lose. She nodded and pulled some bills from her jeans pocket, to let him know she would pay for the extra work. Bo's radiant smile tore at her heart. In the frayed, ill-fitting hand-me-downs his parents provided as work clothes, he was a pitiful figure, yet it took so little to make him happy.

Wishing she could do more to ease Bo's poverty, she went into town and bought some overalls and shirts and a fleece-lined jeans jacket. Rather than have the gift appear to be outright charity, Niki laundered the clothes twice to give them the appearance of past use, then tossed them into the trunk of the Buick. A moment came when she and Bo were able to "discover" the clothes together, and Niki suggested that he take them since she hadn't any need for them.

She doubled up on her weekly purchase of groceries and after the day's work was done, she began inviting her hands—the man who had no one waiting and the boy whose family had too many mouths to feed—to keep her company for supper.

"My daddy used to work for Will's daddy," Jim volunteered one evening, as they finished a meal together with apple pie and coffee.

"What was he like?" Niki asked.

"John Rivers was a hard man, he was, hard as flint. But fair and honest. A God-fearing man and good to his loved ones."

Niki digested this bit of information, then indulged her

own curiosity. "I'm surprised Will isn't married," she ventured.

"Ain't because nobody wants him, that's for sure."

Niki had already figured that out for herself. "But Will never found the right person," she said.

"Oh no, Ma'am. He done that all right," Jim responded. "Charley Connors's youngest girl, Beth. Prettiest girl in the county, Beth was. Right as right could be. Everybody thought they was the perfect couple."

"Then why didn't they get married?" Niki asked.

"Well, they was meanin' to. But then Will lost her."

"Another man—?"

"No, I don't mean like that, Miss. Beth Connors got sick, some kinda thing that took her real fast. She's been dead now a while . . . must be at least ten years. Seems to me, though, that Will maybe ain't over it yet." He shook his head, finishing the conversation with himself if not with Niki, then gathered himself up and left.

Niki sat at the table alone for a long time afterwards, pondering. Yes, Will Rivers was certainly an actor, she thought, and his favorite role was the friendly uncomplicated man whose life was an open book.

In the weeks that followed, Niki learned the truth of Will's warning that tobacco was a demanding crop. As the leaves began to grow and take shape, they became increasingly tempting to sucker bugs and other insects; it was necessary to be ever vigilant, ever ready with the sprays that would destroy them. Then, as soon as the plants bloomed, they had to be "topped," the buds removed to halt further growth.

More and more, Niki came to feel like a protective parent, nurturing her children, keeping them safe from harm. Her days were full, her nights reserved for sleep. Sometimes, after her household chores were done, it was a struggle to stay awake long enough to dash off a hasty letter to Helen or Blake. But she always made the effort. After losing Kate for so many years, Niki had resolved never again to lose touch with the people she cared about. Niki was careful, too, to keep up her contact with Ralph Sandeman. As she imagined his lonely bachelor existence, she could feel no bitterness toward him for what he had done a long time ago.

In fact, Niki came to feel that both her mother and grandmother had to take a degree of responsibility for what happened to them. Monique, the provincial girl, had assumed too quickly that she had been abandoned—and had done nothing to seek out Ralph Sandeman after they were parted, expecting that he would find his way back to her no matter what. She made no allowance for the fact that he might be wounded, separated from her by the horrors of war. And Elle . . . she had also denied herself opportunities. Living again in Willow Cross gave Niki a new perspective on the town, untainted by her mother's bitterness. Seen through Elle's eyes—as Niki had seen it when she was a child—the town and its inhabitants had seemed unwelcoming. But also, her mother had been a woman who took little notice of the people around her, the ordinary workaday citizens of the town. Given a chance, there was evidence that they weren't all narrow-minded and cruel, as Niki had once believed. There were people like Kate and Tim, who cared about making the world they lived in a better place. They did much more than simply tend young children while their parents worked. With a generosity that exceeded their tiny budget, Tim and Kate "adopted" entire families as Kate had once adopted Niki, helping them through hard times, providing food and clothing and even medical and legal advice. The farmers of the cooperative were even more inspirational. If something bad happened to one—a fire, a death, an accident—it was as if it happened to all of them.

At first, Niki went to the meetings of the cooperative to learn. Then she began to look forward to the social activities that eased the loneliness of farm life. Before long, she was working with Will, distributing homemade leaflets, circulating petitions destined for the desks of congressional representatives.

She regarded the work as a way of being meaningfully involved in the community, and partial payment of a debt of honor to Will for the help he'd given her. And when she was completely honest with herself, she thought of it as a way of showing Will Rivers that she was a person of substance, too, that she could live up to the high standards he set for being a good neighbor.

She was complimented when Will began to consult her on the policies that he took a major part in steering through the cooperative. One of his principal concerns was to rouse the other farmers, whose product had long been sold exclusively to Hyland Tobacco, to put pressure on the company not to blend in more than a limited amount of the inferior—and cheaper—foreign leaf. Of course, the other farmers all realized that there was a danger of more and more of the cheap tobacco taking over until their own product could be bought at minimum prices, but they didn't know how to put pressure on the company.

"There's moral pressure," Will said to Niki, when he was outlining the presentation he planned to make at the next cooperative meeting. "We've got to do everything we can to make the company realize that, over the years, they have made themselves responsible for the people of Willow Cross and the surrounding region—and that the responsibility can't just be abdicated. At the same time, we've got to fire up our own people to believe they have a right to share in the general prosperity . . . and that they don't have to be so damn grateful to the company. All that sweet-talk they've had over the years about how good the company has been—providing free turkeys and picnics. That's all well and good, but we've got to teach our folks that they've earned everything they've got—and more. Both sides have to realize it's a partnership."

"It sounds great as an ideal principle," Niki said. "But the truth is, Will, if we fight too hard, we're going way out on a limb. Hyland can break the back of any protest we ever mount simply by letting quality go, and buying everything from abroad.''

''No, they can't, Niki. We just have to believe in our own value to the company, and we can begin to move them in the direction we want.''

Niki wasn't sure that Will was right; she'd had too much direct experience of the ruthlessness of the Hylands. Yet she provided a helpful sounding board as Will ran through the kind of speech he planned to make to rally support.

On the night of the meeting, she planned to go with Will, and was waiting for him to drive by when the phone rang.

It was Will's voice on the line, the first time she'd ever heard him in a breathless panic. ''Niki, Mama's had a bad attack. She didn't respond to the medicine, so I'm rushing her over to the hospital—''

''I'll meet you there,'' she said, thinking he'd be counting on that kind of support.

''No, don't,'' he said. ''What I need for you to do is go to the meeting and say everything I would've said. . . .''

''But Will. They won't listen to anything coming from me. I'm not—''

''You're one of us,'' Will said strongly. ''That's all you need to be heard, Niki. And you know all the right things to say.''

''Do I?'' Niki murmured. Though she knew the broad outlines of Will's intended speech, he always spoke off the cuff, with nothing written down.

''If you really *feel* what needs to be said,'' Will told her, ''then you'll have the words. '' 'Scuse me, hon, I've got to go.'' The line went dead.

When she entered the meeting, she was greeted warmly by most of the other farmers. But Niki was aware, too, of the faint hum of curious whispers that rippled through the hall. So often recently, she had arrived with Will. She knew there would be comment about her appearing alone. Not that she and Will were thought to be a romantic "item." There were enough pretty daughters of the local farmers who still received his invitations to go dancing, or drive to a movie with him, that there was no mistaking that he was still unattached and unclaimed. Niki was known, however, to be under Will's protection while learning the ropes.

She sought out the Reverend Clay, who customarily opened the meetings, to explain why Will would not appear, but the reverend already knew. "I had a call from Will," he said. "He's at the hospital, and his mother's stable, but he's going to stay with her. Told me you'd have some remarks to make in his place. . . ."

"Well, maybe you could do it, Reverend. What Will wanted to talk about, in fact, was—"

The minister cut her off. "Will warned me you'd probably try to push it onto me," he said, and smiled. "But he said I'd be making a mistake—that I'd learn a thing or two about moral pressure if I sat back and listened. Well, seems to me about time we got started. . . ."

There was no way to avoid speaking, Niki realized; she owed it to Will to pass on his ideas. But she dreaded the moment of standing up in front of the crowd. She was sure it would be taken as presumptuous; she was an outsider, after all. . . . More than that: she was the daughter of the foreigner who had been H.D. Hyland's mistress. Without Will to shield her, Niki decided now, she would be mistrusted, regarded perhaps as someone from the enemy camp, an *agent provocateur*, sent to stir them up only so the company could crack down harder. Looking over the crowd, the men and women who stood still murmuring to each other as the meeting got under way, she imagined they might all have unkind things to say . . . echoes of the cruel whispers that had taunted her mother.

". . . our prayers are with Will and his ma, of course. Now I'm going to step aside so you can listen to some words from Will's substitute tonight, Niki Sandeman."

They were all looking at her and waiting before Niki realized the meeting had been underway for a couple of minutes, and she had been announced. She swallowed, trying to moisten a mouth that had gone dry as parchment, and went up to the stage.

As she walked toward the microphone, trying to calm herself and remember the things Will had been telling her, Niki was suddenly overtaken by an odd feeling. She was back on the board, walking slowly toward the edge from which she would spring. Balance, she reminded herself, it was important to take that moment before the dive to achieve the perfect balance.

She came to the microphone, wrapped her hand around it, and looked out at the crowd, taking in the faces one by one. She wasn't her mother, she reminded herself. She was making a life of her own . . . and this could be part of it, having a voice, talking back.

She began to speak. "Hyland Tobacco is ready to put us out of business after lining their pockets with our crops all these years. We've all been worried about how to put pressure on Hyland to keep buying from us, instead of switching to other sources. Well, Will had some ideas on that, and since he can't be here, he left it to me to put them in front of you. . . ."

The words rolled out, fueled by her feeling that she shared the same concerns as her audience—and by the deeper fire of her longing to have justice from the Hylands, if not for herself, then for anyone else who deserved it.

She couldn't have repeated what she said—heard her own voice as if from a distance. But by the end, the attention she had earned from the crowd was absolute. When she came to the end and stood back from the microphone, the silence lasted. She hesitated a moment, nonplussed, and then turned to walk off the stage. At that moment, the clapping and shouting exploded through the hall.

"You bet, Niki, we'll give 'em hell."

"We won't back down this time."

"We'll make 'em see it our way. . . ."

She looked out at the room, then wiped her eyes as if she had just come up from underwater. This dive, she thought, had been almost perfect. It felt so good that she couldn't wait to try it again.

Twenty-two

THE atmosphere in Johnson's Warehouse resembled that of a Middle Eastern bazaar. The dirt floor was piled with bundles of cured tobacco, scores of farmers hovering proudly around them. Over the deep rumble of men's voices trading stories, comparing crops, marking time until the auctioneer's arrival, the air was thick with anticipation. After the long months of hard work, this was the true day of harvest, the time of reward.

The lone woman in a crowd of men, Niki stood near her foreman, Jim Dark, beside the bales of golden leaf they had wrested from the earth. It was prime product, moist and fragrant, reflecting the care and toil that had gone into it from the moment of gestation, through the final stages of delivery—cutting the plant with the stalk split, letting it wilt in the field for a few hours to prevent breaking and bruising during the curing process—being careful not to let the precious leaf burn—spearing it at last on a lath or tobacco stick for the journey to the curing barns.

Niki felt that she, too, had grown and ripened with her crop, strengthened along with the deepening of a commitment to survive here. Laboring from the chill days of winter through the sweltering summer heat, her skin had turned bronze, her hair streaked with gold, her muscles tight and sinewy. Now at last, with the fear of failure banished until another growing season, Niki could relax for a few precious moments, contemplate the pleasure of paying back the personal loans that had sustained her. Perhaps now she might even indulge in a small luxury or two.

Suddenly, a call penetrated the steady hum of conversation around her. "Nicolette—Niki—is that you? Am I seein' straight . . . ?"

Turning, she saw a large man striding towards her. He was deeply tanned, his blond hair streaked like her own, and dressed in clothes far better than those of the farmers who had come to sell their crops. He seemed strikingly familiar, yet Niki couldn't place him.

"Don't you remember me?" he asked, obviously disappointed by her lack of recognition. "Babe Hyland . . . Uncle Babe?" he offered.

Niki stiffened, the welcoming smile on her face pulled into a grimace. "I remember," she said coldly.

Babe Hyland shook his head, clearly perplexed by Niki's reaction. "It really is good to see you again, Niki. Look at you—all grown up. Why, you're as lovely as your—"

"What do you want, Mr. Hyland?" Niki demanded, longing to be rid of Babe. The arrival of one of the enemy threatened to spoil completely what should have been a banner day.

Babe stared back, the hurt showing in his eyes. "Niki, all I wanted was to say hello. . . ."

Forced to think about it, Niki remembered that Babe had never been anything but kind, had been ready to provide for Elle when others in his family abandoned her. Yet he was still one of them. She couldn't offer the hand of reconciliation.

Breaking away from a nearby group of farmers, Jim Dark

moved up beside her. "Anything wrong, ma'am?" he asked, casting his own unfriendly look at Babe.

"Nothing I can't handle, Jim." she replied. But he lingered protectively at her side until she added, "Thanks. It's really all right."

"Just whistle if you need me," Jim said as he moved back to rejoin the circle of other farmers nearby.

"Listen, Mr. Hyland," Niki said then, adhering to formality, "this is going to be a busy day for me. I'm sorry, but I can't make time for small talk."

Babe nodded, and seemed about to accept her dismissal. But then his hand went out to seize her arm imploringly. "Niki, believe me, I mourned hard for your ma. Gabrielle meant a lot to me, too. Can you remember? I wanted to talk to you back when . . . when she died, but you were just a kid, and you were sent away right after. I always regretted not having a chance to see you then. . . ."

"Really?" Niki said coolly. "You could have found where I was easy enough. It's always seemed to me that no Hyland was ever sorry to be rid of my mother or me." She hesitated, not certain it was worth taking the leap into actually accusing H.D. of responsibility for Elle's death. Was anything to be gained now that he was dead? Then she decided that Babe ought to know—if he didn't already: he ought to know that she still held the Hylands to account, all of them. "In fact, you badly wanted to be rid of us—"

An eruption of loud cheers drowned her out, signaling the arrival of the auctioneer. Niki lost the impulse to seek revenge. All she wanted now was to get the best price for her crop. Over the din, she shouted at Babe: "I told you, I don't have time to rake up the past. I've got business to do."

"Niki, please," he said beseechingly, "spend a little time with me after the auction. There're things I want you to know. If you send me away after we talk, I promise I'll never bother you again."

"All right," she agreed, impatient to end Babe's intrusion before the auction began.

As he turned to leave, Niki was struck by the potential irony of the situation. "Wait a minute," she said, "are you going to be bidding on my crop?"

"Not exactly," Babe replied just before he walked away, "I'm here as a kind of official observer. Someone else will be doing the actual bidding for Hyland."

Watching him merge into the crowd, Niki couldn't help feeling a twinge of sympathy. It was clear that Babe had never been given any authority to act for the company that bore his family name.

In the center of the warehouse, Reverend Clay mounted the raised stage, waving cheerfully, calling out greetings to the farmers he knew. Like many Southern preachers, the reverend supplemented his modest income by working as an auctioneer. Taking a drink of cold water from a nearby pitcher, he made a show of wiping his brow. "I'm gonna skip the usual warm-up," he joked, "seeing as how the Lord has already made this beautiful August day hotter than you know what."

Each of the farmers had been assigned a lot number; as a newcomer, Niki had drawn a position near the end. The buyers, far fewer in number and known to the auctioneer by name, were given colored paddles to signal their bids.

"Lot number one," the reverend called out. "I have five thousand pounds of choice Burley here. Give me a dollar a pound to start, I have one dollar, give me one-ten, one-ten, one-ten, one-ten, and now one-twenty, one-twenty, are you done at one-twenty . . . ? I have one-twenty-five . . . twenty-five-twenty-five-twenty-five. . . ." The reverend's delivery had moved into a rapid-fire monotone chant, numbers spilling out of his mouth so quickly one after the other that they became a new language, intelligible only to those who had dwelt for many years in the country of tobacco.

In less than thirty seconds the first lot was knocked down, and with lightning speed, the reverend moved on, his practiced eye darting over the assembly, picking out the subtle movements of the bidders, recognizing gestures that indicated an advance of a nickel or a dime per pound.

Stopping only for an occasional drink of water, the auctioneer worked steadily for five hours, his voice growing hoarse and ragged from the strain. The atmosphere in the warehouse grew lighter, more like a carnival, as farmer after farmer felt the heady relief of solvency.

Yet as the remaining lots dwindled, as the buyers' demand reached the point of satiation, the bidding slowed. Niki began to worry. The price support program protected her, of course. If no one was ready to pay the set price of a dollar and twenty-seven cents a pound (or close to it), her crop would be warehoused. But somehow she felt her leaf deserved better, and as the auctioneer called out her lot number, Niki crossed her fingers and prayed for luck.

"Fine Burley, fine Burley," he chanted, "give me one for this lot, give me one, give me one-one-one-one-one. I have one, give me one-ten, one-ten, one-ten. . . ."

As Niki scanned the dwindling crowd, she saw Babe Hyland earnestly arguing with another man, who was shaking his head. A red paddle went up at the auctioneer's right. "One-fifteen, I have one-fifteen . . ." A blue paddle raised the bid to one-twenty, then another to one-twenty-five. "Are you done, are you done at one-twenty-five?"

The red paddle rose again—and Niki's crop was knocked down at a dollar thirty! A match for the highest prices of the day! She closed her eyes and said a silent thank-you, savoring a sweet moment of triumph and relief.

Niki slid into the front seat of Babe's red Ferrari. He started the engine, listened for a moment with obvious pleasure to its throaty roar, then gunned it so that the wheels spun as they drove off. Up to the moment they departed, Niki was aware of Jim Dark watching from a place outside the warehouse, his scowl sending a silent warning that Babe had better deliver Niki home safely. Niki made a mental note to speak to Jim later, and assure him that Babe was not the sort of threat that Duke Hyland might be. Even if it was on her behalf, she wanted to make sure that Jim's violent side didn't assert itself.

The Ferrari jounced along the rutted country road, then flew onto the main highway, the warm breeze whipping Niki's hair around her face. She glanced at Babe who seemed to be in a private world of speed and motion. Was it an act of courage to hear out this man who once had brought laughter into Elle's life? Or was it a foolhardy mistake to tempt the merciful Fate that had at last allowed Niki's wandering soul to find rest?

When the car passed the town boundary, she began to wonder if Babe was embarrassed to be seen with her, if perhaps he was making something illicit of the meeting she had so reluctantly granted.

At last the car pulled into another dirt road, traveled perhaps a half mile and stopped in front of what appeared to be a tiny, white clapboard inn with neat blue shutters. Babe got out of the car, raced to the passenger side, and helped Niki out. They walked in silence toward the inn. The soft pastel colors of approaching twilight colored the sky above them. Niki inhaled deeply, catching the faint scent of water nearby.

Once inside, a smiling hostess greeted Babe familiarly by his nickname, and escorted them to a corner table in a tiny dining room. Babe busied himself with a menu, as if delaying the moment when he would have to meet Niki's eyes. "May I order for you?" he asked finally.

Niki gave a shrug of assent. Breaking bread with a Hyland was not something she would have chosen to do.

"They make a few things well here," he said lightly. "They all happen to be chicken, so I suppose that's what we should have."

Niki refused to smile, to put him at ease in any way.

He summoned a waiter and ordered a bottle of white wine. "Tell the chef we'd like to try the chicken and dumplings. And some garden salad."

When the waiter left, Babe took a deep breath and began

to speak, eyes cast downward, as if studying the pattern of the blue-and-white checkered cloth. "Niki," he said quietly, "I didn't forget you, ever. I knew there were . . . arrangements made by the family to see that you were educated, and when I inquired about your well-being, I was always told you were happy and well." He looked up and his eyes found hers. "But that didn't relieve me from feeling I should have done more for you. It was just . . . too hard to buck the drift, know what I mean? When H.D. was alive—"

"Don't tell me you're ready to do anything more now that he's dead," Niki cut in sharply. Your sister told me the same thing once, and I made the mistake of believing her. But I won't do that again."

"Pepper?" Babe said, with evident surprise. "She never said anything about seeing you!"

"No, I don't suppose she would have."

"I don't understand. Did Pepper do something to hurt you, Niki? Because if she did—"

"I don't want to talk about that. It was an ugly experience, but it's finished." Niki fought to get control of her temper. "Listen, Babe, you said there were things you thought I should know, and that's why I'm here. But this isn't an easy experience for either of us. So tell me, and then I can go. . . ."

The wine arrived, and after the waiter filled their glasses, Babe emptied his with two quick swallows. "I just wanted to be sure you believed that I truly cared for Gabrielle," he said. "We made each other happy, Niki. You might've been too young to understand, but it was a rare and precious feeling we had for one another. . . ."

Unbidden, unwanted, the memories returned. Of Elle's pleasure in Babe's company, of the laughter that filled their cottage, of the hopes and dreams that had died one horrible night. Then she heard Babe say, "We were even thinking it might be time to get married."

While Niki stared at Babe in astonishment, he grabbed the

bottle out of the wine cooler, filled his glass again, and drank off another huge swallow.

The question came unthinkingly from her lips. "Did H.D. know?" she asked. Was that his motive? she wondered inwardly. Had he been so desperate to keep Elle from laying any claim to the Hyland name that he'd taken the quickest, most brutal path to aborting the marriage plan?

"No," Babe said, "we knew it would be a mistake to tell anyone. We were talking about eloping. I was gonna put Elle—and you—in a car, and drive us all up to Charleston for a quick fix from a justice of the peace."

Niki shook her head, then leaked a smile as she was struck by the absurd irony of the fate that might have been: Babe Hyland could have been her stepfather.

"As I remember," she said, "you weren't at the funeral. If you loved her so much—"

Babe winced with apparently genuine regret. "Like you, Niki, I was sent away. H.D. insisted. He said my presence at Gabrielle's funeral would only cause . . . unpleasant gossip. For you, as much as . . . anyone else."

The excuse seemed more pitiful than irritating to Niki. "You expect me to believe that your father gave a damn what people said about us? He made us outcasts."

Babe bowed his head and refilled his wineglass. The food was set before them, but it was left untouched. "Niki," he said softly, "I can't blame you for feeling as you do. I can't even deny what you say. I was young, I was selfish, I was thoughtless. I didn't have the guts to stand up to H.D. He was . . . he was too powerful. But as God is my witness, I did care for your mother! And I'm ashamed of not having helped you more."

Was it Niki's understanding he wanted? Or was it something else? Suddenly, she had a vivid flash of that fateful vision from her childhood—the man standing in the firelight beside Elle's reclining body. H.D. . . ? Or could it have been Babe. Was he the killer—begging forgiveness?

"You were there, weren't you?" she accused. "You were there the night she died!"

Babe's boyish face froze in an expression of horror.

"My God," he whispered, "you can't believe . . . Niki, you can't believe *that*!"

Niki's eyes narrowed as she studied Babe through the filter of her most bitter memories. He looked as innocent as an angel—but she knew better than anyone that the Hylands were masters of deception.

Suddenly Babe began to cry. Like a child he wept, openly and unashamedly, oblivious to the stares of the waiter, the hostess, and the other diners. Oblivious even to Niki as he traveled back in time to his own buried memories.

"I was there," he said brokenly. "She was so happy, so beautiful. We talked about going away, leaving Willow Cross . . . making a new life somewhere. We were going to be a family, the three of us. We were . . ." he trailed off, eyes unfocused, as if in contemplation of some private vision. "It was my fault," he resumed, in a thin, ghostly voice that raised the hairs on Niki's neck. "It was all my fault. If I'd stayed with her that night the way she asked me to, I could have protected her from that burglar. But I . . . I said no, said we shouldn't flaunt our relationship until we married." There was a long silence. Babe pulled himself back to the present and gazed earnestly into Niki's eyes. "You have every right to hate me. I might have saved her. But I just wasn't there."

Niki believed him. Not because of the tears. Or the words. But because she saw a man who had truly been damaged by Elle's death—as she herself had been. A man who carried a burden of memories as painful as her own. Babe's story made her feel her mother's tragedy all over again. After all the years of empty promises, Elle believed she was going to be a bride at last. How happy she must have been! How heartbreakingly brief her happiness was! But Babe had been a part of it.

Forgiveness came. "You couldn't know what would happen," she said quietly.

"Niki . . ."

"What?"

"Give me the chance to be your friend . . . for Gabrielle's sake."

She paused doubtfully. To believe Babe Hyland was one thing, to go beyond that was more than Niki could imagine. "Friends trust each other," she said, but without bitterness. "I just don't think I could trust *any* Hyland, not even you, Babe."

He nodded. "Then give me the chance to show you I'm not your enemy. Can you do that?"

"I don't know. I've made a life for myself, Babe. It took me a long time to do it. I don't want anything . . . anyone to spoil it." Seeing the sadness in his eyes, she borrowed Helen's favorite way of making peace. "But I'll think about it," she said. "I promise I'll think about it."

Twenty-three

WAKENED by her inner alarm clock, Niki yawned and stretched, enjoying a final few moments of warmth under her cozy down comforter. Outside her window, the trees shimmered with frost. It wasn't the same as a white Christmas, she thought, but it was lovely all the same.

Reluctantly she threw back the covers and reached for her wool robe. She pulled on a pair of thick wool socks and tiptoed to the bathroom, so as not to waken her sleeping guests.

"Merry Christmas," she whispered to her reflection in the medicine cabinet mirror. The reflection smiled back at her, glowing with the same happiness she felt inside.

Hastily she washed her face and brushed her teeth, then padded downstairs to prepare breakfast. Everything felt different today, even smelled different. Was it simply the fragrance of evergreens mingling with the lingering aroma of last night's dinner? Or was it the presence of Helen and Ralph, sleeping upstairs, that made the house feel so cozy and warm?

Christmas had always been a bittersweet holiday for Niki. A season when she felt orphaned and dependent on the bounty of others. This year was different. Her own life seemed rich and full, and for the first time, she felt as if she had an abundance of blessings to share with the people she loved.

She kneaded the dough to start a cherry strudel, covered it with a damp towel, and left it to rise. Humming a chorus of "Jingle Bells," she squeezed a dozen oranges for fresh juice, then filled the automatic coffee maker to capacity. She set a slab of smoked country ham on the butcher block counter, along with a dozen eggs, and when the coffee was ready, she poured herself a cup.

She carried it into the living room and curled up on the couch she'd restored and re-covered, enjoying the rewards of her own labors. Though there was still work to be done, her simple cottage looked and felt like a home. The wood floors had been restored to their original luster, the walls freshened with paint, the kitchen renewed by loving use.

The fireplace was adorned with clusters of holly, the mantel set with thick bayberry candles. In the center of the living room stood a towering fir tree, trimmed with red ribbons and tiny white lights and crowned with a glittering star. All around it, on a red felt skirt, were the brightly wrapped presents Niki had selected with the greatest care. Never before had she bought so many gifts; never before had there been so many people she wanted to remember.

Hearing movement upstairs, Niki returned to the kitchen. With the skill and speed acquired by months of practice, she slipped the strudel into the oven, set the table, and whipped up a fluffy ham omelette.

By the time Helen and Ralph appeared, everything was ready. "Merry Christmas, Niki dear," Helen murmured, drawing the child she had helped raise into her ample bosom.

"Merry Christmas, Helen. I'm so happy you could come."

"It's nice to be here," Ralph said shyly, standing off to one side. "It's been a long time since I had a real Christmas."

"Having you here makes it perfect for me," Niki said, giving her grandfather a hug. Ralph had grown thinner and frailer than when she had first seen him in California. Setting eyes on him yesterday for the first time in two years, Niki had wondered whether her memory was faulty—or how it was possible that he had aged so much.

He didn't eat much, Niki noticed, when they sat down to breakfast. "Is there something else you'd rather have?" she asked. "Some toast, or maybe—"

"I'm fine," he said, squeezing Niki's hand. "It's just part of getting old. Everything kind of breaks down, even your appetite."

"Nonsense," Helen said vehemently. "Properly cared for, the human body is capable of functioning beautifully, well into old age."

Ralph smiled agreeably, reached into his pocket for a package of cigarettes, and lit one up. "There you are, Mr. Sandeman," Helen said, pointing a finger at the offending cigarette. "If you persist in filling your lungs with toxins, what can you expect?"

"I'll put the cigarette out if it bothers you, ma'am," Ralph offered.

"It's not *me* I'm talking about, Mr. Sandeman," Helen responded, warming now to the subject. "It's your health that's on the line every time you light one of those . . . those *coffin nails*!"

"Helen, please . . ." Niki intervened, hoping to rescue the holiday spirit from Helen's pet crusade.

"It's okay," Ralph said. "You're absolutely right, ma'am, and if I were a much younger man, I'd sure pay attention to your good advice. But at my age," he shrugged, "the only thing I know for damn sure is that I'm going to die of something. I figure it might as well be something that gives me pleasure."

Helen's lips compressed with disapproval, but catching

another reproving glance from Niki, she restrained herself from further comment.

Yet a few minutes later, as they were all clearing the breakfast dishes, Ralph began coughing and wheezing. Niki rushed to give her grandfather a glass of water, but he waved her away. Helplessly, she watched as he slumped into a chair, gasping for breath, the color draining from his weathered face. Niki held her own breath, as she waited for whatever it was to subside.

When the wheezing finally stopped, she said: "I think I'd better call the doctor."

Ralph shook his head. "He won't tell me anything I don't already know. It's just a touch of emphysema. Nothing to worry about."

"But it sounds so bad," Niki protested.

Ralph managed a smile. "It'll take more than a little shortness of breath to kill a tough old bird like me. I've been through a couple of wars, remember? Besides, now that I have a beautiful granddaughter, I have a lot more to live for."

"I still wish you'd let me call a doctor," Niki persisted. "There must be *something*—"

"I'll take care of it when I get back to California," Ralph promised. "Now there's something a lot more important I have to do." He took Niki by the hand and led her into the living room. He reached under the tree for the package he'd left there the night before. "Merry Christmas, honey, and many happy returns."

The wrappings were clumsy, as if done by fingers unused to such tasks. Inside the paper was a blue leather album, filled with photographs—harsh but stirring pictures of soldiers at war, of civilians fighting to defend a cause. There were women and children, too, their faces ravaged by the horrors of war, their eyes bereft of innocence. "They aren't pretty," Ralph apologized, "but it's my best work . . . and I wanted you to have it."

Moved beyond words, Niki hugged her grandfather, wishing she could share with him something equally precious, the gift of her own youth and vitality. She handed him a slender package. "This isn't going to seem very original," she said as he undid the ribbon.

But when she saw his tired eyes fill with tears, she knew her gift was perfect. It was a handcrafted walnut picture frame in three parts. In the center was a photograph of Ralph Sandeman, as he had been a long time ago, when his career as a photojournalist was in full flower. To one side was a picture of Elle, seated in this very room, looking young and lovely and full of promise. To the other was a picture of Niki when she was just eight years old, dressed in her finest party frock.

With trembling fingers, Ralph touched the picture of the daughter he'd never seen or known, lovingly tracing its outlines. "My baby," he murmured, his voice filled with wonder and longing. "My Gabrielle."

Niki caressed his cheek gently, wiping away the tears.

"But where did you get this?" he asked, pointing to his own photograph.

"I called the gallery in California. I told them I wanted to surprise my grandfather. They helped me find the picture."

Clasping the gift to his heart, Ralph stood up and left the room.

Niki started to follow, but Helen restrained her. "He wants to be alone with his memories, Niki. Give him a moment."

Niki sat down again.

"I'm very proud of you," Helen said. "What you just did . . . it shows me that you've grown up. That you've learned a great deal about love."

Was it true? Niki wondered. Or had she simply extended her boundaries slightly to include Ralph among those it was safe to love?

"I didn't forget you," she said to Helen, handing over a large satin-lined chest filled with expensive European toiletries, perfumed bath salts, scented lotion, and fine body powder. "Use this stuff when the girls in Vale House get to be a royal pain," she explained. "Just close your door, fill your bathtub with bubbles—and *voila*! Instant relaxation."

"Thank you, Niki. I'll certainly try to take your good advice. If you'll take mine." She waited until Niki opened her gift, a long-sleeved, high neck, creamy silk blouse with an inset of matching handmade lace.

"It's exquisite!" Niki proclaimed.

"Only if you wear it," Helen said. "I want you to indulge your femininity, too, Niki. You may work like a man, but you aren't. Remember that."

"Yes, ma'am," Niki teased, knowing that Helen was talking about something more than bubble baths and lacy clothes.

Suddenly, the sweet sound of Christmas carols was heard outside the house. Niki ran to open the door. It was Kate and Tim and a small band of the older children from the day-care center, three- and four-year-olds, their high, piping voices raised in song. Standing on the threshold, Niki sang with them, wishing once again for a miracle—one that would give Kate and Tim a child of their own.

When the caroling was finished, Niki invited the troupe inside. More gifts were exchanged, and each of the children was given a stocking full of candy. After the carolers moved onto their next stop, Niki went into the kitchen to start dinner. Ralph was standing by the window, staring into the distance, a lit cigarette in his hand. "Maybe you *should* cut those out," she said.

Ralph laughed hoarsely. "You, too? Isn't that a funny position to take when you grow the stuff?"

"I don't think so. I'm not as . . . radical as Helen, but with the problems you have, it would make sense to quit smoking."

"Maybe," he conceded. "But *you* try quitting after you've smoked for forty years. It isn't easy, Niki. Not for me, anyway."

She wanted to say more, do more to help Ralph, but somehow the day slipped away in a steady stream of visitors and celebrations, friends from the co-op, Jim Dark and Jodie McIntyre, the pretty divorcee from the next county who he'd begun dating. Then Bo stopped by with a wreath he'd made of pine cones and bits of greenery. He presented the gift quickly, as if embarrassed by the sentiment that prompted it. Then he indicated he had come to check the Buick in the shed, to make sure it was running well. When Niki called out after him, he kept on walking. She called even louder, but he still didn't stop. With half an idea taking hold in her mind, she took a small paper bag from the kitchen and went to find Bo. She signaled that he should close his eyes, and when he did, she blew up the bag and popped it. Bo didn't move a muscle. Then she clapped her hands loudly and shouted his name, but still he didn't move. Could it be that Bo was hard of hearing and not retarded? And if so, was there any help for his condition? What a New Year's gift that would be, she thought.

Trying to restrain her excitement, Niki gave Bo a nudge, indicating that the game was over. He looked bewildered, but followed her back into the house where she gave him a huge, succulent ham wrapped with a red ribbon, like the one that was baking in her own oven. The teenager's face lit up. He took Niki's hands in his own and held them for a long moment. Then he rushed off, eager no doubt, to turn the ham over to his mother in time for Christmas dinner.

Niki's own dinner was perfect. The food was sumptuous, but it was the spirit of the day, the company—including Jim and Jodie McIntyre—that made it special. Jim said a simple grace, thanking the Lord for his bounty and for the kindness of friends. Niki added a heartfelt "Amen."

When they'd all eaten as much as humanly possible, they moved into the living room for coffee and brandy. Niki laid a fire in the hearth and put seasonal music on the record player. Feeling slightly chilly, she went to the tree and picked up the gift Will had brought early Christmas Eve, a cornflower-blue shawl of fine English wool. As she draped it over her shoulders, its gossamer lightness caressing her cheeks, a gentle sigh escaped Niki's lips.

Had she hoped for something different on the accompanying card, something more personal than "Your good friend, Will"? And if so, why did the card that she'd enclosed with the green checked shirt and matching bandanna say simply "For my favorite country singer"?

No, Niki thought, friends were what they were. And perhaps that was how it should be. As she had told Babe, she had made a good life for herself, one she wasn't ready to risk for anything or anyone.

The church hall was festooned with streamers and balloons. The farmers of the Willow Cross Tobacco Cooperative, their wives and children, were all turned out in their Sunday best. Heeding Helen's advice, Niki, too, had shed her jeans for something more feminine. In her new silk blouse and her flared black velvet skirt, with her golden hair upswept and adorned with velvet ribbons, she looked like a Victorian cameo. No longer a stranger, she was greeted by name and made welcome from the moment she passed through the door, with Kate on one arm and Tim on the other.

"I don't know why you want to spend New Year's Eve with two old married people," Kate said.

"I can't think of anyone else I'd rather be with."

"Oh, really? Do you believe that, Tim?" Kate asked her husband with a nudge and a broad wink.

"Why not?"

"Well, I think our Niki wants us to be chaperones," Kate smiled. "I think she wants us to protect her from you-know-who."

"You-know-who?" Tim repeated. "Is *he* going to be here tonight?"

"There he is," Kate announced. She waved to Will, who was just about to take the stage.

Niki noticed that he was wearing her Christmas gift.

" 'Evening friends and neighbors," Will said. "I'm not an official part of tonight's entertainment, but if it's okay with everyone here, I'd like to try out a new song I wrote."

He waited a moment for the cheers and whistles to subside. "I call this 'Pretty Lady.' " He played a few sweet chords on his guitar, then began to sing the lyric:

"Ev'ry time I close my eyes I see you. Pretty lady, won't you let me hold you? Midnights come and midnights go, and still my arms are empty. Pretty lady, ain't it time I told you . . . ?"

Who was she, Niki wondered, the pretty lady who lived in Will's heart? Was it still the woman Jim had mentioned, was Will singing to a memory?

When his song ended, Will was coaxed into another—and then another. Finally, he begged off the stage, and a bluegrass band struck up a lively dance tempo. A moment later, Will was whirling around the floor with one of his many female admirers.

Responding to a poke from Kate, Tim invited Niki to dance. "Ready to have a good time?" he asked.

"You bet!" she responded. Tim was a playful partner and a good dancer. Round and round he twirled Niki, setting a pace that others tried to follow.

The band segued into a polka, and Reverend Clay cut in. Though he had at least thirty years on Niki, the reverend's dancing was as spirited as his auctioneering, and she was the one left breathless and perspiring when the dance was over.

The first time Will asked her to dance, she felt it was simply a courtesy between friends. It was Will's way, she noticed, to dance with all the ladies—but just once.

"You look beautiful tonight," he said.

"Thank-you," she responded, oddly disappointed at being called "beautiful" rather than "pretty." She inquired about his mother.

"About the same," he said. "She was asking about you."

"I've been meaning to stop by and visit."

"She'd like that."

Darn it, Niki thought, why did this seem like one of those terrible school dances she'd been obliged to attend at Blue Mountain? It was so easy to talk to Will when they were working together. So comfortable to be with him. Why did it have to be different just because music was playing and his arms were around her?

When he asked her for a second dance, she felt an unexpected rush of pleasure at being singled out from the rest. But Niki didn't have to tell herself to be careful. Not anymore. Will obviously had secrets that weren't for sharing. And if he knew more about love than she did, the kind of love that lasted forever, it was more than likely he'd already given that love to someone else.

As the music ended, he released her with a courtly "thank-you, ma'am." Niki smiled a gracious "you're welcome"—and then proceeded to follow his lead—dancing once and once only with anyone who asked. And for good measure, she even did some asking herself, among the older men who were there with wives and grown children.

As midnight approached, Niki's eyes couldn't keep her glance from wandering to where Will was standing. Surrounded as usual by adoring women. The fiddle player shouted out "Happy New Year" and struck up "Auld Lang Syne." Kate and Tim enclosed Niki in their embrace, sharing the shelter of their love. Jim Dark came over to give Niki a hug, then returned to giving Jodie a less chaste embrace.

Niki looked around again for Will. But he was nowhere to be seen, gone with one of his pretty ladies.

Twenty-four

FROM the evening she had filled in for Will as a speaker at the Willow Cross Tobacco Cooperative, Niki had assumed a place of some importance in the community of tobacco growers. As a couple of years passed, and she became more active, she was increasingly recognized as a naturally gifted speaker, someone who was able to stand before a group and command attention with her words—and beyond that to transmute her own concern for issues into a collective willingness to act. Farmers were normally taciturn men; forced to subjugate their own needs and goals to the merciless whims of nature, they were forced to learn humility, patience, and a willingness to accept hardship without complaint. Thus they could be hard to stir to any action. But from the first time Niki had stepped out of the crowd, she had shown a talent as a motivator. She could persuade the most tightfisted of men to contribute something extra for the printing of pamphlets, the most pacifistic or timid to join in a demonstration to be held in front of the Hyland headquarters.

For a time progress was made against the company's plans to increase the percentage of foreign tobacco bought at the expense of local growers.

When she thought about the source of her newly discovered leadership abilities, Niki tended to think it derived mainly from the deep hatred and mistrust she felt for the Hylands. This was a passion that she felt deeper than any other; like a pulsing radioactive force, it affected anybody who came within its field.

At a meeting in the late summer of 1983, Niki raised the idea that the upcoming Hyland Labor Day picnic should be boycotted. The suggestion met with strong disapproval, at first. One farmer after another said that the picnic was a time when the growers and the company people came together as friends.

It was plain "bad manners," one woman said, to be offered anyone's hospitality and then throw it back in his face.

"And what's good manners?" Niki demanded. "To sit quietly and take whatever they put on your plate, and say 'thank-you, boss,' and then walk away hat in hand? What the hell do you think is the purpose of this picnic? What has it been ever since the first one way back in—when was it, 1920 . . . ?"

"It was in 1911," a voice shouted from the back. "My pappy was there. Said he never drank so much dang beer in—"

Niki headed off the nostalgia fest that was apt to develop any time the old days were brought up. "Nineteen-eleven. More than seventy years ago. And let me tell you, the purpose was the same then as now. Fill you up once a year with beer and hot dogs . . . so you won't complain about getting short-changed the rest of the time. We'll it's horseshit, friends. That picnic is supposed to make us think that the Hylands are our friends . . . but it was horseshit then, and horseshit now. And we ought to let them know we're onto the game. 'Cause as long as we go on acting as dumb and grateful and lazy as pigs let loose in a watermelon patch for that one day, we're gonna be herded back to the barnyard by our masters to lie down and sleep off our full bellies in that same damn horseshit."

There were whistles, cheers, and laughter, and when the matter was brought to a vote, the members of the cooperative agreed by a two-thirds majority to boycott the picnic for the first time since 1911.

As Niki left the meeting later, Will came over to commend her for rallying the group. "I've got to admit, I made a halfhearted suggestion to do the same thing five or six years ago when we were in a price squeeze, and there was such a howl I didn't have the guts to try pushing it through. Maybe it's 'cause you're so good to look at when you're up there, but the men sure seem to listen to stuff coming from you that they won't take from anyone else. Anyway, I'm happy I left the talkin' to you."

Niki had grown accustomed to letting Will's flattery slide by. He took every chance to tell her she was attractive, and that was nice. But too often he hopped in his pickup after the flattering was done, and went off to have a drink—or spend the night—with some fluttery-eyed member of his private fan club.

"You know, Will," she said, "I wish you wouldn't be quite so content to let me do the talking. I need you to speak up a little more on this foreign tobacco issue. It's time to take the next steps, do more than gather petitions and send them off to Washington. After all, the manufacturers have an army of lobbyists stationed right there in Washington."

"That's a fact of life," Will agreed. "We sure as hell can't afford to buy an army of our own."

"Maybe not," Niki said, "but we can't ignore it either. Not if we want to hang onto our farms."

Will studied Niki for a moment. "Where's all this stuff coming from? Are you thinking about running for office?" he asked with a teasing grin.

"No. I'm just realizing that we have to find a way to get

our message across to *everybody*, not just to the people who are on our side to begin with. The tobacco companies can afford to buy all the support they need. We have to find ways to get it for free . . ."

Will shook his head and chuckled. "You think you can win people over just by asking? People who don't know anything about farming and don't care to?"

"The least we can do is try to get their attention. You know, Will, when I came back here to live, the thing that impressed me most was the way the people of Willow Cross helped themselves, the way they didn't wait for anyone else to take care of their problems. That's what we have to do now. Face the fact that we have an uphill fight on our hands . . . and do our best to win it. I want to launch a new stage—and I want your help. Are you in?"

He nodded slowly. "Whatever you say, pretty lady," he replied. Then he bid her good night, and drove off in his pickup.

Two weeks later, Will summoned the members of the cooperative to a special rally. The invited guests were a reporter from the *Daily Signal* and one from the local television station, as well as the mayor and the congressman who represented the district in Washington. It was Niki's idea to invite the congressman. "Even if he doesn't come," she said, "at least we'll put him on notice that something's going on in Willow Cross, something he should know about." It was also Niki's idea to keep the rally simple and to the point. After Will opened with a stirring rendition of "Farmer Brown," she gave a speech about how foreign tobacco was produced, about the conditions of near slavery that existed in the plantations of Africa and South America. "It is indecent," she said, "for American manufacturers to exploit the people of other countries. It is inhuman for them to profit from suffering. It would be an unspeakable wrong if we allowed them to impoverish the American farmer with their greed."

As Niki had hoped, the rally made front page news in the *Signal*. Excerpts from her speech—as well as Will's song—were broadcast during several segments of television news.

Persuading Will that they were on the right track, Niki arranged a similar rally in a neighboring district. Soon they were stumping the state, campaigning as vigorously as any political candidates. Whether because of Niki's beauty or Will's talent—or because together they made a strikingly attractive combination—television cameras from the larger stations began to follow them around. Stories about their campaign began to appear in newspapers from nontobacco states.

Yet even as Niki and Will fought the threat of cheap foreign tobacco, another serious threat appeared in the form of a bill to abolish the tobacco price-support program.

On Capitol Hill, while conservatives sought to eliminate vegetables from school lunch programs, liberals countered by attacking the tobacco subsidy. The powerful tobacco lobby looked the other way.

"The manufacturers are letting Congress do their dirty work for them," Will fumed, flinging down a copy of the Raleigh newspaper on Niki's kitchen table. "Doesn't anybody see that? Doesn't anybody care that this could *ruin* thousands of farmers?"

"We've got to make them care, Will," Niki said. "It's past time we went to Washington."

"*You* have to go."

"But you know a lot more about farming than I do."

"Like you said, this isn't about farming, Niki. It's about getting people to pay attention. I figure that's gotta be your show. Hell," he added with a grin, "I can't be singing my songs in the middle of a congressional hearing, can I?"

Niki allowed herself to be convinced. They had come too far to back away from this critical battle that would affect the lives of so many. She called their Congressman and insisted that he arrange for a representative from Willow Cross to speak at hearings on the tobacco subsidy.

* * *

On a mild Tuesday afternoon, with the cherry blossoms beginning to make their appearance along the Potomac, Niki sat in a corridor of the Capitol outside a hearing room, her hands perspiring as she turned over the index cards on which she had scrawled a few notes. In her navy blue suit and white blouse, her thick blond hair tied back demurely, Niki was well aware she bore no resemblance to the popular notion of what a tobacco farmer looked like. Whatever it takes to get their attention, she thought, knowing that the hearing room would be filled with men.

She turned to Jennifer Pierce, the personal aide to Congressman Sumter. "How much longer do we have to wait?"

"I don't know," Miss Pierce said. "The page will come out and tell us when they're ready for you."

Suddenly, a cluster of newcomers came along the corridor led by a tall, silver-haired man wearing an impeccably tailored suit of English pedigree. His carriage was erect, almost military, his manner was formal but polite as he fielded questions from the reporters who trailed him.

"Isn't that Desmond Reece?" Niki asked, recognizing the head of Regal Tobacco from the magazine photos she'd seen.

"The one and only," Miss Pierce responded. "I'll bet he makes an impression . . . no matter what he says."

Grudgingly, Niki had to agree. In spite of her antipathy towards tobacco manufacturers, it was hard not to be impressed by Desmond Reece. Urbane, sophisticated, and refined, Reece had been an outstanding student at Harvard University, a track and field star—and a former Rhodes scholar. The son of middle-class parents, his had been the traditional American Horatio Alger story, refined and revitalized for the twentieth century. Yet what interested Niki most was the fact that Desmond Reece had recently beaten out Duke Hyland for the presidency of the prestigious Association of American Tobacco Manufacturers, a position Duke was known to crave but had never managed to win.

* * *

Nearly half an hour later, the door of the hearing room opened. A young man whispered to Miss Pierce, who passed the message on to Niki.

"They'll be ready for you in a couple of minutes. Go inside and take a seat."

Her heart pounding, Niki followed the page to the rear of the room and found a place to sit. A powerful Northern congressman appeared to be winding down his speech: "Let the tobacco farmer stand on his own two feet," he said in a resonant voice, "as we are asking the welfare recipients and the poor and the needy and all the minorities who depend on programs this country can no longer support. I would be derelict in my duties to my constituents if I did not protest the hypocrisy of allowing Americans to go hungry while we use taxpayer dollars to support an inedible and unhealthy crop like tobacco."

Though she was prepared for opposition, Niki felt herself waver in the face of such an attack. When the congressman finished speaking, the committee chairman stood up. "Our next speaker," he said, "is here by special request of our colleague from North Carolina. Miss Nicolette Sandeman, will you please step forward."

She took a deep breath and walked to the front of the room, trying to exude more confidence than she felt. She was here to serve as the voice of her friends and neighbors, she reminded herself, of all the farmers who depended on the golden leaf for their existence.

As she sat down at the microphone and laid out her notes, Niki was aware of a flurry of picture taking. She forced a smile and began to speak:

"Mr. Chairman, members of the committee . . . I'm here today on behalf of the tobacco farmers of Willow Cross, North Carolina. I'm here to speak for those who have been ignored or forgotten in this debate about budgets, for men—and women like myself—who spend their lives working from sunup till sundown and who would rather die than take welfare. I'm here to remind you that tobacco farming has been an honorable way of life since before America won her independence. The tobacco farmer helped win that battle, just as he helped make America rich, just as he now helps sustain the economy of the South." She paused for breath, studying the faces around her. "I am here to challenge *anyone* who calls the price-support program a handout—or likens it to welfare. It is a national commitment to uphold a way of life that represents the finest and highest traditional American values. Ending the program is not a solution to a budget problem. It's a giveaway to the tobacco companies. If price supports end, then they will control the market, and set the prices wherever they wish—at the expense of the farmers. If, as honorable representatives, you are truly interested in saving taxpayer dollars, then raise the tax on cigarettes. I beg you not to turn your backs on the farmers that have served America so long and so well."

She leaned away from the microphone, then submitted to questioning by the committee members. As if impatient to dismiss her—those opposed to her position thinking she might gain points on her photogenic qualities alone, those in favor thinking she might not be taken seriously enough because she was too attractive to be a *real* tobacco grower—the questions were kept short, and surprisingly neutral. How long had she been farming? Could she be *sure* a return to free market conditions would not benefit the growers . . . ?

As Niki stepped away from the microphone, the cameras followed her all the way to her seat at the back of the hearing room.

The chairman cleared his throat. "Our next speaker," he said, "is also here by special request—of the surgeon general of the United States. This committee agreed to hear his remarks as relevant to the issues at hand. Dr. Alexei Ivanov, will you please come forward. . . ."

Niki snapped to attention, her eyes searching the room. Alexei! But she didn't see him anywhere.

There was a pause then while it was discovered that the

witness wasn't in the room. A page whispered to the committee chairman, who announced that Dr. Ivanov had been called to a telephone on medical business, but would appear in just a minute.

Suddenly there he was, coming through the rear door and striding purposefully towards the witness table, elegant, dashing, self-assured. Even more handsome after the passage of time—if that were possible. Niki wondered if he had any idea that she had appeared before him. . . .

And the answer came at that moment. Just before he seated himself at the table, Alexei scanned around the room quickly until his dark eyes found Niki's. He held them for a moment then, the hint of a smile on his lips, before he faced front again.

Alexei, Alexei Ivanov, she said his name silently as a confusion of old feelings washed over her. Was she glad to see him? Afraid to face him? She wasn't sure, but for only a moment. She wasn't a directionless schoolgirl anymore. She was a woman with purpose, she was part of a community she loved.

But what was Alexei doing here? She listened intently as he began to speak:

"Mr. Chairman, honorable representatives. As a physician specializing in diseases of the heart and circulatory system, I am here to remind you of issues far more pressing than simple economics. I urge you instead to consider the health and welfare of your fellow Americans. To think of what the growing of tobacco means, not in terms of dollars and cents, but in human costs—in death and disease. I have not been practicing my specialty for very long—and yet, in my practice of medicine, I have seen a tremendous amount of unnecessary suffering. There are often problems I see that come from a variety of causes that are neither preventable nor readily treated. Yet far too much of this suffering is caused by smoking. And this I abhor—preventable death, the sheer waste of human life, the needless suffering. . . ."

Niki's heart sank as Alexei talked with conviction and authority of an ever-growing list of illnesses linked to the use of tobacco. His mournful litany began with heart diseases and respiratory ailments, went on to lung cancer and chronic bronchitis—and ended with the danger to unborn infants, at risk of being damaged by the effects of smoking on expectant mothers. Niki had come here to fight indifference and greed, but this . . . this was an attack for which she was unprepared, for which she had no defense.

"In this age of growing consumer awareness," Alexei was saying, "no sensible human being can advocate the support of a crop like tobacco nor any measure which encourages its manufacture. If there lingers in your minds any doubt, remember this: tobacco products, if they are used exactly as intended, will certainly damage the health of the user—and may well result in death."

Niki flushed as Alexei concluded his speech. She felt as if it had been aimed squarely at her. Not being a smoker herself, she had given little thought to the health issue. She had seen her crop in a historic light, even a romantic one. Now Niki was being shown the dark side of her life's work—a side she didn't want to see.

No questioning at all followed Alexei's statement. It had been a courtesy to hear him, but no one on the committee seemed anxious to get into the health issue. That would be for another hearing, another day.

As Alexei walked back along the aisle where she was seated, he suddenly swooped to take Niki's arm and propel her out of the room. Delighted with the opportunity to capture on film two strikingly attractive people on opposite sides of a newsworthy issue, the photographers rapidly snapped pictures, one or two moving with them out of the room.

"What do you think you're doing?" Niki whispered to Alexei. "It won't do my case or yours any good to look so friendly—"

"Never mind. I'll tell you what I felt like doing," Alexei

murmured in reply, smiling at her indignation. "First I felt like shaking you . . . and then," he lowered his voice seductively, "then I felt like taking you in my arms."

Niki had no ready comeback. Whatever changes time had wrought, when it came to the thrust and parry of romantic repartee with Alexei, she still felt like a schoolgirl.

The photographers were left behind, and he released her arm. "Come, Nikuschka, follow me. . . ." He moved quickly, giving her no opportunity to speak as he led her to a nearby garage, where he picked up a silver Mercedes convertible.

"May I ask where you're taking me?" she ventured.

"Somewhere quiet and secluded. Where we can talk."

They drove a short distance to the Jefferson Hotel, a small *beaux-arts* style building a few blocks from the White House. Alexei escorted Niki through an opulent lobby, into an intimate wood-paneled restaurant that resembled a private dining room in a stately manor house. The maitre d' respectfully greeted Alexei by name and showed them to a secluded corner table. This was a very different kind of place from those they had known in New York, yet somehow, Niki thought, it seemed an appropriate setting for Alexei as he was now—mature, confident, burnished by accomplishment.

He ordered a bottle of Cristal champagne. "I hope you don't mind," he said, "but I have an overpowering urge to drink a toast to Fate . . . for bringing us together again."

Though Niki couldn't argue with the sentiment, she shifted to neutral ground. "I'm glad you have the career you always wanted," she said. "Cardiology must be an exciting field . . ."

"As you can understand, perhaps," he said, "I chose it for personal reasons."

Niki was puzzled. When he had been an intern he had not mentioned a special interest in heart problems. "What personal reasons?" she asked.

He looked at her suddenly as if his knowledge of the English language had completely failed. "But you must know. . . ."

Niki shook her head.

"You didn't know," Alexei inquired, speaking very slowly, as if asking a patient for symptoms necessary to make a difficult diagnosis, "that Dmitri died of a massive heart attack?"

Again, Niki shook her head, amazed by his tone of surprise.

"But it was . . . right after you and I were together. He was doing that play in Kansas, and they called me out there. I tried to call you, but you wouldn't speak to me. . . ."

Comprehension crashed in on her. She remembered being angered that he had made such a brief effort to reach her . . . Then recalled that Helen had tried to plead his case, to mention something that had happened—and she had refused to listen, had forbidden Helen to speak about him.

"I'm sorry," Niki said distractedly. "I . . . I wish I had known. I should have. . . ."

But would it have made any difference if she had known then? she asked herself. She had fled from him because she had been frightened by the eruption of passion, afraid it might lead her to the same destructive choices made by the other women of her line. She thought that fear was conquered now—and yet she suspected sometimes that she had unwittingly discouraged Will. . . .

Alexei asked about Helen, and Niki said they kept in touch with calls and letters.

"I hope you realize that won't be enough to satisfy me," Alexei said then. "Now that I've found you again, I intend to come calling on you—and very soon. We have a lot of lost time to make up for . . ." He raised his champagne glass and touched it to hers.

Niki joined his toast in silent assent. It would be pleasant to be courted, she thought. It had been a long time since anyone looked at her the way Alexei did, with admiration and desire. Perhaps they were fated to be together.

"Now," he said sternly, though his dark eyes spoke of far more tender feelings, "I can't ignore the reason you're here in Washington. Will you explain to me what a nice girl like you is doing on the wrong side of a very important issue? How can you be part of such a terrible industry?"

"I never thought of tobacco as terrible," she said slowly. "It's simply what everyone grows in Willow Cross. I love my farm, Alexei, I love the place where I live. It never occurred to me that I might be doing harm."

"If you spent just a week working with me, Niki," Alexei said fervently, "you wouldn't have any doubts. Forgive me if I sound rabid on the subject of cigarettes, but I feel so strongly about it that I have taken a stand against treating patients who continue to smoke. When there are so many who are willing to help themselves, I refuse to sacrifice precious time and valuable techniques on those who insist on destroying themselves."

"But what if people can't stop," she said, recalling Ralph's complaint. "What if it's too hard?"

"Of course it's hard," Alexei said impatiently. "Nicotine is an addictive drug, just like Valium . . . or heroin. But there are ways to kick the addiction. Finding a way depends on making an elementary choice—life over death."

A beeper in Alexei's pocket began to sound its insistent note. He turned it off and excused himself to make a call. "My patients often need emergency attention," he said.

He returned to the table only a couple of minutes later. "Will you forgive me?" he said contritely. "I must leave. Can I drop you somewhere?"

She wanted to think, to digest the happenings of the day. "I'll finish my drink, and get a cab to the airport."

He nodded. "But promise me, you'll give me another chance to see you."

"Of course."

"Thank you, Niki," he said. "Forgive me again." He left some money on the table, and bent to give her a quick kiss.

She smiled. His regret was obviously sincere, and yet she could tell, too, that he loved his calling.

"I want to hear about your work the next time, Alexei," she said as he left. "It sounds exciting . . . important."

"Oh yes, Nikuschka," he answered over his shoulder. "There is nothing more important or exciting than mending a damaged human heart."

She wondered when he was gone if Fate had sent Alexei back to mend her own scarred and imperfect heart.

Shortly after she returned to Willow Cross the issue of the tobacco subsidy came to a vote in Congress. The result went against the farmers and in favor of the growers; henceforth there would be no price supports, no nonrepayable loans for farmers. The cooperatives would now be responsible for tobacco that was not sold at auction. To pay for this, they would be charged a special assessment on a per pound basis.

While the farmers would have to struggle harder, the tobacco companies would get richer and richer.

Upset as she was by the farmers' defeat, Niki was equally troubled by the perception Alexei had left her with that her golden crop was a harmful one. Where once she had paid little attention to health reports, now it seemed she couldn't escape them.

Her new awareness was fed by phone calls that came regularly from Alexei. He was eager to come and visit her, he said, but it was hard to arrange the time. There were so many people who depended on him. . . .

As Niki tended to growing the next crop, she could no longer think of it as the means of her livelihood unconnected to the consequences that might result to others. Unable to ignore her doubts, she took them to Will, who had helped with so many problems in the past.

"Doesn't it bother you to be growing tobacco," she asked one day, after a visit with Charmaine. "Doesn't it bother you to hear about all the harm it does?"

Will appeared surprised by the questions. ''People have been saying those things for a long time,'' he replied. ''I never touch the stuff myself, but I don't see it's much different from growing grain for alcohol, Niki. As long as something's not against the law, people can decide for themselves whether or not to use it. That's the way it's always been in America, and as far as I can see, that's the way it ought to be.''

It was an answer, Niki thought, though not a satisfying one. But the only other answer could mean an end to a way of life she had come to love.

Twenty-five

WHEN Alexei finally came, it was without any warning.

Niki was sitting on her lawn on a quiet Saturday morning, writing a letter to Helen and pausing now and then to watch Bo tinkering contentedly with her car. Helping Bo had been one of the great joys of Niki's life. She had paid for a battery of tests and for the hearing aid he now wore. Tim had been tutoring the boy every Sunday after church. Now every word Bo spoke delighted her, every new achievement thrilled her, just as if he were her own son.

Suddenly, a cloud of dust rose in the distance, signaling the approach of a vehicle. A sleek, silver Mercedes convertible appeared through the dust, honked its horn, and stopped some twenty yards from where she was working. Alexei got out of the car and came hurrying towards her.

Delighted to see him again, Niki ran headlong into a warm embrace. "Why didn't you call? Why didn't you tell me you were coming?'' she asked plaintively, comparing Alexei's dashing sport clothes with her grimy jeans.

"I didn't want to take the chance of being told you were too busy with your harvest. And,'' he confessed, "I was coming anyway. A colleague wanted a second opinion on a patient who lives not far from here. Despite my well-known antismoking position, there seem to be people involved with tobacco who won't hold it against me if they need heart surgery.''

"Come inside,'' Niki said. "I'll give you a cold drink while I clean up.''

She led Alexei into the kitchen, gave him a glass of lemonade, and ran upstairs. Quickly, she peeled off her jeans and work shirt, washed her face and hands, brushed her hair vigorously and tied it back with a ribbon. Then she dressed in a trim ivory skirt and a blouse in a swirling multicolored pattern that had been a recent present from Blake.

Returning downstairs, she found Alexei standing at the back door, looking towards the fields where her golden tobacco was ripening in the sun. "I can see why this place means so much to you,'' he said. "But it's still difficult for me to think of you as a farmer, Niki. Especially growing this. . . .'' He waved disparagingly toward the fields of tobacco.

"Tobacco isn't just a crop here, Alexei, it's a way of life that I've grown to love.'' She took him outside, wanting him to see everything that she saw and smelled and felt every morning of her life here. Even if he couldn't give her his approval, she wanted his understanding.

As they walked together, he reached for her hand and she gave it. She was aware of how solitary her life had been for the past few years, how little experience she'd had of such simple pleasures as a walk on a sunny day in the company of a man who wanted her.

Unconsciously, Niki's gaze strayed to a distant point beyond her own land. Alexei's eyes tracked hers, coming to rest at the same distant point—the Hyland estate. He placed a hand on Niki's shoulder, turning her around until she was facing him.

"Niki," he said, "I've never broken a professional confidence, but I feel now that I must. I want things to be right between us this time. I want to be honest with you in every way. The professional call I mentioned before, the man I came here to see . . . I think you should know that it was Edward Hyland."

Niki stiffened at the mention of Duke's name. Alexei's arm went around her, drawing her closer. "I see that I was right to tell you," he said. "I remember when we met, Niki . . . we both seemed to share a sense of being exiles, of not belonging. I feel that you still carry that with you. I believe it would make a great difference in your life if you could manage to bury the past, forget your grudge. . . ."

"Are you saying I should make friends with Duke Hyland?"

"It was his father who hurt you, Niki. Remember that Edward is, in fact, your half brother—and he's a very sick man. He knows that it's necessary for him to undergo a very delicate bypass procedure. He knows, too, that there is no guarantee of survival—or recovery. If you offer an opportunity to mend fences at this time, he may well grab it."

Niki stopped walking and looked at him. "Alexei, why are you asking me to do this. Did he send you . . . ?"

"No, Niki. I wouldn't act for him in that way. It's for your sake I suggest it, more than his. When anger and hate fill your heart, Niki, there's little room left for love."

She looked up at him and tried to smile. "Is that a professional diagnosis, Dr. Ivanov?"

He touched her cheek with his fingertips. "That's an observation from a man who has never stopped caring for you. Perhaps I'm being selfish as well, but now that I've found you again, I want us to have a chance. I want you to be free of whatever it is that makes you so afraid of love. . . ."

They walked on.

Could she do it, Niki wondered, could she put aside the

bitterness and close the gap that separated her from the Hylands? She had never really known Duke, not the way she knew Pepper and Babe. She could vaguely remember Elle speaking about him, however, a story she'd told about knowing him when he was a very young man . . . how nice he'd been to her then. Of course, the Duke Hyland she'd heard about lately—the one who was cursed by the people at the cooperative, and feared by his other siblings—sounded no better than H.D. Worse, if anything.

But if she listened to that memory of her mother, then perhaps what Alexei suggested was worth trying.

Perhaps.

The hours with Alexei went by almost unnoticed. They went back to the house and Niki talked of what her life in Willow Cross had been; he spoke about his work, of his growing interest in the field of laser surgery. The light of the day dimmed, and suddenly Alexei looked at his watch. "My God, Niki, where are my manners? You must be famished! Let me take you somewhere special for dinner," he offered. "I'm sure that if we drive far enough, we can find a place that serves civilized food and good wine."

The invitation made Niki smile. "Let's stay here," she suggested, thinking how pleasant it would be to share a dinner in her own home. "The wine cellar's rather limited . . . but I think we can manage some civilized food."

After inspecting the contents of Niki's refrigerator, they decided on a menu: chicken *chausseur* and a garden salad, with raspberries and cream for dessert. As they worked together in the spacious kitchen that Elle had loved, they slipped into the kind of gentle reminiscence enjoyed by old friends. Dining by candlelight, Niki felt as if the simple meal had been enriched by Alexei's presence, by the sharing of conversation and laughter.

After dinner, they sat outside on the porch steps, under a canopy of stars, surrounded by the sound of crickets and night creatures. When Alexei put his arm around her, Niki relaxed and leaned back against him. "I've thought of you so often," he said softly. "I've thought of being close to you. After what we shared, it was so hard to believe that you would run from me. If I hadn't lost Dmitri just then, I might have had the sense, the stamina, to go after you. But . . ." He trailed off.

"I didn't know about what had happened to Dmitri," she said. "I must have seemed so cruel to you, so cold not to—"

"No." He touched a finger to her lips to block any self-recrimination. "I understood without being told that you wouldn't deliberately hurt me. But I wished so many times that you could believe the same thing about me. You fled because you thought I had let you down . . . taken advantage . . . when all I wanted to do was love you." He moved around so he could face her directly. "Niki, if I had been older and wiser then, I would have understood your needs—I would have made a better diagnosis from your own special history. But I know now what I should have done then to reassure you." He took a breath. "Marry me," he said then, his dark eyes glowing in the moonlight, his voice husky with longing. "I love you, Niki. I think I've loved you since the day we met. Let me show you that you can count on me . . . always."

There was a magic in the words Alexei spoke, a magic that made Niki feel as if she were the most beautiful and desirable woman in the world. These were the words that made it safe to love—weren't they?—the magic incantation that could have chased away the demons that had destroyed her mother and grandmother.

Yet when she reached for a response, Niki found herself stumbling and faltering. "I . . . I don't know what to say . . ."

"You think I'm crazy to ask this way?"

"Alexei, you just came back into my life. . . ."

"But I have no doubts." Alexei smiled, his confidence unshaken by her hesitation. "And if you need a vow so that you can trust me. . . ."

She shook her head. "No, Alexei, I don't need guarantees from you. I've grown older and wiser, too."

He waited another moment, and then kissed her. As he held her close, she felt his warm breath against her face, the beating of his heart. She stood, keeping hold of his hand, and led him inside.

As they stood in the darkness of her bedroom, he kissed her again and again, murmuring her name. She swayed against him, and soon they sank onto the bed. His hands removed the clothing that separated them. Tenderly, he traced the outlines of her face. "I love you, Niki," he whispered, his breath fluttering against her skin.

She felt as if she were floating in a soft cocoon, where nothing could harm her. Marry me, marry me, the phrase repeated in her mind like a mantra. Yes, the pledge of undying love did banish the ghosts that haunted her heart.

Alexei's fingers worked the muscles in her arms, her thighs and calves, transforming tensions into shivers of pleasure. She sighed, looking at him in the darkness, thinking how beautiful he was. When he felt Niki relax, the pressure of his fingers eased; they moved like butterfly wings along the length of her body. Her breathing quickened as he kissed her breasts, as he flicked his tongue against the nipples, teasing them erect. She reached for him, but he resisted, his fingers traveling downward, parting her legs, kneading and probing until she was ready for him. Straddling Niki's body, his hands seemed to be everywhere, coaxing to life all the sensations that had been asleep so long. When her breathing grew ragged, he entered her quickly, stroking fast and hard until she cried out with pleasure, her back arching in a convulsive spasm of release.

Long after he had fallen asleep, Niki lay awake, warm and secure in the afterglow of his promises. Yet a part of her felt separate from Alexei, apart from him though they had been as physically close as two people could be. Would time make her love and trust him? Or was it true that a heart burdened with hate was unable to love at all? If she did what Alexei said, would she then be free of the burden, free to love?

Habit woke Niki early. After a hasty shower, she inspected her face in the mirror. She didn't think she looked different, but maybe it was too soon to see the miraculous transformation promised in storybooks.

She dressed quickly and went downstairs to prepare a hearty farm breakfast. She took a slab of bacon from the refrigerator and cut off a dozen slices. She broke six eggs into a bowl, and as she started to whip them with a whisk, there was a sharp rap on the back door, followed by an urgent pounding. She looked out the window and saw that it was Will.

Wiping her hands, Niki hurried to open the door. "Is something wrong?" she asked, fearing that Charmaine might be ill.

"Not a damn thing in the world is wrong!" Will exulted, picking Niki up and whirling her around. "You'll never believe what just happened. I can hardly believe it myself! I got a call from a record producer in Nashville. It seems somebody taped me singing 'Farmer Brown' on one of those TV shows we went on . . . then sent the tape to this record producer in Nashville. He called and asked if I had any more songs." Will laughed, clearly relishing every moment of his story. "When I told him I had a trunkful, he said I should send him some tapes. If he likes 'em, he'll sign me up to make an album! With real musicians and a studio, the whole damn works!"

"That's wonderful, Will! Congratulations!"

"I came here to ask you a favor, Niki. Something real important."

"Anything, Will," she answered promptly. After all he had done for her, she was ready to repay him without question.

He was on the verge of explaining when there was a sound of feet thumping down the stairs. Niki glanced through the door of the kitchen, unable to hide her embarrassment as Will's brow furrowed, and the expression of delight vanished from his face.

A moment later, Alexei ambled into the kitchen, wearing a silk robe and rubbing his eyes. "Why did you let me sleep so long, Niki? I would have been happy to help you make breakfast."

Niki was struck dumb as the two men stared at each other.

"Excuse me," Alexei said at last, "I didn't realize you had company."

"I was just leaving," Will said gruffly, and marched out of the house.

Niki went after him and caught him by his truck. "Will . . . Alexei is . . . an old friend," she offered, stumbling over the half-truth.

Will nodded. "No need for explanations, Niki. You're one beautiful woman, and he's one . . . ordinary man. Old friends or not, those are easy numbers to add up." He opened the door of the truck, then paused. "I'll tell you the truth, though, I do wonder why we couldn't make 'em add up for us." He climbed into the seat and slammed the door.

Niki fought against the dismay that swept through her. He wasn't angry, after all, he was only leaving as a gentleman would. Why was she so reluctant to let him go? "You never did tell me what that favor was," she said, trying to recapture the moment of shared celebration that Alexei had interrupted.

He glanced back at the house before answering. "Don't think there's much point to it now. Guess my timing was real bad. . . ." He started the truck.

Niki jumped on the running board. "Will, you came here with something on your mind. I'm not letting you leave until you tell me what it is!"

He responded with a half-smile, as if her show of spirit had revived some of his excitement. "I was going to ask you . . . well, if this record thing works out, I wanted you to come to Nashville with me. For moral support. I suppose that might sound silly—''

''No,'' she said, recalling her own disappointment when there was no one to see her dive. ''No, it doesn't sound silly at all. Name the day, Will, and I'll be there.''

He nodded, then looked to the house again, as if to remind her she was keeping her guest waiting.

There was a silence. Niki stepped down backward off the running board. They looked at each for another second, and then Will drove off.

When she returned to the house, Alexei had taken over the preparation of breakfast. He stood over the pan of sizzling bacon in an attitude of exaggerated absorption, refusing to look up as Niki entered the kitchen.

''That was Will Rivers,'' she said, trying to clear the lingering awkwardness. ''His farm is down the road . . . we belong to the same tobacco cooperative.''

''Ah. So it was farming business that brought Mr. Rivers here this morning?'' Alexei's wry tone implied that he knew better.

Niki was irritated. Somehow both men had managed to make her feel guilty. ''Not business,'' she said. ''He came to ask a favor, and I'll do it because Will's been a good friend to me ever since I got here. If it hadn't been for him, I don't know how I would have survived.''

''That doesn't explain why he was so angry to find me here.''

''He wasn't angry,'' Niki declared quickly. ''Did he look angry?''

Alexei smiled. ''I'm experienced at making diagnoses from X-rays, my dear. I look beneath the surface.'' Moving from the stove, Alexei grasped her gently by the arms. ''I meant everything I said last night, Niki. You may not be ready to share my feelings completely. But I would like to know: should I consider Mr. Rivers to be . . . competition?''

Competition? From a man who collected the adoration of women? "No!" she said decisively, giving the only response she could. "Whatever happens between us, Alexei, Will Rivers is no competition. Any woman who falls in love with him would have to be out of her mind."

Twenty-six

HIGHLANDS was only a few miles away from Niki's cottage, but now, as it had been in her childhood, the sprawling estate was like another world, a place far different from that inhabited by ordinary mortals. As far as the eye could see, there were green rolling lawns, trees of every description, and flowering shrubs. The main house rose like a storybook fantasy in all its antebellum splendor. Nearby, separated by towering trees and dense hedges, was a cluster of smaller houses not unlike Niki's own cottage. For guests? Niki wondered. Or merely for the servants?

As she approached the gate Niki had a fleeting recollection of another day when her mother had driven her there—had raced toward it, the car going so fast that Niki thought they might crash. But on that day, she remembered too, they had turned away.

Today she continued forward, driving on into the sweeping circular driveway. Reminded of Elle's longing to come here—her pitifully futile wish be the mistress of Highland

House—Niki felt a rush of anger. But she forced it down. She had come to make peace, Niki reminded herself, not to fan the embers of old resentments.

She parked her car and walked towards the pristine white door with its gleaming brass knocker. Her hand reached for the knocker, pausing for a moment in midair. What if she was turned away? Could her self-respect stand up to another contemptuous rejection?

Taking a deep breath, Niki commanded her fingers to grasp the knocker, to rap it forcefully against the door. It was better to know what was on the other side than to spend her life battling shadows.

A dark-skinned butler in uniform opened the door.

"I'm here to see Mr. Hyland," Niki said.

"Is Mr. Hyland expecting you?" the butler asked politely.

"No. My name is Nicolette Sandeman. Please tell him I'm here."

"Yes, ma'am," the butler replied, leading Niki into a spacious entrance gallery with a delicately veined marble floor and damask covered walls hung with what appeared to be family portraits. Indicating an antique gilt bench where she might wait, the servant retreated towards the back of the house.

Well, Niki thought, at least she'd gotten this far. It was more than she'd ever managed during H.D.'s lifetime.

The butler returned in a few minutes. "Please follow me," he said, retracing his path through a long narrow hallway, until they reached a glass-enclosed solarium filled with exotic blooms. Reclining on an upholstered lounge, like a ruler in repose, was Duke Hyland. Slowly, he rose to his feet, throwing off the blanket that had covered his knees. Without speaking a word, he studied Niki, his dark eyes lingering on her face. In this warm and sunny room, Duke seemed somehow different from the mysterious looming presence of her childhood. Yet neither did he look like a man who was seriously ill. His body was well fleshed and his complexion was ruddy.

Still, Alexei had said Duke's condition was life-threatening, and Niki had no reason to doubt him.

"You remind me of your mother," Duke said finally, his voice deep, his tone not unfriendly. "Something about the way you carry yourself. . . ."

"Thank-you," Niki said, holding her head up high, as if to affirm she was no longer shamed by a history she had no part in shaping.

Duke gestured towards a chair, then resumed his own place. "Why are you here?" he asked in the same neutral tone.

"I heard . . . it might be a good time to . . . pay my respects," she said, carefully choosing a diplomatic phrase.

"Why would this be a particularly good time?"

"Because . . . you're not well."

Duke frowned. "Who told you that?"

"It doesn't matter," Niki answered quickly, not wanting to compromise Alexei. "I had another reason for coming. . . ."

"I thought so." Duke nodded with a smile of satisfaction. "Well, let's hear it," he said expansively, leaning forward in an attitude of encouragement.

"I came because I thought . . . because I hoped we didn't have to be enemies anymore. I never understood why you were still against me after Mama died, and then H.D., why Sterling Weatherby did everything he could to keep me out of Willow Cross. Even after I put two and two together and figured out you were behind it all. . . ."

"Go on," Duke interjected, his dark eyes glittering at the mention of Weatherby's name.

"I still didn't understand," she continued, "when all I wanted was to make a life for myself, that you would use your power to hurt me . . ."

"And?" Duke prodded, as if he were still trying to uncover the reason for Niki's visit.

"That's all. That's what I came here to say. Maybe you

felt you had reasons to be angry because my mother was . . . involved with your father. That was his doing as much as hers,'' she added quickly, unwilling to blame Elle for H.D.'s sins. ''But it was all a long time ago. It doesn't make sense to go on being angry now. When I heard you were sick, I thought it might make you feel better, too, if we—''

''You mean to say you came here just to make peace with me?'' he asked incredulously. ''That's all? That's all you want?''

Niki thought for a moment, understanding perfectly what Duke was asking. Was she ready to deny here and now that she had any right, any claim to the Hyland name and all that went with it?

''Yes,'' she said finally, ''that's all I want. To put an end to the anger, to close the door on the past. There hasn't been a single day when I've been free of it. I want it to stop. I want some peace in my life.''

Duke stared back at her as if he were memorizing her features. Then she realized he seemed to be looking right through her, as if he were seeing someone else.

He leaned back in his chair. ''Did your mother ever tell you how we met?'' he asked, his voice surprisingly gentle.

''No,'' Niki replied, surprised by the question and the way Duke asked it.

''We met in Monaco on a spring day,'' he said, pausing as if to recapture the memory.

Niki searched her own memory for the story of Elle's meeting with H.D. Hyland in that fairy-tale kingdom—the story in which she had sailed away on his luxurious yacht, visiting romantic places, coming at last to America. There had been no mention of Duke. Niki shook her head. ''Mama never said that. She told me—''

''Told you that's when she met my father,'' Duke finished the sentence. ''She never mentioned, then, that I was the one who found her when she didn't know where her next meal was coming from, that I was the one who brought her aboard the yacht—that H.D. took her away from me . . . ?''

Niki kept shaking her head.

"No, I don't suppose she would have. Do you know what I liked best about her? Gabrielle was the first girl I'd met who didn't know that I was H.D. Hyland's son and heir. She seemed so fresh, so . . . honest . . . I thought we were going to be friends. I thought she was someone who could make a difference in my life. . . ."

As Duke spoke, his face softened and Niki felt herself strangely drawn to him. Was it the tenderness in his voice, the recollection of his youth, the disclosure of a heretofore unknown fondness for her mother?

But suddenly his tone changed, becoming cold and hard. His eyes locked into hers with frightening intensity. "But that isn't how it turned out. No, your mother used me and threw me over. Because H.D. looked like a better deal. And that's why there's no chance for peace between you and me. Do you understand now, Nicolette Sandeman?"

"No!" Niki protested. Shocked though she was by Duke's revelation, she refused to give up hope for reconciliation. She could sense that there was something else between them that had nothing to do with anger or hate. It seemed fairly obvious that he had come close to falling in love with Gabrielle himself. So why wasn't it H.D. he hated for stealing her away? How had that disappointment become transmuted into this vendetta between them?

"Duke," she said, daring to be familiar, "there ought to be more that pulls us together than divides us. And I'm not saying that because I want anything from you but an end to the war. If you were hurt by the past, so was I! Isn't it enough that I grew up without a father? That I lost my mother, too?"

His dark eyes were alert and alive as she made her plea. There was no hint of illness or weakness of any kind. He seemed miraculously energized, as if the old story had revived some vital force within him. "It isn't enough," he said, "it can *never* be enough. No matter what you say or do, you and I are mortal enemies. That's a promise I make to *you* now. Count on it, as long as you live!"

Sickened by the words, the malice behind them, Niki ran from the house. Not until she was outside did she allow herself a moment to recover, breathing in the fresh air as if to cleanse herself of Duke's venom.

Now she knew all too well that her fear of Duke had not been the product of a childish imagination. Yet while she understood the secret of his bitterness towards Elle, Niki still couldn't fathom the depth of his hatred towards her. The promise of his undying enmity filled her with foreboding. It was like a terrible ancient prophecy from which there could be no escape down through the ages.

She was hurrying away from the main house when she saw a man on horseback coming towards her at full gallop. As the horse drew closer, slowing to an easy canter, then a trot, Niki saw that the rider was Babe.

His tanned face crinkled with pleasure as he reined in the horse and dismounted with a single graceful movement. "Niki, what a surprise! What a wonderful surprise!" The warmth of Babe's greeting felt like an antidote to Duke's cold hostility. "Why didn't you tell me you were coming to see me?"

"I came to see Duke," Niki replied, unable to repress a shudder.

"Duke?" Babe repeated, his blue eyes widening with amazement. "Why on earth . . . ?"

"Don't ask me any questions now, Babe . . . please. I have to get out of here." She started walking towards her Buick, but Babe grabbed her hand.

"Leave the car," he said, "I'll get it back to you later."

"No—" She started to pull away.

But Babe held on. "Listen, I can see you're upset. And I know what it's like to run up against Duke. He could give a rattlesnake nightmares when he's in a bad mood. Well, I've got some medicine for clearing him out of my head. Let me share a little with you. . . ."

His cheerful optimism was infectious. Niki let herself be led to a sprawling garage that had once housed H.D.'s collection of classic autos. Now most of the models were of a more recent vintage. "Which one shall we take?" Babe asked, pointing out his cars—a silver Lamborghini, a blue Maserati convertible, and the red Ferrari Niki remembered.

She pointed to the convertible, and Babe smiled his approval, as if to say a fast ride in the open air would do them both good. A minute later, they were off in a roaring burst of speed.

"Tell me why you came to see Duke," Babe said, when they had left Highland House far behind.

"I wanted to . . . offer my friendship because I heard he was sick."

Babe reacted with surprise. "Nobody's supposed to know that."

"You mean nobody who doesn't live at Highland House," she corrected.

Babe nodded. "Duke knows I'm not about to leak his secrets. As far as the press is concerned, the official Hyland line is that Duke will live forever. Just like Hyland Tobacco," he added with a tight smile.

"But how does Duke know you won't say anything?" Niki asked, still trying to comprehend the odd yet powerful relationship between the two brothers.

"Because that's the way H.D. brought us up," Babe replied, as if repeating an article of catechism. "He knew we didn't get along. Sometimes I think he meant it to be that way. But he taught us that when it came to Hyland Tobacco business, we had no choice but to stick together. He made us believe some terrible catastrophe would happen if one of us broke ranks."

Niki thought for a moment. "You know," she said, "I can't remember a single instance when H.D. took the time to teach me anything. Elle tried to tell me that's the way he was, but I don't think I ever believed that. I was sure he was different with his 'real' children. I was sure you all had so much that I didn't. . . ."

"You're not talking about money now, are you, Niki?"

She shook her head. "I used to imagine all the wonderful family things you did in your big house on the hill, how much fun you had together."

Babe laughed mirthlessly. "It's too bad you never got to see the real thing, Niki. What you imagined was just a fairy tale."

Niki believed him. She had seen with her own eyes the wealth and privilege enjoyed by H.D.'s legitimate children, yet she had seen little evidence of real happiness.

They kept on driving until they reached a small marina on the coast. There was but a single vessel moored at the dock, a sailing yacht bearing the Hyland crest. As Babe and Niki got out of the car, an old man wearing a captain's hat emerged from a small weather-beaten shack. "Good day to you, Mr. Hyland . . . miss," the old man said with a smile.

"Hi, Bill," Babe responded.

"Did you come to take the Hyland II out for a test run?" the old man asked.

"Maybe later." Babe discreetly pressed a bill into the old man's hand and led Niki aboard the yacht. "Bill used to work for Hyland Tobacco," Babe explained, "until he got too old to do his job. Now he looks after my boats."

How different the half brothers were, Niki thought. She couldn't imagine Duke being concerned about the welfare of an elderly employee, let alone finding a way to take care of him with no sacrifice of dignity. "Where is the Hyland II?" she asked, curious to see the racing craft that was Babe's pride and joy.

"Over there," he replied, pointing to a metal shed. "I'll show you what she can do after we've had a chance to relax."

Niki leaned against the railing and looked out towards the horizon, where the pale sky met the blue-gray waters of the Atlantic. She felt soothed by the tranquility of her surroundings, the gentle rocking of the boat. Babe went below deck and returned a few minutes later with a bottle of champagne, a tin of beluga caviar, and a box of imported English crackers.

"This looks like a celebration," Niki said ruefully, "but I'm not really in a celebrating mood."

"That's the best time for champagne," Babe said, popping the cork and filling two glasses with the sparkling wine. "You still haven't told me why you came to Highland House today."

"It was another of my fairy-tale ideas," she said quietly. "I thought this might be a good time to make peace with Duke."

"But Duke wasn't interested, right?"

"It wasn't as simple as not being interested," Niki said slowly. "For a minute, I felt that my visit . . . touched him somehow. Then all of a sudden, he was telling me he hated me . . . and I knew he meant it, Babe, I could see it in his eyes."

"I'm sorry he hurt you," Babe said softly. "But that's the way Duke is, Niki. He doesn't make attachments and he doesn't care for anyone."

Yet that wasn't always true, Niki thought. "Did you know he met my mother before H.D. did?" she asked.

Babe was so startled, he spilled his drink. "Did Duke tell you that?"

"He said . . . well, he said that he cared for my mother, that there might have been something between them if she hadn't met H.D."

Babe said nothing to dispute Duke's story. His boyish face was thoughtful, as if he were fitting these new pieces of information into his own fragmented history. "It's possible, I suppose," he said quietly. "It even makes sense. . . ." Noticing Niki's troubled expression, he took her hand and said: "Don't start blaming your mother for what happened a long time ago. She was young and she was all alone. We can't judge her, Niki. Not now. . . ."

Yet even as Babe spoke, Niki could see there was sadness in his blue eyes and she felt as if she should be comforting him. Though he had defended Elle's memory, Niki couldn't help but wonder if that memory had been somehow sullied by her mother's connection with Duke.

She refilled his champagne glass, hoping to lighten the heavy mood. Babe shook his head. "Come on," he said, "I know something that's even better than champagne." Babe ran down the gangway from the sailboat, summoned the watchman, Bill, and together they rolled a long canvas-covered trailer out of the metal shed and down to the water's edge. Babe yanked off the protective canvas, proudly revealing the thirty-foot-long sleek green-and-white craft. To Niki's eyes, there scarcely seemed to be room in it for one person, let alone two, yet when she seemed reluctant to join him, Babe simply laughed. "We'll leave off the helmets and the lifejackets," he said.

"Is that safe?" she asked doubtfully, thinking how slender and delicate the boat looked.

"Of course it isn't safe," he answered, looking like a mischievous young boy. "That's what makes it fun, Niki!"

She squeezed in beside him as Bill carefully eased the boat into the water. It wasn't until they had drifted out about thirty yards, far enough to avoid the risk of scraping bottom, that Babe turned the key in the ignition. As the engine roared to life, he laughed aloud, as if the deafening noise filled him with joy.

Babe shoved a throttle lever forward, and a second later they were flying across the water, the spray pounding their faces, the wind whipping their hair. As Babe accelerated, the boat began to bounce off the tips of the waves, skipping in leaps of five and ten yards as easily as a flat stone hurled over the water by a child. Niki was frightened and exhilarated at the same time. Babe seemed almost mesmerized as he pushed the craft faster and faster. Slow down, Niki wanted to say, slow down a little, but her heart was beating so fast she couldn't speak. Her fists clenched at her sides as the shoreline retreated from view at an alarming speed. The boat seemed to vibrate from the power of the engine.

It seemed an eternity before Babe pulled back on the throttle, slowing to a speed that allowed Niki to relax and breathe. "My God," she said, "I've never felt anything like that in my whole life. . . ."

Babe shook his head with dissatisfaction. "We still have to get some of the kinks worked out. I have to shave some weight off the body without losing the structural strength, and tune up the engine for more power."

"A lighter body?" she repeated, thinking that at top speed the one she was in seemed as fragile as an eggshell. "Won't that be terribly dangerous?"

"Danger is what makes it exciting," Babe said, his blue eyes blazing with a fire she'd never seen. "Knowing it's dangerous, counting on everyone else to back off, to be afraid . . . that's what makes winning so damned exciting."

"What about you, Babe?" Niki asked, her pulse still racing, still pounding. "Aren't you ever afraid?"

"Not here, Niki," he answered with a strange smile. "That's the funny thing. I've been afraid so much . . . terrified of nothing more than sitting in the same room with H.D., or Duke, or trying to live up to being a Hyland. But here . . . this is one place where I'm never afraid."

Twenty-seven

"WHAT time do we get to Nashville?" Niki asked. By a serendipitous coincidence, the Country Music Fan Fair was underway in the city, and she was looking forward to what Will had promised would be a few days of nonstop fun.

"We're not going straight to Nashville . . . if that's okay with you."

"Well, where *are* we going? Is this some kind of a mystery tour?"

"Nope. But it is a surprise."

"Okay," she said agreeably. It was a beautiful June day, it was Will's day, and after all he'd done for her, it was only right that she be here for him. Besides, she thought, it had been ages since she'd taken any kind of holiday, and it felt good to just kick back and forget work for a couple of carefree days.

When the first "Memphis" sign appeared, Niki wondered why on earth they'd come this far out of their way, when they'd only have to double back. But Will kept driving, past Memphis another thirty miles, to an exit sign marked "Whitehaven."

"We aren't!" she laughed. "Are we going where I think we're going?"

"We are!"

"Graceland!" they laughed in unison.

"What on earth made you want to come here?" she asked. "I mean, with an important recording date tomorrow afternoon, I figured you'd want to rest or study your music. Or do whatever it is that musicians do."

"Well," he drawled, "being a farmer myself, I don't exactly know what musicians are supposed to do. So I'm just pleasing myself, if that's okay with you. Hope you don't think it's too corny, coming to Graceland. You being a Yankee," he teased.

"No, you don't, Will Rivers, you aren't going to get me going on that Yankee business again. I made up my mind to be nice to you, and—"

"Well, gosh, Miss Niki," he cut in, "I didn't realize it was such an effort to be nice to me!"

"It isn't!" Niki protested, baffled by Will's sudden touchiness. "All I meant is that I want to be a good friend, like you've been to me."

"A good friend," he repeated, making the phrase sound like an insult. "When did you make up your mind about that?"

Niki fidgeted in her seat, unsettled by this line of questioning—and starting to wonder if this trip was such a good idea after all.

"Did you decide on your own?" Will pressed. "Or did you get some help from that guy I saw at your house?"

"I don't know what you're talking about," she said, "and for your information, 'that guy' is an old friend."

"Another friend," Will said with an odd smile. "I guess I should have known," he added cryptically, then lapsed into silence.

Niki did the same. Her relationship with Alexei was none of Will's business. Wasn't he the one who was still hung up on his "pretty lady"? Did it bother him so much that there was one woman in Willow Cross who wasn't falling at his feet?

She was relieved when they reached their destination: the fourteen-acre estate that the late Elvis Presley had bought in 1957 for about one hundred thousand dollars from a Memphis physician, a place now venerated by millions of fans.

As they climbed out of Will's jeep, he murmured: "The King's castle." Though he smiled, Niki felt he wasn't really joking. "Elvis was only twenty-two when he bought this place. I wonder if he knew," Will mused, "that it was going to become a shrine one day."

They approached the pink field-stone wall that was scrawled with such graffiti declarations as "I Love You Forever, Elvis" or "Elvis Lives." Outside the custom-made wrought-iron gate, they joined the cluster of fans—men, women, children—who were already waiting. A ghostly recorded voice filled the air: it was Elvis wailing "Can't Help Falling in Love."

Niki felt a giggle coming on, but seeing Will's serious expression, she stifled it. When the gate was opened, the visitors filed in quietly, in attitudes of wonder and reverence.

The white-columned portico was an image of classical grace. Inside, the twenty-three-room neoclassical house was a picture-book fantasy of wealth, with its sweeps of off-white and gilt, its crystal chandeliers reflected in blue mirrors.

Will spoke reverently, almost in a whisper, sharing with Niki a favorite Elvis anecdote, of a rock-and-roll legend whose appetites were Rabelaisian, yet whose tastes were often so childishly simple that he'd hop a jet to Denver just to get a certain kind of peanut-butter sandwich.

"This is Elvis's den," he said, pausing in a doorway. "It's called the Jungle Room. According to a story I heard, Elvis furnished the whole place in thirty minutes at a Memphis store called Donald's."

"It's certainly different," Niki said politely, as she took in the huge chairs and sofas covered with what looked like fake monkey fur, the grass-green shag carpet that covered floors and ceiling.

"The room's accoustically perfect," Will said. "Elvis recorded eight hits right here, for his last album 'Moody Blue.' "

As they approached the mirrored television room, with its three huge built-in sets mounted side by side, Niki smelled the unmistakable aroma of Southern home cooking. "I thought this was a museum," she whispered to Will.

"It is . . . and it isn't. Elvis's aunt, Mrs. Delta Biggs, lives downstairs. She cooks for the night cleaning crew."

"You're a regular Elvis encyclopedia," Niki remarked.

Will eyed Niki dubiously. "I suppose this might all seem like a joke to you, especially if all you remember is the way Elvis was at the end. But when he was just starting out, Niki, when he was driving a truck and dreaming about making music, there was nobody in the world who could sing like he did. The music he made . . . it was raw and powerful and full of truth. He *cared* about the music then, it was something he *had* to do, like he couldn't help himself . . ." Will trailed off for a moment, and Niki felt instinctively that he wasn't just talking about Elvis. "Back during those early recording sessions," he continued, "Elvis didn't need drugs or alcohol. He used to sing spirituals to warm up, to free his voice, you know? And then, once he got going, he'd work the whole damn night, clear until the next day, not even stopping for something to eat . . ." As Will spoke, his eyes glowed with such worshipful admiration that Niki felt ashamed of teasing him.

Voices lowered, they entered the Trophy Room, which was like the treasure room of an Egyptian pharaoh. Preserved for posterity were Elvis's motorcycle, his army uniform, his collection of guns and police badges. On faceless mannequins were the King's film and stage costumes, ranging from tailored black leather to the sequined jumpsuits of his Las Vegas shows. "These look awfully small," Niki whispered, recalling the puffiness of Elvis's final years.

Will frowned. "Some say those costumes have been taken in," he admitted finally, "but they're from a time I don't like to remember. That was after success destroyed him, Niki. It made him forget what was real and what wasn't. Success took all the truth out of his music . . . until there was nothing left."

Niki said no more. The clothes Elvis and Priscilla wore on their wedding day were displayed, along with a replica of their wedding cake, evoking in Niki's mind a picture of innocence and hope. Even all the good luck in the world, even a career second to none hadn't been enough to save the marriage—or the singer himself.

Will, too, was lost in thought, as he stood before the collection of some 150 gold and platinums, with an expression of unbridled longing that drew Niki closer. Suddenly, he turned and looked at Niki, as if she, too, were a coveted trophy. His arms went round her, his mouth claimed hers. Caught by surprise, she yielded for one sweet moment, melting into the rugged strength of his body—until an instinct stronger than desire made her pull away.

"So I was right the first time," he said quietly.

"About what?" she demanded, refusing to meet his eyes.

"That guy I saw at your house," he said accusingly.

Niki struggled to mask her confusion with coolness. "I told you before. Alexei is an old friend. Not that it's any damn business of yours," she added.

He tilted her chin up and looked into Niki's eyes, as if he might find there the secret of her true feelings. "You're right," he said finally, "it isn't any of my business."

Niki sighed as Will released her. Was it simply relief she felt?

She followed Will outside, into the Meditation Garden—where Elvis was buried alongside his parents, Gladys and Vernon. Niki and Will stood in awkward silence, watching the fans who plucked at blades of grass to take home for souvenirs, the others who bowed their heads in tribute, or perhaps even in prayer. All around were relics of their devotion—a stuffed hound dog, a vase of flowers wilting in the sun, a Styrofoam cross bearing the message "Rest in peace."

Niki stole a sideward glance at Will, who appeared genuinely touched. She didn't dare reach out to him, she didn't dare bridge the distance that kept them safely apart.

They moved on to a small theater. When the seats were all filled, the lights went down and Elvis appeared on the screen, singing "If I Can Dream." Swaying in their seats, his fans sang along. Will did, too, his voice ringing clear and strong as it joined with Elvis's. Now Niki understood why they had gone two hundred miles out of their way to make this pilgrimage. Will had come here hoping to be touched by the magic that had made his hero a star.

When they got back into Will's pickup, Niki tried to revive the lighthearted camaraderie they had enjoyed during the drive to Memphis. But he wouldn't cooperate. To each question she asked, he gave only a terse answer; when she fell silent, he retreated into his own silence.

As a friend, Will had shown he could be trusted. Yet now that he had revealed feelings and desires of another kind, Niki felt suspicious. Did he have a hidden agenda for this trip? she wondered. Could it be that once away from their everyday environment, he expected her to fall into his arms? Perhaps he had been incited to add her to his list of conquests only by seeing Alexei in her house.

Though it was very late when they reached Nashville, the city was still brightly lit like a giant carnival, and crowds of country-music fans still thronged the streets.

"I didn't realize there would be so many people," she said.

"I told you, the Country Music Fan Fair is the biggest annual event in Nashville."

"So you did." Niki yawned, tired by the long drive and by the strain of the past few hours. "I'm looking forward to the fair,'' she said brightly, ''but what I want right now is a comfortable bed and some sleep.''

But when they reached the motel where Will had made reservations, they were handed just one key.

''There must be some mistake,'' Niki said coldly, her suspicions now bursting into full flower.

''I asked for two rooms when I called,'' Will assured her.

The desk clerk glanced from one to the other. He smiled, as if he had heard this same exchange before, then shrugged helplessly. ''I don't know anything about two rooms,'' he said, ''and if you want my advice,'' he winked, ''you'll take the one we have. At this time of year, you won't find a vacancy anywhere in Nashville.''

Niki restrained herself until they were outside. ''That's a pretty old trick!'' she exploded. ''A damn corny one, too! And if you think I have any intention of sharing a room with you, Will Rivers, I'll tell you right now, you've got another think coming!''

''I made two reservations, damn it,'' Will declared angrily. ''And if you think I need corny tricks to get me a roommate, then you're the one who's got another think coming!''

''I'll sleep in the car,'' she said stiffly. ''You need your rest.''

''I'll decide what I need!'' He grabbed her by the shoulders and shook her hard. ''I don't know what's wrong with you, lady, but it looks to me like you've got a dirty mind to go with that chip on your shoulder!''

''Oh, really?'' she sneered, hands on hips in an attitude of defiance. ''And it looks to me like you have an ego that won't quit! Just because I won't fall into bed with you, then you think there has to be something wrong with me!''

''Well, isn't there?'' They faced one another like gunfighters. Will fired: ''A normal woman doesn't act like she got bit by a rattler when a man kisses her.''

Taking deadly aim, Niki fired back: ''Oh? And does a normal man spend his life mooning over a dead love—at the same time as he goes around chasing every woman in sight?''

Will recoiled, his jaw tightened, his fists clenched at his side as he struggled for control. Suddenly the battle was over. He walked to the jeep, took out Niki's bag, and threw it at her along with the key. A moment later, he drove away.

She let herself into the motel room, undressed quickly, and jumped into bed. Miserably, Niki tossed and turned, sifting through the residue of shouted cruelties. As her own cruel words echoed through her mind, she tried to defend herself. It was all his fault, wasn't it? He was the one who fired the first shot. But wasn't he just speaking the truth? a small voice asked. Well, so was I, she responded. But if all they had done was to speak the truth, why did there have to be such anger in it?

Remembering why they had come to Nashville in the first place, Niki felt a sudden pang of guilt. Imagining Will to be driving around the streets of a city without vacant rooms, on the eve of his recording date, Niki turned her anger on herself. After all Will had done for her, was it fair to sabotage his big chance? Couldn't a mature woman find a way to say no without starting a war?

She fell asleep for a few restless hours, and woke at dawn. She showered quickly and dressed, wondering if Will would bother to come back for her at all, thinking she couldn't blame him if he didn't.

At seven, there was a knock on the door. Niki was ready with an apology as she opened it, but Will skipped over that step. "Hurry up," he said pleasantly, "there's someplace special I want to go for breakfast."

She followed him outside, took her place beside him in the pickup. "Will," she said, as he started the engine, "I'm sorry for fighting with you. I had no right to say those things, to upset you that way, especially when you have to sing this afternoon."

"I'm fine," he said stubbornly, refusing to meet her eyes, "and I was the one who was out of line. A man should know better than to push himself on a woman who's not interested."

"But you didn't do that," she protested, trying to take back the accusation she had made.

"Forget it," he said. "That was last night. We were both tired."

They drove out of town on Route 5, to a nondescript-looking place called the Loveless Motel and Cafe. Niki wondered if there was a hidden meaning in his choice.

"This place is famous for their breakfasts," Will explained, falling back into his role as tour guide and teacher. "A lot of music people eat here. I figured there might be a shot at seeing some today."

Though everyone inside the Loveless looked like "country," Will's search for celebrities proved fruitless. "We'll see the music people later," he said, as if she were the one who'd been disappointed.

The food, however, lived up to its reputation. Niki had the Loveless's renowned fresh buttermilk biscuits with homemade jam. Will went all out and had pan-fried country ham and eggs as well, eating heartily and making favorable comments in between bites, as if to prove that their quarrel had been forgotten. That everything was back to normal between them—whatever that meant.

With a few hours to spare, Will set out to show Niki the city of Nashville. They drove through the central business district, with its reminders of the earliest riverbank settlement, past the state capitol building and Riverfront Park, an open air music theater at the foot of Broadway. Will pointed out the long rows of multi-storied Victorian buildings adjacent to the waterfront, the historic warehouse district.

"Shouldn't we be getting to the recording studio?" she asked.

"Not yet," Will answered. Acting as if he had hours to spare, Will fought the increasing traffic generated by the fair, reminiscing about how he had stopped at one of the fair's autograph booths to get the signature of Hank Williams, Jr. and ended up sharing a long conversation about the singer's legendary father. "Country singers are good people," he said. "Big stars like Dolly Parton and Loretta Lynn compete in all kinds of athletic events during the fair, just to raise money for the Special Olympics."

They meandered slowly along the city's lakes, passing parks and preserved plantation homes. Finally, they approached the legendary Ryman Auditorium.

"That's the place," Will pointed. "That's where the Grand Ole Opry used to be. That's where country music has its roots. A born-again riverboat captain by the name of Tom Ryman built it as a tabernacle. The Opry took it over in 1948, stayed there till 1974."

"Where did it go?"

"It's over in a spot called the Opryland Showpark, east of the city. It's got rides and stage shows and strolling musicians and clowns. But to me, and a lot of other folks, the Ryman Auditorium is still the 'real' Opry. In fact, some say that if you go by Ryman late at night, when Broadway is real quiet, you can hear Roy Acuff singing 'The Wabash Cannonball.' "

With Will calling the shots, they went on touring—to the Parthenon that was an exact replica of the one in Greece, to Andrew Jackson's estate, the Hermitage.

Niki couldn't understand why she practically had to drag Will to the recording session. It didn't occur to her until they were in the building, located on the four-block stretch known as Music Row, and Will paused for a deep breath outside the door to the studio, that he might be afraid—that if his fantasies turned out to be stillborn, they might never revive again.

At last he pulled open the door and Niki followed him in, determined to provide the promised moral support, which now felt more like a penance than a gift.

Yet once he was inside, being greeted by the producer and the studio musicians, Will almost seemed to forget she was there. Within the confines of the glass-enclosed recording booth, Will strummed some warm-up chords on his guitar. Dressed country-fashion, the musicians appeared thoroughly professional and dead serious as they huddled with Will, preparing for the business of making music.

Though she'd heard Will sing any number of times, here it was different. It wasn't just the earphones he wore or the sophisticated electronic equipment that surrounded him. Somewhere between Willow Cross and Nashville, he'd left behind his self-deprecating manner. As he strummed the introductory chords to the familiar "Farmer Brown," he hunched over his guitar, his muscular body taut, his brow furrowed with concentration. At last, with a curt nod, he signaled the downbeat. The introduction was played, and a moment later, his voice rang out, clear and pure and resonant with pride as he sang of the tobacco farmer's life—his life—with all its hardships and triumphs.

When he moved into "Some Rivers Run Deep," Will's eyes clouded over, as if he were feeling for the first time the sorrow of his father's passing. In the intimacy of the recording studio, and with a glass booth separating them, Niki dropped her guard, letting Will's voice wash over her. With his poignant tribute to a father's love, Will's song reached into her own hidden sorrow and brought tears to her eyes. Strange, she thought, how his voice could touch her so deeply, so intimately, how it could evoke feelings she tried so hard to deny.

While the musicians stopped for a brief moment of rest and refreshment, Niki heard Will talking to the record producer about a new song he wanted to use. The producer pointed to the clock on the wall and shook his head, but Will insisted. "I'll pay for the overtime myself," he argued, "but you have to let me do it. 'Dark Side of the Heart' may be the best thing I've done."

After some discussion, an agreement was reached. Will conferred with the musicians and resumed his place. Head thrown back, dark brows knit together, he began to sing. Through the stillness of the studio, over the gentle whisper of her own breathing, Niki listened to the ballad of a man who lived with darkness in his heart, in the place where love had been. As he plaintively sang of summers and winters that were all the same, Niki felt as if the song might be her own.

How could they be so different, she wondered, and yet share so many of the same feelings?

From his place in the glass booth, Will looked directly at her, with an expression that seemed sad and angry at the same time. "I saw love and lightness in her sweet blue eyes," he sang, "she had love to share and I knew it . . ."

He was singing to her, Niki realized, this new song was for her!

"I opened up my heart, I told her come inside, but she didn't know how to start, only knew the way to hide . . . showed me nothin' but the dark side of her heart . . ."

Niki thought she had steeled herself against Will, but she was defenseless against his song. And though she had turned away from the dangers of his kind of love, she felt the sharp sting of rejection in hearing that the door he'd opened for one brief moment was now closed forever against her.

The energy that Will had poured into his performance—as well as the nervous anticipation he had hidden earlier—left him depleted. While Niki drove on the trip back, he slept, his hat tipped down over his eyes. She had to shake him awake when they reached her house at dusk.

"I hope it worked for you, Will," she said as she got out of the truck and he slid over behind the wheel. "I'm sorry if I gave you more trouble than moral support."

He smiled. "I'd say, under the circumstances, you gave me just about the right amount of each."

Niki took her valise from the back of the truck, and said good night. She took a step toward her door, then stopped. "I thought that new song was a winner, Will. A woman could do worse than being the inspiration for something like that. . . ."

Will smiled. "And maybe someday a man could do better than just singin' about it."

Maybe there was hope for them, Niki thought as she snapped on the lights in her dark house.

She had been unpacking her bag for only a minute before the phone rang. "Is this Niki Sandeman?" a man asked.

"Yes . . ."

"My name is Ben Duffy," the voice said. "You don't know me, but I've heard all about you from Ralph. I live next door to him. You might say I'm his best pal."

Niki smiled, remembering her grandfather's visit. "Yes, Mr. Duffy, what can I do for you?"

"Well," he said, "I hope I'm doing the right thing. Ralph didn't want me to call, but to me it didn't seem right. I thought you should know."

"Know what, Mr. Duffy? Is something wrong with my grandfather?"

"Afraid so, Niki. He's not doing well, and I figured that you being his only relative, you had a right to know, no matter what Ralph says."

Niki remembered the coughing, the shortness of breath. But Ralph had assured her he'd seen his doctor and been pronounced "not too bad for an old man of seventy."

"I'll be on the first plane I can get," she said. "And Mr. Duffy . . ."

"Yes, Niki?"

"Please look after him till I get there."

She broke the connection and called her foreman, Jim. He had been watching the farm in her absence, but he had expected her back. Now she would be gone again—perhaps for much longer than the trip to Nashville. Hearing the reason for her trip, Jim agreed to move into the house the next day so he could keep a closer eye on things.

After calling the airport in Charleston to arrange her flight connections, Niki lingered by the phone. Will would be getting home around now. . . . Perhaps she ought to tell him, too, that she would be gone for a while.

But she went to pack some fresh clothes without making the call. She didn't have to report her every move to Will. He might not even miss her.

* * *

As she drove from the Los Angeles airport towards Venice, Niki recalled the first time she came to California. If it hadn't been for Pepper, she might never have found Ralph, never have known him or come to love him. She said a silent, grudging thank-you to her half sister.

The door to Ralph's beach house was opened by a white-haired man. "You can't be anyone but Niki," he said with a smile. "I'm Ben Duffy. Come on in, young lady. The visiting nurse is with him now, giving Ralph his I.P.B. She'll be finished soon."

Niki had braced herself for illness, but she paled when she saw her grandfather, lying on his narrow bed, a mask over his face, making painful, wheezing sounds as he breathed. When he saw Niki, he tried to pull the mask off, but the nurse held it firmly on.

"Just a little longer, Mr. Sandeman," she said with professional cheer. "Just a wee bit longer. We need to build up our supply of good, healthy air, don't we?"

Niki stood in the doorway of Ralph's small bedroom, watching helplessly as the ritual continued. "They call this intermittent positive breathing," Ben explained, *sotto voce*. "The nurse is giving him pressurized puffs of medicated air. He'll feel a little better after she's finished, just wait and see."

Niki waited. When the nurse finally removed the mask and left the room, Niki went to Ralph's bed and kissed him.

Though he didn't look "better" at all, he smiled wanly and shook an accusing finger at his friend, Ben.

"Don't you dare," she said, forcing an artificial lightness into her voice. "You're the one who should be scolded. Telling me all those stories, when you should've been telling me to get myself on a plane and keep you company."

"Sorry you went to so much trouble for such lousy company. You shouldn't be here."

"What do you mean, trouble? I was just looking for an

excuse to get away from that farm. A vacation in California is what I'm after, so don't think you're going to get rid of me so easily."

A few minutes later, she made an excuse to leave the room, so that she might speak privately to the visiting nurse. "Shouldn't he be in a hospital?" Niki asked. "He looks so weak."

The nurse shook her head. "I take him to the hospital once a week to get his lungs checked on a machine that measures the carbon dioxide he expels. There's no other reason for him to be in a hospital now."

"Maybe he should be seeing a specialist," Niki persisted, resisting the ominous implications of what she was hearing. "I want him to have the best care possible. I don't care what it costs. I'll find a way to pay for it."

The nurse dropped her professional manner. "I wish I could say something to make you feel better, miss. But I don't see the sense in that. Your grandfather is a very sick man, and there's not much to be done except make him comfortable. The right side of his heart—the side that pumps to the lungs—is dangerously enlarged. And his lungs," she shook her head solemnly, "there's nothing there but scar tissue. I'm surprised he's hung on this long, to tell you the truth."

"Isn't there anything I can do?" Niki pleaded.

Patting her shoulder, the nurse said softly, "Just be with him. Help him move around, as much as he's able. I try to give him some aerobic activity to supplement the I.P.B." She paused for a moment. "Love him, miss . . . that's the only medicine that's of any real use now."

Emphysema had been only a word, not nearly as lethal-sounding as cancer, yet now as Niki watched it wreak havoc on the body of a man who had survived bullet wounds and shrapnel, she understood how deadly it could be.

With Ben Duffy's help, she tried to follow the nurse's prescription. To make Ralph comfortable, to show him her love. She shopped for groceries and made concentrated broths, coaxing her grandfather to eat when he had no appetite. She changed his bed and fluffed his pillows. She read aloud, mostly Hemingway stories from the glory days Ralph remembered. When he was able, she walked him around the house, or in a tiny circle on the beach, trying to stimulate the circulation of oxygen. He slept a great deal, and Niki was grateful for that, for the moments of peace that sleep allowed him.

Never in her life had Niki appreciated the simple act of breathing until she saw her grandfather gasping and choking and fighting for every tortured breath.

"Didn't expect this," he said, trying heroically to lighten the despair that hung over the sickroom. "Thought that maybe I'd get the big *C*, like the Duke," he joked, referring to the cancer that John Wayne had fought so dramatically.

Niki stayed in Venice for almost two weeks. Not a day went by that Ralph didn't say how much he loved her. Sometimes he repeated himself, forgetting he'd said it before. Sometimes he'd simply stare at her face, as if trying to imprint its memory for eternity.

As Ralph grew weaker, she gave up sleeping on the sofa and spent her nights in a chair near his bed. One Sunday, as the sun was rising, he beckoned Niki closer. She got up from the chair and wrapped her arms around him. "I saw her," he whispered, his pale eyes luminous. "Monique . . . she was here, Niki. She smiled at you. She said . . . she said," he faltered, straining to speak. Then his brave, weary heart gave up its struggle and Ralph Sandeman was at peace.

The doctor who filled out the death certificate named "congestive heart failure" as the cause of death. But Niki felt as if she should be blamed, too.

The funeral service was held in a small establishment not far from where he had lived and died. It was simple and without fanfare, attended by Niki and Ben and a few other neighbors. Each spoke a few words of remembrance. Each spoke of how much finding Niki had brightened the last years of Ralph's life. She thanked Ben for calling her, for allowing her the comfort of knowing her grandfather didn't die alone or unloved.

After the brief service, Niki knelt in front of the casket. Death had somehow softened the tortures of Ralph's final days. His weathered old face seemed peaceful and serene, but Niki felt the weight of a great sadness in her own chest. For the love that had flickered like a candle, lighting ever so briefly Ralph's lonely, solitary life.

"It's time," the funeral director said, tapping her shoulder, then pointing to his watch. "We must be closing the casket soon, Miss Sandeman. They're expecting us at the cemetery."

"Could I have another minute with him? Alone?"

"Of course," he murmured, withdrawing discreetly.

Niki opened her handbag and took out the framed photographs she had given her grandfather for Christmas, the pictures that made them look like a real family. Tenderly, she placed the gift in the casket. "Good-bye, Grandfather," she whispered, hoping that wherever Ralph was, he wouldn't be lonely, praying that somehow, he might once again find his lost love.

Twenty-eight

As Niki drove the short distance to the Rivers farm, she turned on the car radio. It came as no surprise to hear Will's voice, singing "Dark Side of the Heart" again. The record had hit the country charts at number nineteen, but in Willow Cross it was easily number one. The local disc jockeys played it morning, noon, and night, proudly laying claim to "Carolina's own Will Rivers" each time.

Hearing the song on the radio made Niki feel somehow melancholy, as if she were hearing the sound of doors closing over and over again. Why should it matter? she asked herself. Alexei was more attentive than ever, calling two or three times a week, coming to see her whenever his work would allow. And Will had always been wrong for her; with his new-found celebrity, he was more dangerous than ever. Always the darling of local women, he was now sought after by a growing legion of fans, who sent letters signed with kisses, and intimate gifts that made Charmaine Rivers blush.

Yet Niki did mind the distance that Will had put between

them. Though she told herself the calls she made on his mother were simply neighborly, Niki found herself looking for a sign of warmth, even wishing that Will would tease her the way he used to.

As she turned into the Riverses' driveway, Niki noticed a trio of painters working on the facade of the house. So Will was making good on his promise to Charmaine, she thought—in spite of his frequent pronouncements that the success of his record was just a fluke and that nothing about him had changed.

When she knocked on the door, she was admitted by a uniformed nurse, another new addition to the Rivers household. Niki was shown into the kitchen, where Will and his mother were sharing coffee and cake. Will looked surprised to see her, but Charmaine smiled graciously and beckoned Niki to sit down. "You're just in time for dessert, dear," she said. "It's my Sunday special . . . blueberry cobbler."

Niki accepted the dessert and a cup of coffee. "You're looking well," she said to Charmaine, who seemed relaxed and in good spirits.

"Tell that to *him*," Charmaine said, giving her son an affectionate nudge. "*He* seems to think I need a keeper."

"I never said that," Will protested. "I just said I'd feel better, knowing there was someone here in the house all the time."

"And *I* said I'd feel better if you spent some of that record money on yourself, Will Rivers. At least buy those quarter horses you've always wanted." Turning to Niki, Charmaine said: "Why don't you talk some sense into this boy of mine? Tell him to enjoy himself. All he's done is work since his daddy died."

Niki flushed with embarrassment at Charmaine's assumption that she had Will's confidence—and said nothing.

"I keep telling Mama that the music business isn't like farming," Will filled in. "It's more like . . . smoke. You see it in front of you, and then a minute later, it's gone."

"How can you say that, Will?" Charmaine asked indignantly. "After you've been invited to sing at the Opry?"

"You're going to the Opry?" Niki asked, hurt at hearing the news of Will's latest success from Charmaine.

"The Opry's a great honor," Will replied, looking at his mother, "and I'll remember it as long as I live. But that doesn't mean anyone else is going to remember Will Rivers a couple of years from now."

"Nonsense," Charmaine insisted. "You're just being modest, Will. I know your daddy hated the sin of pride, but there's nothing wrong with enjoying your accomplishments . . . and believing in them. After you make this tour of yours, everyone . . ."

"Tour?" Niki cut in, feeling more left out than ever. "What tour is that?"

Charmaine looked from her son to Niki, as if she were just realizing that something had changed between them. "Why, the tour with Loretta Lynn," she said slowly. "Will's going to be her opening act. Didn't Will tell you? I thought he surely would have said something, the two of you being such good friends . . ."

"It isn't definite yet," Will said defensively. "I still don't like the idea of leaving Mama alone . . . or leaving the farm, for that matter."

"If you don't say yes, then you're a damn fool, Will Rivers," Charmaine said, her worn cheeks pink with indignation. "When you love something, you reach out and take it! You don't sit around making excuses to let it pass you by."

"She's right," Niki said quietly. "Sometimes you don't get a second chance."

Once again Charmaine looked from Niki to her son, as if she were hearing more than talk of Will's career. "The farm will be fine," she said finally, "and so will I. What's the sense of hiring a keeper, if you don't let her do her job?" she added, as a final argument.

Will threw up his hands in mock surrender. "I seem to be outnumbered," he said with a laugh.

When Niki was ready to leave, Will got up and walked with her to the car. "Good luck on the tour," she said politely. "I'm sure it's going to be a great success."

"Are you going to miss me?" he asked with a grin—and a hint of the old teasing manner.

Niki mustered a jaunty smile and a voice to match. "Of course I'm going to miss you! Who am I going to call for advice when something goes wrong? Who's going to keep me from making mistakes I can't afford?"

The grin faded. "I guess there's lots of people you could call on for those things, Niki."

No, there aren't, she wanted to say, there aren't lots of people like you. But all she could manage was: "I'll miss you anyway."

"Maybe you can come see me sing. Maybe when I play Raleigh or Durham. If you have the time, that is . . ."

"Maybe I will," she said. "If I have the time."

Not until Will had gone did Niki realize how much she had come to depend on him. Not just for advice, as she'd told him, but simply to . . . be there. She missed his presence, his easy smiles, his songs—the way he used to sing them for the farmers of Willow Cross. And she envied Will his new career, for with every passing day, she felt her own sense of purpose slipping away.

Much as she loved her farm, much as she cared about her fellow growers, her "golden" crop now seemed somehow . . . sinister. Since Ralph's death, it seemed harder and harder to justify growing the very leaf that had caused such terrible suffering. Somehow her conscience was no longer satisfied by the argument that smoking, like drinking, was a matter of choice—and that tobacco growers were no more responsible for smoking-related diseases than the growers of malt and barley were for alcoholism.

Seeing her indecision, Alexei renewed his proposal as they

walked through the fields that would soon deliver another harvest, a harvest that might well be Niki's last. "Keep the farm," he said, "if you love it so much. Grow flowers, grow alfalfa, grow anything but tobacco. We can come here for holidays . . ."

"And what would I do?" she asked with a sad smile. "Other than grow flowers or alfalfa?"

"You can be a part of my antismoking campaign," he replied promptly, as if he had already given the question some thought. "With your help, I could devote more time to my practice . . ."

"What about my credibility?" she asked, only half joking. "After all the noise I made on behalf of the tobacco farmers?"

"Who better to talk about the evils of the tobacco industry?" he countered. "Think of what you can do in Washington if you're on the right side, Niki. The tobacco industry is virtually *immune* from government regulation, a law unto itself. Consumers demand to know what they eat and drink, yet tobacco products can not be regulated for wholesomeness by the Food and Drug Administration—or for safety by the Consumer Product Safety Commission. The tobacco manufacturers use thousands of additives to add flavor or make their cigarettes burn longer—and the government is powerless to regulate them, no matter how toxic or carcinogenic they might be!"

Niki nodded. Everything Alexei said was true—and yet she couldn't bring herself to take up his arguments as her own. Just as she couldn't bring herself to accept the security of being his wife.

Late in June, Niki received a special-delivery letter. The envelope was embossed with the seal of the Regal Tobacco Company. The letter inside was cryptically brief:

Dear Miss Sandeman,

I would like to discuss with you a matter of some importance and mutual interest. My secretary will contact you to arrange, at your convenience, transportation to our corporate offices in Atlanta.

Very truly yours,
Desmond Reece
Chief Executive Officer

What possible "mutual interest" could she have with the head of Regal Tobacco? Niki asked herself. It was like getting one of those telegrams telling you that you'd won a contest you never entered.

If the letter had been from anyone else, Niki might have tossed it into the garbage. Yet in spite of his connection with Regal, Desmond Reece was not a man to be so quickly dismissed.

After seeing Reece in Washington, she had made a point of finding out more about him—and what she learned had impressed her. Reece was a self-made man, an entrepreneur since his student days at Harvard. According to one story, young Desmond had a craving for pizza late one evening during his freshman year. After calling a dozen numbers from the Boston yellow pages, he found that none of the local pizzerias would deliver. Frustrated in his personal desire for a convenient late-night snack, Reece did further research. He soon discovered that while there was an enormous student population in the greater Boston area, virtually no restaurants provided delivery service. Recognizing a great untapped market, Reece solicited funds from his more affluent classmates and formed a small company. Its assets were three mini-vans, a multi-line telephone, and contracts with a score of restaurants. By his sophomore year, Reece was virtually self-supporting; by the time he graduated, he was earning in excess of ten thousand dollars a year.

When he completed his postgraduate education, Reece was recruited by the chairman of Regal Tobacco. In the twenty odd years of service that followed, Reece was groomed to be the chairman's natural successor.

All of this Niki found interesting, but in a general way. What struck a personal chord were the comparisons reporters often drew between Reece and Duke Hyland—between Reece's gentlemanly managerial style and Hyland's tyrannical "iron fist in an iron glove" methods. In spite of Hyland's heavyweight public relations, the press by far seemed to favor the "gentleman scholar." When, in search of good copy, a reporter once needled Duke about his more popular competitor, Hyland replied: "I'd rather win than be loved any day." Reece countered with: "I don't see the two conditions as mutually exclusive."

As the business and popular press kept score of wins and losses on each side, it became very clear that within tobacco's "big happy family," Desmond Reece and Duke Hyland had a very bad case of sibling rivalry.

It was that rivalry—and simple curiosity—that made Niki accept the invitation to visit Atlanta.

Amidst the burgeoning construction in downtown Atlanta, the luxury hotels and the glass-and-steel office towers, the Regal Building stood out from the rest. Classically simple in design, constructed of the finest materials and with the greatest attention to detail, the building was said to reflect the personality of its chief executive officer.

The atmosphere that greeted Niki, from the moment she entered the outer reception area was one of traditional elegance—restrained, refined, and very, very costly. The walls were paneled in burled wood, the carpet oriental, the furnishings handcrafted. The receptionist sat at a desk that might well have been authentically Chippendale. When she greeted Niki, her manner was gracious, her accent upper-class British.

From the manner in which she was welcomed, it was clear that Niki had been designated a V.I.P. The receptionist murmured a few words into her intercom and within seconds, a young man wearing a conservatively cut, pin-striped suit appeared. "I'm Timothy Hale, Mr. Reece's assistant," he said.

"Welcome to Regal Tobacco. I hope you enjoyed your flight on the Regal jet."

Niki said she had. The opportunity to fly aboard a private Regal jet had been a final inducement in bringing her to Atlanta, and Niki had enjoyed every moment of the all too brief trip, surrounded by luxury and service beyond anything she'd experienced before.

As she followed Hale through the glass doors that led to the executive territory, walking past half-open doors, she glimpsed furnishings fit for English manor houses, paintings worthy of museums.

None of it prepared her for Desmond Reece's office, which at first glance seemed to be as big as a basketball court. Floor-to-ceiling windows offering a bird's eye view of the city were the only modern touch. Everything else in the room was rare or beyond price. On one wall hung a Van Gogh, on another a Cezanne and a Matisse. In a custom-made vitrine, there was a magnificent collection of glass—Venini from Italy, Lalique from France, antique Steuben—all rare and unusual pieces.

Like a photograph from *Gentleman's Quarterly*, Desmond Reece was leaning against the carved mantel of a wood-burning fireplace, pipe in hand. All that was missing from the scene was an Irish setter or trusty hound to complete the living portrait of a country squire.

"So good of you to come," he said, just as if Niki's time were as valuable as his—and with an accent that like so much at Regal, hinted of England. "We'll be dining in a few minutes." He nodded at his assistant, who offered Niki a drink.

Niki accepted a glass of bottled water. She was much too curious to dull her senses with anything alcoholic.

When Reece was satisfied that she was comfortably settled, he shifted positions, to a wing chair of mellow, old leather. "I'll come straight to the point," he said—and then proceeded to wander afield. "It's not often I indulge myself in a leisurely midday meal. I do so today in your honor. I confess to you, Miss Sandeman, that I am what is popularly known as a 'workaholic.' As Voltaire once said: 'Work keeps at bay three great evils: boredom, vice, and need.' And while I agree with that philosophic sentiment, I do find it refreshing to experience occasionally a few simple pleasures."

Niki hung on his every word, waiting for the promised "point."

"I would like to offer you a position with Regal Tobacco," he said finally. "I sincerely hope I can persuade you to accept it," he added, playing the courtier.

"I'm not looking for a job. And if I were, I wouldn't be . . ."

"You wouldn't be interested in working for a tobacco manufacturer," he finished with a smile. "Yes, I thought you'd say that, Miss Sandeman."

How was it that rich and powerful people were able to convey an impression of omniscience? she wondered. As if they knew everything about you before you knew it yourself.

"I'm well aware of your position and your work on behalf of the tobacco growers." Reece's smile broadened, became almost beatific. Not only did he not seem angry, he seemed to wholeheartedly approve of every damning thing Niki had said.

"And that is precisely why I invited you here—so that I'd have the opportunity of changing your mind."

"Mr. Reece, I don't know where you got the idea that I'd be of any use to your company. What I know about is growing tobacco. So I won't waste your time, I'll tell you that I've been giving serious thought to closing down my farm. I believe cigarettes are harmful and I don't want to be a part of producing them."

"Well, then," he nodded, "if you're ready to consider a newer, more exciting career, it seems my timing is perfect."

Niki shook her head. Was this man hard of hearing—or was he playing with her? Didn't he understand that she didn't want any part of tobacco?

"I don't wish to exert any undue pressure, Miss Sandeman. What Regal has to offer will become very clear if you open your mind to it. As Grotius once said: 'Not to know things is a great part of wisdom.' " Reece rose from behind his antique partner's desk. "Let me offer you a pleasant lunch and the opportunity to consider what you don't know."

As if by magic, a pair of doors were thrown open to reveal an enormous dining room that could seat a squadron of executives—but which now had been set for two. Bouquets of tropical blooms—anthurium and birds of paradise—gave a whimsical touch to a room that was otherwise stately. An old Baccarat chandelier hung over the linen-draped table. At the antique sideboard hovered a chef and a butler in livery. Reece took Niki's arm in a courtly old-fashioned gesture, escorted her to the mahogany table, held her chair, and then took his own.

As she inhaled the tantalizing aromas that filled the air, Niki felt a pang of regret. This was a magnificent place and Desmond Reece certainly seemed to be a gentleman. It was too bad he was in the business of tobacco—the one business in the world she wanted no part of. Oh, well, she thought, the trip to Atlanta had been fun and the meal promised to be a fine one.

The wine steward offered, for Desmond's approval, a rare Margaux, previously decanted. Desmond sniffed the bouquet, tasted the wine, paused thoughtfully, then nodded. "It'll do," he said.

The first course was a light consomme; in its center, a perfect, tiny poached pheasant egg.

Reece raised his wineglass and said, "To your good health, Miss Sandeman, and to an association I hope will be interesting and profitable."

Niki sipped her wine, wondering again at the kind of confidence that didn't admit the word *no*.

"Miss Sandeman," he said, "I am a man who deals in realities, in corporate strategy and balance sheets and such. Yet I like to think that my small success at Regal," here he gave a smile of winsome modesty, "is in some part due to my instincts about people. It was my instinct that led me to contact you. Let me be frank. I am impressed with the level of public attention you were able to gain for the farmers' plight. A remarkable achievement, since it was accomplished without financial backing, without benefit of such professional image makers as we in the industry employ."

Niki sampled her soup, refraining from comment on the tobacco industry's "image makers."

"And if I may say so," Reece continued with a smile, "I am impressed with your beauty and presence—valuable assets in any profession, as you will no doubt agree."

Niki nodded cautiously as the butler removed the soup dishes. A filet of venison was being served as Reece came to the point. "As I'm certain you already know, the tobacco industry has withstood the test of time, the rigors of economic cycles. I like to believe it's because we offer products that are uniquely recession-proof, even depression-proof."

Niki was tempted to interrupt. If there was one thing she didn't want to hear, it was the kind of self-serving public relations garbage Reece was spouting.

"Now, however, those of us who captain these ships of industry must reevaluate the courses we chart. We must look beyond the coming fiscal year. We must examine our responsibility to our shareholders and balance that with our responsibility to the American public."

Where on earth was this leading? Niki wondered. And why was Desmond Reece making a speech for an audience of one?

"My plan, my five-year plan," he said, "is to diversify Regal's holdings in the nontobacco area. Like you, Miss Sandeman, I have come to realize that my fiscal health—Regal's—need not be achieved by compromising the health of the American public. As they like to say of us in the business press, we are a progressive company with a leadership position.

"In short, Miss Sandeman, I would like you to work in our newly expanded acquisitions department. I want you to put your enthusiasm and dedication into helping Regal diversify. To assist in my long-term goal of divesting Regal of its tobacco holdings.''

"Are you saying that you want to take Regal out of the tobacco business?'' Niki could scarcely believe what she was hearing. Did Reece think he was some kind of superman? Or was he a madman in Saville Row clothing?

When he responded, it was clear he was neither. "I am saying that yes, that is our goal for the future. My intention is to make this possible in a manner that ensures the ongoing health of our company and the welfare of our stockholders. That is why I recently made the decision to move our corporate headquarters here to Atlanta—away from what is commonly thought of as 'tobacco country' to symbolize Regal's commitment to change.''

Niki was impressed. No other tobacco executive had the courage to say what Reece was saying. But while she admired his goal, she felt inadequate to the position he was offering. "I have no training for corporate work,'' she admitted—reluctantly—for Reece's proposal seemed not only exciting but . . . evangelical. "In fact, I should tell you that I didn't even finish my undergraduate degree.''

"Miss Sandeman,'' he said with a smile. "Here at Regal we employ MBAs by the dozen. Some start work in the mailroom, some as assistants to minor executives. As Shaw once said: 'What we call education and culture is for the most part nothing but the substitution of reading for experience, of literature for life.' What I want from you is the commitment and the intelligence you've *already* demonstrated on behalf of the tobacco farmers. I want you to put those qualities to work for Regal, to be part of our plan for the future. You will, of course, be trained in the mechanics of corporate work. In time, Miss Sandeman, I think you will find there are virtually no limits to the career you can build at Regal. The starting salary and benefits we offer are, I believe, competitive.'' Reece went on to outline a compensation package that seemed not only generous, but downright dazzling.

There was just one thing wrong. Relieved as she was to be offered an answer to her own dilemma, Niki felt she couldn't just abandon her community of fellow farmers. If she helped Regal to get out of the tobacco business, what would happen to them? "Mr. Reece," she said slowly, "I'm very tempted by your offer."

"I sense a 'but' in the air," he said.

She nodded. "Working for Regal would solve my personal problem with tobacco. But I'm thinking that it isn't right for me to just walk away from people who don't have any choices. Not when the land they own isn't fit for much else but growing tobacco."

"Miss Sandeman, your loyalty is truly admirable. Let me suggest yet another solution to the problem you've posed. You recognize, of course, that there are farmers who will refuse to do anything but grow tobacco until the day they die—regardless of any other options that might be presented."

Niki nodded. That was true enough.

"Now as for the others . . . I put to you the example of George Washington Carver, who began growing peanuts in soil nutritionally depleted by generations of cotton crops. I believe that there are similar solutions in store for the tobacco farmer. In fact," he said, leaning closer and dropping his voice, "we at Regal have been exploring just such possibilities, involving the growing of selected strains of tea."

"Really? I didn't know we could grow tea in America."

"With the proper technology, Miss Sandeman, with Regal's resources, I believe we may yet pioneer another 'first.' In any case, I can assure you that by taking a position with us, you will be in a far better position to aid your fellow farmers. As a member of our acquisitions team, you may, for example, search out firms whose expertise may well hold the key to a new prosperity in tobacco country."

Niki's admiration for Desmond Reece was now bordering on awe. Not only did he have a social conscience, he had the power and the corporate wealth that could make miracles happen.

By the time the espresso and raspberry mousse were served, Niki's mind was racing ahead. With the money she earned here, she could keep her home in Willow Cross. She could even continue to employ Jim and Bo as caretakers. The Atlanta airport was the busiest in the country. Weekends, she could hop a plane to almost anywhere. To visit Willow Cross, to see Helen—even, she admitted, to see Will. Best of all, this was work she could believe in.

Reece offered a final inducement. "I understand that you may be hesitant to resettle until you've had an opportunity to explore your new position. We can offer you the use of a corporate suite at the Hyatt Regency for a trial period. Say, ninty days? If, at the end of that time, you decide to come aboard, we will of course, offer any assistance you require in leasing or purchasing an apartment."

Niki was thinking quickly. The way the deal was structured, what did she have to lose?

Reece closed in with a postscript. "We at Regal are in for some challenging years, Miss Sandeman. As you are no doubt aware, our competitors are pursuing their own vigorous plans for the future. We need talents such as yours, if we are to maintain parity with such firms as . . . Hyland Tobacco."

Yes, she thought, yes, Mr. Reece, you've just said the magic words.

"Perhaps you'd like to think my proposition over," he said.

Niki had one fleeting thought of Alexei and how he might react, and then she dismissed it quickly. If he truly cared for her, he couldn't expect her to live as her mother had done, always subservient to a man's whims and desires. "No, Mr. Reece," she said. "I don't have to think about it. I accept your offer. When can I start?"

She was standing in the living room, surrounded by cartons she had packed, when she heard the car turn into her drive, a slight sound since it was still near the road and the wheels were turning very slowly. She had been organizing her things all day, what to take, what to leave; though she would be living in Atlanta most of the time, she had no intention of ever giving up the farm. Niki pushed back the hair that had fallen over her face, lank from the sweat of the day's exertions, and glanced through a doorway to the kitchen clock and saw that it was almost two A.M.

Who would be coming now? she wondered. Will . . . Jim . . . Alexei? She expected no one.

She threaded her way out of the maze of cartons, and went to open the front door. Looking out into the night, she saw no headlights. Had she imagined the sound? Perhaps it was only a car driving by, continuing up the public road.

Yet she sensed some imperceptible change in the familiar music of the night, the breeze, the cricket sounds, that warned of another presence.

She took a step outside and peered along the path of light that was thrown onto the drive from her open doorway. "Hello . . . ?" she called.

The silence that came back was chilling. She was sure there was someone watching her from out there in the dark. And then a memory came back to her of another night, years ago, when she had been troubled by the same kind of mysterious disturbance. It occurred to her suddenly that even if she had only been aware these two times of such strange visits, they might have happened often without her detecting them.

"Who's there?" she shouted, already retreating a few steps, drawn back to the refuge of her house.

And then she froze. At the farthest reach of the light cast through the open doorway, a figure moved into view. A man, in a plain white shirt and dark pants. It was so dim out there that Niki couldn't discern his features.

But then, as though he saw that she was having difficulty recognizing him, the man moved slightly forward—just enough so that she could recognize him.

Duke.

She stared for a moment, and then the cry erupted from her. "What do you want? Why, Duke . . . why do you come here?" Unafraid now, she started to walk toward him. "Why? What are you looking for . . . ?" She moved faster, wanting to seize him.

But then he was gone again into the darkness, and there was the sound of a car door slamming, and the motor revving. The headlights blazed on, then the car spun away and disappeared into the night.

It was still troubling her, long after she had gotten into bed.

Remembering the malevolent declarations he had made when she had gone to Highlands, Niki could only interpret it one way. Obsessed with getting rid of her, he came to refuel his hatred, to plot and dream of the day when she would be gone. Perhaps his visit tonight was his most satisfying, and he had shown himself at last since she was leaving. It was his way of saying that even if his victory was not yet total, he was winning.

Thinking of the crusade she was about to begin, Niki could almost feel sorry for Duke.

☆

BOOK IV

Twenty-nine

NIKI let herself into the luxurious corporate suite that was her home away from home, dropped her bulging leather briefcase on the floor, and kicked off her stylish but confining pumps. After yet another in a long series of twelve-hour days, she craved a warm bath and a light supper. The jangle of the telephone intervened.

Wearily she picked up the receiver.

"It's about time," a familiar voice chided. "Some friend you are, Ms. Sandeman. You don't even return my messages."

"I just got in, Blake. I haven't even had time to check my messages."

"Does that mean you're staying in tonight? Again?"

Niki sighed. "I'm sorry, Blake, really I am . . ."

"I don't believe you're sorry at all. I think you've snuggled into that same old rut and wrapped it around you. Have you ever stopped to ask yourself what that means, Niki?"

Niki sighed again. Last night she had spent an hour on the

telephone trying to convince Alexei that she couldn't possibly take the entire weekend off to be with him; she was simply too exhausted now to go through the same kind of argument again. "Please, Blake," she said, "couldn't we talk about this some other time? I really am beat tonight. . . ."

"When, then?" Blake persisted. "I have a busy and demanding career, too, you know. But I manage to have a life as well." After years in the design business, in Paris, then in New York, Blake had stopped running from the opportunities offered by her father. She had returned to join the executive ranks of Underwood's stores.

"Okay, Blake," Niki conceded, "you've made your point. Why don't I pick you up at the store tomorrow? We can have dinner . . . and I promise not to say a word about my job."

"Seven o'clock. And you'd better not cancel—or I'll revoke your discount privileges at Underwood's!"

"I'll be there," Niki laughed. "I can't afford your inflated prices without my discount."

Dear Blake, she thought, as she hung up the telephone. Niki had looked her up as soon as she had arrived in Atlanta. Ever since then, Blake had made her irrepressible presence felt in Niki's life. Even with her demanding position as head of Underwood's marketing division, she still found time to campaign for her personal causes. Socializing Niki was but one of these causes; another was to make herself into Atlanta's premier hostess and party giver, the city's answer to Perle Mesta.

Niki peeled off her tailored navy suit and hung it in the closet, alongside a dozen similar uniforms—the "power suits" Blake suggested to enhance her corporate image. She ran a scented bath and sank into the warm, soapy water, luxuriating in the sweet release of the day's tensions. Though she was no stranger to hard labor, her job at Regal was even more demanding than her work on the farm. It hadn't been easy learning how to become a productive part of a huge corporate machine. Regal was a sky-high complex of divisions, each with its own hierarchy—each speaking a particular dialect of the universal corporate language that had challenged and mystified her.

With her customary determination, Niki had crammed a year's worth of education into months. Rotating through Regal's various divisions, she learned at the hands of men who worshipped the bottom line. She attended seminars and read voraciously—books, business magazines, even copies of computerized files and memos. Every morning she studied the *Wall Street Journal*. At night, she researched the annual reports of companies that were prospective candidates for acquisition. There was little time or energy left for anything so mundane as finding and furnishing an apartment. After several extensions, her temporary stay at the Hyatt had taken on a kind of permanence.

Relaxed and refreshed by her bath, Niki wrapped herself in a terry-cloth robe and ordered a chef's salad and a glass of white wine from room service. When her supper arrived, she had the waiter set it on the table beside the window, then signed the check, adding a generous tip.

With the dazzling city panorama before her, Niki reached into her briefcase for the letter from Will she had been saving for a quiet moment. Sipping her wine slowly, she read the letter in the same way, lingering over every sentence. "This is a hell of a way to see America," he wrote. "I've lost count of how many states we've passed through. They're all starting to look the same, just hotels and restaurants, theaters and stadiums. My manager says it's time to cut a new album, but I hate the idea of staying on the road to promote it. I miss Willow Cross. I flew back to see Mama last week, but I could only stay one day. She misses you—and I guess I do, too." The letter was signed "Yours, Will," followed by: "P.S. When are you coming to see me? I already guaranteed you'd have a room of your own. We can even make it a separate hotel. P.P.S. I met Randy Travis last week. He said he had my album. Can you imagine that?"

Niki smiled. With all his success, Will was still a fan, too. He had become exactly the kind of entertainer he had always admired himself, unassuming and—as far as Niki could tell from his letters—unspoiled by the money and adulation he received.

Though she had promised to catch one of his performances, Niki knew it was more than being busy that kept her away. Maybe Will was able to joke about their time in Nashville, but she still didn't think it was funny. Nor was she about to risk another similar disaster. Why should she risk anything for a man whose heart belonged to someone else? She added Will's letter to the others that had come before, all carefully tucked away in her lingerie drawer. After consuming her light supper, she took a thick stack of annual reports to bed with her.

Thus far, Niki's role had been limited to research, the gathering of data on companies ripe for acquisition. Now she was ready to take a giant step forward—to recommend to Mr. Reece that Regal acquire Freshfruit, Inc. She had been tracking Freshfruit ever since she read an interview with the firm's founder in *Forbes* magazine.

She reviewed the documents spread out before her, hoping to justify Mr. Reece's confidence in her abilities. On paper, Freshfruit was the kind of company that made a raider's mouth water. The current price of its stock was below the book value of its assets, excluding such intangibles as goodwill and standing in the marketplace, but including "young receivables," payments due in ninty days or less.

With a company in such peak health, Regal could easily do a leveraged buyout and make the purchase with a bank loan secured by Freshfruit's own assets. In fact, as Niki rechecked the numbers, she thought it likely that Regal could borrow even more against Freshfruit than the total cost of the buyout. On paper, the deal seemed not only exciting, but also virtually risk-proof—and Niki could almost taste the sweetness of a new kind of success.

As a small tobacco farmer, she'd been nothing more than a tiny dot in Hyland country. Being part of the Regal team, she belonged to the powerful armies of the boardroom, a combatant in an arena where Hyland sometimes came out second best. On behalf of the farmers, she had raised her voice for a losing cause. But now she was on the side of the angels, the side that would show Hyland, and all America, that it was possible to give up the manufacture of a death-dealing product without sacrificing profits or compromising corporate health.

In anticipation of this noble goal, surrounded by the documents that would bring it closer, Niki fell asleep in her solitary bed.

At eight o'clock the following morning, Niki entered Desmond Reece's inner sanctum. Declining his assistant's offer of coffee, she took the "hot seat," facing Reece across his massive partner's desk.

"Please proceed, Miss Sandeman," he said. "I'm most eager to hear your recommendations."

"I believe we have an excellent prospect in Freshfruit, Mr. Reece. Though the company's only been in business for five years, you can see from the figures I've prepared that they're already showing impressive profits."

"I've looked at the figures, Miss Sandeman. And while I agree that Freshfruit is a healthy little company, I feel the operative word here is 'little.' What makes you believe it's a suitable property for us?"

Niki smiled. She had anticipated this objection. "Freshfruit is small, Mr. Reece, but a tiny perfect jewel can be a better investment than a larger one that's flawed. In my opinion, the profit potential here has just barely been tapped. The company has already achieved a substantial market share in its home state of California. With the kind of capitalization Regal can put behind it, Freshfruit products can be successfully marketed nationally. I believe the possibility for rapid growth is enormous."

"I agree. What else, Miss Sandeman?"

"I think Freshfruit has the kind of image that Regal wants . . . and needs. Its 'natural' soft drinks are made without refined sugar and without additives. They're perceived to be healthy and nourishing. The packaging is excellent. The bottles are made of glass; they have an old-fashioned, almost quaint design that evokes the kind of nostalgia that's very popular now."

Reece's smile was more than reassuring. "You mean it evokes those endangered species, old-fashioned moms and homemade apple pie?"

"Exactly," she smiled back. "It's a powerful concept, Mr. Reece. I think the association would be a positive one for Regal. It would demonstrate exactly what it is you're trying to do here. Furthermore," she added, "I believe that the Freshfruit line can be successfully expanded, beyond soft drinks, into a variety of fruit-based natural products."

Reece nodded. "You've done your homework, Miss Sandeman. I think you may have found a winner for us."

"Then if you don't mind my saying so, Mr. Reece, I think we should move quickly."

"And why is that, Miss Sandeman? Has one of our competitors shown an interest in Freshfruit?" Reece's eyes twinkled, as they often did when he mentioned "the competition."

"Not yet," she said, "but if we move now, the buyout can be quick and bloodless. As you can see, the majority of the stock is held by the company's founder, a Mr. Harvey Benson. I've done some investigating into Mr. Benson's personal finances, and it seems he's experiencing some personal cash-flow problems due to heavy investments in California real estate. I believe that if you make him an offer now, if you sweeten it with a long-term management contract, Mr. Benson's problems would be solved. And you would have the benefit of his expertise."

"I shall take all your recommendations under advisement, Miss Sandeman. And now, if you'll excuse me . . ."

"Mr. Reece, if I could have just another minute or two," Niki asked nervously, realizing her allotted time was up.

Reece glanced at his watch and nodded.

She pulled a newspaper clipping from her briefcase. "I'm sure you've seen this item," she said, handing over the story of a current lawsuit filed against Hyland Tobacco by the widower of a woman who had died of lung cancer after smoking Hyland cigarettes for thirty years.

Reece frowned. "There's nothing new here," he said, waving away the clipping. "Product liability lawsuits are a reflection of the litigious times we live in, Miss Sandeman."

Despite his cool reaction, Niki pressed on. "I thought," she said, "that with all the negative publicity the lawsuit is generating for Hyland, this might be an excellent time for Regal to reveal some of its own plans for the future."

"I take your point," Reece said with a nod. "However, there is an equal danger in being premature, Miss Sandeman. If we speak now of plans that will not be in place for several years, we may well generate media cynicism, rather than goodwill."

"I see," she said slowly.

"But," he added with a smile, "since you have such a keen interest in Regal's public image, please feel free to bring me any other ideas you may have. I do value your commitment, Miss Sandeman, and your dedication. As I told you at our first meeting, I think you have a promising future here at Regal. Very promising indeed."

Niki left Reece's office with mixed feelings. Gratified as she was by his commendation, she was disappointed that Reece couldn't seem to see the merit in her suggestion.

Surely, he had seen the increasing number of stories attacking the special privileges enjoyed by the tobacco companies, as well as their deadly products. Surely, he was aware of the growing strength of the antismoking movement. Now that Hyland was being publicly charged with death-by-smoking, why wouldn't Desmond seize the opportunity to distance Regal from the other companies? Why couldn't he see that a statement of intent was better than a complicitous silence?

* * *

Standing before her mirror, Niki adjusted the beaded headband that completed her costume for the Underwood benefit ball. Her pleated, white flapper dress, acquired at one of Atlanta's antique shops, was a perfect fit, as were the vintage evening slippers.

When the hotel operator called to announce the arrival of her escort, Niki added a bit more blush to her cheeks and a second layer of red lipstick, to give her mouth the "bee-stung" look of the twenties. Much as she'd complained when Blake had announced her plans for a costume party, Niki found that it was fun to wear a disguise, to be someone else for a night.

She opened the door to admit Alexei, who was just about to knock.

"You look stunning, Niki," he said, "absolutely magnificent."

"You look pretty good yourself," she said, admiring Alexei's impeccably cut evening clothes, the silk scarf casually draped around his neck. And as she glimpsed their reflection in the mirror, Niki had to admit they made a good-looking couple. Yet the more she came to know and appreciate Alexei, the farther away she seemed from marrying him. *What's wrong with me?* she asked herself on more than one occasion. All her life she had shied away from men, especially from those who seemed likely to love and leave. Alexei wanted nothing more than to provide the security she'd always craved, yet all Niki could manage to give him was affection and excuses.

"Thanks for coming," she said, brushing his lips with a kiss that was warm but not passionate. "Blake was threatening me with all kinds of mayhem if I didn't get you down here this weekend."

"Glad to be of service," he said gallantly, "though I still don't understand why you go on living like this. I respect your independence, Niki, and I understand how important your work is. If a company of Regal's stature voluntarily divests its tobacco interests, if a man like Desmond Reece makes just one public statement against the manufacture of cigarettes, the entire industry will be shaken. But what I don't understand is why you can't have a normal life in addition to your work. Isn't it time you got out of this hotel and—"

"There isn't any time to think about finding an apartment, let alone doing it," Niki cut in, before Alexei could say any more.

His dark eyes flickered. "I wasn't talking about details," he said quietly.

"I know," she sighed. "I'm sorry, Alexei. I just can't give you the answer you want." She reached out and touched his face; he took her hand and held it for a long moment.

"Is there someone else?" he asked softly. "Someone you could love?"

"No!" she answered quickly, shaking her head as if to exorcise the image of Will that flashed through her mind. Inexplicably, she was annoyed with Alexei for asking the question to which she had no safe answer.

The Underwood Ball, for the benefit of a half-dozen local charities, was expected to be the highlight of Atlanta's social season. Blake's antebellum palace, a gift to herself with the proceeds of her trust fund, was filled with fresh flowers and lit with crystal chandeliers. An army of caterers, costumed as Confederate soldiers, served champagne and canapés, while a Peter Duchin band played show tunes for the dancing pleasure of the city's social set.

Dutifully, Niki presented herself to Blake, who was dressed as a daughter of the Old South in a scarlet gown of daring décolleté. "Well," she drawled, "it's about time you showed yourself in public, Niki Sandeman. And it's about time you produced this handsome and elegant man instead of keeping him all to yourself."

"It's good to see you again, Blake," Alexei said with a courtly bow, bringing her hand to his lips.

Blake sighed dramatically. "Now why can't I find someone

as perfect as you? Niki, you don't mind if I borrow this lovely man for a dance or two . . . do you?'' She linked arms with Alexei and prepared to drag him away. Mindful of her duties as hostess, however, Blake scanned the room. Her gaze lighting on a man in a business suit, she beckoned him over just as he plucked a drink from a passing tray.

"Now let me introduce you to a fascinating gentleman," she said. "Niki, this my uncle, John Cromwell. He's from the Northern side of the family. And he works for a living, which is no excuse for being unsuitably attired for my party. Uncle John's planning to leave Atlanta tomorrow, but perhaps if we show him Southern hospitality, Niki, we can persuade him to stay." Her duty done, Blake firmly propelled Alexei towards the dance floor.

"Uncle John" wore a serious expression that matched his somber, dark-gray suit. But since he appeared to be at least sixty years old, Niki felt perfectly comfortable about engaging him in conversation. "And what is it you do that Blake disapproves of, Mr. Cromwell?" she asked.

"I'm a lawyer, Miss Sandeman," he replied. "Cromwell, Baggett and Constantine. Of Trenton, New Jersey."

"Your name sounds familiar."

"I'm the chief counsel in the Troiano case. Maybe you've read about it."

"Isn't that the—"

"Yes, Miss Sandeman," he put in grimly, "the case against Hyland Tobacco. I consider it a victory that we even got to court, after all they did to bury us."

Niki had been following the trial in the papers. "But you seem to have a strong case, Mr. Cromwell. The dead woman's doctors said if she'd stopped smoking, she might still be alive. Her husband testified she tried many times but couldn't. Don't you think the jury will be sympathetic?"

Cromwell shook his head. "We have a long way to go, Miss Sandeman, and we'll need a lot more than sympathy to win."

"Then why did you take the case if you didn't think you

could win?'' she asked, grateful now that Blake had provided her with such a fascinating companion.

''Because it had to be done. My partners and I knew going in that this was going to be a *pro bono* situation. Do you know what it cost my firm to pursue it? Millions of dollars in billable hours and years of preliminary work. I didn't kid myself—or my client—that it was going to be easy. After all, the companies have been bracing for this kind of lawsuit for maybe thirty years. They're ready to outspend, outlitigate and outmaneuver. They make you reinvent the wheel every step you take. They use gag orders to keep you from information you need, and just when you find an opening, they try to paper you to death.''

Niki listened with growing revulsion as Cromwell described the stonewalling tactics of Hyland's lawyers. ''If the judge hadn't cut us a couple of breaks, we'd still be in preliminary hearings.''

''But your case is getting a lot more publicity than I've ever seen before,'' she said. ''It seems as if the press is on your side, at least. Maybe that will encourage other people to sue.''

''Maybe,'' he agreed. ''But Miss Sandeman, take a look at the cold hard facts. In recent years, the tobacco industry has spent anywhere from $800 million to $1 billion on defending lawsuits. That's more than the national budget of many small countries. Who's got that kind of money to fight them?''

''But if they start losing,'' she pressed, sickened by the idea of a colossal Goliath fighting off all comers, wondering if a giant like Hyland could ever be toppled.

''Even if they lose ten or fifteen thousand cases a year—think of that, when we're not sure we can win a single case—even then, Miss Sandeman, they can afford to pay damages of $5 or $6 *billion* just by raising the price of their cigarettes a mere twenty-five cents a pack. Money the addicted will willingly pay, for a defense fund that may someday keep them from collecting their own damages. Quite a turn, wouldn't you say? In effect, you have cigarette smokers paying to defend the companies against themselves."

"But that's monstrous!" Niki exclaimed.

John Cromwell smiled grimly. "My sentiments exactly. Tell me, Miss Sandeman, how is it you're so interested in the Troiano case? Are you by any chance a member of the local press?"

Niki blushed under her makeup. "I work for Regal Tobacco," she said quietly.

Cromwell grimaced with distaste. "So," he said sarcastically, "you'd like to see Hyland beaten, but you don't see anything wrong in working for Regal."

"It isn't like that," she protested, caring very much about John Cromwell's good opinion. "I'm not at liberty to explain right now, but I can assure you that Regal isn't like Hyland. Our management does care about the health issue."

Cromwell shook his head. "I stopped believing in the tooth fairy a long time ago, Miss Sandeman. I'm not about to start believing in the benevolence of anyone connected with the tobacco industry. But since you seem interested, I'll tell you my personal reason for taking the case. I think the verdict is going to be political, not financial. I think we hurt the tobacco industry any time we can strip away all that glitzy public relations crap they surround themselves with. No matter how the Troiano case turns out, we've managed to show just how sinister the industry is, how far they're willing to go with their 'big lie' tactics. And even though they're as rich and powerful as ever, I think people are getting disgusted enough and forcing their congressmen to listen."

"I think you're right," Niki affirmed. "What you're saying is exactly what I believe."

"Well, then, Miss Sandeman, I think you have to know that your boss has to be as worried as Mr. Hyland. Because if *any* company loses one case—just one—the whole corporate body will start to bleed badly. And that's when the sharks will come in for the kill."

Thirty

"WE need more companies that have a positive image, not just good balance sheets," Niki argued. Buoyed by her success in the bloodless buyout of Freshfruit, Inc., she had become bolder and more confident in her search for acquisitions. She placed on Reece's desk her research on two firms: one that manufactured "natural" vitamins and another that produced "natural" cosmetics. Leaning forward in the executive hot seat across from Reece, she went on: "If you don't mind my saying so, Mr. Reece, the tobacco companies get a lot of mileage from their association with the farmers."

"I don't mind your saying so," Reece replied with an amused smile.

"Well, then, we need to find new ways to show that Regal stands for something good. That it has *class*. That it's different from the other tobacco companies."

"Exactly so," Reece agreed with a sage nod, "and I shall give your new proposals every consideration." Like a schoolmaster with a favored pupil, he added a cautionary note: "Diversity and variety, Miss Sandeman, that's what I want you to remember in the future. We cannot limit our vision to the so-called health market. We are indeed different from our competitors, but I want you to pay careful attention to what they are doing and learn whatever you can."

Niki complied. After verifying a rumor that Hyland Tobacco had made overtures to Barclay, Inc., a prestigious wine-distributing firm, she went straight to Reece and urged him to buy the company for Regal.

He was noncommittal to start. "What makes you think Hyland won't come back with another bid?" he asked. "What makes you think we'll succeed in doing anything more than driving up the price?"

"It could happen," she acknowledged. "But suppose we make just one good offer . . . and make it conditional on an immediate response. If Barclay understands we won't be part of a bidding war, they couldn't say no without taking a big gamble. They'd be facing the possibility of having to settle for a lower price than ours if we drop out."

Reece leaned back in his chair and studied Niki. "You know, Miss Sandeman," he remarked at last, "you remind me of myself—at a much younger age, of course. You have a problem-solving instinct that is as refreshing as it is rare." He smiled. "Take the ball and run with it."

Two weeks later, Niki was celebrating over oysters and champagne at Brennan's restaurant in New Orleans, with none other than Babe Hyland. Still dressed in a navy business suit, having come straight from a long day at the office, she listened eagerly as he regaled her with news of Duke's reaction to Regal's latest coup. "It would have been bad enough to lose out to old Desmond Reece," he laughed, "but knowing that *you* were involved . . . well, I'd tell you exactly what he said but none of it was fit, even for the ears of a veteran tobacco farmer."

Niki laughed with him. A mutual interest in Duke's distress

had become a part of the camaraderie she shared with Babe. He didn't have any trouble cheering Niki on in her work, even though her successes enriched the competition.

"I'm not finished yet," Niki said. "I have my eye on something that will make all the deals I've done look like small change."

"Oh? Something that will get Duke's ulcer in an uproar?" Babe smiled, his blue eyes crinkling mischievously; at this moment he looked young and handsome and carefree, a different man from Duke Hyland's disenfranchised brother.

"More than that," Niki said. Not for the first time, as she looked at Babe she thought how attractive he'd become as he acquired the look of maturity. How would she feel about him, she wondered, if they weren't related?

"Tell me about it," Babe urged, his voice dropped conspiratorially as he leaned across the table.

"Can't just yet. It's still very hush-hush."

"Don't tell me you and old Reece are planning a run on Hyland?" he joked.

The sheer boldness of the suggestion, an idea undreamed of, startled Niki. For a moment, she was silent. Could it be done . . . ?

"No," she said finally, "as far as I know, Mr. Reece has no plans whatever for Hyland. But," she smiled, "speaking theoretically, of course, whose side would you be on, if we did go after Hyland?"

"Why yours, of course," Babe said gallantly. "Speaking theoretically."

After dinner they walked through the French Quarter hand in hand, hearing the sounds of jazz from the tiny clubs that lined the narrow streets. The night was balmy and the area was crowded with tourists and locals alike. Dressed in a creamy-white Italian suit, his golden hair set off by his year-round tan, Babe drew as many admiring glances as Niki did.

"I still can't believe you brought me here for dinner," she said, savoring the European atmosphere of the port city.

"When you said you were coming in the Hyland jet, I assumed we'd be going somewhere in Atlanta."

Babe shrugged with the easy manner of a man long accustomed to the best that money could buy. "I thought the occasion called for something special. Your mother always loved New Orleans," he added quietly. "We talked about coming here for our honeymoon . . . then maybe sailing somewhere. Elle loved the sea as much as I did. She . . ."

Niki listened as Babe reminisced; in his recollections of Elle, she recovered some of her own lost memories. As he spoke, Niki could almost imagine the childhood that might have been hers, but for the tragedy that had snuffed out Elle's life. Of all the Hylands, Babe was the only one who never married, though his name had been linked with many beautiful and wealthy women. Now she wondered if it was because he was true to the memory of a lost love. Just as Will Rivers seemed to be.

As she had hinted to Babe, Niki had set her sights on a company that was no less a giant than Régal itself: Homepride Foods. In the prepared food industry, Homepride towered over the rest. With a score of thriving divisions, Homepride turned out everything from a baking mix launched in 1925 to microwave meals that required no refrigeration. In virtually every American pantry, there was bound to be at least one Homepride product, just as every school lunch box was likely to hold one variety of Homepride cookies or snacks. This, Niki felt, was the company that could provide Regâl with a successful transition away from tobacco. Equally important, it would protect Regal from outside takeovers.

Regal's success had an almost Biblical cadence: tobacco profits begat improved technology; technology begat greater profits, which in turn begat diversification. Now Regal was generating an annual surplus of over $1 billion in cash receipts—more than $100,000 an hour—which made it a desirable takeover target, a company that could be bought with its own income.

Armed with meticulous documentation, Niki made her recommendations to Reece: Homepride earnings were both stable and high. Its pension plan was overfunded, it carried very little debt, and could therefore borrow heavily to fund its own demise as an independent entity. Homepride stock, trading at around sixty dollars a share, was seriously undervalued. All of these signals were red flags in a business environment where takeovers had become everyday occurrences.

In an atmosphere of utmost secrecy, so as not to drive up the price of Homepride stock, Niki laid the groundwork. Using a dummy corporation formed for this purpose, she purchased a tiny bloc of Homepride stock, which entitled Regal to a list of Homepride shareholders. By keeping the purchase well under 5 percent of the company's outstanding stock, Niki was not required to register the purchase with the Securities and Exchange Commission—a move which would alert every brokerage house in America as to Regal's intentions. The next step was to secure the necessary financing.

Niki's personal life ground to a halt for the next several weeks as she met with the representatives of banks from all over the globe. Most were eager to service a company as powerful and prosperous as Regal.

Though Niki had taken a leadership position in smaller acquisitions, here, it was Desmond Reece himself who fired the opening gun. Promptly at nine o'clock on a Monday morning, he placed a telephone call to Charles Storr, the chairman and chief executive officer of Homepride, at his corporate headquarters in a Chicago suburb.

In short, Regal offered $90 a share for all the stock in Homepride. It was to be an all-cash deal in the sum of $12.5 billion: $2.5 billion in corporate funds and $10 billion at the ready from a consortium of foreign banks. Though secrecy had been maintained to prevent a last-minute increase in the price, Reece made his first bid large enough—a "preemptive strike," he called it—to drive any competitive bidders from the field.

Now it was time to call in the press. By noon of the same

day, Niki assembled more than a hundred journalists in Regal's ballroom-size conference quarters. Introducing her employer, she said: "You all know Desmond Reece. His skill as a man of business is exceeded only by his personal integrity. Under his stewardship, Regal has experienced an era of dynamic growth and remarkable prosperity. But Desmond Reece's vision reaches far beyond the bottom line, and today, Regal stands on the brink of unparalleled and exciting changes. Ladies and gentlemen of the press, I give you Mr. Desmond Reece."

Reece stilled the smattering of polite applause. Understanding his audience, he omitted his usual philosophic meanderings. "I know you all have deadlines to meet," he said, "so I shall be brief and to the point. This morning I had an amiable and gentlemanly conversation with Charles Storr of Homepride Foods." The hum and buzz of whispered asides filled the air as the press anticipated what was to come.

"Yes, ladies and gentlemen," Reece said with a smile, "we have made a bid to acquire Homepride Foods. We have made an offer of ninty dollars per share."

There was a collective intake of breath and then a hand shot up.

"Yes, Mr. Baron," Reece said, recognizing the *Business Week* columnist by name.

"How high are you willing to go?" Baron asked.

"I believe we have already made a most generous and substantial offer," was Reece's noncommittal reply.

"What are your plans for Homepride's management?" another reporter asked.

"We have made no such plans," Reece said smoothly. "However, rest assured that you will be informed, in a timely fashion, of any and all developments. Now," he added, "let me turn this meeting back to my able associate, Niki Sandeman."

Reece withdrew from the room, leaving Niki to explain the details of the deal and to parry the reporters' speculations as to what might follow.

Did she think that Homepride might try to find a "white knight"—another buyer who would agree to keep the present management in place?

Following Desmond's lead, Niki declined to speculate, but expressed confidence that Regal would prevail.

Immediately after Reece's phone call, Homepride began buying back its stock as rapidly as possible, hoping to drive up its price beyond Regal's reach. The chief executive officer Charles Storr, then called a press conference of his own.

Denying vehemently that Homepride's goose was cooked (as a columnist had declared), Storr proclaimed his intention to preserve the company's independence. He announced a plan to execute a $14 billion recapitalization, which would award Homepride stockholders an estimated $110 per share dividend—while greatly increasing the company's debt. To help finance this move, Storr said he would sell off divisions worth some $3 billion. To underscore the seriousness of his intentions, Storr added that steps had already been taken to begin divestiture.

Late one evening, after the Regal Building had been virtually emptied of employees, there was a closed meeting in Reece's office. Present were three senior vice-presidents, Niki Sandeman, and Reece himself.

"In the light of Mr. Storr's strategy," Reece said, "it's time to consider carefully our next move."

"He's bluffing," stated the vice-president who was in line to take over Storr's job.

"It could prove very expensive for Regal to call his hand," Reece said mildly. "What do you think, Miss Sandeman?"

"I think he's prepared to do exactly what he announced," Niki responded, with a confidence gained from a thorough investigation into Storr's background. "A takeover bid is every chief executive's worst nightmare. As head of Homepride, Storr enjoys a benefit package in excess of $5 million per annum. If he loses that, he loses more than money.

Storr is sixty-two years old, a widower with no children. He lives for his work—and if he loses Homepride, he'll be forced to retire. That's why I think he's ready to cripple the company with debt to keep Regal from taking it."

Reece smiled. "And your recommendation is . . . ?"

"I think you should meet with Storr. Find out what it will take to get him on our side." Hearing a rumble of disagreement, she raised her voice: "Storr has been a good manager, Mr. Reece. It would be in Regal's best interest to keep him." Defiantly, she stared down the man who hoped to take Storr's job.

Reece smiled again. "Your thinking is harmonious with mine, Miss Sandeman. Whenever possible, I prefer to make an enemy into a friend."

Two days later, Reece and Niki flew to Chicago. In an anonymous suite in an airport hotel, they met with Charles Storr and his personal assistant. Serious negotiations began at ten P.M. and continued, uninterrupted, for three hours. Shortly after one A.M., Reece and Storr shook hands. Homepride Foods was sold for some $12 billion, slightly more than $100 per share. Charles Storr was made vice-chairman of Regal, in charge of combining and managing all the parent company's food divisions.

It was a deal of almost unprecedented proportions. While Reece was lionized in the business press, he graciously shared the spotlight with Niki, and rewarded her with a substantial raise and a new position: vice-president in charge of special projects.

She was tested almost immediately, even as the papers for the Homepride deal were being drafted.

In the Congress and in the liberal press, questions were raised about the enormous power Regal would now have—power that could be used to silence critics of the tobacco industry. With magazines and newspapers so dependent on advertising, who would dare to offend a company like Regal?

Niki flew to Washington at once for a series of secret meetings with the federal regulatory authorities. Passionately, she pleaded Regal's case, pointing to Reece's exemplary record of social commitment, outlining his plans for divestiture. "While other tobacco companies may seek to protect themselves by manipulating public opinion," she said, "we have no reason to do so. Regal will soon enjoy a unique position of public trust, a position we will rightfully earn."

The deal went unchallenged, and the Regal family of companies became the fifth largest conglomerate in the United States.

Secure in her status as the ranking favorite in Reece's personal court, Niki suggested that Regal now begin divesting its tobacco interests.

Reece smiled indulgently. "Miss Sandeman, even the Lord rested on the seventh day. Surely we all deserve a respite, a moment of ease? How long has it been since you've had a real holiday?"

Niki reflected. "I can't remember," she said.

"Take a few days off. Buy yourself some new things, or whatever it is that young women like to do nowadays. Then I would like you to fly to London. Take one of the Regal jets and . . ."

"London?" she repeated. Will had written that he would be in London, inviting her once again to come.

"Is there a problem, Miss Sandeman?"

"No problem," she replied. But she hesitated. Was Fate—in the form of Desmond Reece—telling her it was time to stop running away from Will? "What is it you want me to do?"

"Be our contact to a Mr. Philip Tennyson, the curator of the British Museum. I have agreed to lend the Regal art collection to the museum for a special exhibition, providing satisfactory arrangements can be made as to security, insurance, and, of course—"

"Publicity," Niki supplied.

"Exactly. After you've seen Mr. Tennyson, I want you to enjoy London. Reward yourself fully for a job well done. I insist on it."

Exhilarated by her success, Niki followed Reece's advice. Throwing aside her usual caution, she indulged in an extravagant shopping spree at Underwood's, buying everything from designer dresses to flimsy evening slippers. Nothing she bought had anything to do with her job at Regal. It was simply the reward she'd earned—though there was an underlying purpose she could barely admit to herself, a desire to look her absolute best when she saw Will again.

Thirty-one

FROM the air, London had a patchwork look. It was a great river port with enormous cruise ships and freighters side by side; it was a sprawling metropolis with towers of glass and concrete; it was a city of lush green gardens.

For the seven hours she had been in the air, Niki had enjoyed nonstop luxury. In the solitary opulence of the Regal corporate jet, she had slept in the comfort of a queen-size bed and wakened to a breakfast served on fine china.

As she thought about seeing Will, she counted the ways in which she had changed. She was stronger now, more assured, a woman to whom travel by private jet was no longer a novelty, and putting together a multi-billion dollar business deal was undaunting. She had earned her own place in the world, with less reason to fear a fate like Elle's. She looked different, too. As Niki contemplated her impeccably manicured fingernails, she thought back to the days when her hands had been red, rough, and calloused from work in the fields.

Will had liked her then, had liked her in jeans and plaid work shirts—and she had liked herself, too. Of course, she had no complaint about being elegantly clothed—as today, in the black silk suit from Valentino. And perhaps she even attracted a few more glances as she walked through an airport with her natural beauty enhanced by French cosmetics, her thick blond hair styled by the best hairdresser in Atlanta.

But how much difference would it make to Will? He was in the ranks of the top country stars now, had won awards in the record industry, had a string of songs that were in the top ten. In just the past year, his latest album had reached the number-one position on the lists devoted to country and western music, and had hovered near the top on overall national lists. He was famous, probably earning several million dollars a year. And yet, Niki knew, Will being Will, he probably hadn't changed at all. The same, Niki realized, couldn't be said of her.

When the plane landed at Heathrow Airport, she was met by a chauffeur in livery. He introduced himself by the single name "Hardy," and explained that he was assigned to look after her needs as long as she was in London. As the chauffeur collected her luggage and placed it in the trunk of the black Bentley, Niki reveled in her status as a top-ranking Regal executive.

Her pleasure heightened when Hardy delivered her to the splendor of Claridge's, where she was checked in with the same pomp and ceremony accorded to the heads of state who stayed at the hotel. She was charmed by the hotel's dated grandeur, the art deco style, with its wrought-iron balconies and sweeping foyer staircase. To her delight, she found that her suite had a wood-burning fireplace. As she stripped off her clothes and curled up for a nap in the antique canopied bed, she imagined herself and Will sitting in front of a cozy fire, sharing stories of how their lives had changed, laughing together. As she drifted into sleep, half dreaming, half awake, Niki saw herself in Will's arms.

* * *

When she awoke from her nap, Niki showered quickly and dressed, eager to begin her exploration of the city. Tomorrow she would see Mr. Tennyson at the British Museum; the day after that, Will would arrive to begin his engagement at the Palladium. But today was hers, to fill as she pleased.

Hardy was waiting outside the hotel, and when he saw Niki, he pulled the Bentley out of the long lineup of limousines, drove it to the entrance, then jumped out to hold the door. "Where to, Madame?" he asked.

"I'll leave that up to you, Hardy. This is my first time in London, and today I just want to be a tourist."

"Very good, Madame."

Their first stop was the Tower of London, where Niki exclaimed over the crown jewels and the implements of torture. She pitied Sir Walter Raleigh, who languished in the tower for more than a dozen years, and the two little princes who were murdered there in 1485.

Next she visited the stately Hampton Court Palace, where Henry VIII lived occasionally with most of his six wives, and the Banqueting House on Whitehall, where King Charles I was beheaded by his subjects—a full century before the French got the idea of changing governments by regicide.

She browsed in Harrods, the ultimate department store, where a customer could find everything from a mortuary to a bank, or arrange a sightseeing tour in the store's vintage Rolls-Royce, the "Flying Lady."

She bought cashmere sweaters at the Scotch House and a jade pin for Blake in an antique shop on Portobello Road. As it struck her that she hadn't even thought of Alexei in days, Niki felt a pang of guilt which impelled her to buy him a hundred-year-old book on diseases of the circulatory system, written by a physician to the British court.

Thoroughly exhausted, she returned to the hotel for a light dinner and a long night's sleep.

The following day, Niki met with the curator of the British

Museum to fulfill the special assignment Desmond Reece had entrusted to her. It required quite a shift in gears, yet she felt that being delegated to handle the cultural project so important to Regal's public relations, was the best barometer of the way he had come to rely on her, and it was important to do it well.

As Niki discussed with Philip Tennyson the details of the forthcoming loan of the Regal art collection over tea and biscuits, a representative of Lloyd's of London was also present. Soon they were all talking of insurance in the hundreds of millions, of armored cars and an elaborate security system involving the latest electronic equipment and a squadron of additional guards. Niki couldn't help but marvel at the wealth and power that enabled Regal to acquire a collection that even a national museum would covet.

Mindful of the need to publicize Regal's largesse, Niki proposed a gala ball at the museum, to be attended by members of the peerage, as well as distinguished representatives of the various arts. Perhaps someone from the royal family might be persuaded to attend as well, Niki suggested. When the curator gently reminded her that all members of the royal family were exceedingly busy, their schedules filled for as long as two years in advance, Niki didn't argue. Instead, she answered as Reece himself might: "I'll leave that to your discretion, Mr. Tennyson. Let me say, however, that if the queen . . . or Prince Charles is able to be at the ball, then Regal will be very happy to underwrite all expenses connected with the exhibit."

When Niki got back to her hotel, she found a message from Will. "Leaving Paris late tonight. See you at eight in the morning. I don't get up as early as I used to."

Niki rose early, and treated herself to a long, luxurious bubble bath in the oversize porcelain tub, sinking deep into its recesses, feeling pampered and sensual. As she began to sponge her muscular arms and gently rounded breasts, Niki recalled the instructions of diving coaches who had told her to trust the power of her own body. But there was another kind of power locked within the physical, she knew, and she wondered if she would ever be able to fully unleash it—to trust her womanhood, without fear of betrayal or worse.

She stepped out of the tub and wrapped herself in a thick terry-cloth robe. Skillfully, she applied her daytime makeup and brushed her shoulder-length blond hair until it shone. She put on a pair of sapphire wool slacks, a matching sweater, and a cashmere blazer.

She ordered coffee and muffins from room service. When her breakfast arrived, Niki was too nervous to eat. It had been a long time since they had been together—and even longer since he had shown any real pleasure in her company. As she paced the room, checking her watch every few minutes, she began to wonder if his invitations had been given in the same way she had received them—with mixed feelings, a sense that they wouldn't be accepted? Or—worse—was he driven by that male ego which once had basked happily in the adoration of every woman he knew? Being idolized by the legions who heard him sing might have only made him more accustomed to being loved by many.

When she finally heard a knock on the door, Niki rushed to answer it. Barely glimpsing Will's rugged face, his familiar grin, she found herself enveloped by a powerful bearhug that took her breath away. "It's about time," he said huskily. "I was starting to think you'd never come."

"Never's a long time," she murmured against his chest.

"Hey," he laughed, "that sounds like a song title. Want to help me write it?" He began to sing at the top of his voice: "My lady let me go away sad, I thought she'd never want to see me . . . she said, darlin', you were wrong, 'cause never is a long, long time."

She laughed and told him to stop, but she didn't mean it. The silly song seemed to revive the old Will, the one who teased and joked about so many things she took seriously.

A moment later, Will drew back and looked at her. "You're different," he said. "What have you done to yourself?" Seeing the disappointment in her eyes, he quickly added, "You look beautiful, Niki . . . just different from the way I remember you."

"I left my shirts and jeans in Willow Cross, if that's what you mean," she said, a slight edge in her voice.

Will grinned, as if pleased by her response. "Well, darlin'," he said, "*that's* reassuring . . . you still sound the same, even if you do look like a magazine cover." Before she could say anything, he walked through the suite, examining the luxurious furnishings. He looked the same, she thought, in his denim jacket and jeans. A little thinner, perhaps, but that was to be expected, with the late hours and the irregular meals of a hectic road schedule. "How much are you paying for this place?" he asked.

Niki was startled by the question. With all the money Will must be earning, why would he even think about the price of hotel accommodations? "I'm not paying for the suite," she replied. "Regal's picking up the tab for the whole trip."

The answer didn't seem to satisfy Will. "So this is the way you're living these days," he said slowly. "Looks like you've really taken to this 'corporate' stuff . . ."

"What's wrong with that? I thought I explained in my letters . . . I love my farm, Will, but I just can't love tobacco anymore. That's why I went to Regal, why I . . ."

"Hey," he cut in with a laugh, "let's not stand here all day. The sun's shining, and we've got better things to do than talk about Regal Tobacco. Let's go," he said, taking her arm.

When they reached the entrance to the hotel, she indicated the waiting Bentley outside. "I don't suppose you'd care to make use of the Regal car. . . ."

"You've got that right." He hailed a passing taxi.

The London Will showed Niki was different from the one she had seen on her own. They rambled through the ethnic neighborhoods that reflected the days of England's empire—mingling with Indians and Pakistanis in West London's Southall district, taking in the Caribbean flavor of Brixton and the oriental atmosphere of Chinatown and Gerrard Street. They browsed the Cypriot shops in Camden town and admired the Islamic mosque that stood, majestic and serene, on the fringe of Regent's Park.

With his ear for music, Will mimicked London's varied accents—the lilt of cockney, the twang of Australia, the Scottish burr, the rarefied upper-class sounds bred in British public schools.

At eleven-thirty, they watched the changing of the guard in the forecourt of Buckingham Palace. At twelve-thirty, Will bought sausage rolls and soda pop from a street vendor and announced they would eat outdoors, in St. James Park. Once the royal domain of Henry VIII, it was now inhabited by pelicans and wildfowl, and enjoyed by businessmen and lovers alike. "Is all this your way of telling me that Will Rivers hasn't changed?" Niki asked, as she settled herself on a patch of green grass, trying to eat the sausage roll without dripping grease on her sweater.

"Not exactly," Will replied, passing her a clean handkerchief. "I've found out there's a hell of a lot in the music business that's phony and rotten. And if I had my way," he said dreamily, "I'd be back in Willow Cross, maybe cutting a new album every so often. Living with real people who don't lie as naturally as they breathe." Casting a mischievous look at Niki, he added, "You and I don't always see eye to eye, but I figure I can at least count on you to tell me the truth."

Niki said nothing. Did she really deserve to be called truthful when she hid so much from Will? Yet why would he even expect total honesty from anyone, when he had so many secrets of his own?

"I can't say I liked it when you told me what a jerk I was," he said, as if reading Niki's mind.

"I never did that!"

"Hey," he laughed, "we're talking about truth now. Remember Nashville?"

Niki winced. How could she forget?

"Anyway," Will continued, "I thought about the things you said. I was mad at you, all right, but I knew you weren't the kind of person who gets mean for no reason. I figured there *was* something wrong with the way I was hanging on to Beth."

He said the name of his lost love so tenderly that Niki felt a pang of jealousy. Yet she was pleased that Will thought about her when they were apart, touched that he wanted to share with her a secret memory.

"I was only fifteen when I met Beth," he was saying, "but I knew she was the one I wanted." Simply, eloquently, he talked of first love and innocence, of pledging his undying love to the girl who'd captured his heart. "We always talked about 'forever.' We didn't know it was going to be so short. Beth got leukemia when she was seventeen. She fought so hard, Niki," Will continued brokenly. "She wanted to live so bad . . . God, *I* wanted her to live. But she died just before graduation . . . buried her in the dress she was going to wear, pink ruffly thing with . . ." he trailed off, his hazel eyes drifting to some distant point beyond the trees and flowers.

Niki touched his hand sympathetically. He smiled reassuringly, as if to say he was here with Niki now. "After that blowup you and I had in Nashville, I went to visit Beth's grave. I used to do that a lot. . . ."

"I never knew."

" 'Course you didn't. I didn't tell you anything about her. Even when I was . . . well, even when I was thinking you just might be somebody I could care for. . . ."

Somebody I could care for . . . it sounded like the lyric of a song; to Niki's ears it was a revelation. Will seemed to be waiting for some response from her, but she was wondering how a man who cared could have acted the way he did.

"Anyway," he continued, "I went to the cemetery and I talked to her, but something was different. I always used to imagine I heard her voice. Not out loud," he added hastily, "I wasn't crazy. But I used to hear her inside my head, like she was still with me—and as long as I had that, there was always somebody to go back to. But that day, I was . . . well, I was just a man standing by the grave of the lady he loved. It was like . . . it was like she died all over again. And I knew she wasn't ever coming back."

His voice was so soft, so gentle, yet Niki felt no jealousy now, just a sadness for his pain. "I'm sorry I hurt you that way," she apologized. "I had no right . . ."

He tipped her chin up and looked into her eyes. "If you were starting to care for me, you had every right . . ."

She dropped her eyes. Maybe it was easier for him, she thought, laying to rest the ghost of a dead love. Maybe it was much harder to bury the fears that were still very much alive.

They spent the afternoon climbing Parliament Hill—and stood on the southern rim, with the city spread out before them like a great checkered village. Will put his arm around her shoulder and she didn't pull away.

Since Will had to perform at eight, they decided to have an early dinner. Niki suggested Le Gavroche, which Hardy had mentioned was the best French restaurant in London. Will made a face. He promised her the best food this side of the Atlantic, flagged a cab, and gave an address in Piccadilly Circus. When she saw what Will had in mind—a tiny storefront, adorned only with a sign that said "Soul Food," Niki made a face.

"Give it a chance," Will said earnestly. "Just because something doesn't look fancy doesn't mean it isn't good!"

"Doesn't mean it is, either," Niki said, wondering why Will had to work so hard at proving that success hadn't changed him.

Will dined on what purported to be catfish and greens, but which didn't bear the slightest resemblance to anything Niki had seen, let alone cared to eat.

Niki ate a salad and lots of bread and butter, fending off Will's mention of snobbery by saying she'd rather be a healthy snob than a good sport with food poisoning. Yet though they argued spiritedly, Niki was more at ease with Will than she had been for a long time. Was it because he had shown her the shuttered places of his own heart? Because he seemed to be inviting her in?

After dinner, Will dropped Niki off at her hotel, handing her an envelope containing a backstage pass and a single ticket. "I have to go now, darlin'," he said, but I'll be waiting for you after the show."

Niki hurried to her room, eager to freshen up. After a quick shower, she dressed carefully, starting with her newly purchased silk underwear, then slipping into a softly draped sea-green silk sheath by Carolyn Roehm and delicate sling-back evening slippers. She applied fresh makeup, blushing her cheekbones and shadowing her eyelids, thickening her luxurious lashes with dark mascara. She completed her toilette with an upswept hairdo that showed off the graceful unbroken sweep of her long neck. As she gave herself a final inspection in the mirror, she recalled Will's earlier remark about her appearance. Well, she thought, just because he was going to be so . . . so militantly Willow Cross-ish, that was no reason for her to go to a concert looking like a field hand. She added a pair of diamond studs, slipped on a silk evening coat, and went to meet Hardy with his Bentley.

Outside the Palladium were signs and posters bearing Will's name and likeness; the tall, muscular body, the strong, masculine face with its dark brows and sensual lower lip. As she pulled out her ticket from her evening bag, Niki was carried along by the milling throngs into the huge and already crowded theater.

Most of the audience seemed to be young and female, just as it had been in Willow Cross. Niki's seat in the center orchestra was perfectly positioned for sight and hearing.

There was a quickening excitement in the theater as the band moved into place. Through the sound system came a disembodied voice: "Ladies and gentlemen, the Palladium proudly presents . . . Will Rivers!"

Applause and cheers rose to the rafters as he strode onto

the stage, wearing his familiar costume, his walk springy and buoyant. He tossed a jaunty salute to the audience and, over the thunder of approval, opened with his current hit, "Small Changes," which recounted the little things a man noticed in a woman he lived with that told him she no longer loved him. "Used to work beside me, she'd be there right up to sundown . . . now I'm in the field alone, she tells me she's so run-down . . ."

Listening, Niki was aware not only of Will's poetry, but of his knowledge of love, of women, the customs of the people and places he came from. It was clear that he hadn't lost touch. But she wondered whether he had chosen the song partly because it spoke to her—about the kind of changes that she feared would raise a barrier between them.

His voice was richer, deeper, more finely tuned, and he used it confidently. Amidst sighs and squeals and youthful shrieks of delight, he worked without pause, singing songs she knew by heart and songs she'd never heard. In an atmosphere that was palpably sexual, Will's performance was assured, his eyes traveling the front rows, making each woman feel as if he were singing to her.

It was only when he began to sing his classic "Dark Side of the Heart" that his gaze finally reached the place where Niki sat. Through one line after another, his eyes lingered and she felt him reaching out to her as he sang of his loneliness and his longing for love. Under the hot stage lights, his craggy face glowed with sweat. His voice grew ragged, yet that, too, seemed irresistibly sexy, like his crooked grin. When his eyes finally moved on, Niki felt as though the sun had gone behind a cloud.

He sang for almost two hours, but when he tried to say good night, the audience screamed for more, and so he gave them a couple more songs, new ones that he said he was trying out for the first time, and then reprised a couple of "classics"—inviting the audience to sing along with the chorus of "Farmer Brown," exactly as he had done at the co-op dances in Willow Cross.

The performance was finally ended after an ovation of shouting, clapping, and stomping that lasted a quarter of an hour. When Niki went around to the stage door, she had to push her way through a wall of teenage girls to reach it. They looked at her with undisguised envy as she presented her pass and was admitted. "Bleeding groupie!" one of them shouted. Niki shook her head and smiled.

A stagehand directed her to a dressing room adorned with a glittering star. She tapped on the door and walked inside. Will lay on a couch, exhausted, his clothes plastered to his body with sweat, looking even sexier in his disarray. When Niki came in, he jumped up and gave her a quick hug.

"I'm your biggest bleedin' groupie," she said. "Will, you're . . . you're the best dang shout-'n-holler feller I ever heared," she put on a playful country accent to camouflage, however slightly, the full extent of her genuine admiration.

He laughed, and then ducked behind a screen. "Just give me a minute to look my Sunday best."

"There's a big crowd outside," she said, as he changed his clothes. "Maybe I should call Hardy at the hotel and tell him to pick us up."

"Not necessary," he called out. "I hate all that star stuff, the limousines and the bodyguards and the hangers-on. It's bullshit, Niki, it has nothing to do with music." A few minutes later, he reappeared in a fresh denim uniform. "Usually I stay a while and say hi to the fans. Like Elvis did," he added with a grin. "But tonight I'll make an exception. There's a fire exit we can use. We'll walk a block or two and then we can catch a cab."

Niki cast a doubtful glance at her flimsy evening slippers, at the slender line of her dress. Will took her hand and led her down a long corridor and around a corner. He pushed open a heavy metal door, looked up and down the street, then nodded for her to follow. Her heels clicking on the pavement, Niki walked quickly, trying to keep up with Will. Suddenly, as they reached an intersection, there was a shriek of recognition—and a mob of teenagers in eager pursuit. Tightening his grip on Niki, Will ran, half pulling, half dragging her. She heard her dress tear just as one of her shoes fell off. She stumbled over a crack in the pavement—and kicked off the other shoe to keep from falling.

Panic overtook Niki, she found it hard to breathe, as the mob chased them down street after street. The concrete hurt her stockinged feet, but she ran and ran, until Will finally pushed her into a dark, dank alley. They waited a long time, shivering in the night chill, until the sound of voices and footsteps disappeared. "For God's sake, Will, why couldn't you just let me call Hardy?" Niki demanded, her panic barely subsiding. "Why do you have to work so hard at pretending you're still in Willow Cross?"

"Is that what you think I'm doing?"

Niki peered out of the alley and down the street. She didn't have the slightest idea of how to get back to Claridge's. "I don't want to stand here and argue with you, Will. I want to go back to my hotel. And if you think it's too . . . too *corporate*, well that's just too bad!"

Silently, Will walked out into the street and hailed a passing taxi. When they reached the hotel, he walked Niki up to her room. "Good night," she said coolly, "and thanks for a memorable evening."

His jaw tightened, but then he laughed. "No, you don't, Niki, not this time. After all we've been through, the least you can do is invite me in for a drink. Let me warm up for a few minutes before you send me away."

After a moment of thought, Niki relented. There had been no harm done, other than the loss of her new shoes. She lit the logs in the fireplace and poured two brandies from the bar. Handing one to Will, she sat beside him on the carpet. "I'm sorry about what just happened, Niki. I don't blame you for being mad . . ."

What was this? Will Rivers apologizing?

". . . But the way I feel, it's like I have to keep fighting to stay the way I am. I love my music, Niki, and hell, yes, sometimes I like the applause, but I hate everything that comes with it. Promoters who lie. Managers who steal your money . . ."

"Is that what's been happening to you?" she asked, her indignation melting in the warmth of the room. She understood all too well about lies and betrayal.

He nodded. "It isn't the money, Niki. Hell, if somebody asked me for a few bagfuls, I'd probably give it away. It's being dealt a crooked hand by people I've trusted."

Niki reached out and covered his hand with hers, understanding exactly what he meant. Both their lives had changed. She felt that hers was going in the right direction, but Will still seemed to be struggling to find his way. "Beware of answered prayers," she mused, recalling how Will had dreamed of the career he had now.

"Yeah," he said, "I guess there's a lot of truth in that." He was silent for a moment. "I always figured that you and I were two sides of the same coin, Niki. You always seemed to be running hard, running away. From yourself, from your past. Me, I had a past, too, but I didn't run away from it. I kept it real close, all the time, but in the end, it's the same thing. We both used the past to keep from loving anybody. Not one hundred percent. I guess we figured if we didn't take too many chances, we didn't ever have to get hurt real bad. But it doesn't work that way, Niki. You get hurt anyway . . . and you end up being alone."

The room was quiet and still, save for the sound of a grandfather clock, ticking like a single heartbeat. Sitting together on the floor beside the hearth, bathed in the gentle glow of fire light, they watched the smoldering embers. She turned her face toward him, seeing herself in his eyes, feeling the heat of his desire. He kissed her tenderly, twining her fingers with his own.

"I missed you," he said softly. "I got used to having you around. All those places I've been, I kept thinking about you being there with me. . . ."

"I missed you, too," she whispered. "I . . ."

He stopped the flow of words with another kiss. Scooping

her up in his arms, Will laid her gently on the bed. She stiffened and pulled inside herself. Will somehow seemed to know. He stroked her forehead, brushed her hair with his fingertips, as if to say there was time, all the time in the world.

"I guess I love you, Niki Sandeman," he murmured. "I love you and there's nothing to be done about that."

The simple declaration was spoken softly; it hung in the air, waiting to find a home. Niki's lips moved but no words came. She reached for Will, pressing her mouth to his, her heart pounding with fear and anticipation. "Don't be afraid, darlin'," he murmured, "I won't hurt you. I just want to love you . . ."

I won't be afraid, she told herself. Loving Will didn't have to be a bad thing, not if she was careful . . .

They tugged at the clothes that separated them, until they lay naked together. He buried his face in her breasts, his hands moving along the smooth, silky flesh of her thighs.

Desire warmed Niki's body as Will's love warmed her soul. With trembling fingers, she stroked the arms that held her, the tight, hard muscles of his legs.

She moaned softly as he caressed her breasts, her nipples quickening with arousal, her senses coming alive after long years of sleep. Her legs parted and wrapped around his strong back, the boundaries of flesh dissolving as their bodies merged. Gently, he stroked at first, teasingly, fueling the heat of desire. Her body arched, her muscles tensed, urging him to ride the wave of sensation that rippled and rose, building higher and stronger . . . cresting at last, engulfing them both in a great, crashing shudder of release.

Wrapped in the newness and wonder of love, Niki lay still and quiet in Will's arms, scarcely breathing, afraid to shatter the moment with words. He smiled at her in the darkness, kissing her face almost reverently, the light in his eyes revealing feelings like her own. They slept for a while, until Will reached for her again, as urgently as if they had never made love, rousing her need, bringing her flesh to life with the touch of his hands, his sensual mouth.

Waking up in a man's arms was new and strange. As she looked at Will's face, she found in herself a tenderness that hadn't been there before. Thinking to surprise him with a sumptuous breakfast, she tiptoed into the sitting room and called room service. She ordered every item on the menu. "And some flowers," she said. "And a bottle of champagne, too."

Will was still asleep when the smartly uniformed waiter arrived, wheeling in a linen-covered table. A few minutes later, wakened perhaps by the fragrance of fresh coffee, Will opened one eye and propped himself on one elbow. He smiled at Niki—until he glimpsed the waiter arranging the table with crystal goblets and gold-rimmed china.

" 'Morning," she said cheerfully after the waiter left. "I hope you're hungry."

Will sat up. He looked at the baskets of fruit and muffins, the covered salvers of eggs and bacon and sausage and ham. The pitcher of orange juice, the silver champagne bucket, the crystal vase filled with roses. "Lord, Niki, why did you have to go and do that?" he asked. "All that stuff, just for show . . ."

Niki's lower lip trembled. Will had made her glow in the light of his desire and now, when she was vulnerable and defenseless, he was frowning at her, acting like she had done something bad.

"I wanted to surprise you," she said quietly.

He shook his head in bewilderment, as if he, too, were disappointed. "And *this* is what you thought of? All it would have taken to make me happy was a simple 'I love you, Will' . . . or anything halfway there."

Will's words seemed like a challenge, suddenly defining a distance he was demanding she cross. The thought made her angry. "Why can't you understand my feelings the way

I tried to understand yours?'' she asked heatedly. ''I ate the crummy food you wanted, I ruined my dress and had to run for my life, all because we had to do things your way. Now you're telling me what to say, what to do, how to look, for God's sake! Why can't you leave some room for *me*, Will? Why can't you . . . ?''

''Why are you trying so hard to be somebody I don't like?'' he cut in. ''Why can't you be the Niki Sandeman I came looking for?''

''Damn you, Will!'' she fought back, anger making her stronger. ''Who do you think you are? Maybe you think you're the same Will Rivers I knew in Willow Cross—but you aren't! You're worse!''

Will half rose from the bed, the deep creases of his face set with anger and hurt. ''If that's what you think, then what was last night about, Niki? Can you tell me that?''

''Last night,'' she said, wrapping her robe around her and sweeping into the bathroom, ''was a mistake! Just like I thought it would be!''

''Is that so?'' he shouted after her. ''Did you ever stop to think that maybe it's you who makes things turn out bad? Do you ever really stop being sorry for yourself and think about somebody else's feelings?''

She slammed the door by way of reply.

A few minutes later, Will added his postscript with an even more resounding slam.

Niki forced herself to spend another few days in London, just as Reece told her to do. She need to convince herself she was fine. To prove that her life wasn't going to change for the worse just because Will Rivers was as impossible as ever.

Yet she felt as if she were going through the motions, even during a solemn moment in Westminster Abbey, even as she walked the picturesque and disreputable streets of Piccadilly Circus, and then all through a stunning performance of *King*

Lear by the Royal Shakespeare Company, and while she tried to laugh at the bawdy antics of the female impersonators at the Union Tavern.

Somehow it had all been spoiled by one brief moment when she was almost happy.

Thirty-two

THERE must be some mistake, Niki thought, as she read the item in *Business Week*. It stated that shortly after the Homepride buyout, all the "No Smoking" signs had been removed from the company's offices, restrooms, and cafeteria. It concluded: "At a time when thinking Americans have raised their voices in favor of a smoke-free society, Regal's move would seem to be curiously reactionary. Is this simply Regal's way of saying 'Welcome to the family'? Or is it something more sinister, Regal's way of encouraging Homepride staff to consume more of the parent company's tobacco products? This reporter wonders if the new management will be raising salaries, or offering combat pay, to compensate for the added risks of working in a smoke-filled environment."

Who could have authorized such a stupid and damaging step? Niki wondered. To darken Regal's luster now, when it was in a position to show the entire business community that an enlightened management could achieve profitability without sacrificing conscience.

Angered by this ugly postscript to her own success, Niki took the article to Reece.

His solemn manner led Niki to believe he'd already seen it. Tenting his fingers together, he assumed a clerical stance and began to pontificate: "It was in 1604, Niki, that King James I of England wrote of tobacco and its role in the 'rumors and tumors of the spirit.' Yet in their infinite wisdom, the founding fathers of our country adopted tobacco as our national crop. I daresay it remains more uniquely American than any other product. Now, as conscientious executives of a distinguished American company, we have complex and far-reaching responsibilities: our responsibility to the public at large and our duties to the shareholders who look to us to shepherd their investments. After all," he said, allowing himself a thin smile, "you do realize that Regal is the bluest of blue chips. That it has a prominent place in the portfolios of pension fund managers everywhere. I think, and I hope you will agree, that even the most fervent antismoking advocate would not wish to see that goal accomplished at the expense of America's widows and orphans . . ."

"But we've already covered this ground, Mr. Reece," Niki cut in impatiently. "I understand the need for careful, well-planned divestiture. What I'm asking about is the change in smoking policy at Homepride Foods."

"Ah, yes, well that, too, is part and parcel of our overall plan, Miss Sandeman. It was felt by several Regal executives—and I was in total agreement—that as long as we *were* in the business of manufacturing cigarettes, it would be hypocritical to prohibit their use."

This seemed like a chicken-and-egg argument to Niki. "We have to start *somewhere*, Mr. Reece. Why not with a gesture as simple as saying: 'Look, we can't turn on a dime, but here are our intentions: we will divest, we will do so judiciously, and we will protect the investments of our shareholders.

Meanwhile, we will encourage good health practices among our employees by supporting a smoke-free environment.' "

Reece nodded. "I understand your point, Miss Sandeman. Why don't you write me a memo and we'll review the matter at the next executive meeting?" He rose to his feet, a signal that Niki was dismissed.

She went straight to her office and drafted a one-page memo, to which she clipped a photocopy of the newspaper story. On it, she wrote: "Can we afford this kind of adverse publicity? I think we *must* heed the message here to protect Regal's credibility."

The red light on Niki's private line flashed. When she picked up the receiver she heard Alexei's voice. "Welcome back," he said. "I hope your trip to London was a success."

"I'm sorry I went," she blurted out. "I mean, I shouldn't have taken so much time away from the office," she added, trying to cover her guilt and remorse. Damn Will Rivers, she thought, damn him for being like a . . . a nagging toothache that just wouldn't go away.

"I hope that doesn't mean you're too busy to come to Baltimore this weekend . . ."

"Of course, I'll come," Niki agreed. Alexei's constancy was a healing balm.

"Good. There's something I want to show you."

"What?" she asked.

"You'll see when you get here."

They stood on a grassy knoll in a quiet suburban area.

"What do you think?" Alexei asked, indicating a stretch of land dotted with trees and a tranquil pond. In casual slacks and an open neck sweater, his black hair combed back, Alexei looked more like a film star than a cardiologist.

"It's lovely," Niki said. "A beautiful place for a picnic."

"It's more than that," Alexei said proudly. "It's where I'm going to build my new home."

Niki was startled. She had assumed that Alexei was content

with apartment living, the conveniences it offered. "When did all this happen?"

"I put a deposit on the property last week. But I've been thinking about it a long time." His dark eyes grew dreamy. "This will be the home I've always imagined, Niki. All those years Dmitri and I were moving around, I promised myself that one day I would have something . . . solid, lasting. I've interviewed several architects. I think I've found the right one. There aren't any plans yet, but it's going to be a traditional house, yet with many windows. When I'm here, I want to see sunshine all day. I want the living room to overlook the pond, the bedrooms to . . ."

As Alexei described his dream house, Niki became uncomfortable, anticipating what might come next. Curiously enough, her quarrel with Will had done nothing to heighten her feelings for Alexei. All it had done was create new doubts. Though she had come to care for him deeply, she found it harder than ever to believe, as Alexei did, that love would come after marriage. And even if it did, wasn't love the problem?

Yet Alexei didn't renew his proposal. He seemed instead to be showing Niki he was making changes in his life. With or without her. Was this a change of tactic on Alexei's part? she wondered, feeling deflated and relieved at the same time. Or had he given up on their being more than friends?

They returned to Alexei's apartment, which was a few blocks from the hospital. Though the building was modern, Alexei's place was much like the one he'd had in New York—Old World in style and atmosphere, though far more luxurious. The carpets were oriental, the furnishings antiques, mostly from eastern Europe. The library was filled with souvenirs of Dmitri's career—playbills and posters, theatrical photographs and scripts—keeping alive the memories of a troubled but binding relationship.

As Alexei went into the kitchen to make coffee and sandwiches, Niki turned on the radio, searching for the classical music he liked. Hearing the urgent sound of a news bulletin, she stopped to listen. "Early today Hurricane Hannah struck the Carolina coast with winds of up to 120 miles an hour, leaving in its wake a broad path of death and destruction. Several coastal communities have been evacuated. Residents farther inland have been advised to secure their homes against the driving winds and heavy rains. Stay tuned for further reports as they are received. . . ."

My God, Niki thought, Willow Cross was less than forty miles from the coast. Was that enough distance to keep her friends safe from danger? Would Kate and Tim be all right? Jim and Bo and Charmaine Rivers? And Will . . . was he back in Willow Cross, or still safely far away?

She picked up the phone immediately and dialed Jim Dark's number. A recorded voice said her call could not be completed as dialed. She tried the Hansen farm—and everyone else she knew, with the same results. "I have to leave," she told Alexei when he returned with the coffee.

"Why? What's wrong?" he asked, seeing the worry on her face.

"North Carolina's been hit by a hurricane. A bad one. I have to get back to Willow Cross. I tried to call, but I can't get through. I have to see for myself if everyone's all right. And my home . . ."

"You can't go now," Alexei cut in. "If the storm is really bad, the airports will be closed. I'm sure your friends have had ample warning to protect themselves. And as for your house, surely your hands will have done whatever's possible to fortify it. Stay until tomorrow, Niki, get some rest. Perhaps the phone service will be restored then. Perhaps there's no need to make the trip."

Niki shook her head. Everything Alexei said was perfectly reasonable, yet the way she felt about Willow Cross had nothing to do with reason.

An hour later, she was in Dulles Airport, beginning what would be a very long wait. As she sat in the departure lounge, drinking bad coffee and checking her watch every few minutes, Niki realized that she, too, had given Alexei a message.

She had shown him where her feelings were most deeply rooted.

It wasn't until the following morning that she finally reached the Raleigh airport. She found a working telephone and tried Kate's number again. This time she got through.

"Thank God," she said, heaving a sigh of relief. "Are you all right? I've been worried sick since I heard about the storm."

"Hannah gave us a bad time," Kate said, her voice crackling over the wire. "I can't remember anything like it, Niki. We lost electricity. All the telephones went down. Most of them are still out, except for a few in town. We didn't get hit as badly as the outlying areas."

"Do you know anything about Bo and Jim?"

"And Will?" Kate added pointedly. "You haven't asked about him. He's back at his farm, you know."

Niki didn't comment.

"You know that's funny," Kate said.

"What's funny?"

"Will had the same reaction when I mentioned your name the other day."

"Kate, I'll see you and Tim later. We can talk then."

It had been a long time since Niki had been home. And now to see it like this, she thought, as she drove her rented car slowly along half-flooded roads, easing her way through fallen branches, keeping a sharp eye open for electrical wires. It wasn't just Hannah that had wrought such cruel damage, uprooting trees and battering flimsy frame houses until they collapsed. All around her, Niki could see the signs of the losing battle being fought by the tobacco farmers—in the fallow fields choked with weeds and the abandoned curing barns, in the clusters of tree stumps, the dead remains of the state's tall pines, cut down to be sold for desperately needed cash.

In good times, a farm half the size of Will's could support

several families, even allowing the farmers to send a fortunate youngster or two to college. Now it seemed certain that the good times would never return.

Before 1984, it had been rare for 10 percent of the tobacco crop to go under loan to the farmers' cooperatives. Niki knew all too well how quickly that percentage was rising, how heavy surpluses were building—because the tobacco companies could afford to bide their time and wait for the prices to drop.

Already, Niki was hearing predictions more dire than any Will had made. It was said that the small tobacco farmer would soon become a historical curiosity, like the blacksmith or the carter. And soon, it was said, the tobacco companies would take over the growing of tobacco, not only in foreign countries, but in America as well.

From the highway, Niki saw "For Sale" signs on land that had been family-owned for generations. Where would they go, these people who had built lives and raised families on the golden leaf? To soulless factories in other towns? It wasn't fair that the best they could hope for was the sale of their land to developers. It just wasn't fair, Niki thought, feeling a pang of guilt that she had escaped their fate. And it was hard to believe that all this suffering was necessary, when the people being hurt were her friends and neighbors. There had to be some way to help them, there just had to be.

When Reece hired Niki, he said Regal shared her concern for displaced farmers. Could she persuade him to do some thing now? With a depressed economy, Willow Cross and the surrounding communities might never recover from the hurricane.

As she approached her own property, Niki held her breath. Let the house be all right, she prayed silently, let Mama's house be all right.

The driveway was heaped high with rubble and tree branches. She left the car in the roadway and began slogging through ankle-deep mud. She saw Bo and Jim working on the roof, a portion of which had been torn away. Half her windows were still boarded up, but those Niki could see were intact.

She called out to the men on the roof. They waved and Jim began descending the ladder.

"You don't know how glad I am to see you," she said, as Jim approached. "I tried to call you last night, but I couldn't get through."

Jim nodded. "No telephones out here, Miss Niki. Most of us didn't miss 'em till this morning. We were too busy trying to stay ahead of the wind and the water." He pointed to the roof. "That's the worst of it for you, ma'am. You've got some water damage upstairs. Me and Bo tried to mop it up this morning, but some of the floor boards buckled."

She was one of the lucky ones, Niki thought. Her house was still standing, and she had the money to repair whatever was damaged.

"There's something you should see," Jim said. He went into the house. A few moments later, he reappeared, carrying something in his arms. It was a rusted metal box. "We found this when we took down a section of damaged roof. It was in a hollow place just over the ceiling in your bedroom."

"Looks like those Martin people left behind some hidden treasure," she joked. "Do you think you can open it?"

"Yes, ma'am. It's pretty corroded. I guess a couple of whacks with a chisel and a hammer should do the trick." Jim set the box on the muddy ground and went to fetch his tools.

Niki didn't expect much. She had no qualms whatever about invading the box, not after what the Martins had done to her house. It was probably nothing but junk anyway, just like the rest of the stuff they'd left behind.

With two sharp blows, Jim shattered the rusty lock, then went back to his work, leaving Niki to inspect the contents of the box in private.

She lifted the lid. Inside was a sheaf of official-looking certificates secured with a rubber band that fell apart at Niki's touch.

She stared at the printed words, rubbing her eyes as if to make them clearer. It was Hyland Tobacco stock—and it was all in Niki's name!

But how? she asked herself. And who . . . when? And why had she never received any of the usual shareholder mailings?

The answers were on a ruled piece of copybook paper, carefully printed in Elle's neat, precise European hand, noting the date of purchase of ten separate blocs of shares, each acquired on Niki's birthday. Alongside each purchase was a notation regarding the sale of one of Elle's possessions, first a string of pearls, then a pair of earrings and so on. Obviously, she must have felt the need to keep her transactions a secret, for there was, at the top of the page, a Willow Cross Post Office box number. True to her peasant roots, Elle had hidden the legacy in her house, not knowing she wouldn't be alive to give it to her daughter. A gift that, in its way, would bestow a taste of legitimacy.

How ironic, Niki thought, that she should own anything that bore the hated name of Hyland. And to find it now, admidst all this devastation, gave Niki an eerie feeling, as if the heavens had opened and revealed some purpose yet unknown to her.

But what to do with this unwanted, yet strangely compelling gift? The stock must have split several times since Elle had bought the first lot, multiplying the original number of shares. She could, of course, sell the stock and donate the money to a charity, perhaps the American Cancer Society, in Ralph's memory. No, a voice in her head said. Not after Elle had sold her jewels to leave this legacy. Not after Fate had miraculously spared this one portion of Elle's estate from Weatherby's plundering.

Niki closed the box and took it into the house, placing it on a shelf in her bedroom closet. Let it stay there, she thought, until she understood what she was meant to do. She picked up the silver-framed photograph on her dresser, as she had not done in a long time, touched it as she had seen Elle do, invoking the power of the past for guidance.

Glancing through the unboarded window, Niki saw a familiar vehicle driving up on what had been her front lawn. She ran down the stairs and opened the door just as Will was getting out of his jeep.

"What are you doing here?" she asked.

"I could ask you the same thing."

"I live here . . . at least some of the time."

"Didn't know you'd be here," he said, with obvious embarrassment. "Just wanted to come by and make sure your place was all right." He glanced around. "Looks like Jim and Bo have everything under control, so I guess I'll be going." Will turned to leave.

"Wait," she said, suddenly realizing how rude she'd been—and how generous Will had been to come.

He paused, a quizzical look on his face.

"Would you like to come in?" she asked. "I can't offer you much . . . maybe a cup of instant coffee?"

Will followed her into the house and sat down at the kitchen table.

"I wanted to ask about your mother," Niki said, as she poured some bottled water into the kettle and set it on the stove to boil. "And your housc . . . I hope that wasn't damaged too badly?

"Mama's fine. It takes more than a big wind and lot of rain to scare her," he replied with a grudging smile. "The house is too stubborn to give way."

"Like some people we know," Niki blurted out before she could stop herself. "Sorry," she said, clapping her hand over her mouth. She sat down at the table, across from Will.

"No need to be sorry," he said, his smile broadening now. "I do know somebody who fits that description."

Niki let the remark pass. "When did you get back?" she asked.

"Couple of days ago. That's it for me. No more touring, no more months on the road."

"Just like that?" Niki asked. She understood Will's distaste for being on the road, his love for his roots and staying close to them, yet she didn't understand how he could truncate his career when it had so recently reached its peak. "How does your recording company feel about your decision?" Will shrugged, a gesture she didn't quite believe. "I told them I'd make records as long as somebody would buy them, but I wasn't going to spend my life in hotels and airplanes. They didn't like it. They said maybe later, but right now I had to keep a 'high profile.' "

"And you said if you couldn't do things your way, you weren't going to do them at all."

Will grinned sheepishly. "Have you been listening in on my private conversations, Niki?"

"Call it a lucky guess," she said, a smile tugging at the corners of her mouth. The kettle began to whistle. Niki poured the water over the instant coffee and handed Will a mug. "So where does that leave you?" she asked.

He shrugged again. "Cooling my heels, I guess. Trying to figure things out." His eyes caught hers and held them for a long moment.

Niki sipped her coffee, thinking what a waste it would be if yet another of Willow Cross's resources were dissipated. Whatever problems she had with Will personally, she loved his singing. It was wrong for his talent to lie fallow, as wrong as it would be for this town to just lay down and die.

"You look like you're trying to solve the world's problems," he said.

She shook her head. "Not today. I'm thinking about Willow Cross. Driving in today . . . I felt bad seeing what was happening here. Not just a hurricane, but the rest of it."

Will nodded. "I know what you mean. I felt it, too, Niki. Maybe that's one of the reasons I don't want to leave again."

"Will," Niki said, an idea beginning to take shape in her head, "what if you could get a 'high profile' without leaving? If you could help the farmers here at the same time? Would you do it?"

"Is this a trick question, Niki? Of course, I'd do it. But what?"

"It isn't all clear in my mind yet, but I'm thinking about a benefit, Will. Something big. Maybe like a Woodstock for country music, right here in Willow Cross. If I can get Regal Tobacco to cover the cost, to pay for a lot of publicity, we could probably get a lot of other country singers to volunteer, too. Some record company would certainly be interested in an album. And we could get television coverage, too. I think we could raise a lot of money, what with souvenirs and T-shirts and album sales."

"That sounds real interesting," Will said cautiously, the gleam in his eyes belying his tone. "I don't know if I like the idea of getting mixed up with Regal. . . ."

"Don't be so prejudiced! Regal has the money to finance an event like this, to do it right. Think of it, Will, the money that's raised can help the farmers rebuild their houses. And their lives, too. Say yes and I'll have the idea in front of Mr. Reece before the week is up."

Will said yes.

Niki made the return flight to Atlanta filled with anticipation. Helping the farmers, lending the Regal name to a benefit would be a brilliant stroke of public relations. Especially now, she thought, glancing at the *Wall Street Journal* on her lap. Four years after the Troiano lawsuit was filed against Hyland Tobacco, the jury had awarded Mary Troiano's family half a million dollars. It was far from a stunning defeat for Hyland. A half million, as Blake's uncle had so cynically observed, was little more than pocket change for Hyland. But this was the first time any award had been made, the first time the invincible defenses of the "tobacco axis" had been penetrated.

According to the article, Hyland's lawyers planned an immediate appeal. "Let me make this crystal clear," announced the chief counsel. "We will fight and we will win any and every action brought against us. There will be no out-of-court settlement. Their will be no monies paid to rid ourselves of nuisance lawsuits."

The Hyland defense team charged that the judge in the Troiano case was biased. As evidence, they cited the judge's own words, when he denied a Hyland motion to dismiss: "I believe," he had said, "that there is ample evidence of a tobacco industry conspiracy, vast in its scope, devious in its purpose, and devastating in its results."

Niki was jubilant that Hyland had been publicly tarnished. Yet unless steps were taken to show that her company stood apart from the "tobacco industry conspiracy" of which the judge spoke, she saw in the decision ominous implications for Regal as well.

She could scarcely contain her enthusiasm as she described to Reece her plans for the Carolina Country Music Jamboree, starring Will Rivers. "I don't have a complete lineup yet," she said apologetically, "but I'm sure I can get at least a dozen more performers. We can make this a really important event, Mr. Reece. Bigger than the sporting events we sponsor. The proceeds can be used for hurricane relief—and to establish a fund that will help the farmers phase out their tobacco crops. It can be used to rehabilitate the soil, so other crops can be grown. We could even fund a job-training program . . ." Niki waited for the benevolent smile that had signaled a winning idea in the past.

"Your idea has merit, Miss Sandeman," Reece said, "a great deal of merit. Yes, I believe Regal could underwrite the costs of such a venture. We might even make a substantial cash donation . . ."

"That's wonderful!" Niki exclaimed, her eyes shining with excitement. "You don't know what this will mean to so many people, to . . ."

"However," he cut in sharply, "this will have to be a charity function. We will help the farmers rebuild their homes, we will assist them in repairing all damage caused by the hurricane. As for the other,'' he shook his head, ''I think not, Miss Sandeman.''

''But why?'' she argued, bewildered by this turn of events. ''You said there was a need for transition programs. You agreed that Regal should be a part of that transition.''

''Indeed I did. But the time is not right for such a move.''

''Not right?'' she echoed. ''If you had seen what I've seen, Mr. Reece . . . all the farms going under in Willow Cross alone . . . with hundreds more like them throughout the state.''

''I don't doubt the hardship, Miss Sandeman. I'm simply saying that at this time, Regal cannot endorse, let alone underwrite, any project that would seem to undermine the industry.''

''When?'' she demanded, angered by hearing the same answers yet again. ''What *is* Regal's calendar on this issue? On *any* issue relating to divestiture?''

''I understand your disappointment,'' he said, a sharp edge to his voice. ''And much as I appreciate the enthusiasm with which you do your job, I cannot tolerate discourtesy in this office.''

Suddenly, it was as if all the small signals she'd picked up had coalesced into a blinding flash of light. ''You were never serious about taking Regal out of the tobacco business, were you?'' she asked quietly.

''Are you questioning my integrity, Miss Sandeman?''

She looked closely at the gentleman scholar, the man she had so admired. Was he, after all, a liar like the rest? ''I think you were conning me,'' she said evenly. ''Maybe you were conning yourself, too.''

''What a choice of words, Miss Sandeman,'' he reproved. ''I do feel so much is lost when the language is abused.''

''Why did you ever hire me in the first place? Was it just to shut me up? To get me out of the way?'' The thought that she'd been used only to fatten Regal's bloated profit sheets made Niki feel sick.

"Miss Sandeman, while my stated policy is to make an enemy into a friend, it certainly does not extend to employing those who can serve no function. No," he continued, "you have more than justified my confidence in your abilities. With time, I feel you will outgrow your, shall we say, quixotic tendencies. With maturity, I feel you can achieve a senior position of great responsibility."

Niki stared at her employer, incredulous at his sublime disregard of what she'd been saying. "Don't you understand that I didn't come here to achieve a senior position? Don't you realize I came here because I believed in *you*? Because I thought you wanted to do something *good*—and I wanted to be a part of it."

"And we have done a great deal of good here at Regal . . ."

Niki shook her head. What a fool she had been to be taken in by good manners and high-flown speeches. "Spare me," she said, "spare me the tobacco industry's party line. If you weren't blinded by your own smoke screens, you could have seen the big picture, Mr. Reece. You could have done what you promised and still come out a winner. Not only because it's the decent thing to do. Because the time *is* right for it."

Reece glanced at his watch. "If you'll excuse me, please . . ."

"I'm going," she said grimly. "I won't take up any more of your precious hundred-thousand-dollar-an-hour time. But I don't excuse you. You're no better than the drug dealers who sell poison in the streets. Your friends in Washington won't be able to protect you much longer, to cover up Regal's callousness and greed . . ."

Reece smiled sadly, as if his star pupil had just failed an important exam. "What you call greed, Miss Sandeman, is the basis of every successful business. If you haven't learned that here, I'm sure you will in your next place of employment. Wait and see . . ."

"No," she cut in, "I'm through waiting for people like you to teach me anything. It's my turn, Mr. Reece. I don't know how yet, and I don't know when, but I'm making you a promise I intend to keep. I'm going to show you that you threw away a chance you'll never get again. I'm going to show you just how pitiful and corrupt your so-called philosophy of business is. Count on it!"

Thirty-three

"TO hell with Regal!" Will exploded. "And to hell with that sonofabitch, Desmond Reece!"

Niki followed as Will paced the length of her driveway, his lean body taut with anger, oblivious to the rain that was drenching his clothes and soaking his dark-brown hair. Suddenly he stopped and turned. "Wait a minute, Niki. Why should we let Regal decide what we do or don't do? A benefit is a damn good idea. Why can't we do it the old-fashioned country way? Help ourselves the way we always have, instead of waiting for somebody else to do it."

Brushing her wet hair from her face, Niki smiled in spite of her own anger and disappointment. For once, she and Will were on the same wavelength. "To tell you the truth, I was thinking we should go ahead anyway. I don't have a job. I have all the time in the world to organize and coordinate a benefit. It's still a good cause and I'm sure we can get help from other sources."

"I'll put up the seed money," Will volunteered, then

looked at Niki quizzically. "Why didn't you say you still wanted to go ahead in the first place?"

"I figured I'd wait until you were finished saying 'I told you so.' "

"If that's what you were expecting, you were wrong. Hell, Niki, people like Reece have been lying and cheating since before you were born. You can't win when you play their games. If you learned that, you came out ahead."

"Oh, I learned that, all right," she said. "I just haven't figured out what to do about it."

"Forget about it," Will said decisively. "You're back where you belong and that's all that matters."

Is it? Niki wondered. She'd lost more than a job when she left Regal. The purpose she felt, the identity she'd achieved, they were gone now, and she would have to start all over again.

She told Will she would draw up some preliminary plans for the benefit and arranged to meet with him in a few days.

That evening, she received a call from Alexei. "What's going on?" he asked, his voice betraying feelings of hurt, as well as worry. "I've been trying to reach you for days. The hotel said you'd gone; the operator at Regal acted like they never heard of you."

"That's just what I'd expect them to do," she said bitterly. "Erase me. I should be used to that by now."

"Were you fired? Is that why you left so suddenly? Is that why you went back to Willow Cross?"

"I quit," she said flatly.

"But why? I thought you were determined to stay, at least until Regal completed its divestiture program, until . . ."

"There wasn't any divestiture program," she cut in. "It was all a lie. A big lie. That's what Regal is all about, just like the rest of them."

"I'm so sorry, Niki." Alexei was silent for a moment. "But why didn't you call me?" he asked reproachfully.

"I guess I didn't want to talk about it. Maybe I didn't want to admit I was a fool. Again.'' Yet even as Niki offered the explanation, she knew it was only half-true. There had been so many betrayals, so many lies. She couldn't help but wonder if this was the lesson life had to teach each time she searched for the destiny that was hers. Riddled with self-doubt, she had run back to Willow Cross to lick her wounds. And to make the Carolina Country Music Jamboree a reality.

Yet after she convinced him she was fine, Alexei sounded almost relieved that Niki was no longer Desmond Reece's dedicated disciple. ''We could easily solve your unemployment problem,'' he offered half-jokingly.

''I may be out of a job, but I'm not exactly unemployed,'' she replied with some annoyance. ''I'm in the middle of an important project. I'm working on a benefit for the farmers here,'' she said, going on to explain about the jamboree.

''You've found another cause? So quickly?''

Something about the way he said ''cause'' made Niki defensive. ''What's wrong with that? The farmers need help. God knows they're not getting it anywhere else . . .''

There was a pause. ''That isn't what I meant, Niki. I wasn't talking about the farmers.''

''What then?'' Niki pushed, daring Alexei to challenge her latest commitment.

''I was talking about you. In your personal relationships, you're so tentative, so cautious . . .''

''Go on,'' she said.

''You don't ever give yourself completely, heart and soul, to some*one*—only to a some*thing* . . . a cause, a sport, a job. When is that going to change?''

She had no answer. She couldn't disagree with what Alexei had said. She knew it was true—as she knew *why* it was true. And she wanted to change it.

But she had no answer for his question, and no certain hope that there would ever be one.

Within two weeks, the Carolina Country Music Jamboree was underway. Soon after that, it seemed as if all of Willow

Cross was involved and at work. The editor of the *Daily Signal* gave Niki office space and the use of his copying and facsimile machines, so she could prepare press releases at no cost. The president of the First Farmers' Bank personally took care of Niki as she set up a special operating account, extending a generous line of credit on the strength of Will's name. The local television station, a network affiliate, began shooting promotional spots of Will, to be distributed to other affiliates across the country.

Niki persuaded Will to call each and every member of the country-music community to ask on the farmers' behalf, if they would perform free.

The owner of the fairgrounds agreed to donate the land for a day. Seniors from the local high school were enlisted to clean up the grounds after the jamboree. Kate and Tim headed a squadron of volunteers whose job it was to prepare souvenir "thank-you" packets for anyone who donated goods or services or money.

Grateful for her Regal training, Niki handled all the business details herself. She registered the event as an official charity, so that the proceeds would not be taxed, so that those who gave to it could claim a tax deduction. As the official representative of the jamboree, she began calling record companies, in Nashville and New York, stimulating interest in a souvenir album—and creating an auctionlike atmosphere in order to get the best possible terms. She convinced a Raleigh manufacturer of cotton goods to produce souvenir T-shirts below cost.

Working with Will again was almost like old times. Almost. As their benefit gathered momentum, getting bigger by the day, he offered Niki what sounded like an apology. "I was out of line thinking you'd changed for the worse, Niki. I can see now you meant what you said—about loving Willow Cross."

She nodded cautiously. She could see that Will *had* changed some, from the man who never admitted he was wrong. But she didn't doubt that he was still the man who could easily hurt her, if she let him.

All the while Niki was working on the jamboree, she was thinking of the Hyland stock in the rusted strongbox. It had split four times since Elle had purchased the first lot. If she sold it now, the proceeds could fund a new business, or support her until she found a new career. But it wasn't money Niki was thinking of; it was a way to regain what should have been hers all along. A way to make up for the betrayals, to fulfill the destiny that had eluded her for so long.

As she watched the benefit take shape, seeing the results of a good idea and determination, another idea was born. It was as bold as it was daring. It would take her into the heart of what had always been enemy territory: Hyland Tobacco. But did she dare? Could she succeed against an opponent more formidable than Desmond Reece—Duke Hyland himself?

At seven o'clock on a Saturday morning, the deserted fairgrounds outside Willow Cross came to life. Work crews began setting up the planked stage, the auxiliary lights, and sound equipment. On the periphery of the area designated for the jamboree, food vendors parked their trucks, stringing colorful banners across their cabs. Souvenir merchants assembled their makeshift booths, decorating them with T-shirts and postcards and posters.

The weather was uncommonly balmy for February—a good sign, Niki thought when she got up and saw the bright sun and blue sky. She dressed quickly in jeans and a plaid shirt, pulling her golden hair back into a pony tail. She drove to the fairgrounds to meet with the heads of various committees for a final run-through of the day's agenda.

Will was already there, busy overseeing the work of the sound technicians, awaiting the arrival of the other entertainers.

By ten o'clock, a steady stream of cars moved slowly along

the narrow highway leading to the fairgrounds. The state police were out in force, doing their best to control and direct the heavy traffic—and keeping watch for signs of drunkenness or drug abuse.

By noon there were at least two or three thousand people in the fairgrounds, sitting on blankets, enjoying the mild weather. Each of them had paid ten dollars' admission to see a lineup of stars that would do even the Opry proud.

From the air, where a helicopter from one of the networks hovered, a well-known disc jockey described the scene as "part Woodstock, part country fair . . . a down-home celebration of America at its best."

Promptly at noon, Will greeted the crowd. "We all know why we're here, folks. To have a good time and help out our friends and neighbors. So sit back and enjoy the music . . . and don't forget to open your hearts and your pocketbooks. I'm going to open the show with 'Farmer Brown' . . . sing along if the spirit moves you."

By three o'clock the crowd had swelled to ten thousand. From the air the fairgrounds resembled a colorful pointillist painting. All over the country, television sets were being turned on as the three-hour telecast began with Loretta Lynn singing a medley of her favorite songs. Telephone numbers flashed on television screens as volunteers answered ringing telephones to accept pledges.

At the fairgrounds, cheers and whistles rose to the sky as an honor roll of country musicians took the stage—Randy Travis and Keith Whitley, Dolly Parton and Tanya Tucker, Dwight Yoakam and dozens more.

A local bluegrass band filled in the spaces between the stars, encouraging the crowd to sing along. As the afternoon wore on, refreshment sales grew brisker, as did the sale of souvenirs. Niki moved through the crowds, trying to estimate the day's receipts, knowing that these would be a small portion of the total proceeds. From time to time, she ducked inside a mobile television unit to see what everyone in America was seeing, to hear the tallies of money raised.

At ten to six, Will took the stage. In a rousing finale, with ten thousand voices joining him, he closed the show with "Some Rivers Run Deep."

When the television cameras shut down, the local police chief stepped forward to ask the crowd's cooperation in making an orderly departure. Miraculously, there had been no arrests, no major disturbances; the most serious problem had been the reuniting of lost children with their parents.

Later that night, as the workmen took apart the stage, as the volunteers walked through the fairgrounds collecting litter, Will and Niki stood together, exhausted but triumphant. "We sure make a good team when we're on the same side," he said with a smile.

Niki smiled back. "I guess after this, you won't have a problem getting the record company to see things your way."

He nodded. "What about you, Niki? I've been thinking, with you being out of a job and all, if there's anything I can do . . . I mean if you need money," Will faltered, noticeably embarrassed by what he was trying to say. "We can call it a loan," he added quickly. "Or if there's anything I can do to help you find work . . ."

Niki shook her head. "Thanks for the offer, Will, but I don't think I'll be looking for work right now."

"Oh? What are you up to, Niki?" he asked with obvious curiosity.

She hesitated. Her idea had not yet been put into words. Could she expose it now, while it was still new and fragile? "Something I've been thinking about for weeks," she said slowly. "I mean to go after a seat on the Hyland board."

"What?" he looked at her incredulously, as she'd feared he might. "With all the jobs in the world, why the hell would you want to mess around with Hyland? I didn't say 'I told you so' after you got burned at Regal . . . but somebody ought to be saying it now."

"Forget it," she cut in, "forget I said anything. I didn't think you'd understand."

"Okay, then, educate me. In case you hadn't noticed, I can learn a new trick every once in a while."

"I had noticed," she admitted. "I just don't know if someone like you . . ."

"What's that supposed to mean . . . someone like me?"

"Someone who grew up with roots and a family. Someone who never had reason to doubt who he was."

Will nodded, waiting for her to go on.

"This isn't about a job or work, Will. It's something bigger, much more important. Maybe the most important thing I've done in my whole life."

Will listened as Niki told the story of the strongbox, of her growing conviction that she was meant to use it in just one way: to take what had been denied her, to establish once and for all the legitimacy she had craved.

Comprehension dawned in his eyes. "Do you mean to tell me this is about a grudge? An old, old grudge?"

"That's a small word for what I'm feeling, Will."

"Maybe so, but feelings don't change what is. Why, what you're proposing is like . . . like if I went after old man Scranton because his daddy cheated mine on a land deal."

"It isn't the same," she said stiffly. "The Hylands owe me something more than land or money. They cheated me of a name, an identity . . ."

Will was shaking his head. "Looks to me like you've made that for yourself, Niki. What you're talking about means going backwards."

"No!" Niki said sharply, then whirled away and ran to her car, afraid he would cheapen her sense of destiny with petty criticisms and words like *grudge*. Obviously, she and Will could only get along when they were doing something he believed in.

Yet saying the idea out loud had made it real. Her bloc of Hyland shares was the beginning. In the end she would claim what Elle had struggled to provide—Niki's rightful place beside H.D.'s legitimate children.

So what if it was they, the legitimate ones, who held a majority of the company stock? All she needed was enough backing to win a single seat—to replace one of the Hyland puppets that sat year after year, rubber-stamping Duke's authority. Once inside, she could raise enough hell to force the kind of changes she had tried to peacefully implement at Regal.

She smiled as she contemplated what the press would do with the spectacle of a board member speaking out all over the country against the manufacture of tobacco, writing letters to shareholders, urging them to support divestiture.

The key to her plan was Babe. She was sure he'd help her. How could he not? He had almost as many reasons to despise Duke as Niki did. He, too, had been cheated of a birthright, not just by way of H.D.'s will, but also by Duke's constant devaluation.

She invited him to dinner, hinting mysteriously that she had something of great importance to discuss, but refusing to explain any further.

Babe arrived in high spirits, bearing an enormous bouquet of flowers, a chilled bottle of Dom Perignon, and a box of pastries flown in from Paris. Recently returned from the Caribbean, where his new boat had shown record-breaking potential, Babe looked as happy and relaxed as she had ever seen him. He popped the cork on the champagne with an expert hand, filled two slender crystal flutes, and handed one to Niki. "Now tell me what it is you're celebrating tonight," he said, "so we can make a toast."

"What makes you think this is a celebration?"

"Your voice, when you called me," he replied. "I knew you had something special to tell me."

"It's not a celebration yet," she said, lifting her glass. "It's a . . . a beginning. We can drink to that."

Slowly and with deliberate care, Niki put the flowers in water, teasing Babe with evasions and hints as to her purpose.

It wasn't until she served the partridges *en croute*, that she revealed her intentions. "All I need is your backing," she said, "and I'm certain of a seat on the board. We can make a difference, you and I together," she continued, her excitement mounting as she envisioned the plan she'd intended for Regal coming true at Hyland. Making the name that had been denied her stand for something good.

Babe put his fork down and looked at her.

"What's wrong?" she asked. "Don't you believe we can do it?"

"It can't go that far, Niki," he said, a sharp tone of warning in his voice. "Don't even *think* about tangling with Duke. For your sake."

Whatever Niki expected, it wasn't this. Babe was looking at her as if she'd grown another head. "But I thought you hated the way Duke runs the company. I thought you hated not having a place there. Or were you lying to me?" she asked, her old suspicion of anything Hyland resurfacing now.

"I do hate the way things are. Pepper and I have never gotten along with Duke. But when there's trouble from the outside, we stick together." He laughed bitterly. "It's the only time we do."

"But I'm not an outsider," she said softly. "Have you forgotten, Babe?"

"To me, you've never been an outsider," Babe said, speaking slowly as he reached for words of explanation. "But when it comes to Hyland Tobacco, only H.D. could decide who had a place and who didn't. His was the only word that counted, Niki. He made us both outsiders, in a way, even if he did give me his name."

Niki stood up. "I want you to leave my house, Babe," she said coldly.

"Niki, don't," he said, reaching for her hand.

She moved away. "At least Duke said he hated me right to my face. You say you care for me, but you won't stand behind that. Not when it counts. I'm glad my mother didn't marry you!'' she lashed out, in a final condemnation. ''Having you for a father would have been worse than no father at all!''

Slamming the door behind him, Niki was still shaking with anger. How many times did she have to learn the same damn lesson? How much did it take to convince her she couldn't trust a Hyland?

All right, she thought, she would do it without Babe. It would be harder, it would take more time, but the farmers' benefit had shown her that determination always found a way.

Thirty-four

SEATED behind a desk heaped with documents and law books, John Cromwell looked more like an overworked college professor than a high-powered lawyer. His Trenton, New Jersey law office was relatively modest, yet Cromwell had succeeded where so many others had failed. He had scored a direct hit on the tobacco industry.

"What can I do for you, Miss Sandeman?" he asked.

"You were right about Desmond Reece and Regal Tobacco," she said. "That's why I don't work there anymore."

"It seems I owe you an apology. But I don't think you came all the way to Trenton just for that."

"I'm here because I intend to 'infiltrate' Hyland Tobacco."

"Oh?" Cromwell smiled at the mention of his greatest adversary. "And just how do you intend to manage that?"

"With financial backing from investors who care about more than money."

"A small and extremely rare species," he said, the smile broadening, "but I believe they do exist."

"As you know," she said, "the Hyland family controls fifty-one percent of the company stock—so the usual takeover procedures won't work here. My plan, if I can find investors who'll make a commitment to the divestiture of all tobacco divisions, is to agitate from within. To force the issue into the public eye."

"You mean what the anti-war protestors and the civil rights people did in the sixties."

"Exactly."

"But why come to me?" he asked. "Surely there are many capable lawyers in North Carolina who can handle stock transfers. . . ."

"I'm not sure they'd all fight as hard as you. I know you hate all that the tobacco companies stand for—and you know at least as much about Hyland Tobacco as any lawyer alive. I think I can trust you, too, that you're someone who'll stick with this no matter how nasty it gets."

Cromwell nodded thoughtfully. "And it could get very ugly indeed."

"But you'll do it . . . ?"

He hesitated only another moment. "I'm your man. In fact," he added, "I may be able to assist you in the search for investors."

She leaned forward eagerly. "That could save me a lot of time," she said. "I doubt very much that the bankers I worked with at Regal would be interested in the kind of commitment I need. They're all bottom-line people."

"I understand. But during the course of the Troiano case, I've spoken to a number of people who have personal reasons to share your convictions. Let me make some telephone calls on your behalf, Miss Sandeman—and the rest, of course, is up to you."

In Detroit, Niki talked to an automobile manufacturer whose son had died horribly of tongue cancer after dipping snuff since the age of fifteen. "I'm not here for charity," she said, "or a donation to a good cause. I'm here because someone I loved died from tobacco, too. I believe that if we can get one company to voluntarily stop the manufacture of tobacco, there's no limit to what people like us can accomplish." Briefly she described her accomplishments at Regal Tobacco. "I know I can do the same at Hyland," she said. "If you're willing to back me, I'll do my damndest to protect your investment and to see that you get a fair return on your money."

Niki left Detroit with a commitment for two million dollars.

In New York, she made the same speech to a real estate magnate whose wife had recently died of throat cancer. Even before she'd finished, the man had pulled out his checkbook. "I was going to make a sizable donation to the American Cancer Society, in my wife's memory," he said. "But maybe my money will do more good spent on the kind of prevention you're talking about."

Niki left New York with five million dollars.

She swung through Baltimore and made a stop at Johns Hopkins to pick up some recent medical data that Alexei had promised to prepare for her. She found him hard at work in his spacious sunny office, surrounded by green plants, one wall lined with books, another with plaques and awards attesting to his distinguished career. "You look tired," he observed as he greeted Niki with a warm hug and kiss. "Have you been forgetting to eat and sleep?" he asked, his tone more loving than clinical, as his long tapering fingers brushed a stray tendril of blond hair from her eyes.

"Guilty," she replied with a rueful laugh, "but it's all in a good cause, Alexei. If I'm to have even a fighting chance, I have to make every day count for two."

"Making every day count is an admirable philosophy," he said, leading Niki to a sofa upholstered in green oriental silk and sitting down beside her. "But you seem to apply it only to work."

"What I'm doing now isn't just work," she said quickly.

"I know. It's never *just* work with you, Niki. It's always more like . . . religion, like a quest."

Yes, she thought, perhaps the road she was taking now would be the last in a lifelong quest. "How am I so different from you?" she asked, thinking of how Alexei had spent his life. "You're dedicated to healing people, to fighting disease and pain. Isn't that why you've achieved so much?"

"Perhaps," he agreed, "yet we are different in one way, Niki. My work is important, but it has never consumed me. The goals you set seem somehow less important than the inner fixation that drives you." Alexei paused and smiled. "Am I sounding more like a doctor than a friend?"

She shook her head, her blue eyes clouding. "Maybe you're right. I can't remember being any other way. I keep reaching, I keep thinking if only I get to this place . . . and then when I get there, it isn't where I want to be at all."

"That sounds like a Russian way of seeing things, Niki. So dark and brooding and pessimistic. There, it goes with the climate and the long months of darkness. But you were raised in the South, with sunshine and warmth."

"On the outside," she said softly, "only on the outside."

He drew her towards him, held her quietly for a long moment. "And this latest crusade," he said, "do you really believe it will be different?"

"I have to believe that," she said fervently.

"In that case, I won't even try to divert you." He rose from the couch and picked up a large manila envelope from his desk. "I hope you'll find this material helpful. I've provided you with all the latest medical statistics related to tobacco. Use it well, Niki."

"I will," she promised, taking his hand. "You've been such a good friend. Better than I deserve," she added, thinking how unfair, how complicated love seemed to be.

Alexei smiled again, but there was a sadness in his dark eyes, as if he could read her thoughts. "Love isn't something that's earned, Niki. We love who we love because that's simply the way it is. Because it doesn't seem possible to love someone else."

* * *

Niki's odyssey took her all over the country. She visited the owner of a hotel chain in Chicago, a shopping-center tycoon in Indianapolis, a reclusive billionaire in Palm Springs.

She felt like a revivalist preacher, traveling from city to city to spread the word, just as she had done on behalf of the tobacco farmers. Yet this time she felt a conviction that could not—would not—be diminished, no matter what the odds.

Her life seemed to be like one of those puzzle boxes, with one container nesting inside the other; each time she thought she had come to the last, she found yet another piece inside.

Learning the lesson of secrecy from Desmond Reece, Niki kept her intentions quiet until she had sufficient capital to purchase 5 percent of Hyland's outstanding stock. Having done so, she was obliged to register the purchase with the Securities and Exchange Commission.

Then she went public with an offer to all Hyland shareholders: seventy-five dollars a share.

The business press immediately picked up the story, and since there was no possibility of a takeover, everyone wanted to know what Niki Sandeman thought she was doing.

Niki obliged by calling a press conference, much like those she had arranged for Desmond Reece. "It is my intention," she announced, "to purchase Hyland stock to the fullest extent possible."

"But why?" asked the reporter from *Business Week*.

"Would you believe me if I said I thought Hyland was a good investment?" she joked.

There was a ripple of laughter.

"That's good," she said. "It's also my intention to seek voting proxies from those shareholders who do not wish to sell."

"Are you going one-on-one with Duke Hyland?" the reporter from *Fortune* asked with a smile.

"I just might do that," she replied, "if that's what it takes to get Hyland out of the tobacco business."

There was a quick flurry of excitement. Now *that* was a story. Crazy, maybe, but a story nevertheless.

Swallowing her pride, Niki made a trip to the Rivers farm to see Will. In the months following the benefit, his popularity had soared to the point that he felt he no longer needed to stay on the road to maintain his following. He had the luxury of being able to stay home where, among the other improvements, he had now installed a completely professional sound studio, so he no longer had to leave to make his records. The Rivers property was a showplace now, as it might have been a long time ago in the days when tobacco was king.

Niki found Will walking one of his quarter horses on his new land, acreage which his father had once sold off, now reclaimed. When he saw Niki, he turned the horse over to one of his hands and walked over to meet her.

"It looks like you have everything you ever wanted," she observed.

He shaded his eyes from the sun and looked closely into her face, as if searching for hidden meanings in her words. "Don't know if anybody gets 'everything,' " he said cautiously, "but I'm not complaining. What brings you here?" he asked. "Didn't think you had much time for Willow Cross these days, what with traveling from one soapbox to the next."

"That is why I'm here," she said evenly. "To ask for your help. You're a much more popular story than tobacco. If you'd come with me on some of the talk shows, maybe sing a song, I can reach people who don't read the business news. They have a stake in what I'm trying to do, Will. I just need a way to get their attention."

"How far would you want me to go?" he cut in, a strange expression on his face. "Would you like me to romance the lady reporters? Maybe bribe the men?"

Niki thought he was teasing her. "I wouldn't dream of telling you what to do or how to do it," she said. "I'm only asking you to help a good cause. No matter what you think of me, you have to admit . . ."

"But it isn't my cause," he said quietly, and now his face was serious. "I know *you* believe you're doing a good thing, Niki. And Lord knows I have no love for the tobacco companies. But I can't help you put more farmers out of business, I just can't do it. Ask me to sing for the homeless. Or to feed hungry children. I'll do it in a minute."

"I see."

"No, you don't, dammit! I can tell by that look on your face. You're so damned . . . obsessed with this Hyland thing, there's no room in your head to understand anybody else's way of thinking! Just like there's no room in your heart for—"

"I don't want to hear it, Will Rivers!" she broke in. "I don't want to hear what's wrong with me one more time—not even in one of your songs!" She turned on her heel and left.

All right, she thought, if Will wouldn't help, she would find another way to tell the American public the truth about tobacco. Recognizing the media's hunger for a new story every day, Niki decided to give just that, tailoring a different approach to every publication and every television program.

To the *Washington Post* reporter, she talked about tobacco's invasion of foreign countries. "I'm shocked," she said, "that, with the support of our politicians, we allow the seduction of children by companies like Hyland. Do you know that Hyland offers Japanese teenagers free admission to rock concerts in return for empty packages of their cigarettes? Would we tolerate this in the United States? Is it any less wrong in another country?"

To the *New York Times*, she spoke of Hyland's devious advertising methods, citing a series of ads that looked like editorials but were filled with pro-tobacco propaganda. As the stories about Niki Sandeman multiplied, she was likened to Joan of Arc and to Don Quixote. "Just spell it right," was her attitude; it didn't matter whether she was praised or ridiculed, as long as millions of people heard the message.

Her original group of investors was growing every day, encompassing men and women from all walks of life. Cromwell's office found it necessary to add another associate to help handle Niki's business. Her 10 percent holdings grew to 12, then 15 and 18 percent. Voting proxies were coming in, as well, slowly at first, then with greater volume as Niki's name became almost as familiar as Will's.

On the occasion of the thirteenth annual Great American Smokeout, she appeared on the Oprah Winfrey show and talked of how smoking had become a major killer of women. "This isn't what equality is about," she said. "I think women need to take a role in stopping this poison. And that's what I intend to do when I sit on the Hyland Board."

Right after the show, Niki received a telegram from Helen: "I always knew you were a thoroughbred. Now it seems that you, too, have discovered that 'special something' within you. I will pray for your success."

As the annual stockholders' meeting drew near, Niki's campaign gathered momentum. Then, fortuitously, she was given a powerful new piece of ammunition. An article on the business pages of the *New York Times* reported that Regal Tobacco posted a $447 million third-quarter loss as income from domestic cigarettes declined—compared with a net profit of $355 million in the same period the year before. The story noted that these domestic losses were offset by strong performance by the food divisions.

Niki had the article reproduced and sent to all Hyland shareholders along with a letter warning that under the present management, Hyland would soon face the same kind of decline.

Speaking as a former Regal executive, she called the *Wall Street Journal* and gave the following quote: "If Regal didn't have its food divisions, it would be in real trouble now. Hyland would be in even worse trouble, if it weren't for the company's foreign markets.

"To me, it makes better sense to lead a trend than go against it. Americans are spending more than $100 million a year on ways to quit smoking. They get hypnotized, they listen to subliminal records, they try acupuncture or ear staples, they chew nicotine gum or Chinese herbal medicine. There's even a Smokers Anonymous program modeled after Alcoholics Anonymous. Doesn't that tell the tobacco industry *anything*?"

The invitation to come to Flamingo Island came the morning after the day that the *Wall Street Journal* published her remarks. It came by overnight courier service, delivered in a letter with an engraved Hyland Tobacco Company letterhead. The message on the paper was handwritten in ink in a scrawl that seemed to have been done hastily—or energized by anger:

> I have a proposition to make that could end all of our problems. Please contact my secretary to make arrangements to be flown to Flamingo Island tomorrow.

It was unsigned. Duke had assumed rightly that Niki would never wonder for a second who the invitation had come from.

He had assumed wrongly, however, that Niki would be swayed by his proposition. In her visit to the island, she had refused the offered bribe of $50 million dollars to end her takeover bid. The battle went on.

The stockholders' meeting was to be held at the Breakers Hotel in Palm Beach. Niki flew down a week early, in the hopes of generating more local press coverage.

As she stood in the arrival area of the West Palm Beach airport awaiting her luggage, she saw a man in a chauffeur's uniform holding up a sign that said "Sandeman." Thinking he had been sent from the hotel, she pointed out her bags when they hit the carousel, then followed him outside.

He led Niki to the longest stretch limousine she'd ever seen and held the door open.

Sitting inside was a man wearing a suit and a cheerful grin. It was Will Rivers.

Niki's eyes opened wide. "What are you doing here? How did you know I'd be on this flight?"

Will reached out his hand and drew her into the car. "Just because we're not speaking doesn't mean I don't know where you are and what you're doing."

"And what are you supposed to be doing? I thought you hated limousines and suits—and everything that doesn't fit on a farm."

"I do. Hell, I especially hate this suit."

"So?" she demanded.

"So call it a peace offering," Will said. "I figured you'd believe it if I wore your uniform instead of mine. Do you think this suit makes me look more sincere?" He made an appropriately somber face.

Niki laughed in spite of herself. It was impossible to stay mad at Will when he was determined to make up.

"That's better," he said approvingly.

"Does all this mean you've decided to help me?"

"What it means, darlin', is that I'm not your enemy. Never have been, even when you treat me like one. Now don't go getting that righteous look on your face, Niki. I came here because I care about you, even when you're wrong . . ."

"You sure have a funny way of making peace, Will. It sounds to me like you're trying to pick another fight."

Will laughed. "Fighting can be a part of loving, Niki. Hell, it can be fun, too, if you don't let it scare you. I remember hearing my folks chewing on this and that . . . and a little while later, Mama would be laughing, telling my father how he'd better mend his ways—or else. I figured it out pretty early on that they didn't mean half of the bad things they said, that the other half wasn't going to change the way they felt about each other."

As Niki listened, she recalled the many arguments she and Will had had. Did he expect her to be like Charmaine, no matter what he said or did? She had never seen a love that worked that way. Or any other way, she thought.

"Look," he said as the limousine pulled up to the luxurious oceanfront hotel, "look how far I'm willing to go for you, Niki. I'm even going to stay in this fancy place, just so you'll have me around if the fighting gets mean."

"Oh, it will," she said. "I have *that* promise from Duke Hyland himself. He—"

"Niki," Will interrupted, "do you think you can forget Hyland Tobacco long enough to say you're glad to see me?"

She looked into the face that had laughed with her, at her, bedeviled and beguiled her. The face that invaded her thoughts even when she tried to banish its owner from her life. "Yes," she said finally, "I'm very glad to see you, Will. I needed you here."

As Niki settled into her luxurious ocean-view suite, the telephone shrilled. She picked up the receiver expecting to hear Will's voice. When she heard that of Babe Hyland, she almost hung up.

"I need to see you right away," he said. "It's about the stockholders' meeting."

"Tell your brother I'm still not interested," she said coldly. "You can't bribe me and you can't scare me."

"I'm not speaking for Duke, Niki, not this time. I've been waiting for you to arrive. It's urgent that we talk now. You won't be sorry, I promise."

"I've learned that your promises count for nothing, Babe."

"It's different this time, Niki. I want to help you."

She didn't trust a word he said. Yet she wasn't so foolish or prideful as to ignore the possibility of help. "All right," she said. "I'll see you now. Make sure you come alone."

Babe gave a short laugh. "Don't worry, Niki. If Duke even suspected I was talking to you, he'd skin me alive."

Ten minutes later, Babe arrived—and promptly asked for a drink. Niki gave him a scotch from the mini bar, and as she handed him the glass, she could smell alcohol on his breath. Though he looked tan and dapper in his yachtsman's clothes, his eyes were red, his face was haggard.

"You said you wanted to help me," she said, coming straight to the point. "Why should I believe you?"

He took a deep shuddering breath. "Because I'm forty-five years old, Niki. Because to H.D. I was a second son. To Duke I've never been anything more than a bloc of voting stock. Dammit, Niki, a man's life has to count for more than that!"

"Then why didn't you help me when I asked you before?"

"Because I've never had the guts to stand up to my brother. You were right about that, Niki. You were right about a lot of things."

"What are you saying, Babe? Are you going to back me?"

Babe gave a sad smile. "Not exactly."

"Then what—?"

"I'm giving you my proxy, Niki. It's in the hotel safe—in your name. Seventeen percent of Hyland's stock to vote any way you want."

"Seventeen percent!" Niki's eyes flashed with excitement. This was beyond her greatest expectations. With Babe's proxy in hand, she could take over the whole damn company! "But what about you?" she asked. "What will you do at the meeting?"

He shook his head. "I'm not going, Niki. I still don't have the guts to cross Duke. I'm racing the Highland III tomorrow. After that I'm taking off . . . to Greece, maybe Sardinia. Maybe I'll come back in a year or so. . . ."

"I don't know what to say," Niki said.

Babe smiled again, and for a moment, Niki glimpsed the young man her mother had loved. "Just make it count for something," he said. "Then at least I'll know I did something good . . . for you, for Elle. Maybe even for Hyland."

"I will," she promised fervently, "you bet I will."

"There is something else you can do for me," he said shyly.

"Anything."

"Come and watch me race the Highland III. I'd like it if my little sister was cheering me on."

"I'll be there."

"And Niki . . . please keep the business of the proxy confidential until the meeting. I just . . . well, I don't want any unpleasantness with Duke before I leave."

"I understand," she said. It was hard to break the habits of a lifetime, and Babe was doing the best he could.

The Florida sun was dazzlingly bright for a winter day; the sea was blue and calm. A perfect day for a race. Niki and Will stood on the forward deck of the *Sally Ann*, a sailing yacht owned by a friend of Babe's. The yacht was moored a half mile from the finish line.

As the warm sea breeze caressed her face, Niki felt almost serene. Soon her life's pilgrimage would be over. "I'm going to do this right," she said to Will. "I'm not just going to take Babe's proxy and steamroller the meeting. I'm going to convince everyone there that what I'm doing is right."

"And you're so sure of that, you're willing to sacrifice everything . . . ?"

Sure? Was there anything in her life she'd been more sure of than settling the score with the Hylands? Didn't Will understand there were things you couldn't help doing? Things you *had* to do because there could be no peace, no rest until you did?

The starting gun went off and Niki raised her binoculars to her eyes. She cheered as the The Highland III took an early lead. From the distance its fluid fiberglass body seemed to be flying over the water.

"He's got to win," Niki said. "Babe's got to win this one, he's just got to!"

Will was silent, his gaze fixed on some distant point on the horizon. Niki didn't notice. She was far too intent on following the feather-light craft that was Babe's pride—and perhaps only joy.

At the halfway mark, the Highland III was still leading, but two other boats were closing quickly.

Niki held her breath as Babe accelerated. The other boats followed suit.

A dazzling burst of speed shot the Highland III straight for the finish line. Suddenly, the boat veered sharply to one side and flipped over. There was an ominous rumble—and then a blinding sheet of flames.

"Babe!" Niki screamed. "Somebody's got to save Babe!"

A second later, a deafening explosion threw jagged shards of metal into the air and blackened the sky with thick coils of smoke.

Will grabbed Niki and pulled her around to hide the shattering vision. But she had already seen a horror she would never forget. Babe's life had ended just at the moment when there was hope that it was really beginning.

Thirty-five

THE grand ballroom of the Breakers Hotel was filled to capacity. Never before had a Hyland stockholders' meeting generated such crowds and such excitement, not to mention a record turnout by members of the press. The battle lines had been drawn long before this day, and now the atmosphere was as charged with anticipation as the smokey air of a sports arena before a heavyweight title prizefight.

For the stockholders who had arrived in Palm Beach undecided as to which side they would back, the past few days had been a nonstop courtship of cocktail parties and promises. For the principal players in this high-stakes game, the past few days had been filled with tension and anxiety. Amidst other scenes in the drama, Babe's death was quickly pushed off center stage; it provided a day's headline, a few tributes were spoken by those who had known him, and thereafter his name was raised only in connection with questions about how, and by whom, Babe's holdings in Hyland Tobacco would be voted. It was assumed that Duke was the principal heir, and that his position had thus been strengthened.

Now, as Niki Sandeman entered the ballroom, flanked by her supporters, there was a palpable crackle of excitement. She glanced only briefly at the conference table where her enemies were seated, Duke and Pepper and their puppet board members, before taking her own seat in a forward row of the audience.

The meeting was called to order by Henry Lowell, an elderly nabob who had earned his place years ago as a manufacturer of the cellulose filaments used in cigarette filters. Lowell made a few opening remarks about Hyland Tobacco's continued success, and then introduced the man who was responsible: the chairman, Duke Hyland.

Dressed in a white linen suit that made him look every inch like a successful plantation owner from bygone days, Duke nodded graciously at the applause which greeted him before he began to speak. "Ladies and gentlemen, I will not bore you with long speeches. I put to you instead the old American adage that says: 'if it ain't broke, don't fix it.' " He paused, waiting for the ripple of laughter to die down. "You've all read the annual report, you've all received your dividend checks, which I am sure you have noticed represent a sizable increase over last year. These accomplishments speak to you more eloquently than I ever could." There were murmurs of agreement from the crowd.

Refusing to look in Niki's direction, to even acknowledge her presence, Duke continued: "You will hear today some talk, which in my opinion, is more suitable for street-corner revivals than it is for a place of business. You will be asked to support a young woman whose only qualification for leadership is a failed career at another tobacco company."

Niki almost sprang to her feet, the word *liar* on her lips, but John Cromwell restrained her. "Not now," he whispered.

"You will be asked to throw away your investments, to support the bizarre notion that some good can come of Hyland Tobacco going out of the tobacco business." Duke chuckled amiably, as if to include his listeners in a private joke. "I'm not a man to point fingers," he said, "but I wouldn't be at all surprised if this idea didn't come from Hyland competitors." Niki's fists clenched at her sides, her jaw tightened, as if to force back the angry words that threatened to spill over.

"Yes, indeed," he continued, "I'm sure that our competitors would be mighty pleased to pick up our foreign markets, our tobacco farms in Brazil and Africa."

Duke paused, and when he resumed speaking, his manner was serious. "I see something mighty wrong with business practices that can only profit other companies, ladies and gentlemen. I put it to you that when you're feeling charitable, why, then, you ought to just put an extra few dollars in the collection plate on Sunday." There was another murmur of agreement. "I promised I would be brief, so I won't go on to describe my plans for Hyland's future. I will say only that it will surpass anything we have done in the past." He smiled graciously and left the podium to the accompaniment of enthusiastic applause.

Henry Lowell then passed over several pieces of routine business, and asked if there were any shareholders who wanted to speak.

A single hand went up. It stuck out like a flag raised at the summit of mountain, and everyone in the room turned to look at Niki Sandeman.

"Will the young lady in the third row please step forward then?" Lowell said. Though he knew who Niki was he refused to acknowledge her by name.

Niki stepped forward to the podium. She took a deep breath, and began to speak. "Ladies and gentlemen, my name is Niki Sandeman. Contrary to what you may have heard, I am not asking you to throw away your investment in Hyland Tobacco. All I ask is that you think about the kind of glorious future Mr. Hyland has in mind." She paused to cast a scornful glance at Duke, who was busy whispering to Pepper as if to underline his view that Niki was merely an insignificant nuisance. "Mr. Hyland has gratified you with his reference to your growing dividend. But I want you to think about where those dividends will be coming from, if Mr. Hyland has his way." Her voice rising with conviction, she went on, "Make no mistake about it: Hyland Tobacco, like every one of its competitors in the lucrative business of selling tobacco products is a merchant of death. Respectable, yes—when compared to the dealers of dope who do business in the alleyways and street corners of our dying cities. But are they any less deadly? Do they cost this nation any less every year in the billions of additional health care dollars required to deal with the effects of smoking? In lost productivity? Not to mention the sheer human cost in suffering. These 'respectable' merchants of death are, in fact, far more deadly, I promise you. We now have the truth before us," she said, holding up the latest surgeon general's report for emphasis, "the truth that even millions of dollars of tobacco money could no longer hide. Tobacco is as addictive as heroin! Think of that, ladies and gentlemen. And what is even more frightening, tobacco kills thirty times more people *every* year than *all* narcotics-related deaths combined."

She paused dramatically, then continued: "Each night, as you watch your evening news, you look with horror on the footage of war, of death from AIDS, from accidents and crime. Not one of you would pretend that any of these tragedies is somehow a benefit to humanity—or that it should be allowed to exist. Yet each and every year, there are more deaths from smoking than from AIDS, heroin, crack, cocaine, alcohol, fires, murders, and auto accidents . . . *combined*!" Niki roared the final word in a way that made her fury at the needless death very personal.

"Think of it, ladies and gentlemen, think of it, I beg you. This year alone, more than a half-million Americans will die of lung cancer and smoking-related diseases. And there are those who say that my war . . . my crusade against the tobacco companies is hopeless and foolish. But have we not all wished we could end the futile death that has come from wars of guns and bullets? One more thing to think about, my friends: the half-million Americans who will die this year—and who might have lived if they did not smoke—number more than the sum total of this nation's battle fatalities in World War II, *and* the Vietnam War together.

"Cigarette advertising tries to make us believe that smoking is as American as apple pie," she said sarcastically. "They never mention that this all-American habit costs us $100 billion every year in medical bills and lost productivity. What could America do with that money if it were spent for the homeless, for the poor, for education!

"Think of the costs that can't be measured—the cost in death and human suffering. Think of how we pollute and corrupt our own children. We tell them to say no to drugs, and then by our own example, we say yes, yes, yes to cigarettes. They get the message, too, my friends. Every day, an estimated three to five thousand kids light up for the first time. And they join the march of those gray battalions that will die . . . if I lose my 'hopeless and foolish' crusade."

Niki paused to wipe the beads of perspiration from her brow. She looked out at the rows of men and women who had applauded Duke Hyland only minutes ago and wondered if she could possibly be making an impact on them. Was she, as Reece had said, a Don Quixote to imagine that there was in most human beings a decency strong enough to overcome greed?

"If I gain control of Hyland Tobacco," Niki resumed, "it is my intention, ladies and gentlemen, to diversify into harmless products. To divest all tobacco divisions—and to rename the company Hyland, Incorporated. Your present chairman says that if Hyland divests, someone else will reap the profits from its tobacco divisions. I say this is an argument spoken of greed. An argument that ignores what is happening in our country today. In 1986, for the first time in thirty years, unit sales of all tobacco products fell. They have declined steadily since. Tobacco's death grip on this nation's lawmakers is falling away, too. In 1986, there were only eighty-nine municipal laws restricting smoking. By the end of 1988, there were nearly four hundred, with hundreds more in the works.

"Oh, yes," she continued, "*your* company has been working very hard to void or weaken these laws. But in the long run, they will fail."

Niki looked hard at Duke, as if to fix everyone's attention upon him. "Your chairman knows that the American market for tobacco will never again recover. His response: 'let's sell death to other countries, friend and foe alike. Let's force their governments to let us in, let's invoke free trade, let's squeeze *their* politicians the way we squeezed our own.' What I am proposing is not the sacrifice of your investments. What I want is good business, long term, without selling deadly products here or abroad." From the corner of her eye, Niki saw Duke point to his watch. A moment later, Lowell got up from his chair at the conference table.

"Miss," he said, "I must remind you that we have important business to transact today. As a shareholder, you have been given the courtesy of the floor, but—"

Niki rode over him. "As a *majority* shareholder, I don't need your courtesy or your permission to speak."

There was a stunned silence, and then a hasty conference between Pepper and Duke.

Unable to ignore Niki any longer, Duke stepped forward. "What do you mean 'majority shareholder'?" he demanded.

Triumphantly, she produced a copy of Babe's proxy and shoved it in Duke's face. She waited, enjoying his shock and his silent anger.

The room was buzzing now. The combat had begun.

Suddenly Duke smiled broadly. "No, Miss Sandeman," he said, "I believe you have made yet another mistake. If you had taken the time to examine the bylaws of this corporation, you would know that the proxy you're holding is null and void."

How could that be? Niki reached for the briefcase she had set to the side of the rostrum while she spoke. He must be stalling, she thought, he must be trying to buy time. She pulled out the original documents Babe had given her. They were duly signed, dated and, notarized.

"I think you're the one who's made the mistake," she declared coldly, handing over the documents. "This was given to me by William Hyland. The signature was authenticated by a notary public."

"I'm not questioning my brother's signature," Duke answered. "Or his right to assign a proxy. But I do not accept that it's *your* right to vote such proxy. As I said before, if you had bothered to read the *original* shareholders agreement, you would know that stock owned by the Hyland family may not be transferred in any arrangement that would result in the stock being voted by anyone *other* than a member of the Hyland family." He paused, letting the impact of his bombshell sink in.

Niki's ears rang with the words: "a member of the Hyland family." Her cheeks flushed with embarrassment. Was she to be forced here and now—in a room packed with strangers—to fight against the shame of her childhood? To choose between broadcasting her mother's humiliation or being publicly denied once more?

Duke's smile of victory gave her a powerful reminder. What she was doing was more important than pride or personal feelings. What she was doing could make a difference. Not just to her and Will, but to millions of people. Standing erect, she announced in a clear voice. "I think you know very well, sir, that I *am* a member of the Hyland family. Your brother, Mr. William Hyland knew that as well—which is why he gave me the proxy."

The room was suddenly still. The personal drama unfolding eclipsed for the moment the simple matter of finances. Duke feigned a look of surprise. He shook his head, his manner shifting suddenly, now the Southern gentleman again. "Miss Sandeman, I deeply regret that you feel the need to embarrass us all in this way. May I ask with which branch of the family you claim a connection?"

A snicker came from someone in the audience, sparking a larger wave of nervous laughter.

Niki's cheeks flamed scarlet, and a tide of rage began to course through her. Duke was treating her as if she was simply a deluded lunatic—and it was working; she could feel support in the room slipping away from her, as the mass gravitated towards the one who held the power, the wealthy, trusted man who stood at the head of the room with such assurance.

Striving for dignity, Niki said, "You know as well as I do, Duke, that you and I had the same father—Henry David Hyland."

Now there was a collective intake of breath, a renewed babble from all corners of the room. Never before had the dull, routine Hyland stockholders' meetings resembled a nighttime soap opera.

Duke chuckled. "Well, that's a mighty convenient thing to say, Miss Sandeman, since my daddy's been gone lo these many years, and can't defend himself. But I don't recall that you were ever mentioned as a family member. I don't recall that you received any inheritance. I don't ever recall you so much as coming through the front door of our house." Duke was clearly reveling in this moment, taunting her with the hard and painful truth that while they may have shared H.D. Hyland's genes and chromosomes, that was all they'd ever shared. Reminding her that she had no more right to call H.D. "father" now than when he was alive. "But perhaps it wouldn't be asking too much for you to produce some small proof of your claim?" he said with exaggerated patience, speaking as if to placate a mind that was simple or unsound.

Niki was tortured by the knowledge that the only birth certificate she could produce clearly stated, "Father unknown."

"Well, speak up, Miss Sandeman," Duke goaded her. "A legitimate claimant to membership in my family shouldn't be having the kind of difficulty you seem to be experiencing."

She was silent a long moment. Would this be the end

then—a certain victory turned into a public humiliation, to be trumpeted far and wide in tomorrow's newspapers? She cursed herself for overconfidence, for failing to do the necessary homework.

"I think that if Miss Sandeman has nothing more to say, we had best get to the business at hand."

"No, Mr. Hyland," she shouted out, grasping at a last straw. "I think you'll find that if you disqualify my proxy, there will be no business conducted today. According to my arithmetic, you will not have the necessary fifty-one percent to make up a quorum. Read your bylaws, Mr. Hyland. You'll see I'm right."

There was a loud rumble of disappointment from the stockholders. Duke's eyes blazed. He looked as if he'd be capable of murdering Niki where she stood.

"This isn't the end of it," she said. "Until you address my claim properly, you can damn well consider Hyland Tobacco in a state of limbo!"

She picked up her briefcase and started to leave the room. A moment later, Will was at Niki's side, leading the way as she dodged the waiting reporters and photographers. "No comment," she said to the questions, yet knowing all too well that every juicy detail of this meeting would soon be public knowledge. No pictures, she pleaded silently, covering her face until Will pulled her hand away.

"Head up, darlin'," he whispered, "don't let the bastards make you hide."

"This is all your fault," Pepper said accusingly, when she and Duke were alone in a suite at the Breakers Hotel after the meeting. "Babe never would have given her his proxy if you hadn't treated him so bad. You drove him to it, Duke, and now he's paying you back!"

"Shut up," Duke snapped. "Nobody drove Babe anywhere. He was weak and he was stupid, Pepper. Just because he's dead doesn't change a damn thing."

Pepper's surgically youthful face hardened. "Don't push,"

she warned. "You need me, Duke . . . you need my backing more than you ever did. So I'm warning you now, if you *ever* say another mean word about Babe . . ."

Duke retrenched. "Okay, okay, I'm sorry about Babe. I know how close the two of you were. But this is no time for threats, Pepper. In fact, this is no time for anything but sticking together and getting rid of that bitch."

"She seemed awfully confident," Pepper suggested.

"She's just blowing smoke. After today, I think we have a good shot at discrediting her altogether. In fact, I'm going to put out a letter to the stockholders today, showing her up as a gold-digging troublemaker who's going to cost them money."

"Are you sure it's going to be that simple?"

"I'm sure." Duke's jaw muscle twitched, giving the lie to his confidence.

Pepper didn't appear convinced. "I don't know, Duke. It looks to me like she's going to get her foot in the door, pick up one board seat at least."

"Over my dead body."

"Duke, be realistic."

Duke attempted a smile. "Don't worry, Sister dear. I'm going to do what I should have done a long time ago. I told her this was war, and now she's going to find out exactly what I meant."

Thirty-six

THE team of Hyland lawyers moved with lightning speed and the force of a well-trained army. Within two days of the aborted stockholders' meeting, a federal judge in Raleigh had been petitioned to nullify the stock proxy assigned by the late William Hyland to Nicolette Sandeman. Immediate relief was requested in this most pressing matter, the petition said, in order to prevent grievous damage to the business of Hyland Tobacco.

As Niki had feared, the media had a field day with this new and startling development in her crusade against Hyland Tobacco. Suddenly, her personal history seemed of far more interest than her humanitarian vision.

She was besieged by reporters in search of a juicy tidbit or two to flesh out their stories of an illegitimate child seeking recognition by one of America's richest and most newsworthy families. Digging into Niki's past, they found the unexpected bonus of Gabrielle Sandeman's still unsolved murder. Faced with reporters who raised the titillating mystery, Niki had to fight down the urge to suggest that H.D. Hyland had committed the crime. There was no proof, after all; it would only make her look more disturbed. But she bought no peace with her silence. When she refused to comment, the reporters prowled the streets of Willow Cross, interviewing senior locals, some of whom remembered—or claimed to remember—the late Gabrielle Sandeman as a high-living foreign hussy who "put on airs" and was given to unspeakable practices before she came to "a bad end."

One enterprising television newshound dug even deeper than the rest. Discovering that Elle Sandeman was herself an illegitimate daughter—the child of the French Olympian, Monique Veraix—he expanded the fact into an item about illegitimate children of the "rich and famous." And he asked, as part of it, whether Niki might not run true to form—and have an illegitimate child of her own.

Heartsick over the erupting scandal, Niki barricaded herself in her cottage. Will had gone to California to discuss a TV special and called offering to return and provide support, but she was anxious to keep him away. His career, she felt, might be damaged if he was linked with her as a "love interest."

Alexei came unannounced, however. Unconcerned about the photographers and television cameramen who camped around Niki's driveway, he brushed past them as he got out of his car, letting himself be photographed as he went to her door carrying the suitcase he removed from the trunk.

"Marry me now," he urged Niki after she had welcomed him in. "There's no need for you to put yourself through all this . . . ugliness. You don't need the Hyland money. You don't need *anything* from the Hylands, Niki. If you want a new name, take mine! Leave Willow Cross, come back with me to Baltimore."

"I can't leave Willow Cross. Not now, not because of anything people say about me. Or because they're trying to make me feel dirty. I should be used to it," she added softly, "but I'm not. It feels just as bad now as it did when I was a kid."

"But why, then, won't you give up this battle? So far you're the only casualty, and I don't want to see you—"

"I have no choice but to go on," she cried passionately. "Don't you understand, Alexei. I won't be whole until it's finished! It isn't the Hyland money I want, Alexei! And it isn't the Hyland name. It's *me* I'm fighting for . . . can't you understand that?"

He was silent for a long moment, as though listening to more than Niki's words, as if he were hearing at last a message he had always refused to hear.

"If the stories bother you," Niki said softly, "if you feel they might hurt your career in any way, maybe it would be best if you went back to Baltimore. I'd understand, Alexei, really I would."

A flicker of pain crossed Alexei's face. "I promised you once I wouldn't leave you, Niki. So if you mean to see this thing through, then I shall stay here until it's all over."

Niki had believed that taking her place on the Hyland board would somehow validate and legitimize her. Yet now it seemed she would have to fight that battle in a courtroom—and risk being told, once again, that in the eyes of the world, she did not officially exist.

In spite of all the gossip and the scandal, she was ready to take that risk. What hurt was that Will had neither been seen nor heard from since Alexei arrived in Willow Cross. That he had believed what was being said about Niki without even giving her a chance to speak.

She drove to Raleigh the day before the hearing to meet with Cromwell, who was headquartered in a local hotel, working around the clock to prepare his brief.

"What are my chances?" she asked, knowing he would be candid to the point of bluntness.

"About fifty-fifty," he replied. "In the state of North Carolina, the last similar case was in 1954. A wealthy Raleigh businessman left his estate to his wife and children, to be divided equally. He had an illegitimate son who argued that he should be included because he was born before the will was drawn up. He claimed that he hadn't been specifically named in the will because the father didn't want to embarrass the legitimate children."

"What happened?" Niki asked.

Cromwell grimaced. "The court ruled against him. The judge reasoned that if an illegitimate child wasn't recognized by his father, the court wasn't empowered to legitimize the offspring of an illicit union."

"I see. That doesn't sound like a fifty-fifty chance to me."

"That decision is more than thirty-five years old," Cromwell reminded her. "Even then, if the man had the resources to carry the fight through the appeals process, the decision might have been reversed. Furthermore," he added, "there have been a great many similar cases in other states, cases where the judge ruled *for* the illegitimate child. Even in the South, Niki, there's been an awakening on this issue. All we have to do is convince the court that by supporting you and your mother when she had no other visible means of support, that H.D. Hyland did, in fact, recognize you as his family."

"I've been trying to convince myself of that all my life," Niki said bitterly.

"None of that," Cromwell warned. "I've been up against those Hyland lawyers before, Niki. They're damn good—and damn quick to spot *any* sign of weakness, so don't you be the one to show them hesitation or doubt. Our position *has* to be this: that you are, without any doubt, the daughter of H.D. Hyland; that Duke Hyland is now attempting to deny a rightful claim."

"But that's true," Niki cut in eagerly, "that's just the way it's always been."

"All right," Cromwell said with a rare smile. "Remember that when we're in court—and maybe we can do better than fifty-fifty."

The courtroom was filled, with reporters occupying the back rows and television cameras clustered near the entrance.

As Niki entered and saw Duke and Pepper seated with their cadre of lawyers, her step faltered for an instant. But Alexei, at her side, gave her hand a reassuring squeeze and she continued forward. It was fortifying to feel she had the love of this man who had promised always to be there. There were others, too, whose unstinting love and support she depended on to see her through—Helen, Blake, and Kate. Even Jim and Bo had come.

And yet as she scanned the spectator gallery, she half-hoped, half-expected to see the face of another who had made no promises. A man who had turned away from her, perhaps for the last time.

The clerk sounded the traditional "oyez, oyez" as Judge Harrison Petty entered the room. Casting a disapproving eye on the media group, Judge Petty issued a stern warning: "Ladies and gentlemen of the press, you are here at my discretion. If your presence proves to be in any way intrusive or disruptive, you will be ejected from my courtroom."

"What do you know about this judge?" Niki whispered to Cromwell.

"The Hylands don't own him, if that's what you're asking."

"I suppose that's something to be grateful for."

Cromwell shook his head. "That's defeatist talk, Niki. Remember what we planned? There's strength in confidence. So even if you don't feel it . . . pretend."

Niki nodded. A moment later, she was treated to a genuine display of confidence when the chief counsel for Hyland—Quentin "Pappy" Lombard—stepped forward to make his opening remarks. A former all-American quarterback, Lombard's courtroom skills were as legendary as his wins for the Blue Devils of Duke.

In a leisurely and meandering speech, Lombard said the facts of the case were plain and simple. Through "unknown means" (and here he paused to leave room for innuendo), and for "reasons known best to herself" (again a pregnant pause) Miss Nicolette Sandeman had "procured" the proxy of William Hyland. "Finding this proxy to be invalid under the original bylaws of the Hyland Tobacco Company," he continued, "Miss Sandeman has put forth a claim of kinship. Though this claim has no basis whatever in legal fact, it has obstructed and delayed the proper business of the Hyland Company. On behalf of my clients, I am obliged to ask the court for a just and speedy verdict."

By contrast, John Cromwell seemed the quintessential Northern lawyer—brisk, efficient and matter-of-fact. Yet he, too, asked the court to be speedy and fair in rendering what was the only just decision: to grant Nicolette Sandeman the legitimacy she had long been denied.

Lombard called three witnesses—Duke, Pepper, and the lawyer who had prepared H.D. Hyland's will—with one intent: to follow the form of the 1954 case and to force a similar verdict. All the witnesses stated under oath that H.D. had never mentioned the existence of a child, nor had he expressed any interest in providing for Nicolette Sandeman.

Cromwell declined to cross-examine any of these witnesses. "Calling the liars isn't going to make a damn bit of difference," he told Niki, "not without any documentation to prove it."

With a winner's smile, Lombard took his place at the plaintiff's table. Now it was Cromwell's turn. His single witness, indeed his entire case, was Niki Sandeman herself.

Though Cromwell had rehearsed her, Niki all but forgot his admonitions when she took the stand. Stumbling and blushing over the phrase "my father," she tried to describe, with conviction, the years when H.D. Hyland had been a regular part of her life and Elle's.

"Was your mother employed during the years in question, Miss Sandeman?"

"She was not," Niki admitted, though not without shame.

"And how did you live during this period?"

"Objection," Lombard cut in. "A minor child could not know the financial details of her mother's life. Anything she has to say now would be hearsay."

"Your honor, we ask the court's indulgence in allowing some latitude here," Cromwell said. "Though Miss Sandeman was a minor, she can testify, of her own knowledge, to certain financial arrangements."

"The court will allow the question," Judge Petty ruled.

"My father sent a check every month," Niki replied. "My mother showed them to me when . . . when I was unhappy because he wasn't with us."

"Tell the court in your own words, Miss Sandeman, about the kind of presence your father maintained in your home."

Haltingly, Niki spoke of the wardrobe H.D. kept at the cottage, the special wines he sent from his private cellar and the stock of personal cigarettes.

"Thank you, Miss Sandeman. Now I show you this document—which I request to be entered in evidence. Do you recognize it?"

"I do. It's my mother's citizenship application."

"Will you read aloud the name of your mother's sponsor?"

"Henry David Hyland," Niki said in a loud, ringing voice.

"The defense rests," Cromwell said.

Like the proverbial cat who ate the canary, "Pappy" Lombard stepped forward to cross-examine Niki. "I know this must be mighty hard on you, Miss Sandeman," he said, all gallantry and sympathy. "And I deeply regret any discomfort my questions might bring you. I know it must have been mighty painful growing up without a daddy . . ."

"Yes," she agreed, her voice barely audible, "it was."

Pappy nodded. "I know it must have been mighty difficult on your mama, too. But she tried her best, didn't she, to raise you and make you feel like you had a place."

"Yes," Niki answered, drawn in spite of herself into a thick blanket of memories. "She tried, but it wasn't possible. Not the way things were here. She—"

Lombard cut her off. "I'm sure. And she told you that H.D. Hyland was your daddy and that he cared for you."

"Yes," Niki said, blinking back her tears.

"And, of course, you believed your mama."

Niki stiffened now, suddenly alert. "Yes, I believed her," she said coldly. "My mother wasn't a liar."

"Of course not," Pappy said softly. "But you know, Miss Sandeman, sometimes when we love our children and we want the best for them, sometimes we try to protect them from information that would cause them pain and sadness."

"Objection!" Cromwell shouted, springing to his feet. "Mr. Lombard is editorializing and making speeches."

"Sustained," Judge Petty said. "Mr. Lombard, if you have a question of this witness, please ask it."

"I will, your honor, I surely will. Miss Sandeman," he said, "isn't it possible that your mother told you that H.D. Hyland was your father simply because he was a wealthy and distinguished man? Isn't it possible she was trying to protect you, in her own way? Isn't it possible . . ."

"No!" Niki shouted, wanting to staunch the flow of evil conjectures, "it isn't possible! *He* put you up to this!" she cried out, pointing at Duke, who sat smug and smiling throughout her ordeal. "He's trying to smear my mother now because she isn't here to defend herself. He's—"

"Order, order," the judge said, with an explosive rap of his gavel. "The witness will refrain from further outbursts, or I may have to issue a citation for contempt."

"I understand how you feel," Lombard continued, "I surely do. And it pains me to cause you any more distress, Miss Sandeman, truly it does. I'm only trying to arrive at the truth."

"Truth," she echoed bitterly. "Or whatever passes for it and satisfies your client."

"Miss Sandeman," the judge remonstrated, "I've already warned you once . . ."

Suddenly the courtroom door opened. After a brief exchange with a bailiff, a man was admitted. He signaled to Lombard.

"Your honor, may I request a five-minute recess?" Lombard asked. "I believe we can clear this entire matter up without further delay, if the court will indulge me."

"Very well, Mr. Lombard. Five minutes."

Niki stepped off the witness stand and hurried towards Cromwell. "What's going on?" she asked.

Cromwell shook his head. "I don't know. But if he's going to introduce evidence we haven't seen, I can challenge him on the rules of disclosure. Just keep calm, Niki. Don't allow Lombard to provoke you."

Niki took a drink of water and tried to compose herself. All too soon she was recalled to the stand and reminded that she was still under oath.

"Miss Sandeman," Lombard began, "do you recall an accident you had when you were just a little girl, about four years old?"

"Objection, your honor. Relevancy?"

Lombard held up his hand. "Your honor, if you'll give me just a moment or two, I think you'll find this line of questioning is not only relevant, but crucial."

"Overruled. Please get to the point. The witness will answer."

"Yes," Niki replied. "I did have such an accident."

"Do you remember being taken to the Willow Cross Hospital? Where you received a blood transfusion during the course of your treatment?"

"I don't remember that. My mother told me that's what happened."

"Well," Lombard smiled broadly, "fortunately, we have no need to rely on your mother's word in this case. We have hospital records of your treatment—just as we have hospital records relating to Mr. Hyland's final illness. Your blood type is B positive, Miss Sandeman. Mr. Hyland's type is . . . was A negative . . ."

He paused dramatically, to heighten the impact of his final pronouncement: "It is therefore medically impossible for Mr. Henry David Hyland to be your father."

"Objection!" Cromwell shouted. "No foundation, your honor, we object!"

Niki went rigid, as if a bolt of electricity had shot through her body. The room began to spin, and then she lost consciousness.

Thirty-seven

"THINK, Kate, please," Niki begged, as she sat in her friend's kitchen, her shoulders slumped in an attitude of dejection. "Your father delivered me. Isn't there some chance he wrote down something, *anything* to confirm who my father was?"

Kate's brow furrowed with concentration. "As far as I can recall, Mama put all of Papa's things in a warehouse after he died. In River Junction, I think. She wouldn't give it away or throw it away, so unless she changed her mind, it would probably still be there. But Niki," she added, reaching out to clutch her friend's hand, "even if that's so, I don't think you should get your hopes up."

"I know, Kate. I just feel like I have to do *something*." How many times Niki had wished someone else were her father—someone other than the distant, cold man who had never hugged or kissed her? Yet now that it seemed the wish had been granted—that she had been released from the curse of Hyland parentage—she was devastated.

"She lied to me," Niki said brokenly. "How could she have done that to me? Was she so obsessed with the Hylands that she made it all up? Did she lie to him, too?"

Kate tried to soothe her friend, to find a blessing somehow in this shocking discovery. "Niki," she said, "we may never have an answer. All we know is that for some reason your true father had to step aside . . . and then perhaps Elle gave herself to H.D. for your sake—to survive. But you hated him, remember? Wouldn't it be nice to think that maybe your father was someone your mother truly loved—that you could have loved?"

Niki refused to be comforted. "I don't believe that for a minute, Kate. If there was *anything* good about my real father, wouldn't she have told me? She knew how miserable I was about the way H.D. treated us. No," she insisted, and released a ragged sigh, "if Elle kept it a secret, it probably means that the truth is worse, much worse, than what I grew up believing."

"It doesn't have to mean that," Kate argued. "It could be she planned to tell you the truth one day, Niki. After all," Kate added gently, "she didn't expect to die before you grew up."

Parson's warehouse in River Junction was piled high with cardboard cartons and dusty furniture. After paying Mr. Parson twenty dollars for the privilege of rummaging through her father's belongings, Kate and Niki were allowed inside.

The remains of Dr. Charles Boynton's thirty-five years of practice consisted of a roll-top desk, a leather-covered examining table, a metal cabinet filled with instruments, a bulky sterilizer, and an oak filing cabinet bulging with papers. Dr. Boynton's records, like the man himself, were kept in a neat, old-fashioned way.

With trembling fingers, Niki dug out the slender file bearing her name. It detailed the history of her childhood illnesses—measles, mumps, chickenpox—as well as her fateful accident. There were several neat notations on house calls made when Niki had tonsillitis, followed by his recommendation that the tonsils be removed. ''Patient's mother declined,'' he wrote. Later, there was another note: ''Patient's mother apparently right. Symptoms have disappeared. Wait and see.''

Not a word anywhere about her father.

Sighing heavily, Niki handed back the folder to Kate. ''You were right,'' she said. ''I was just grasping at straws.''

''Well, now that we're here, don't be so quick to give up,'' Kate said, pulling out another folder—marked ''Sandeman, Gabrielle.'' The first page was a copy of the death certificate Charles Boynton had prepared.

''I can't,'' Niki said, pushing it away. ''I can't look at that.''

''Then I will,'' Kate said, leafing through the pages.

Suddenly she gasped. ''Niki . . . oh, my God, Niki . . .''

The look on Kate's face frightened her, but Niki had come too far to stop now. She leaned over Kate's shoulder and read an entry dated December 15, 1958. It detailed a house call made at midnight. ''Patient was hysterical. Contusions around the face and shoulders. Hematoma on left cheek. Patient said she had fallen accidently. Nature of injuries suggest violent assault. Upon further questioning, patient said she had been raped.''

The blood drained from Niki's face and she felt sick to her stomach. Was there no end to the horrors of the past? Was her father a monster even worse than the one she'd known? As Kate rummaged through the file, Niki began to wish she could go back to the moment before she had declared open war on the Hylands. It had seemed so noble and so right at the start—yet all she'd done so far was to uncover a a filthy, ugly swamp that threatened to swallow up all her hard-won self-respect.

Kate pulled a sealed envelope from the file. Inside they found a history of Elle's pregnancy. ''Patient has agreed that when the child is born, father will be listed as 'unknown.' For the child's sake, I have urged patient to share with me the identity of her assailant, with full assurance that such disclosure will remain ever confidential—to be used only by me and only in case of medical emergency."

The name that followed was Edward Hyland.

Never in her life had Niki been so ill. Lying in the bedroom of her childhood, she shook with fever, retching violently, as if her body were struggling to exorcise some terrible demon. Sick to her very soul, she was beyond comfort.

"It's going to be all right," Alexei murmured, as he applied a cool compress to her forehead. "We'll make it all right, Niki."

Yet his soothing words only seemed to make Niki more desperate. Wildly, she thrashed against Alexei's healing hands, struggling against the nightmare from which she couldn't wake up. "It's never going to be all right!" she cried out. "I have to get out of here, Alexei! I have to get away!"

Yet even as she uttered her desperate cry, Niki knew there was nowhere to run and nowhere to hide. For so many years she had been at war with herself, unable to either live with or forget the Hyland part of her. For each victory, there had been a defeat. Each time she was about to triumph over it, the dark monster took another shape, threatening to consume her with its evil.

"If that's what you want, we *can* go away," Alexei murmured. "It's what I've hoped you would say . . ."

Was that the answer? she asked herself. Was that what it came to after all these years? A retreat? A surrender to shame?

She shook her head in silent despair. Alexei sat with her for a long time, until exhaustion made her eyelids heavy. He murmured something about driving to town to pick up some groceries. "I won't be long," he promised. "Try to get some rest while I'm gone."

She closed her eyes, drifting off into a restless, feverish sleep.

She was jarred awake by the sound of footsteps on the stairs. Thinking it was Alexei, she tried to sit up. A moment later Will was in the doorway, his face somber. When he saw Niki lying in bed, his expression softened. "I'm sorry for barging in," he said apologetically, "but I knocked a couple of times. I tried the door . . . and it wasn't locked."

"It's all right," she said quietly. "Why are you here?"

"Because I'm through backing off, Niki," he began, as if reciting a prepared speech. "You can send me away if you want to, but first you're going to hear me out." He stopped, suddenly aware of Niki's pallor, the dark circles under her red-rimmed eyes. "What's wrong, darlin'?" he asked, kneeling beside her. "What's happened to you? I've been half out of my mind, thinking you didn't want to see me. Figuring you'd made up your mind to marry that guy without giving me a chance to speak my piece."

Niki half-smiled through her misery. Even now, Will refused to give Alexei any other name but 'that guy.'

"I thought you didn't want to see me anymore," she said softly. "I thought you were starting to believe all the terrible things people said about me. And now that I know the truth about what I am, it's even worse."

"What are you talking about, Niki?" Will asked, as he sat down on the bed, his face creased with worry.

"You were right," she said brokenly, "about the darkness inside me. And now I know why it was there. My father wasn't H.D. It was another Hyland—his son, Duke. I was conceived when he raped my mother, Will . . . and I can't stop thinking about that. I can't make those awful pictures go away. Oh, God, I feel so dirty, so . . . worthless." She began to cry softly.

Will's fists clenched, his hazel eyes blazed with anger. With a visible effort, he forced himself to speak calmly. "And what do you figure to do about that?" he asked.

"Do?" she asked dully. "What can I—?"

He interrupted at the same moment that he put his arms around her, pulling her into a sheltering embrace. "Niki, do you remember how it was when you first came back to Willow Cross? How you had to burn the rotted tobacco stalks in the fields—so the new plants could have a fresh start? If you don't see this thing through, if you don't burn away the rot and decay, it'll always be there, choking off everything you do. I figure you deserve better than that, darlin'. I figure there's a reason why you found out about your father. And I don't think it's about quitting."

Niki said nothing as she weighed what he had said. Of course, he was right. It was the circle of her own life she was struggling to complete. Elle had reached out once again, beyond death and beyond the years that had all but obscured her life, to help her daughter find the identity that had eluded her.

"And no matter how it turns out," Will said, brushing the tears from her cheeks, "I'm declaring myself here and now. Maybe I've been a damn fool to wait so long. Maybe you're already spoken for—but I know nothing in this world comes with a guarantee . . . and I'm hoping you know that, too, Niki, that you'll take me just the way I am."

Niki raised herself on the pillow to look at him with inquiring eyes. "Are you saying—?"

"Hell, yes," he erupted, and gave her a broad grin. "Don't suppose this is the most romantic way to do this, darlin', but I'm asking you to marry me."

Niki closed her eyes for a moment, reaching deep inside herself for an answer. She had it now, didn't she, the proof that it was safe to love Will? He was giving her the kind of commitment her mother had longed for—saying the words that Monique had never heard. If Will had broken the mold of Niki's past and set her free, why then couldn't she speak?

"Hey, say something," Will coaxed nervously, taking her hand—which was now ice cold. "Dammit, if you're going to marry that Russkie, tell me now and put me out of my misery!"

"Will," she choked out, "I can't marry anyone. Not you. Not Alexei. Not until . . . until . . ."

"Until you finish this thing with the Hylands."

Niki nodded. She braced herself for Will's anger. For the accusation that her obsession was greater than her capacity for love.

Instead, he put his arms around her. "All right," he said huskily, "I can't say I like it. I can't even say I understand what you're feeling. But I still don't want you to quit, Niki. I want you to think about the family we're going to have. Think about the lessons you can teach our kids, about taking something ugly and making it good. They'll be proud of you, sweetheart, just the way I am now."

Niki sat up straighter, her eyes became brighter, as Will's words painted a picture she had never really seen clearly before—not just man and woman together, but a whole family built on love. A love that could overcome the lies and the hatred—and the deadly obsessions.

"I see I've got your attention," he said with obvious relief. "Now you concentrate on getting yourself well. You've got some fields to burn, darlin' . . . so you'd better figure out which way the wind is going to blow."

Though she was still weak and feverish, Will's pep talk had forced her to start thinking again. Could she find a way to defeat the man who had violated her mother? Who'd publicly desecrated Elle's memory to hide his own heinous crime? Niki's throat constricted, her stomach lurched, as the word *father* crossed her mind. Yet Duke Hyland was her father. And it was he who had sown the seeds of the putrefying harvest that must now be destroyed.

A few minutes after Will left, Alexei came back into Niki's room. Realizing that he must have been in the house for at least part of Will's visit, she found it difficult to meet Alexei's eyes, to see his unspoken questions. Yet she felt she must recognize and answer them. Even if she were never able to marry Will, she knew now that she couldn't share the life of a man she didn't love.

As he sat down beside her, she said quietly, "It isn't fair to keep you here, to let you believe there's a chance we might have a future together. I do care for you, but . . ."

He gave her a smile that conveyed sadness mixed with bravery. "It's Will you love," he said.

She wanted to be as honest as she could. "I've never been sure when it comes to loving a man. I've never even been able to say the words. Maybe it's because it's been so hard for me to love myself, when there was always the knowledge of a man who hadn't wanted me—the memory of my mother suffering because love had poisoned her life instead of fulfilling it. I don't expect you to understand . . . I just hope you can forgive me . . ."

"There's nothing to forgive, Nikuschka. And perhaps I understand more than you imagine. At least on the subject of love," he added with a heartrending smile. "I know why you've never been able to say yes . . . either to me or to Mr. Rivers. If you never choose a man, if you insist on 'maybe'—but never 'yes, this is the one I love'—then you never have to risk whatever it is you're afraid of. I had hoped that when you conquered that fear, it would be me you would reach out to."

Niki's eyes glistened with fresh tears. For Alexei. For herself. For the pain that always seemed to follow the elusive promise of love.

Two days later, Niki met with John Cromwell. She told him what she had learned of her parentage and showed him Charles Boynton's file. "Couldn't we take this into court?" she asked. "If we get an expert to swear that the handwriting's authentic, wouldn't that convince a judge that I'm entitled to vote Babe's proxy?"

Cromwell frowned, then shook his head. "Not necessarily," he said slowly. "All we have is hearsay evidence. A dead man's evidence of what a dead woman told him."

"But she *was* raped!" Niki shouted, seeing her slender hope of victory slipping away. "Doesn't that count for anything? Dammit, John, that monster sat in court and spit on my mother! He called her a lying tramp and the judge believed him! I'm not going to let him get away with that!"

"Calm down, Niki, calm down. I'm not suggesting we let Duke Hyland get away with anything. I merely said that Dr. Boynton's file alone won't prove your case. However," he added, "there may be another way of substantiating paternity. A DNA test, for example . . ."

"Then let's do it," she cut in eagerly.

Once again, Cromwell shook his head. "In cases of rape," he explained, "the court can order a DNA test. But here, where there's no possibility of *proving* rape, we might have a difficult time getting the court to order a DNA test on a man who isn't willing to have one."

"What about medical records then?" she asked. "Can't we find out *his* blood type, the way he did."

"Not good enough," Cromwell cut in. "It would be easy enough to find out Duke Hyland's blood type—but all we'd be showing is a possibility that he could be your father. It wouldn't be proof. Blood tests are only conclusive in cases where paternity is impossible."

"Well, what are we going to do then?" Niki demanded, realizing the irony of trying to prove that a man she loathed was indeed her father.

"There's a private detective we employed during the Troiano litigation," Cromwell said. "His investigation into the affairs of Hyland Tobacco and all its executives was very extensive. Perhaps he can help us get what we need."

As Cromwell explained his intentions, Niki smiled.

"It may not stand up in a court of law," Cromwell cautioned.

"Get it," Niki said. "Maybe there's a higher court for someone like Duke Hyland."

Alone in his book-lined study, Duke poured himself a double shot of bourbon and drank it down. He picked up the telephone and dialed the number of his personal physician. Though the hour was late, Duke was unconcerned about intruding into the man's personal life. People who served him were well paid, and he expected them to be on call, day or night. Fingers drumming impatiently on his desk, Duke waited for his summons to be answered.

"Kendrick," he said, upon hearing the familiar voice, "Duke Hyland here. That business I needed to take care of—it's almost done now. Give me a couple of weeks to tie up the loose ends . . . schedule that surgery we talked about for the first of next month."

The doctor's response brought a frown of annoyance. "That's your business, to make sure it isn't too late," Duke said harshly. "If you can't do the job right when I'm ready, I'll get someone who can!"

Slamming down the receiver, he muttered, "Doctors, they're worse than lawyers." They were always trying to scare you, he thought, trying to pump up their fees. Hadn't they made all kinds of dire predictions five years ago? He'd pulled through then—and he would now. Not a word of his illness had ever become public. And he certainly couldn't afford to have that happen now. Not when he was about to consolidate his power at Hyland so that it could never be threatened again. His lawyers had already filed a petition to void Babe's proxy. Once that was done, Babe's stock would belong to Pepper, and Duke was prepared to make her an offer she wouldn't dare refuse. He had beaten Elle's trouble-making daughter, and he had beaten her good. He'd had the satisfaction of seeing her crumble before his very eyes.

Suddenly, there was the sound of voices loudly raised. A moment later, Niki invaded Duke's office, his butler trailing behind. "I'm sorry, Mr. Duke," he apologized. "I told the young lady you were busy, but she just came on in."

"That's because she isn't a lady," Duke said with a nasty smile. Caught by surprise, he hesitated, undecided as to whether it would give him greater pleasure to throw her out—or to hear what she had to say, and then throw her out. "Leave us," he said to the butler, then leaned back in his chair. "I told you you'd be sorry," he gloated. "I told you it was war if you didn't accept my offer."

Alone together they stared for a long moment into each

other's eyes. Duke saw something in her eyes that he had never seen there before.

Could she know? he wondered. Could she know it *all*?

For a few seconds, Niki went on staring into the face of her father.

Goaded by her silence, her unflinching gaze, Duke spoke again. "If you think you can make some kind of a deal now, forget it. You're finished, Niki. You played your hand and you lost."

"I didn't come to make any deal," she said with quiet force.

"Then why—"

"I know what you did to my mother," she said, her voice trembling with anger. "I know that you raped her! And if I didn't have something worse in mind, I'd kill you right now like the dog you are!"

Duke's mouth was etched by a cruel smile. "Nobody ever had to rape that money-grubbing bitch," he sneered. "Hell, she even died like the whore she was, half-naked. She was always ready to spread her legs for anyone who'd make it worth her while. I didn't have to rape her."

"Rotten liar! You beat her, forced yourself on her!"

Duke shrugged, as if Elle was no longer of any consequence.

"And you got her pregnant," Niki spat out, grimacing as she spoke of her own conception.

Alert now to danger, Duke sat up in his chair. "You're losing it, Niki. Don't you know you can't go around slandering people?" he asked, his voice edged with menace. "I might just have to call my lawyers and have them sue you."

"Do that. And tell them what a lowlife you are. And while you're at it, show them this!" She pulled a document from her bag and threw it on his desk.

Duke barely glanced at the papers.

"What's the matter?" she demanded. "Not interested in the truth? *That* is the result of a DNA test—*Father*! It makes me sick to say it, and it makes me sick to look at you, but that test is as good as a fingerprint. You left your mark on me, Duke Hyland, and now I'm giving it back to you in spades.''

''You're bluffing,'' he said. ''I didn't take any damn test!''

''You didn't have to,'' she shot back. ''You just had your usual weekly haircut, Duke, remember that? I persuaded your barber to part with a lock of your hair—for sentimental reasons,'' she said sarcastically. ''That's all I needed. The lab did the rest.''

Duke picked up the report and started to read it, his brow furrowed with puzzlement.

''Go ahead,'' she said, ''look for a loophole, Duke, because you won't find any. So go ahead and call your lawyers—because the next time we meet, it will be in court. And after that, you'll be seeing me in your office! After I take it, *Father*!''

She turned on her heel and stormed out, slamming the study door behind her.

Duke slumped into his chair. He poured another drink and downed it quickly, but the alcohol gave no relief from the gnawing pain in his gut. He closed his eyes, remembering the day he'd picked up a young Frenchwoman in a cafe in Monaco. He tried to remember how he felt that day, but those feelings had long been buried. Just as the boy he'd been was buried within the man he'd become. Yet she had refused to go away, haunting and plaguing his life. She was like his Delilah, he thought bitterly; even in death, she had sent someone to steal his hair, to steal his power, to ruin him in what should have been the moment of his greatest triumph.

Could his lawyers beat her again? he wondered. Ignoring the pain that cut through him like a hot knife, he refilled his glass once more, trying to think, to plan. But all Duke could see was her face, laughing at him; a dark vision unfolded before him—of being dethroned by his own bastard child.

Lying alone in bed, Niki felt weary. She had won at last, and this time there would be no more tricks and no more delays. There would be a new day at Hyland, a new hand at the helm. She would never bear the Hyland name—she didn't want it—yet she was on the brink of fulfilling a dream beyond anything Elle had ever imagined. She would have the kind of legitimacy that was earned and not granted by someone else. Yet even as she had seen her own victory in Duke's hate-filled eyes, she had seen something else, too—the frightening power of a consuming obsession, devouring everything that stood in its way . . . even the ability to love.

She thought of Will, of the sad waste of so many years. Everything she needed had always been there for the taking, if only she'd known where to look.

When she finally fell asleep, a dream came. Visions of a night so long ago. . . . A little girl on the stairs, wakened by the sound of thunder. A man bent over her mother, fumbling with her clothes, undressing her—

Suddenly, Niki found herself sitting up in bed, shivering. Across the gap between the world seen in sleep and the memory of conscious reality, a spark had been thrown that had jolted her into full wakefulness. Had she heard a noise in the house, the sound of a gun? Her tired, confused mind was still lost in the limbo between the real and the remembered. Perhaps what she had thought was her life was the dream—and she was still the child, needing to go downstairs and find her mother to be reassured.

The shapes of the room became more solid, and she knew where she was. But the image of the nightmare stayed with her—H.D. leaning over the reclining body of her mother, undressing her.

H.D.?

Then it came to her—the truth, a blue spark leaping out of the darkness. And she knew why. It was something Duke had said: "She died half-naked, just like the whore she was!"

But Elle had been found by the window, with her robe on.

A comprehension denied her for decades by the mistaken perception of a child—the child she had been—finally formed. The figure she had seen bending over her mother that night. He hadn't been *un*dressing her . . . he had been covering her nakedness, dressing her so that she could be found in a way that would make it seem a prowler had killed her. But it was Duke who had murdered her. Elle had been dead already when the child tiptoed downstairs.

Suddenly, she heard a sound from downstairs, a sound that made Niki feel as if she were still in the dream. Terrified, she wrapped herself in a robe and tiptoed downstairs, as she had done so many years ago. As she inched towards the door, she saw Jim's toolbox lying open on the hall table. She picked up a wrench and raised her arm.

"Who's there?" she called out in a trembling voice.

"Pepper Hyland . . . for God's sake, let me in!"

Limp with relief, Niki dropped the wrench and opened the door.

Illuminated by the thin yellow beam of the porch light, Pepper looked ghastly and ill.

"What do you want?" Niki asked wearily, too spent to fight or argue.

Pepper stepped inside, uninvited, and slumped into the living room sofa. "He's dead," she said. "Duke's dead."

Niki recoiled in shock. She opened her mouth to speak but no words came. Feeling her knees give way, she half-fell onto the sofa facing Pepper.

"Do you want to know how he died?" Pepper asked.

Still dazed, Niki could only think of those awful moments when she and her father had been locked in mortal combat; of her own realization that he had murdered her mother and stolen her childhood.

"He shot himself."

Niki winced, but said nothing.

"Do you hate us that much?" Pepper asked softly, showing her years in spite of all the surgeon's skills.

"I don't hate anyone anymore," Niki said quietly. "I just want it all to be over."

Pepper stared at Niki's face, as if taking a measure of the younger woman's suffering. Her own expression softened.

"It didn't work out the last time I offered to be a friend. I was too wild—too corrupt, I guess, and you were too innocent. But maybe we can try it again," she offered tentatively. "There's just the two of us left now. Even if we aren't related, we—"

"But we are," Niki cut in, determined never to hide again. "We are related. Duke was my father."

Pepper began to laugh and cry all at once. "Oh, God," she said, "Oh, God, what a family!"

Taking pity on Pepper, Niki brought her a snifter of brandy.

"You might as well know the rest of it," she said. "He killed my mother."

Pepper's eyes flew open, her hand clutched at her throat, as Niki recounted Duke's final legacy to the daughter he'd hated before she was even born. "I still don't know how it happened," Niki said. "I guess I'll never know."

"Duke said he was only trying to protect Babe," Pepper cut in, her voice hoarse, her hands trembling as she clutched the brandy. "When he found out that Babe was sneaking around with Elle, Duke went to see her. He told me he offered her money to get out of town, to leave Babe alone. He said she laughed at him, told him she was going to be Mrs. Hyland, no matter what he did . . ."

"So he killed her. He told you that."

Pepper shook her head so violently that her drink spilled onto her lap. "I never knew," she said, "I swear to God, I never knew. All he told me was that they argued, that he threatened to tell Babe something that would make him leave her . . ."

Niki realized what it must have been "That I was his bastard child—and not H.D.'s." Niki closed her eyes. The rest of the scene was as clear as if she had been there to see it. A fierce struggle between two deadly obsessions . . . ended by a gunshot. Duke clothing Elle to support the tale of an unknown intruder, to remove any suspicion that she had been entertaining a lover during the evening of her death.

"Poor Babe was so broken up," Pepper continued, caught

up now in her own memories. "That's why we sent him away. Duke said that if anyone asked him, Babe would be stupid enough to admit he had been with Elle. Maybe even say they were planning to get married . . ."

Niki paled as she absorbed the full impact of Duke's hatred. Of how he had taken away her freedom to love and trust, leaving only a legacy of fear and suspicion.

Pepper drained her brandy and when she was finished, she rose to her feet. "All right," she said, "it's going to be over, here and now, Niki. No more lawyers, no more courtrooms. We'll do it your way—Hyland, Incorporated" She held out her hand and Niki took it.

A moment later, she was gone.

Niki stood in the doorway, watching the delicate pink light of the rising sun burn away the last patchy traces of night and unfold the promise of a new day.

She ran upstairs, washed her face with cold water and threw on a shirt and jeans. She drove to the Rivers farm as if her life depended on it, unable to bear the waste of another precious moment.

When she saw him in the distance, hunched over a length of broken fence, she drove as far as the road would go and left the car. Leaping over the split-rail fence, she ran across the open field. "Will!" she called out, laughing with joy as she rushed towards him, her blond hair flying in the breeze.

His arms opened wide to welcome her, his hazel eyes bright with hope.

"I love you, Will," she cried out, exhilarated by the words and the freedom to say them. "I'll love you forever and ever!"

As his arms closed around her, the past fell away like the withered tobacco leaf when summer was over. There were no more secrets, there would be no more ghostly obsessions. Now it was just the two of them, and together they would build a life on love and caring and trust.

"Hey, you know what?" Will said suddenly. "I feel like writin' a dozen new songs." He looked into her face and smiled. ''Hell, you always were my very best inspiration. Gave me the song that really made me. . . .''

''Dark Side of the Heart,'' she said. ''But now the dark side is gone, Will.''

''You sure, pretty lady?''

She smiled as he reminded her of another inspiration. ''I'm sure.''

''Well, don't you worry, I know you'll give me plenty of other things to write about.'' He kissed her, and then lifted her up in his arms. ''How's this for a title: I feel like makin' love right now.''

''Top of the charts, for sure.''

As he carried her toward the house, he was already humming something new. It sounded, Niki thought happily, like a lullaby.